ALSO BY RANDY SUE COBURN

Owl Island

Remembering Jody

A Better View of Paradise

Randy Sue Coburn

A Better View of Paradise

A NOVEL

Ballantine Books *New York*

A Better View of Paradise is a work of fiction. Names, characters, places, and incidents are the products of the author's imagination or are used fictitiously. Any resemblance to actual events, locales, or persons, living or dead, is entirely coincidental.

Published in the United States by Ballantine Books, an imprint of The Random House Publishing Group, a division of Random House, Inc., New York.

BALLANTINE and colophon are registered trademarks of Random House, Inc.

Grateful acknowledgment is made to the following for permission to reprint previously published material:

Coleman Barks: "Love Dogs" by Rumi from "The Essential Rume," translated by Coleman Barks, courtesy of Coleman Barks.

Doubleday: excerpt from "From the Notebooks" from *Straw for the Fire* by Theodore Roethke courtesy of Doubleday, a division of Random House, Inc. Copyright © 1972 by Beatrice Roethke.

Tim Owens: lyric excerpt from "Princess Pupule," music and lyrics by Harry Owens, courtesy of Tim Owens. Copyright © 1940. Used by permission. Royal Music Publishers.

ISBN 978-0-345-49036-0

Printed in the United States of America on acid-free paper

www.ballantinebooks.com

9 8 7 6 5 4 3 2 1

First Edition

Book design by Laurie Jewell

For my mother, Bette Lee Coburn

To be loved means
to be ablaze.
To love is to shine
with inexhaustible oil.
To be loved is to pass away;
to love is to last.

—RAINER MARIA RILKE

I ka ʻolelo no ka ola
I ka ʻolelo no ka make.

In the word is life
In the word is death.

—HAWAIIAN PROVERB

A Better View of Paradise

Prologue

Just one long-ago day on the island remains so alive for Stevie that it returns less as memory than emotion. It is a day that begins out on the lanai, eating breakfast while she watches a gecko swell up and pulse its throat, the liquid trill of mating cardinals in her ears. It is a day before anyone ever forced her to wear tights, or Wellingtons, or endure the insult of scratchy Fair Isle sweaters against her skin. It is a day that will forever mark the freest part of childhood, when time slipped through soft, silken air scented with ginger and night jasmine. A day when her family is whole.

After breakfast she sets out to bike topless to the beach in a pair of faded blue *palaka*-cloth shorts, binoculars dangling from the handlebars of a green Schwinn with fenders rusted from salt air. "Shirt, Stevie," Lila calls from the kitchen, and runs out waving a thin orange tank top that's almost as nice as nothing at all, but not quite. "I know," Lila says, "but you're nearly six now." Still straddling the bike, Stevie pulls the top over her head, and then she pedals off to look for spinner dolphins. Lila said she saw some earlier this morning while out gathering *ogo,* the seaweed that she chops into salty *poke* made with fresh-caught tuna.

Stevie means to figure out, once and for all, why the dolphins spin. Do they spin because they're catching fish? Do they spin because they're sending a signal? Or do they spin because they're doing a dance? She knows why red-and-black butterflies float among koa trees in the forest; they're looking for sweet sap ooze on broken branches. But the dolphins are a mystery. She's asked every adult around the house why they spin, and none of them can say for certain.

At the beach Stevie leans her bike against an ironwood tree, then walks around the bend, past lava rocks where Lila hunts her *ogo.* She's headed for a big driftwood log where she plans to sit and watch the sea, glittering now with low morning light.

But when she arrives at the log, someone is already there: a beautiful lady with long, straight hair dark as a *kukui* nut. She's barefoot, like Stevie, and her shimmery red dress is singed at the hem. She sits in front of a blackened pit where many fires have blazed, smoking a hand-rolled cigarette. She must be a tourist, what Lila calls a hippie chick. Tourists often camp out in little clumps along the beach here, where riptides make it too dangerous to swim. But this lady is alone. Besides, she doesn't have a tent or sleeping bag or any of the other usual camping gear. "Hello," Stevie murmurs, trying not to stare. It's rude to stare—she's heard that a lot from Momma and Grammy.

The lady looks up and picks a fleck of tobacco off her tongue. "Finally," she says, as though Stevie's kept her waiting. "Did you bring matches?"

What a strange question. Especially from a big person smoking a cigarette. Especially when she's talking to a small person who's been warned over and over not to play with fire. Stevie shakes her head with a little shiver, though the sea breeze is warm.

"I need matches," the lady says. "Will you go get me some?"

Stevie knows what she ought to do: say she's sorry, but no, she can't, and anyway, she's here this morning to decide why spinners spin. But as she gazes into this amazing creature's dark, expectant eyes, something keeps her from refusing. She just says yes, runs for her bike, and races back home, where she snatches a box of Diamond strike-anywhere matches from the garden-shed shelf and tosses it into her bicycle basket. She doesn't wear a watch and she doesn't think in terms of minutes, but her trip takes no time at all.

Setting the bike aside once again, Stevie sprints down the beach with the matchbox, forgetting her binoculars. But when she reaches the log, the beautiful lady is gone. The only sign that anyone else has been here is the makings of an enormous bonfire, laid above a nest of crisscrossed kindling. How did this happen so fast? Not a stick of wood was stacked anywhere close by before.

If the lady expected Stevie would bring matches, then the fire must be Stevie's to light. And so she opens the matchbox and pulls out a red-tipped stick. But her hand hovers over the striker strip on the side of the box as she wonders what the punishment would be for setting off a big blaze. Something even worse than what happens if she talks back, or loses her temper, or breaks a special china cup she had no business playing tea party with. The match goes back into its box. She needs a grown-up to light this fire, and her best bet there is Lila. Who, unlike her parents, has never once swatted Stevie's bottom in anger or sent her to her room in broad daylight.

And so she flies home again to tell Lila what's happened. Lila gets a strange look on her face. Then she covers the bowl of *poke,* washes her hands, puts on her palm-frond hat, and drives Stevie straight back to the beach in her beat-up station wagon.

Neither of them speaks as they walk together to the driftwood log. When they get there, the bonfire is burnt to ash, still smoking. Another impossibility! As Stevie starts to protest, to swear that she was telling the truth, a sob catches in her throat and her eyes fill. But Lila isn't mad. She pulls a soft kitchen cloth from her pocket to dab at tears. "It's all right, *ku'uipo.* Puff your nose." While Stevie blows into the cloth for her, Lila heaves a sigh somewhere between puzzled and thunderstruck. "First time ever," she says, "I hear of her coming to a *keiki.*"

Ku'uipo—that means sweetheart. *Keiki*—that means someone like

Stevie, who orders from the *keiki* menu at Daddy's hotel, or someone even littler, who splashes in the tiny *keiki* pool. "Do you know the lady, Lila?"

"I know *'bout* her. Everybody does. That was no hippie chick, Stevie. That was Pele."

"Pele?"

"She made these islands, with her volcanoes. Nevah seen her myself, but I hear plenty stories—the kind that spook you into chicken skin, like I got now." Lila holds out her arm so Stevie can touch the fine, raised hairs. "Sometimes she's old," Lila goes on, "sometimes she's young, but always she asks for something. And maybe you do the thing she wants, but before you know it, poof—she's gone, nowhere 'round. You turn her down, though, bad things happen."

"Will bad things happen to me?"

Lila shakes her head. "You got the matches. You did just like she said."

"I didn't light the fire."

"She must've done that all by herself."

"Then why did she want me to bring matches?"

Lila just laughs. "Ask her yourself, Stevie, next time she comes around."

But she doesn't come around again. And bad things happen anyway.

Chapter 1

Pele is far from Stevie's mind on the warm September morning that her new garden is scheduled to open. For one thing, she's a long way from Hawai'i—in Chicago, a tough-guy city if ever there was one. And for another, she's all grown up. Thirty-six years old. An age that, in her better moods, on her better days, seems in perfect balance. Eighteen years of living as somebody's daughter, under parental control, followed by eighteen years of independence. By her reckoning, that means she ought to have a pretty fair shot at being her own person. A person who calls home a Brooklyn Heights floor-through apartment with eye-catching French flea market linens on the bed and well-used chef-grade cookware in the kitchen. A person with reliable friends and a regularly exercised passport. A professional person, too—one who is, to be exact, making her mark upon the land. What's more, this person is determined not to let *anything* interfere with a day on which both she and the elaborate garden she designed are going to be celebrated. Not even the fact that somebody just dumped her. Especially not that.

When Stevie gets out of bed in her room at a small, European-style hotel on East Delaware Place, her head aches and her mouth is dry. She fights the urge to rush out and buy herself coffee, pastries, and a pack of the American Spirit cigarettes she still craves whenever something major goes wrong. Instead, she clips back her hair and puts on running clothes—an athletic bra engineered to immobilize C-cup breasts, loose-legged purple shorts, and a mustard-yellow T-shirt decorated with a big bunned wiener that reads:

HOT DOG!
JOHNNY'S
ROUTE 46
BUTZVILLE, N.J.

Soon she's jogging along a lakeside path, red-faced already in this low late-summer sun, glad for the sweet-smelling freshwater breeze. Fog hugs the waterfront, the shoreline that is Stevie's favorite thing about the city, and through the fog she catches glimpses that remind her of a veiled belly dancer, undulating against the Gold Coast's rigid street grid. Land curves in and out, so sensuous, so seductive, it's easy to imagine that only some supreme feminine force of nature could have shaped it. Stevie knows better.

Her research into all things Chicago has taught her that most of the shore, like the rest of the city, is man-made, an illusion created with ton upon ton of dumped landfill. "Shit," Stevie hisses. Just thinking of dumped landfill is enough to bring her own dumping front and center again.

She's told no one any details of the breakup. Not even Lorna, her best friend since college. Especially not Lorna. And that's because she knows exactly what Lorna will say: "First words, Stevie. Let's talk about first words."

Lorna has a theory—annoyingly accurate by now—that every man, right off the bat, says something that reveals with astonishing precision what your relationship with him will be like. "And you'd pay attention, too," Lorna contends, "if only you weren't stone-deaf to anything but that sneaky devil with the romance-o-meter whispering in your ear. Telling you not who they are, but who you *want* them to be. So you miss what really matters. When some guy says 'I don't deserve you,' listen up, Stevie. That guy is not flattering you. That guy is preaching the goddamn gospel."

That guy was just Exhibit A. Over the years, Stevie has given Lorna ample additional evidence to prove her point, standouts being the lover who said "You are exactly the kind of woman I should fall for" (Stevie had failed to give proper emphasis to the word "should") and another who claimed "You make my life so full" (soon enough, he'd sink back into depression).

What was the first important thing Brian had revealed? The words that, in the world according to Lorna, contained the tiny, tightly coiled kernels of their future—or, rather, their past. Nothing comes. It's easier to recall how she met Brian than what tumbled out of his mouth after she did.

They were collaborating on a symphony hall that his firm had designed, and no sooner did they shake hands than he presented her with an architectural drawing of the building, complete with computer-generated landscapes. Not only had Brian done her job for her, he'd done it in a completely crappy, generic way. What was he thinking, plopping down a woodland-style trout stream right beside a sleek modern building in downtown Pittsburgh? Every bit as ridiculous, in Stevie's opinion, as garnishing a plate of lox and bagels with bean sprouts—a textbook example of what she calls Fake Nature. How did Brian explain himself? He must have said *something.* Oh, yes. Now she has it. "This ought to give you an idea," he'd told her, "of what works for me."

At the time, she'd taken his remark only as an indication that it would require a jolt into hyperspace to bring this bucko in the stylish black-framed eyeglasses up to speed. And though every fired-up fiber in her body wanted to, she couldn't do it by yelling at him. If she tried, she'd only sputter and lose steam, like some worn-out machine, and then on top of being frustrated and upset, she'd be humiliated. In situations like this, Stevie's quiver held only one arrow—a well-earned professional reputation for walking at the first sign of disrespect. "If all you want is some toady to haul around rocks and shove shrubs," Stevie informed Brian, "find somebody else."

He wasn't the first arrogant architect she'd encountered, not by a long shot. But he was by far the best-dressed, most attractive, age-appropriate one who, according to advance reports, also happened to be divorced. Leaving the room, certain that he'd come after her, she was glad that the asymmetrically cropped skirt she was wearing gave him a damn good look at her legs.

Brian made it up over good wine and lamb shanks at a little Italian place in the West Village, his treat. "We just got off on the wrong foot," he told her. "Forget what I said. Let's start over from scratch. What are *your* ideas? How do *you* think it should look?"

So she took out a felt-tip pen to sketch on the back of her menu. A tree-lined promenade alongside a shallow, shimmering ribbon of water. Dramatic high-tech lighting for the evening, a friendly park-like feeling for the day, and a sloped entryway to emphasize the site's steep grade changes. When she put down her pen, all the anger that had backed up on her like a bad case of indigestion was gone, released by that little burst of creativity. Brian not only praised her concepts but wore a persuasively contrite expression. Stevie, at least, was persuaded.

"First time I've ever been out front on a project this big," he said. "Guess I got a little carried away. That's an amazing shape you want to build everything around. How'd you come up with that?"

"Oh," she'd said, "it just seemed appropriate to the site." She didn't want to risk her credibility with the truth. Which was that the shape had come to her before she ever saw the site, the sort of fantastic confluence that happened sometimes before a big project beckoned.

Then Brian pointed to the window by their table and she saw fat flakes of snow dancing down to powder the narrow cobblestone street and storybook townhouses. A sight that notched their dinner way into red on the romance-o-meter. This was at a time in New York when even if by some miracle you lived a day without hearing or uttering a single sentence connected to the catastrophe, the tendrils of 9/11 were always there, entwined with the heightened reality of ordinary needs—

for sustenance, connection, and, of course, sex. Making all more urgent, somehow. More necessary.

When Stevie left the restaurant with Brian hours later, the sidewalk wore a thick coat of snow. They held on to each other to keep from slipping, and skittered sideways into their first kiss, one that started out all cozy and considering, but soon grew greedy enough to knock them off their feet—a slapstick beginning that did nothing to chill the heat between them. After scrambling upright again, they forgot about getting Stevie a taxi. Instead, Brian steered her to his place on Hudson Street, where they made love until morning. Flinging themselves on his Italian leather sofa. Falling onto his low-slung platform bed. Sloshing around in his canted-stone-slab bathtub. He was every bit as good at kissing as the perpetually broke artist Stevie had had a fling with in her twenties, the one whose best quality, apart from his kissing, turned out to be that he was a dead ringer for Adrien Brody (though who knew that then?), and Brian had the far bigger plus of being successful enough—or so she imagined—not to be threatened by *her* success. And he wasn't. Not yet, anyway.

By the time Stevie returned to Brooklyn Heights to change clothes for work, she had done what Brian asked. She had forgotten he'd ever uttered those lousy first words about what worked for him (and never mind her). It would be quite a while before she began to suspect that apart from the wild, athletic lovemaking that had hooked her, Brian went in for Fake Intimacy just like he went in for Fake Nature, and the mingy amounts that satisfied him would leave her starving.

But the first-words theory is Lorna's, not Stevie's, and what Stevie whips herself for now is not paying closer attention to the Jamaica sago tree that was in Brian's living room, its jungly fronds brown-tipped and shriveling. It wasn't that Stevie ignored the plant itself. In fact, she insisted on taking it home, where she repotted it, sunned it in a westward-facing window, left a classical music radio station on during the day to soothe it, and carried it into the bathroom for an extra dose of humidity when she showered. The plant thanked her, too, with sturdy new growth. The important thing she overlooked, the thing that should have set off alarms, was how, once the tree was healthy and happy again, she could not bring herself to return it to Brian. And who did *that* say the most about—him or her?

As if mistakes could be outrun, Stevie quickens her pace on the lakeshore path. She needs to mold her heartbreak into something more manageable. *You're just being tested,* she tells herself. *And this time it's your final exam. Once you ace it, Stephanie Anne Pollack will graduate and get a diploma. No more knocking yourself out to earn love from difficult, demanding men.*

Later, doubling back past Oak Street Beach, she's convinced that this little dream will come true. Riding the hotel elevator up to the sixth floor, red-faced and still panting, she can see herself ready to cross the stage to accept her imaginary diploma, flushed now not with exertion but a sense of achievement.

It is still too soon for her to realize just how long her walk across that stage will be. It is still too soon for her to feel the core of her life heating up, threatening to erupt.

There is a page in Stevie's red leather-bound journal reserved for an ever-lengthening list of prominent people who had flaws that should have disqualified them from their chosen professions. The fashion designer who couldn't sew. The songwriter unable to read music. The balding, pigeon-toed dancer with terrible posture. In every case, the flaw was what ended up making that person distinctive. The fashion designer compensated with brilliant fabric draping. The songwriter compensated with extraordinary productivity. The dancer compensated by making hats, pigeon toes, and terrible posture the trademarks of his louche, sexy style. The list helps Stevie feel better about her own flaw, which is that in a business where so much depends upon the ability to stake out boundaries and translate blueprints with cartographic precision, she has absolutely no sense of direction. None. Not in the way of her colleagues, anyhow, each of whom seems to have sprung from the womb with an unerring, built-in compass. If any of them were to catch Stevie assessing a site with her battery-operated global positioning device, they'd laugh their asses off.

Stevie has no doubts about the cause of her deficiency. The island world where she came into consciousness was a small, swirling wonder, an orb spat out by Pele, with spellbinding cathedrals of precipitous, uninhabitable mountains in the center and—past verdant water-carved lava ridges, closer to shore—the gentle slope of places where people lived. Roads meandered, twisting to accommodate a wily old banyan, curving to the course of a rascally little stream, mindful of how every living thing had a personality, if not a tongue to tell its story. Neither towns nor land fit into tidy rectangles, and there were just two directions people ever discussed as they went about their routine business: *makai,* toward the sea, and *mauka,* toward the mountains.

And so it is that whether she's walking a site or creating a blueprint of her own, the only way Stevie can tell east from west, north from south, is to remember the glossy Rand McNally map on Miss Nishamura's classroom wall in Kōloa and make rapid mental equations: her right and left hands are east and west, her front and back sides are north and south. It's difficult not to move her arms while she calculates, but once she's done she's set. She's oriented. She knows her place in this other world, the one with precise grids, the one in which she's calibrated to achieve.

Like an actress practicing her Oscar speech in the shower, Stevie imagines how she'll reveal her flaw someday: *My designs depend on water and earthen shapes reminiscent of mountains because I am literally lost without them.* Or, less formally: *There's this glitch in my brain because I was born on a dot in the middle of the Pacific Ocean.*

She'll have it down by the time her work is published, her reputation secure. But for now, she worries that this flaw might make her seem gender-afflicted, like a girl who can't cut it in calculus. Adding other people to her list is a million times easier than assuming that she belongs on it herself. Anyway, she can't decide whether she's compensating for her flaw or camouflaging it. Though the best argument she can think of for full disclosure is that it would contradict the way she's been labeled: "the New York minimalist."

That's what the *Chicago Tribune* architecture critic called Stevie when she was selected to design the city's new garden. Damned if she's going to play into that stereotype today. No dressing in structured black Issey Miyake; no twisting her dark, wavy hair into a sleek roll at the nape of her neck. Which was how she looked in the photo of her that the paper had run, all cheekbones and angles—precise, powerful, urban, and, no doubt about it, minimal. At this event, she'll show them a little of her island-girl side, the side she often reaches for in fraught moments, like when she moved to New York and decided to live in Brooklyn Heights for no better reason than that there was an apartment available on Pineapple Street. Her usual island-girl fixes are simpler. Cheaper, too. Listening to Ray Kane's slack-key guitar, mixing up a pitcher of mai tais, setting a gardenia in a dish of water by the bed to perfume her sleep.

Now, after showering, she steps into a vintage dress from a Honolulu resale shop, a sleek rayon cheongsam from the forties that accentuates her short, tidy torso and skims her long legs at the calf. The pattern is floral, but not one of those fussy prints she can't stand, the kind that shrills: "I am a flower." This one says something bolder, smarter, and says it in a strong, low-pitched voice similar to Stevie's: *I know how to handle flowers—and you, too, probably.*

Considering the doubt that drives her, it's amazing how often such a performance succeeds. Especially with men. Until she needs something from them. Or that's how it seems this morning, as the memory of Brian's *final* words returns: *There's no comfort zone with you.* How could he say such a thing after all she'd done for his pleasure, his happiness, not to mention his comfort? And not just in bed, either.

"You're crazy," she had told him. "That's not true."

But the part of her talking was the part too proud, too vulnerable to admit mistakes, much less tell him off in any sort of gratifying way. Not with another huge, hurt part of her believing him. Believing him still. Which is why she longs for that damn diploma. Enough already.

Last night's crying jag has taken a toll on her eyes, and all she can do about it is use drops to erase the red and hope to disguise dark circles and puffy lids with concealer, mascara, and eyeliner. Not much of an improvement. Good thing the entire event is scheduled for outdoors; she can keep her sunglasses on without seeming weird or pretentious. Stevie rejects the high-heeled sandals she wore on the plane for a pair of glossy red flats resembling ballet slippers—sensible shoes, since she expects to be on her feet for a long while.

Untying a small velveteen bag, Stevie pulls out a pair of clustered aventurine earrings and her least expensive but oldest, most treasured bracelet—a thin silver band engraved on the inside with her secret name. Her Hawaiian name. Makalani. Eyes of Heaven. She slides the band onto her right wrist. It's a snug fit, but then she's worn it since the age of twelve.

As Stevie peers into a large gilt-framed mirror by the fireplace to put on the earrings, one of them slips from her hand. When she steps back to find it, her foot lands on the earring post, wedging it into a crevice in the gleaming old walnut parquet. She stoops to jiggle and pull, but the earring is stuck so tight that she has to call the concierge for a pair of scissors and use blade tips to dig it out. Along with the earring, she raises a chunk of parquet. Easy enough to lay the wood back in place, but before she does, a bit of red fabric beneath the adjacent floorboard catches her eye. She tugs, working the material loose, then gives a hard yank. Up comes a rectangular piece of red wool shaped into the letter "P." She sniffs the wool—pretty musty—and moves to throw the thing away. But no sooner does the letter land in the trash basket than she scoops it back up again.

Who knows? Maybe the "P" stands for Pollack. A sign that this will be a red-letter day for her after all.

Stevie's garden is part of a large new park built on the site of an old steel mill that once forged metal for Chicago's skyscrapers. She'd been invited to submit her plans for the garden because of rave reviews for a similar project in Belgium, made on land reclaimed from a defunct gasworks. "Pollack's design," one influential critic wrote, "can be interpreted as a surgical act of healing, with the land skillfully draped and sown as if to hide past torments."

It wasn't long before Stevie ranked among the country's top young landscape architects, someone to watch. And in Chicago, everyone *is* watching. Not just because of the ambitious, expensive fountain that's the jewel in her garden's crown, but because the garden itself is supposed to do so many grand things. Make a new bridge to Lake Michigan's waterfront. Restore polluted land. Lift long-neglected neighborhoods out of oblivion. Celebrate not dead generals or presidents, like so many public places in Chicago, but working people, the laborers who built this city. And it was nothing but a bunch of theories until Stevie sat down with her sketch pad and modeling clay to devise a tribute expressing all the migrations that brought all those people here.

She divided the garden into a shaded lower level, to represent struggles and injustices, and an elevated grassy area with plenty of light, to convey hope for the future. The Shadow Plate is shaped like a piece of protective armor, a breastplate that might have come from her professional wardrobe, while the Light Plate's form suggests the heart within. She chose every one of the garden's hundreds of young trees herself, running her hands over their trunks, branches, and leaves the way an empathic racetrack trainer inspects a promising colt. The only flowers that will be in bloom today are a splash of buttery dahlias, a small legion of late summer delphiniums, and a bed of red flowering hibiscus (not the Hawaiian sort, but a species native to prairies), all punching up from the Light Plate's sloping, sculpted soil. When it comes to flowers, Stevie is something like a three-year-old who doesn't want the mashed potatoes touching the green beans. She never mixes them up. She likes to give them plenty of room to be full of themselves, every chance to grow into what they are. Just the thought of killing a plant that fails to thrive—one of her mother's trusty gardening techniques—sours her stomach.

Another signature feature in her new garden is what she calls the Shoulder Hedge, named for the City of the Big Shoulders. The hedge lies between the garden's Shadow and Light Plates, with steel training frames that evoke the not-so-distant urban towers made possible by the mill. The chest, the heart, the shoulders—always there are body parts hidden in her designs.

But none of these elements is what beat out every other landscape architect who vied for this commission. Just two factors counted there, the first being Stevie's feeling for the city, something handed down from her father, Hank—the first difficult, demanding man she ever loved.

Before competing for the garden, she had come to Chicago only once, with Hank. It was long after the divorce, long after her mother had hauled her off to England. At sixteen, Stevie considered time alone with her father precious, rare. Hotels were Hank's livelihood, and he had reserved rooms for them at the Drake, his idea of the best. They caught the Chicago Avenue El on a fine October morning, and when the train turned the corner after Dempster Station, Hank all but genuflected as the tip of Wrigley Field came into view. He took Stevie to Murphy's Bleachers for bratwurst and cream soda. While the jukebox thumped out the same song over and over—"Men in Blue," a novelty tune recorded by five Cubs players—Hank taught her how to keep track of the game on a scorecard. Then they yelled their throats raw from seats low on the first-base line while the Cubs won their first National League play-off game against the Padres, and they returned the next day to watch their team bag the second.

"I can just about guarantee they'll break my heart again," Hank said. Still, he bought her a prematurely manufactured pennant proclaiming the Cubs league champions in case he was wrong. He wasn't. One win away from playing in the World Series, the Cubs flamed out. Perhaps the most pertinent fact Stevie knew about her father's past was that his team hadn't played in the Series since 1945, when he was almost thirteen.

But the Cubs were still golden on that first trip of Stevie's to Chicago, and, elated by their victories, Hank took her to visit the planetarium, the Museum of Science and Industry, the zoo, his favorite steak house, his favorite deli, and even, at Stevie's insistence, the Art Institute, though there Hank stayed outside to smoke and read the *Trib* while she went through with a tour group. Stevie knew her father to be an only child, like her, and he said there weren't any relatives left to meet, so by the end of that visit, she had extended a lifelong yearning for more family to the city itself.

When it came to her father, the Chicago project has been her *secret* garden. She hasn't mentioned anything about it to him—and neither, it appears, has anyone else. All in keeping with her plan: wait until the stress passes, give the garden time to mature, invite Hank for a Cubs game in May or June, and spring the surprise on him then. It's tough for someone aspiring to be her own person to admit, but nothing she does is so real to her as when it stirs pride in Hank. At least when she worked for *his* approval as a kid, she could tell when she got it. Sure, he had a temper, and was more apt to express affection with some sort of jock-like swat than with a hug, much less a kiss. But difficult as it was for him to voice emotions, she almost always understood how he felt about things. Not so with Beryl, her mother, who *belonged* back in England, with everybody else who'd rather die than let you know.

The other factor that cinched the South Side garden for Stevie was her fountain, set to dazzle in the Light Plate's center. Inside the fountain's sweeping oval expanse, water appears to shift and turn and change direction over carved granite surfaces—an elegant echo not just of history itself, but of how, more than a hundred years ago, the city's engineers and hordes of laborers reversed the Chicago River's flow to protect citizens from disease. Reversing a river! A feat so dramatic it reminds Stevie of Moses parting the Red Sea.

She imagines that contemplating her garden will encourage people to shed all the daily distractions of their world, to consider the meaning of their ancestors' lives—and maybe even their own. That's what she's told the press, anyway. She has no idea what effect the garden will have on other people, how it will make them feel. She only knows what she hopes they will notice.

Stevie arrives at the park by taxi, amazed at the sight of visitor parking lots packed with cars. Openings for her previous projects have been more subdued—a smattering of politicians, a few boring speeches, and maybe, if she's lucky, someone in the crowd of civic activists, architects, and artists who's interesting enough to talk to for more than two minutes. She makes her way on foot to the tented area where all the other principal designers and their staffs are gathered before the ceremony.

"Look at you," cries Enrico, the architect who did the park's band shell and boardwalk. "A rose among the brambles. Oops—sorry! Forgot you don't like roses."

"It's not that Stevie doesn't like roses." This from Larry, the master plantsman who selected the remainder of the park's foliage and looks like he could be Denzel Washington's twin. "Stevie *loves* roses. She just doesn't think they're right for Chicago. Anyway, those blossoms on her dress aren't roses, they're orchids." He puts an arm around Stevie's shoulders and hands her a plastic flute filled with champagne. "Courage," he tells her.

"That's right," Enrico says. "Don't pay any attention to that asshole."

"I'm not." Stevie assumes they're referring to Brian. Sunglasses or no, her expressions have always been transparent, and after all, Brian was supposed to have been here with her today.

"Good," Larry says. "If writing about jazz is like dancing about architecture, well, I mean, what can you expect?"

The muscles in Stevie's jaw draw so tight they make a small, audible pop when at last she speaks. "The question, Larry, is this: What did I get?"

"You didn't see today's paper?"

Stevie's heart stutters like a broken metronome. "I didn't think they'd run anything until tomorrow. Plus, nobody told me—"

"Their critic jumped the gun." Enrico raises an eyebrow while Stevie drains her flute in two swallows. Then he speaks to her as he always does, as if she were one of the boys. "So fuck him, right? It's not the end of the world until it's the end of the world, and anyway, you'll have the last laugh, Stevie—you'll outlive him. So will your trees. So will your fountain."

This could be her father talking, only his signature "buck-up" comment to her was always the same: "Don't be so sensitive." Then, after that, a whole familiar litany of tough-guy truisms: "In this life, you've got to take the bitter with the sweet," "There are more horses' asses than there are horses," and "I don't care who he is, everybody puts his pants on one leg at a time." But Hank says these things when she's being hard on herself, not when *he* thinks she's erred. Which has happened a mere handful of times since she outgrew spankings. That's how good she's become at protecting herself. That's how good she's become at being successful.

Less than a foot away lies a copy of the *Tribune,* folded over someone's briefcase, but before Stevie can snatch it up, she hears her name called out by Claudia, her assistant, who flew in days ago to oversee last-minute details. "It's the fountain," Claudia says, a frown puckering her otherwise smooth little moon face. "The pump broke last night, and by the time it was fixed, all the grass got really wet. I tried to call, but—"

"Oh, God," Stevie groans. What had she been doing while this was going on? Polishing off the better part of a bottle of wine with an early dinner in her room. Sniveling, feeling sorry for herself. Then, before going to bed, asking the front-desk clerk to block all calls and turning off her cell. Until now, she's forgotten about the phones.

"It would be okay if there weren't so many people," Claudia adds. "They're all over the place. It's unbelievable. I mean, their *dogs* are jumping into the fountain."

"Their dogs?" Stevie repeats. Before she can say something more intelligent, the city parks commissioner introduces the mayor over a public address system, and Stevie, along with everybody else, has to go stand behind him, in full view of those assembled for the ceremony. But first she grabs the newspaper, pulls out the arts section, and scans a long article praising everything about the park. Everything but her garden. The most damning sentences jump off the page and smack her in the face:

> Stephanie Pollack's much-vaunted fountain says nothing so much as *look at me.*
>
> Her benches are too much like tombstones for comfort.
>
> In a garden that's a tribute to workers, you'd think there'd be a few more comfortable places for ordinary folks to sit and eat their lunch.
>
> The flowers and plants are all lined up like little soldiers in Pollack's service.
>
> One is left gasping for touches that enrich the human spirit.
>
> The problem with Pollack is that she is too much of a sculptor, too much invested in order and control.

And, worst of all:

> She doesn't know how to fit people—actual people—into her designs.

How could something so public turn into something so, well, personal? It is imperative that Stevie take the pummeling and remain on her feet, walking to the podium with a mask of attentiveness that holds firm through a South Side junior high's choral rendition of "This Land

Is Your Land." Then, while the crowd applauds, she slips away unnoticed to her garden.

So much for her red-letter day.

So many people are milling around the garden's Light Plate that a swath of grass close to where the pump broke is already turning to mud. No dogs are in the fountain at the moment, but a panting golden retriever perches with its paws on the rim, lapping water. What *is* in the fountain is a toddler with what may well be a full diaper; the child is squealing with delight as his mother dips him in and out of the water. Stevie wonders if it's been a failure of imagination on her part not to have anticipated this particular activity. It could be worse, she supposes. If the situation were the other way around, with the baby drinking water tainted by dog shit, there would be an E. coli mess on top of every other awful thing happening today.

When a muscular guy in a Sox T-shirt overthrows a freestyle Frisbee, it lands in the fountain, too—near the curve where Stevie stands. As one of the Sox guy's teammates sheds his Nikes to go in after it, she wants to shout, "No, you're not supposed to do that!" But she remains mute while he wades over the slippery granite, loses his footing, and falls. All of which has captured the attention of a television news crew that keeps shooting as he climbs out of the fountain with a skinned knee. This must be what happens when you don't know how to fit people into your designs. They get hurt.

The news crew moves on—in search, no doubt, of more colorful behavior. "Are you all right?" Stevie asks the Frisbee guy.

He hurls the Frisbee back into play and grins at her. "That depends," he says. "If I'm not, will you kiss it and make it better?"

How refreshing—a male who wants to flirt instead of attack her. And he *is* cute, in an overgrown adolescent way. "No, thanks."

"Are you a lawyer, then? Want to sue the city for me?"

At that, Stevie manages a defensive little huff. "I hardly think that what you just did to yourself is anybody else's fault."

"I get it, you're a lawyer *for* the city."

"I'm not a lawyer at all." She realizes that she can tell him anything, it won't make any difference. "What I am is . . . a professional hula dancer."

"Really? That's amazing."

"I know. It is. I am. *Aloha nui loa,*" she adds with a hip-swiveling sidestep and a gesture that suggests rippling waves. *"A hui hou!"*

With that, she turns and heads for one of her tombstone benches in the Shadow Plate, where there aren't so many people.

Deeply as Stevie had felt this land inside her, she must have misread it. She must have misread her history. She must have misread her mission. All she wants now is to stop what she's feeling, and what she's feeling is that every awful thing written about her in that article is true, and everyone who reads it will know it's true—and in the face of that, how can she survive? No sooner does she sit than her eyes sting with tears. She worked so hard. She doesn't deserve this. Then it's back to square one: She must deserve this, or this wouldn't be happening.

Stevie removes her sunglasses to fumble for a Kleenex in the slim clutch she's carrying, and when she doesn't find one, swipes a wrist under her eyes.

"Here," a voice says.

She looks up to see a tall, angular woman in a persimmon-colored linen dress whose hair is an uncombable riot of short salt-and-pepper curls. In her extended hand, she holds a tissue.

"Thank you," Stevie says, hearing Lila's voice in her head—*Puff your nose, Stevie*—as she dries her eyes and then blows. "Thank you so much."

When the salt-and-pepper woman smiles, her pale, fine-boned face radiates a mature, off-center sort of prettiness just shy of exquisite. She pulls another tissue from her leather knapsack-style purse. "You've got a little of that raccoon thing going on," she says. Then, sitting down beside Stevie, she sighs and shakes her head. "You must be mad enough to murder that guy."

The accent is pure Chicago, galumphing with flat-footed vowels, but somehow Stevie feels sure that this woman is talking about the architecture-critic guy, not the Frisbee guy. "Actually," she says with a lame little chuckle, "I'm mad enough to murder *myself.*" No sooner are the words out of her mouth than she regrets speaking this way to a stranger who, for all she knows, might be a reporter, or an architecture critic herself. Her pale blue eyes have the kind of penetrating, preternatural look of curiosity that Stevie associates with media people.

"Are you sure," the woman says, laughing, "that you're Henry Pollack's daughter?"

Stevie swivels around to face her. "I'm sorry if this sounds rude, but I don't know you, do I?"

"Not really," the woman exclaims. "And *I'm* sorry about *that.* God, isn't this hilarious? Here we are, already apologizing to each other, and they'd all rather die than say they're sorry."

No, Stevie thinks, *she's not a journalist—she's a nicely dressed lunatic.*

"Wait a second, let me back up here," the woman says, then makes an odd noise—*"erck!"*—that Stevie imagines must be meant to approximate the sound of a car changing gears. "I'm Margo Gaynor, and I think it's high time we got to know each other. I have to tell you, though, you are *so* much more attractive than that picture in the paper."

Now she sounds like a stalker, one who picks victims out of the *Trib* then digs for deeper background on the Internet. Stevie's expression must radiate suspicion, but Margo Gaynor rattles on, oblivious. "You should always wear your hair down, except maybe when you have to look sophisticated. Or older. And that dress—my God, it could have been made for you." The only way Stevie can hear this as normal conversation from a stranger is if she pictures herself trapped on a Greyhound bus next to someone who's not allowed to drive.

"Seems to me," Margo is saying now, "that a few drops of Hawaiian blood go a long, long way."

"Hold on, I—"

"You want to hear something funny? When I was little, I had this fantasy that I'd grow up and marry Hank myself."

"Are you referring to my father?"

"I told you it was funny. I'd grown out of it by the time I met your mother, which was a good thing, since a scrawny girl like me didn't stand a chance against someone with breasts like hers! But what am I saying? I didn't come here to tell you that." She lays a long, slender hand on Stevie's shoulder. "I came here to say I think it's silly for us to carry on their feud. Don't you?"

Whose feud? Stevie might ask if she weren't such a wreck. Okay, so maybe this Margo person isn't certifiable. But in the middle of a full-blown existential crisis, who has time for strolling down some drama queen's memory lane? "It's sounds as though you knew my parents when you were a kid," she says, shrugging away from Margo's touch, slipping her sunglasses back on. "Some other time, I'd be interested. But I'm having a horrible day that has nothing to do with my family, and I have no idea what you're talking about."

Margo cocks her head at Stevie as if *she's* the one who's nuts. "You're serious?"

"I promise you, I did not come out here because I'm in a mood for kidding around."

"Okay, okay. My timing stinks. Just let me ask you this. Is your father still alive?"

Stevie scoots along the bench to put even more distance between them. "Of course he's still alive."

"Then tell him you met Margo in Chicago, and she sends her love. Oh, and here . . ." Margo scrambles through her bag for a card with contact information and a computer disc and presses them into Stevie's hands. "I hope you'll feel like getting in touch later."

Stevie nods, stands, and smoothes her dress as she speaks. "All right. Well. Thanks again for the Kleenex. Bye."

After escaping, she flips open her cell to call a taxi.

During the ride back to East Delaware Place, Stevie's phone beeps with a voice-mail alert, but upon hearing that she has thirty new messages, she turns the damn thing off again. There's no one she wants to talk to now, no one except her father.

Chapter 2

That bizarre woman in the park might think having a crush on Hank when she was a kid makes her special, but honestly, she ought to take a number and get in line behind all of Stevie's classmates, friends, and a few friends' mothers who felt that way about him, too.

At seventy, Hank remains the sort of man people notice. Tan and fit-looking, with a prominent cleft chin, he has a full head of thick, wavy hair, which, now that it's silver, contrasts with his ultramarine eyes almost as much as when it was the color of dark chocolate. Hank sometimes walks with a cane, but in the cashmere sweaters, knife-pleated khakis, and crisp chambray shirts he favors, he still has enough vitality to appear dashing instead of weak. There always seems to be an age-appropriate woman in the background of Hank's busy life, someone he's met at the Seattle health club where he swims laps, or at one of the hotel management conferences where, as a top consultant in the field, he often speaks. In Stevie's opinion, they are all attractive, pleasant, interesting individuals. But she's had her fill. "Even after you stop seeing them," she's told Hank, "they're still calling me to talk about you. Don't bring anybody else around unless you're going to marry her." Not that Stevie's holding her breath there, any more than she now expects her father to hold her hand about her terrible review. Charming as Hank can be—with clients, employees, even strangers—there is never anything the least bit warm or fuzzy about him unless he's been drugged for surgery.

What Hank is best at providing when Stevie's down is not praise or comfort but an infusion of his high-octane doggedness—the sort of stubborn, resilient stuff with which he battled back from a freak case of polio, not letting his withered left leg keep him out of the ocean or off the golf course. When Stevie learned how to ride her green Schwinn, it was Hank who kept running alongside with a stiff-kneed, choppy gallop, holding the bike stable by its seat until she balanced well enough to pedal on her own. When Stevie decided to pursue landscape architecture, it was Hank who arranged interviews at American universities with cutting-edge departments, and Hank who flew her in from Dorking—the all-too-aptly-named town in Surrey where Beryl had opened her antiques shop, catering to a tweedy clientele that defined minimalism as a six-place Royal Doulton setting instead of a twelve. By then, Beryl had slipped into a lackluster second marriage with George Branscomb, an orthodontist who, even now, thinks of Stevie's profession as glorified gardening. When he thinks about it at all.

At the New York landscape architecture firm where Stevie is the youngest partner, the staff has always had a hard time understanding why a rising LA star like her obsesses over all the inevitable little setbacks and never seems to celebrate the successes, not even when she wins awards. Desperate as Stevie is to be her own person, she can nevertheless recognize this as another trait inherited from Hank. Excellence is expected, mistakes are not to be tolerated, particularly when they're your own. Lest Hank surmise that she's blaming him, Stevie to this day avoids mentioning his and Beryl's divorce—an effort that erases how hard she's struggled not to blame herself.

Still, the last thing she wants from her father now is for him to order her back into the fray. She wishes to call him because her current cavalcade of disasters is well beyond being soothed by things that merely remind her of the islands. What she needs now *is* an island. *Her* island—Kaua'i, Pele's first creation. And the most essential function Hank can perform is to tell her whether the house he's kept in Kōloa is available at the moment. If it is, she can hide out there, where no one knows her as the New York minimalist, much less as a hotshot architect's dumped lover. She can lose herself. Swimming along the reef at Māhā'ulepū, where few tourists go. Walking into Kōloa town past carpets of fallen plumeria blossoms. Bringing home succulent, fat-laden pork *laulau* wrapped in ti leaves from Sueoka's Snack Shop, and having a wedge of Lila's *liliko'i* pie for dessert. Hiking for miles on the Waimea Canyon's lofty lip amid all the plants that first colonized the island, inflicting none of the bloodshed, disease, or ongoing grief of colonizing humans. Sleeping on the lanai beneath her great-grandmother's pineapple quilt, awakening just before a flower headache sets in.

She can do all the things she hasn't done for far too long. All the things that, come to think of it, she finds impossible to imagine Brian enjoying.

Based on the evidence of other vacations Stevie's taken with Brian, he would require tablecloth restaurants, not the place mat joints she favors, plus daily room service and visits to the most expensive properties for sale—not that he would buy anything, just for the kick of imagining how he'd redesign them. He would be wary of beaches that lacked the right number of intriguing-looking people necessary to validate his own appearance there. Even worse, he would wear one of those European-style swimsuits that the local boys called cheap hotels—no ball room. Small wonder she never took Brian to Hawai'i. So what had she been doing with him?

Good question, but her mind's too clogged with wondering what *he'll* make of her public trashing to figure out an answer that doesn't sound as if she's just trashing him. An answer smarter than an excuse—that would be nice, too.

❁

Though Stevie talks to Hank on a fairly regular basis, he isn't much for chitchat and she hasn't seen him for six months, since the Chicago deadline heated up. When she calls Hank at his Seattle condo, his voice-mail message says he can be reached at a number she recognizes as belonging to the Kōloa house. Well, she isn't about to go there at the same time as Hank, especially since he's probably not alone, and alone is what *she* wants to be. At a safe distance from all those people, actual people, who—if the hopeless way she's feeling now is any measure—she'll never, ever be able to fit into her designs. But on the chance Hank might be returning to Seattle soon, she calls anyway.

"I've been trying to get you for two days," he says. "Don't you check your messages?"

A minor complaint. But his testy tone sets off such a swell of emotion that her father might as well be the *Tribune* architecture critic. She chokes it back, removes a shoe, hurls it at a pillow, and covers the receiver as she screams a scream that feels as though it ought to summon hotel security, but leaves her body sounding more like a rodent's peeved squeak. "Why don't you call me back later," Stevie tells Hank, "when you're not angry."

She clicks off, hefts her suitcase onto the bed, and starts flinging things inside as her cell phone chimes out the first notes of Beethoven's Ninth. "I'm not angry, honey," Hank says when she answers. "I'm upset. There's a difference."

Honey? Since when does Hank call her honey? On the line, she hears the once-familiar sound of Hank taking a drag on a cigarette. When he quit ten years ago, at his doctor's insistence, Stevie told him she would quit, too, in solidarity with him, as if proposing some kind of union program instead of an act of love. But he didn't need her support; he went off tobacco cold turkey, no problem, while Stevie required patches and gum and a three-month prescription of Xanax. Now she's tempted to relapse right along with him. "Dad, why are you smoking?"

"Why not? I'm old enough to be playing with house money."

"What does *that* mean?"

"It means that I'm not risking anything. I'm going to die anyway. Sooner than I thought, it turns out. That's why I've been calling, to let you know. I want you to go over my will with my attorney, so you won't be confused about anything after I'm gone."

"Gone?" The Johnny's hot dog T-shirt she's been about to pack falls from her hand, and when she speaks again, her voice is faint. "What's happened?"

"They found two tumors on my lungs."

Stevie sinks to the bed, arms wrapped tight around her middle as she rocks from the waist like a pump being primed. Eventually, words flow. "That doesn't mean you're dying. People live for years after getting diagnosed. You will, too."

"Nope," he says flatly.

"But that can't be right!"

"The tumors are inoperable. And it's spread to my liver."

"Do you want me to tell Mother?" Stevie whispers.

"No! Let her come to the funeral. Only I don't want a funeral—that's something else important for you to know. Nobody tells the truth about anyone at those things. And I don't want you paying a fortune to bury me somewhere, either. Cremation's just fine."

"There has to be a treatment, Dad."

Stevie hears him take another drag. "I've already decided the treatment issue with my team. You can't get a terminal illness these days without a team."

"Aren't I on your team?"

"You? You throw like a girl."

"No I don't." She bends for the dropped shirt, tosses it into her suitcase, and summons a louder, more adult tone. "I can't let you do this alone."

"Don't be ridiculous. We all do this alone, kiddo."

Ridiculous? Fury surges again, but this time transforms instantly into pain. As is often the case with him, with her, with them. "I wish you hadn't said that."

"Oh, come on, Stevie. How long have you known me?" Then Hank's the one growing louder. "I refuse to be a burden. I am not one of those people who had a child just so there'd be someone to take care of them when they got old. That's irresponsible, nothing but poor planning."

"Poor planning, my ass."

"I didn't call for this, Stevie. What the hell is wrong with *you*?"

"I am not a child and you are not a burden. I'm coming out there."

"You've got your work. Besides, it's not time."

"I'm on the next flight out of O'Hare."

"You're just being obstinate."

"I'm my father's daughter."

"If I say black, you say white."

"I love you, too, Daddy." The words slip out so easily that she wonders if she's ever said them before. Perhaps she did, once, at a time she can no longer remember. Perhaps he even answered in kind.

"O'Hare?" Hank says. "You're in Chicago?"

"That's not important now. I need to book my flights." She paws through her computer carrying case for a United schedule.

"Where are you staying?" Hank asks.

"I can probably get there late tonight your time, but I have to hurry."

"Are you at the Drake?"

Oh, God, Stevie thinks, *he must be in denial.* But if Hank needs to talk hotels instead of cancer, who is she to refuse him? "A little place on the Gold Coast—the Raphael Hotel." And because he knows Chicago so well, she adds the address: "201 East Delaware."

"It's a hotel now?"

"Uh-huh. A pretty nice one, too."

"Well, it used to be an apartment building. We lived there after the war."

"You lived at 201 East Delaware?" The flesh on Stevie's arms prickles into chicken skin, and as the cell phone knocks against her ear, she realizes she must be trembling. "Are you sure you've got that right?"

"Apartment 604—I can guarantee it. Why are *you* there?"

"Somebody I work with recommended it."

"Funny," Hank says in a musing tone, "I've never heard of the place. You'd think I would have known."

"Known what? That I was staying here?"

"No! That the building where I lived turned into a hotel. Have you got a job in Chicago?"

"Let's talk about that when we're together." Stevie raises a shoulder to hold the phone because it seems both hands are required to check her watch—one to raise a wrist, the other to clear her eyes. "I'll see you in the morning."

❁

Stevie shakes a cigarette out of her newly purchased pack of American Spirits and smokes one down to the filter while she races over to Michigan Avenue, dragging wheeled luggage behind her. After tossing the butt into a trash can, she doubles back to throw the rest of the pack away, too, then flags a cab. Once she's settled in the back seat, the gray-haired driver merges his Crown Victoria into traffic and flashes a tolerant smile in the rearview mirror. "Want to tell me where you're going, or should I just read your mind?"

"Sorry." Stevie pops an Altoid into her mouth. But instead of focusing on his request, she's distracted by the driver's livery license, by the fact that he's named for two different dead presidents, plus one probably dead father, and by how his license photo shows a wider version of the grin he just gave her, teeth gleaming against skin the color of a coconut shell. Once more she starts to answer, but what diverts her now is a bluesy spiritual playing low through the speakers by her head. "That song," she says. "Could you please turn it up?"

"You got it."

A big, booming refrain fills the cab:

"Ain't no grave can hold my body down."

Chicken skin again. While it's hardly unusual to hear a song like this in Chicago, which is, after all, home of the Chicago blues—another nugget from her garden research—it feels as though some Divine Deejay just spun through every composition in the universe and decided that this particular song was the one that Stevie needed to hear.

"When that final trumpet sounds, I'll be gettin' up and walkin' around."

Stevie's certain that the muscular, inflamed voice singing a capella belongs to a white woman possessed by the spirit of an elderly black man. Normally, she wouldn't even consider such a possibility. Where is all this information coming from? She has no earthly idea. Maybe the same place that put her in a hotel where her father once lived.

"Ain't no grave can hold my body down."

Difficult to decide, though, what meaning she's supposed to take from the song. Should she fight for the life of her father—the life that already seems to be escaping his body, releasing into the atmosphere, permeating everything around her—or should she accept that it's coming to an end? Not that she's currently capable of either, cocooned in this eerie fog. Besides, Hank has always done his own fighting.

After the song ends, the driver lowers the volume and speaks. "I suppose it could be Union Station you're heading for, or Midway." Traffic is thick; they're still poking along Michigan Avenue. "But my money," he says, "is on O'Hare."

"Yes, sorry—sorry again." Stevie bends over her knees, light-headed from the cigarette, from the song, from the all-at-once inevitable yet inconceivable conclusion to the situation she's traveling toward. After five deep breaths, she straightens up to tell the driver her airline, and as the Crown Victoria ramps onto the expressway named for Kennedy—*another dead president*—she shifts her sputtering mind to the tasks at hand. Leaving a message for Lorna, telling her where she's headed and why. Arranging for Claudia to take care of her plants while she's gone. Counting out the fare and a generous tip for Roosevelt Jefferson Jr. as he reaches into the trunk for her suitcase.

After he drives off, she tucks his receipt into her wallet and sees that he's scribbled something on the back:

"Blessings on your journey home."

At the airport ticket counter, Stevie spends frequent-flier miles for a first-class upgrade, the better to get a drink into her hand before takeoff.

She clears security and then, thinking of what an avid reader her father is, stops at a concourse bookstore, where she alights on a huge new hardcover biography of FDR—over a thousand pages. It seems like another sign, going directly to a book about the man who is her father's favorite president, a fellow polio survivor, and also links up to the taxi driver. She wonders if everything in her world is *always* so connected, if she'd pay attention. Or is she just too panicked right now to function on a more rational level? A more Hank-ish level. She remembers how, on her third birthday, she howled because Hank wouldn't allow her to take her bottle to bed that night. According to his reasoning, she was now too old for a bottle, and if she didn't stop crying for it, he had to conclude that she wasn't really three and all her birthday presents would have to be returned. Another battle Hank won. Not that a three-year-old could put up much of a fight. Maybe giving her father this biography is just a magical version of the same bargain; since she's never known him *not* to finish a book he's started, a massive one like this ought to keep him alive for quite a while. Long enough so that she might finally figure out how to win at least one battle for herself.

As the plane passes over Minnesota, Stevie's already starting her second vodka martini, grateful to be spared the obligation of small talk by the empty seat beside her. "Ain't No Grave" returns, playing on a continuous loop in her head. She closes her eyes and thinks of the Night Marchers, those ghostly warriors Lila used to spook her with back in the days when she came to the Kōloa house to cook and take care of Stevie. You were always supposed to leave the doors to your house unlocked, front and back, so the Night Marchers might pass through on their way to the sea. Lila would understand this song. So would Stevie's British grandfather, a wispy, ethereal figure long before he died, always whistling "Clair de lune." She remembers talking with him about spirits when she was small—this was something they had to do while tending orchids in the greenhouse, where the air was thick with the smell of humus and they couldn't be overheard. According to Grandpa's wife and daughter, talking to spirits was the dreadful reason for his family's downfall, their forced migration from England to Oahu, their mandatory metamorphosis from heavy tweeds to tropical-weight wools, and they did *not* enjoy being reminded.

"I've been noticing how Hawaiians often speak of their dead in the present tense," Grandpa said once as Stevie helped him make beds for his hybrid seedlings. "Over them, death truly hath no dominion."

"Momma says they're just superstitious," Stevie told him.

"Well, you might say that your mother fell a bit far from the tree."

"You mean she's *haole*?" It was a new word for Stevie then, something she herself had been called by some tough local kids, and she'd known by the way they'd spat it out at her—*"Stevie's a fish-belly howl-ee"*—that it couldn't be nice.

"*I'm* the *haole* here," Grandpa had said. "In the word's colloquial sense." Stevie's Hawaiian great-great grandmother wasn't Grandpa's ancestor, she was his wife's, so far removed that only a whisper of her amber, Polynesian beauty could be seen in Beryl's elegant skin and bone structure, barely a sigh in Stevie, with her coal black hair and ashy gray, almond-shaped eyes. Stevie knew the story's essentials. Her Oahu-born great-great-*tūtū* had married a British naval officer who never went home, and *her* eldest daughter had married another Brit, who did, sailing back with his bride to raise a family in Surrey. Stevie wouldn't dream of using the word *"haole"* around her mother or grandmother, those strict enforcers of refined manners. But Grandpa was the one who lived by language, equally devoted to his unabridged Oxford and Hawaiian dictionaries. He knew enough to tell Stevie that *"haole"* didn't really mean white.

"In point of fact," he said, "Hawaiians used the word to describe ghosts. That's what the first whites looked like to them. But the real meaning keeps unfolding. If you translate *haole* from the Hawaiian literally, it's a little poem of a word. What *haole* means is being without breath, without spirit."

Well, Grandpa had enough breath for everyone, if you asked Beryl or Grammy. Maybe right at this moment, he's parsing a sonnet with Shakespeare, or the Earl of Oxford, or another one of those loquacious Elizabethans Grandpa had hired a literary-minded psychic in London to channel for him.

"Poor dear," Grammy would say. "The Blitz did him in. Otherwise, he would *never* have published that book."

"That book" was Grandpa's meticulous record of how his conversations with the dead had revealed who *really* wrote everything attributed to Shakespeare—every play, every sonnet—and his insistence on publishing it had destroyed his academic career, forcing Grammy to solicit help from family connections in Hawai'i, where spirits held such sway that not nearly so many people thought Grandpa ought to be institutionalized. He hired on to teach literature at Punahou, Honolulu's most prestigious private school. A comedown from Cambridge, to be sure, but plenty tony by island standards. They were a fertile bunch, those missionary families who came to Hawai'i to do good, then ended up doing well. Their descendants made Punahou a bastion for the islands' white elite, and so long as Grandpa didn't shove down their throats the Oxford earl—Grandpa's pick in the Will the Real William Shakespeare Please Stand Up Sweepstakes—Grandpa had a job.

Stevie guessed he was the only member of her family who wouldn't laugh at her—or be horrified—if she revealed that she had seen Pele. "No, no, my dear," Grandpa corrected. "You didn't *see* Pele."

"I didn't?"she said, deflating.

"No. She *showed* herself to you."

"So you believe it happened?"

He shrugged as he nodded, and even Stevie, young though she was, recognized the gestures of a person with no real alternative. "But learn a lesson from your grandfather—don't waste your time trying to convince anybody else. It's a private honor, and the only question that matters is why she chose you. You're so young, it may be a long while before you find an answer, so there's no point fretting over it now, is there? Someday we'll go to the Big Island together, visit the volcano where Pele finally found a home for all her fire."

But they never did. He tried to arrange a trip for just the two of them, but Stevie's mother refused to let her go. Grandpa went anyway, by himself. Then he died, when the cooling fresh-lava bench on which he stood broke away and fell into the ocean. Soon after came Grammy's death, then Stevie's parents' divorce. Now the piece of Grandpa that she cherishes is the bracelet on her wrist. Still, their forgotten conversation coming back to her in such detail makes Stevie wonder if the same gene responsible for unhinging Grandpa is surging up in *her,* exacerbated by fractional Hawaiian blood. And Hank? As much time as he's spent on the islands, her father is the ultimate *haole* rationalist, shaped by the stormy, brawling, husky City of the Big Shoulders. He believes only in this life. Which was probably why Beryl had married him—someone as different from her own dreamy, distracted, disgraced father as she could find. And when that didn't work, she chose a paler, less passionate man who was content to worship her, requiring little in return.

Stevie finishes her drink with a groan. Thumbing the text of her parents' incompatibility was useful, once. It helped her stop thinking that *she* was responsible for their breakup, that a more lovable child might have inspired them to have extra children and glued them together for keeps. But what possible good can it do now? Her usual crisis mode, which is to spring into action with a game plan, is thwarted by Hank's resistance to her even playing on his team.

Mindless entertainment—that ought to help stop all the churning inside. Stevie puts on headphones to watch the movie that has just started on overhead screens, about a small-town girl determined to play Olympic-level soccer. But when the girl's father appears, coaching her on to victory against all odds, Stevie bursts into tears.

She takes off the headphones, mops her face with a cocktail napkin, and reaches into her computer bag for a book on desert succulents. It's her custom to spend half an hour every morning reading about plants she's unfamiliar with, and in the normal course of events, she would be riveted enough to lose herself in all the particular properties of the claret cup hedgehog cactus. Now, though, her eyes glaze over. Putting the book away, she notices the CD case given to her by Margo, that Kleenex woman in the park. Tempted as she is to toss it into the trash bag that a flight attendant is hauling down the aisle—why clutter things up at this point with peripheral people from the past?—she's also curious. Just what would someone like Margo want her to see?

Once her laptop powers up, Stevie inserts the disc, expecting some sort of written document to announce itself in the computer directory. Instead, a DVD program starts to play what looks to be a grainy film-to-video-to-digital transfer of old family movies. As if to leave no doubt, a title appears: *Gaynor Family Home Movies.* Oh, swell. A soundless record of some stranger's milestone events. First up is what must be meant as an establishing shot of the Drake Hotel, with big-finned cars whizzing by. Just begun and already bland as milk. But something keeps Stevie watching the wedding reception that follows—probably the same fascination that, while her parents were divorcing, had her hooked on a TV program called *Family,* in which there were three siblings, count 'em, with perfectly mated parents dispensing psychologically sound solutions for every conceivable problem. An alien universe.

The bride in this production is a tall, slender beauty with dark hair and piercing blue eyes. Must be Margo's mother, to judge by their resemblance. The era would be right, too, as indicated by women in tidy fifties-style perms, men in severe side parts and brush cuts. Was there ever a decade that tried harder to make everybody look so absolutely grown-up? Even the children seem like miniature adults, goofy edges all combed down and polished. The only visual comic relief comes from older ladies in hats that threaten to fly off with their faces. Next is the wedding dinner, with the camera zooming in on table after table of people looking up from plates of prime rib to wave. The ritual is familiar enough to Stevie; this is nothing but a dated version of all the hotel weddings she's ever attended. Seen one, seen 'em all.

Stevie yawns and stretches. Maybe this cinematic sedative will help her catch up on some sleep. She *ought* to sleep, with a tight connection in Los Angeles and a long flight to Līhuʻe ahead of her. But before Stevie can shut down her computer, there appears a face that she recognizes. Hank's. And oh, he's so whole and so young—younger than Stevie is now, by quite a bit—with a pretty redhead by his side. Once, long before Stevie ever watched any science fiction movies, she time-traveled in a dream and saw her father as a boy her age—eight at the time—but just as they were about to speak, the sheer excitement of finding him cut down to her size woke her. Replaying this footage of Hank is about as near as she'll ever come to that dream in reality. She moves in closer to the screen to watch it over and over, then leans back to see if he'll appear again.

He does. Clapping as a curly-headed little girl—Margo?—blows out several candles on her birthday cake, which has a ballerina figure stuck in chocolate icing; sitting in the bleachers of Wrigley Field with this same child, older now, perched solidly on his shoulders for the seventh-inning stretch; walking by giraffes at the Lincoln Park Zoo with her hand in his. And later, in somebody's living room, ascending a short flight of steps to stand beside Beryl, who's tan and lovely in a pale blue cheongsam, a fringed black shawl around her shoulders. Stevie can tell by her father's easy, even-footed navigation of those steps that polio is still ahead of him. Ever since she can remember, he's climbed only with his good right leg in the lead, bearing his full weight.

In Beryl's arms is a baby gnawing on her own fist. A baby who can only be Stevie. After an abrupt cut, Stevie shows up again, this time held by the bride from the earlier footage—older and more matronly looking in gray flannel slacks and a nubby sweater. Then there's the little girl, who might be ten by now, tickling the baby's tummy until she kicks her feet and obliges with a gleeful, gummy grin. In another shot, Stevie's baby self bawls in the arms of an obviously ill, thin-lipped older woman with tightly coiled gray hair.

Stevie didn't watch all those episodes of *Family* for nothing. People appear repeatedly in scenes like these only if they're tied by blood to most everybody else around them.

After landing in Los Angeles, she races to the airline's executive lounge and pulls out Margo's card to send an e-mail. Her message contains only four words:

How are we related?

Chapter 3

Sometimes Margo thinks that her mother's death certificate was a permission slip, freeing her at last from the pressure to do things mandated by Evelyn. Oh, she'd battled Evelyn. After all, they both had Pollack tempers. But for so many years, Margo had succumbed to Evelyn's if-you-don't-I'll-never-speak-to-you-again ultimatums. She got married at the Drake, the way Evelyn did. Went to the same obstetrician. Lived in a North Shore suburb close to Evelyn's house on Deere Park Drive. If there were a muscle in the body for making independent decisions, hers would have atrophied by the time she was thirty, when she began long-overdue resistance training, and ever since Evelyn's death two years ago, it seems as though that conjectural muscle of Margo's has gotten pumped up on steroids. She threw herself into community politics, took tango lessons, tutored at-risk children. She learned to knit, creating wildly colored, somewhat lopsided scarves for everyone in her family. She counseled at a clinic for teenagers with sexually transmitted diseases and is now enrolled, as a forty-six-year-old graduate student, to earn a degree in marital and family therapy.

Still, it came almost as a shock when, as she proceeded from one new endeavor to the next, no one told her she'd made a mistake. No one told her she'd failed. Better yet, no one faulted her for moving back to the city. Or for letting her hair go gray. Or for wearing a pair of panties that, were she to be run down by one of Evelyn's proverbial buses, everyone in the emergency room would see bore the legend, *I ♥ My Cunt.* In fact, the only terrible criticism Margo endures comes from the part of Evelyn that lives on inside, always ready to carp. *You're such a dilettante. How do you expect anyone to take you seriously? They're all snickering up their sleeves at your antics.* Sometimes Evelyn's so nasty that Margo talks back while riding the El or getting groceries at the Jewel—"Oh, just shut up, Mother, would you?"—and other people change seats or swing their carts in wide arcs to avoid her.

Once Margo's nest was empty, it seemed amazing that someone with her background had sent a couple of decently adjusted, well-grounded kids out into the world. Now she wants to put all that nurturing energy to work on a broader scale. One requirement for her degree program is that each student must write a family history. "Pay particular attention," the professor advised, "to surgical cuts. Family members who no longer speak or have anything to do with one another. Be sure to note the cause of the cut, and the cut's ongoing ramifications. If possible, get both sides of the story."

Margo could hear Evelyn shrieking. *All you need to know is I hate Hank, and I'm right to hate Hank, and if you don't hate Hank, you're wrong. Not only wrong, but disloyal. Insensitive. Spiteful, too. So just leave it alone.*

Margo had managed to track Hank down to Seattle, but his address and phone were unlisted, as if he'd no desire to be found. Then, while stacking a mess of old newspapers for pickup, Margo noticed an article she'd neglected to read, about a new South Side park with a garden funded by one of Evelyn's old charity-committee pals. The piece included a photograph of the landscape architect who had won the garden commission and would be attending the dedication ceremony. The name might as well have been neon-lit, the way it leapt out at her: STEPHANIE POLLACK.

Could this sophisticated, solemn-eyed young woman be little Stevie? And if it was, did she swim so far out on her own? No one could ever accuse *her* of being a dilettante. Just look at all the awards, all the validation. Still, different as their lives appeared, might Hank be as big a storm inside Stevie as Evelyn is in Margo?

So Margo went to the opening for Stevie's garden to find out, and came home with Evelyn in full cry. *I don't care what she told you—he's poisoned her against us, you should have listened to me.* But Margo's heart had gone out to Stevie the minute she saw her on that bench, trying not to cry, and she's not about to harden it now.

When Stevie's cryptic e-mail arrives that very night, Margo's reply all but writes itself, a whoosh of right-brained words pouring through her keyboard-crabbed hands and flying fingers. Not so much a description of her feelings but the feelings themselves, giddy at being released. She doesn't bother with rereading, rewriting, or standard punctuation. She just punches the "send" button and then checks her e-mail every half hour for a response, as if she'd just written a love letter. In a way, Margo supposes, she has.

Chapter 4

No other customer is in the Līhu'e airport Avis office as Stevie signs papers for an economy-class roller skate of a car. It is almost eleven p.m. Hawaiian time but four in the morning by her body clock, and she's running on such jumpy, mixed-up emotions that instead of reveling in her return to the place she so often aches for in homesick fevers, she might as well have just landed in Detroit. Where she is doesn't matter at this moment, only her mission. Which right now means making sure that Hank receives whatever state-of-the-art treatment is available, wherever he has to go in order to get it, and that his cigarettes are tossed—to hell with his house money. Never mind that her own plan had been to run away from everything wrong in her life by coming here; if that's what Hank has in mind, he'll have to fight her to do it. Bad enough he's hidden his illness from her until now, but if she learns from Margo that he's been hiding relatives, too, well, there's another tempest brewing.

"Want me to mark your map?" the rental clerk asks. She wears a company-issued red-hibiscus-print blouse, has a fresh plumeria blossom clipped into her hair, and is attractive in the way of so many island women—an intriguing blend of bloodlines.

"Oh, I don't need a map," Stevie tells her.

"You must come here plenty, not to need a map at night."

"I used to, but it's been four years."

"Bet you're glad to be back."

"Not exactly," Stevie says. "My father's ill. Which car is mine?"

The clerk steps out from behind the counter and startles Stevie with a hug. "Welcome home," she says.

The New Yorker part of Stevie, tempered by routine doses of irony and sarcasm, is suspicious. *Is my tiny piece of native sending signals to her way-bigger piece of native? Or is she just dishing out* aloha *kitsch for the* haole *girl?* But deeper down, Stevie is aware that to question this sincere, once-familiar warmth, to do anything at all but bask in it, would be ridiculous.

Instead of the roller-skate car, the clerk upgrades her at no extra charge to a roomier red Mustang convertible. "*Kama'āina* discount," she explains. *Kama'āina* means local—or as local as a largely *haole* person like Stevie can get.

What it really means, she can hear Grandpa saying, *is child of the land.* A label that describes how Stevie once lived, nurtured by her physical experiences of Kaua'i, its steep canyons and lush valleys, taro patches and tasseled cane fields, waterfalls and beaches, and all the gods and goddesses whose permission Lila had taught her to ask before plucking a flower, entering the ocean, stepping through a stream. It's no accident she chose a job that lets her be outside so much of the time, amid all the elements that make her feel most at ease in the world—water, stone, sunlight, living things. But that's a career, a matter of being someone who does something. Here, as a kid, it was always just a matter of being, period.

Island-born though she is, Stevie is such a stickler for truth that she wouldn't have claimed *kama'āina* status for herself because of her long absence—much longer than those four years, really, if you added it all up. Then, too, she learned some time ago that while there were those like Lila, who felt that deep love for this place meant you belonged on the island, *haole* or not, there were others who felt differently. Still, it's as nice as being embraced, having *kama'āina* hung on her like a homemade lei.

Stevie only napped fitfully for an hour or two on her last flight, but driving beneath this crescent moon sky and breathing this tender air again is so stirring that she stays alert all the way to the Kōloa district.

On the long grass drive that leads to her father's house is an old plantation cottage, once part of a cane workers' camp, that Hank had moved onto his property before restoring it. For years it's been rented to an ever-changing cast. Whoever lives there now is having a typical Saturday-night party—everybody out in the yard, eating off the grill, pouring out drinks from pitchers, and shaking their hips to Willie K music. As Stevie drives by, a few people she doesn't recognize raise a hand with thumb and pinkie extended, giving her a "hang loose" shaka wiggle that she returns while thinking, *Fat chance.* Hanging loose, really loose, is something she can do only when escaping her real life. A stranger's hug and a couple of waves, no matter how genuine, aren't enough to alter the fact that this trip promises to be less an escape than a head-on collision.

The lone outward sign that Hank's house gives of expecting Stevie is a floodlight left on. The house itself is a more spacious version of the rental cottage, with better materials, maybe, but the same board-and-batten construction painted in the same shade of palm-frond Hawai'i green. Nothing fancy, but all at once so simple and welcoming that just the sight of it breathes a little calm into Stevie's heart.

She parks next to Hank's prized old white Land Rover Defender. He can't pump a clutch with his polio-withered left leg, and she remembers how excited he was when they came out with a model that had an automatic transmission.

The first scent to hit her nose is intense, almost narcotic—sweet as *pīkake* petals that open in the dark, but shot through with something savory, more like cloves. Unable to resist, she follows the fragrance to a stand of flowering lady-of-the-night shrubs that she now remembers planting on the shady side of the house, then snaps off three clusters to take inside. While a frog chorus ratchets up in a nearby pond, Stevie climbs wide steps that lead to unlocked double doors. As little time as she's been here, a fine powdering of red dirt already clings to the soles of her shoes. She leaves them alongside Hank's scruffy Top-Siders and enters the screened lanai that hugs two sides of the house, flipping off the light behind her. Navigating now by moon glow, she sets her suitcase aside and opens another door to step soundlessly over bamboo floors and *lauhala* mats into the high-ceilinged center of the house.

The master bedroom door is closed, with no telltale strip of light underneath. Though everything points to Hank's being asleep, she's desperate to knock, desperate to find proof of him alive and breathing. But before her knuckles hit the door she stops. Why disturb his rest because she's overamping on fear? Besides, she won't be much good for anything if she doesn't get some sleep herself. But where? There are choices: her childhood room (now fitted out with a double bed to accommodate couples when the house is leased to tourists), one of two other bedrooms, or the lanai, where there's a futon. She'd have no privacy on the lanai come morning, but that doesn't matter so much as the trade winds she'll be able to feel more fully from there. She would also be better situated to hear Hank when he gets up to make coffee and join him first thing. Maybe if they're both still sleepy, anxieties and defenses down, they'll get off to a better start.

Stevie turns a lamp on low, finds a slender ceramic vase to fill with water, and snips her lady-of-the-night stems into an arrangement for the polished koa dining table. Then she changes into an oversize Yankees T-shirt and goes to the closet where family things are kept to pull out her great-grandmother's quilt, a splash of stylized green-and-gold pineapples on a field of creamy moiré silk, wave-patterned to glisten like water. Beryl took nothing of her life in Hawai'i back to England, save her daughter.

Within minutes of crawling underneath the quilt, Stevie falls into a thick, heavy sleep.

The breeze brushing her cheek floats her in dreams to an ocean pier, where she fishes alongside a frail old man who sits in a striped beach chair, struggling to hold his rod steady. Stevie stands to reel in her catch—an improbable marlin, a gorgeous trophy fish she has no wish to eat, or hang mounted on the wall, or destroy for any other reason. *I release you,* she thinks, and instantly her line returns, hook and all. While she reaches into a bucket for more bait, she sees the old man scoot his chair to the edge of the pier and tip into the transparent water below, as if on purpose. She dives in right away, swimming through schools of yellow tangs and turquoise wrasses, but doesn't see him anywhere, and only when he shouts to her does she realize that this man is her father.

"Stevie! Come here!"

She starts to panic, she's running out of air, but still she keeps searching.

"Stevie?" His voice is loud and pained and clear, not burbling through water unintelligibly the way hers does when she tries to answer.

"Stevie," he cries again. "Where are you?"

Stevie bolts upright on the futon and switches on a lamp. It's three a.m., dead-of-night dark outside, and that's where her father is.

"I'm coming," she shouts, then jumps out of bed, pulls on a pair of sweatpants, flips the floodlight switch, and runs barefoot down the steps to hover over Hank, who lies on the ground. His silk kimono has come untied over his pajama bottoms. The ankle of his good leg is bruised and swollen. The arm that must have broken his fall is bloody. A half-smoked cigarette smolders on the bottom step.

"Help me up," he commands.

"How long have you been calling?"

"Never mind that, just get me to the stairs—I can stand from there."

"Put your arms around my neck." It seems as though lifting him should be easy because Hank has lost an astonishing amount of weight since the last time she saw him. Even his hair looks thinner. His skin, too—tan though he is. "Hold tight," Stevie says, all the while wondering if she's really awake, if this old man from her dream could really be her father, if the smoky, sickly scent that's knocking all the ginger and jasmine and lady-of-the-night right out of her head might really belong to him.

She bends, takes a deep breath, and strains to bring Hank up with her on the exhale. If they were truly in water, his weight buoyant, maybe she'd succeed. But he's still a big man, taller than she by almost a foot, and hard as he tries, strong as she is, she can't lift him to his feet.

"This isn't going to work," Stevie says, dropping to her knees beside him. "I'll call the medics."

"No!" Hank bellows. "You can't call the medics."

Yes, this is her father, all right—her insisting, resisting, overruling father. For as long as she can remember, just the fact of his yelling has triggered tears, and even though she's at least enough of her own person to realize that she has nothing to do with why he's so upset, this time is no exception. She works to quell all her quaverings, to sound calm. "Why not?"

"Because you have to call the goddamn hospice people—they won't let you call an ambulance."

"Hospice?" A gut-punch of a word. Only people who aren't being treated qualify for hospice care. Lost causes. "What were you going to do, Dad? Wait until you were dead to ask me out here?"

Struggling to right himself, Hank moans. "This is no way to live." His hands press into tiny ironwood tree cones and his skin is so fragile that cuts appear.

"Stop," she says, taking hold of his shoulders. "You're hurting yourself. You have to be still."

He's short of breath—shivering, too. "Get a chair," he barks. "I'll pull myself up on the chair."

"I know you hate giving up, but, Dad, this really could kill you!"

"Get it."

From force of habit, Stevie obeys. Before returning with the chair, though, she grabs a phone and the pineapple quilt.

Hank is so exhausted now that the chair is no help, either. And while all their efforts have somehow brought him closer to the steps, within a few feet, they might as well be miles away.

Stevie measures her words out flat and firm. "I don't care what you say, I'm calling for help."

"Is that right?" Hanks rasps. "You're just lucky they've got me on Prozac."

Another shocker, but she can tell he meant to be funny, and being able to laugh, even for a few seconds, seems like a step in the right direction. "Thank God for small favors."

"Call Lila. She'll know what to do."

At last, something that makes sense. Lila's a registered nurse—has been for years. She answers on the first ring.

"Oh, my girl," Lila says after hearing what happened. "Such a lucky thing you were there."

She knows more than I do, Stevie thinks. And, as usual, Lila is right. If Stevie hadn't flown in last night, someone else might be finding Hank—much later, and in much worse shape. Maybe even dead. A thought awful enough to diminish her wild, out-of-control sense of having failed her father—for not hearing him sooner, for not being able to get him back on his feet.

With Hank cooperating now, Stevie rolls him onto the quilt, and while she's wrapping it tight around him Lila pulls into the drive—not behind the wheel of a car but straddling a motorcycle, a sleek old Honda Nighthawk. She takes off a helmet emblazoned with the words *Hula Tūtū* and bustles over with confident concern. But how on earth is one other woman, even if she is a leather-wearing, motorcycle-riding, hula-dancing grandma, going to be able to do with Hank what Stevie couldn't?

By using the blanket to lift Hank up to a sitting position, for starters. Then Lila flips a long braid shot through with gray over her shoulder and turns her broad, honey-hued face to Stevie. "Run get the oxygen tank," she says.

"Oxygen tank?" One more sign of death's proximity, but with the ballast of Lila's efficiency, Stevie only adds, "Where?"

"In his bedroom."

Sure enough, there's a small metal canister by Hank's nightstand.

Lila hooks the breathing apparatus over his ears, turns a knob, and as Hank's inhalations extend, steady, then strengthen, she speaks to him sweetly. "You're a stubborn old man, aren't you, Hank? *Pa'akik'ī* to the max, eh?"

With that, Stevie's what-I-don't-know-is-a-lot list lengthens. She's always thought of Lila as hers, but now, amazingly, it seems Lila also belongs to Hank. There's no other possible explanation for how, after all her years of saying "Mr. Pollack"—in front of Stevie, anyway—Lila has progressed to not only a first-name basis, but lighthearted banter, with a little Hawaiian-language lesson thrown in. Next thing you know, she'll be slipping into pidgin, the Hawaiian creole that Beryl could never bear to hear her daughter use. And it's impossible for Stevie to tell if the awful little stab of jealousy she feels comes from reluctance to share Lila, or to share the father whose time she could never get enough of when he was well. Whom she was always too impressed by, too intimidated by, to banter with herself.

Lila pockets Hank's cigarette butt, extinguished now, and gives his chest a gentle poke. "I think I've got a pretty good idea what went down. You couldn't sleep, took another pain pill, and didn't bring your cane when you sashayed out here for a smoke. Then you got all light-headed and tripped on that last step, didn't you? And don't give me any stink-eye, mister—I'm not gonna spank you."

After Hank's had enough oxygen, Lila puts the tank aside. Using the blanket again to leverage his weight, she and Stevie draw him onto the first step. "Can you get up the rest on your *ōkole*?" Lila asks, but before the words are out of her mouth Hank is already doing this, using his arms, slack-muscled but strong enough still to lift his butt onto the next step. When he reaches the top, the women raise him to his feet and then, leaning on them, he's able to hobble all the way to his bedroom.

"Bet you're thinking that bed never looked so good," Lila tells Hank. "I'm tempted to crawl right in myself."

"Be my guest," Hank says. "I have to warn you, though. Nothing's going to happen."

"No problem, Hank," Lila says as she sits beside him. "You're not the first man who can't keep up with me."

Stevie winces when she sees how Hank needs both hands to swing up his withered left leg and lie down. For all she knows, never having watched him go to bed before, he's had to do this for quite a while. But her newly heightened awareness tells her no, this development is recent.

Once Hank is comfortable, Lila checks his wrist and ankle to make sure they aren't broken. Stevie fills a small plastic bucket with warm, soapy water so Lila can clean his cuts.

While Lila works, Hank points an accusing finger at Stevie's chest. "Traitor," he says. "I can't believe my eyes."

Stevie braces for reproach, an old reflex with Hank, before realizing what it is he's talking about. "It's the Yankees T-shirt," she explains to Lila. "National League pitchers have to take their turn at bat, but American League teams have pinch hitters. Heresy, according to Dad."

"That's not the only reason I loathe the Yankees," Hank says. "It's a hell of a lot tougher to build a great team than it is to buy a good one."

"I'm just glad you weren't hallucinating," Lila tells him, then goes back outside to retrieve the oxygen tank and her duty bag.

Hank sinks into his pillows and sighs. "Stevie?"

"Yes?" Now that they're alone again, she waits for him to tell her something important, something maybe even profound. But what he says is, "Turn on the TV, would you? I want to see how the Cubs did."

Hank's old television set, the only one in the house, is on the blink. The basic cable sports channel's picture is ghostly, hard to look at, but the announcer's voice is clear. While Lila administers more oxygen and takes Hank's blood pressure, the news he wants comes: "The Cubs beat the Brewers in Milwaukee last night, eight to four, with Mark Prior the winning pitcher."

"Know what that means?" Hank says.

"No," Lila says, "but I bet you're gonna tell us."

"The first Cubs pitcher since '98 to win seven straight decisions. Remember the last one, Stevie?"

Since the Cubs are the safest, most neutral topic between them—the closest thing they have to a shared religion—Stevie hesitates only a second before answering. "Kevin Tapani?"

"Atta girl. You learned a lot from your old man. No—don't turn it off. Let's see how Houston did with the Padres." It's almost as if the oxygen's made Hank high. Or maybe it's that extra pain pill he took kicking all the way in. If Stevie could just close her eyes and listen only to Hank's vigorous-again voice, only to his Cubs talk, she might be able to convince herself that nothing terrible happened tonight, and nothing terrible is wrong with him.

The Padres lost, as it turns out. Not the outcome Hank wanted. "That leaves the Cubs still half a game behind the Astros."

Lila switches off the TV. "Enough. They'll play again tomorrow."

"Can we watch?" Stevie asks.

Hank shakes his head. "The game's not on any of my channels."

Stevie's brain hums into strategizing mode. "Then I'll hook up my computer so we can get coverage on the Internet."

Hank shrugs. "Whatever that means."

"It means we can listen on WGN Radio, get the game with good old-fashioned play-by-play. Mai tais and the Cubs out on the lanai—how's that sound?"

"Great," Hank says. "But hold the rum for the seventh-inning stretch. It's not yet noon here when they start. When I was a small boy, you know, I'd listen to all the Cubs' away games on the radio."

A piece of buried treasure there, spoken with an unfamiliar, reminiscent timbre. "Who did you listen with then?" Stevie asks.

"Just Pepper."

"Who was Pepper?"

"Smartest dog you ever saw. A fox terrier. Floppy little ears, one bent over higher than the other. Before the game started, I'd put down napkins at every corner of the dining room table, pretending they were bases."

"Then what did you do?"

"Stand at home plate to take the pitch, bunt, swing—whatever the announcer said the Cubs batter was doing. Pepper ran the bases with me."

"Was this on East Delaware?" Stevie's thinking of the hotel where she'd stayed.

"No." Hank gives a long, loud yawn. "This was on Bittersweet Place."

"You're kidding. You actually lived on a street called Bittersweet?"

"What's so strange about that?"

"Oh, nothing. Just how you always say, 'In this life you've got to take the bitter with the sweet.' "

"Huh," Lila snorts. "Sounds like an ulcer recipe to me."

When Hank yawns again, Lila crosses the room to fold Stevie into an embrace so big and firmly grounded, so like Lila herself, that by its end their hearts once more seem set in sympathy. "I can finish up here," Lila says. "You both need sleep."

Closing the bedroom door behind her, Stevie lingers long enough to hear Hank speak—"We're going down a bad road now, aren't we?"—and Lila answer, "Not yet. Meanwhile, you got what you wanted, yeah? You got your girl here."

Stevie leans against the door and muffles a sob with the flat of her hand, wishing she could believe that Lila's words were true.

Stevie's in the kitchen, rubbing at the last stubborn bloodstain on the pineapple quilt, when her first memory of Hank hits so hard that she gasps for air. And it's not just her first memory of Hank. It's her first memory, period.

Could it be that first memories are even more important than Lorna thinks a man's first words are? And if so, how reliable is this one, coming from a time before she could even speak a complete sentence? Its specifics aren't recorded in home movies, or snapshots, or lovingly told, oft-repeated stories. As far as Stevie knows, the details exist only inside her. And it's the details that convince her. She couldn't have made them up. What she remembers must have happened.

She's in her mother's arms, going to visit Hank in the Honolulu hospital where he went to recover from polio. He stands gripping parallel bars in what must be the physical therapy facility, and a nurse watches while he strains to propel himself forward with his stricken left leg. At the sight of his wife and daughter, Hank's face lights up. Beryl sets Stevie down on the floor at the end of the bars, facing her father, so he can see not just how she's grown, but even more important, how's she's now able to stand on her own, to maybe even reach him on her own. They are both the same. They are both learning to walk, Stevie for the first time, her father for the second. And their mission is identical: to keep walking, unsteady and awkward, until at last they reach each other.

The memory stops there, with her achieving this hard thing that's made easier not only by how eager she is for a hug, for a kiss, for his applause and amazement, but by the sense that in doing this, she will heal her father. At least, that's how the memory seems now, though the meanings she's put to it are so delicate, so evanescent, that she doesn't trust herself to speak of them when Lila emerges from Hank's room and joins her at the sink.

"I've seen plenty pineapple quilts," Lila says. "Even made one myself. But your great-*tūtū*'s? Still my favorite. And if what the aunties say is right, she was sewing her descendants into this quilt. There's a space for you between the stitches."

"Grammy said the creamy fabric came from her wedding dress."

"Big-time prudes, those missionaries. But they did a good thing, teaching *wahine* to quilt. One like that would bring money today. Three thousand, at least. The Bishop Museum folks—they'd frame it."

"Not with this bloodstain," Stevie says. "I should have grabbed a different cover."

"Let's see about that. Got some shampoo?"

While Lila goes to work with a bottle of Aveda, energy leaves Stevie's body all at once, like a supercharged sugar crash. "Guess I better call the hospice people," Stevie says. "Let them know what happened."

"*I'll* let them know. That's who I work for."

"I thought you worked for the hospital."

"Not anymore. I'm on the clock, my girl."

Watching Lila massage suds into the stain with her fingertips, Stevie thinks of when they were last together. In New York, at Christmastime, almost a year ago. Lila had insisted on flying out to nurse Stevie through the aftermath of a tubular pregnancy that took her right ovary and fallopian tube. Looking back, it was the beginning of the end with Brian. "He should be here taking care of you, too," Lila had said at the time, and Stevie rushed to his defense.

"Don't be so hard on him, Lila. When I went to the hospital, it was an emergency. He didn't know I was pregnant. I didn't know myself! My periods have always been weird, and the home test I did was negative. It's not like we were trying. Brian already has a child, and he's not at all keen on having another. Besides, you're forgetting everything he's sent over for us—the food, the movies, the books."

"I'll tell you what's worse," Lila said. "*You're* forgetting *you.*"

Stevie couldn't let herself agree, not then, so Lila was the one she distanced herself from, not Brian.

Now Stevie wonders whether the pineapple quilt contains any stitches for the imperfectly planted life she'd lost and has never known how to grieve, unless chalking up extra mileage when she ran counted as a denial mode of mourning. Maybe Great-*Tūtū* possessed the power to see that Stevie would be the end of her fractured little family's line.

Lila points to a carefully patched place by the Hawaiian-flag appliqué that's sewn onto the quilt's underside, near the bloodstain. "I did that," Lila says, "after you cut into it by accident with your scissors. You were scared to death what would happen when your mother found out. But she never even noticed."

Stevie shrugs. "Mother's roots here didn't go deep enough for her to care. Our one similarity is that she got yanked from England the way I got yanked from Hawai'i."

With a fingertip, Stevie traces the Union Jack that fills the Hawaiian flag's right-hand corner, a symbol she took personally as a child, a mark of her mother's torn loyalties instead of the state's. Beryl's favorite thing about this Kōloa house was that it had a good view of Queen Victoria's Profile—what *haole* call the Ha'upu Range summit. It seemed to comfort Beryl somehow, living in the shadow of that revered chinless monarch, and to this day there are die-hard Anglophiles like her in Hawai'i, people who maintain that the islands would have been better off under the protection of England, a country of islands itself and, even more important, a country that understood how to honor sovereigns instead of one that grew up rebelling against a king. Then, the fantasy went, Hawaiians would still have royals of their own in 'Iolani Palace, there would be more tea orchards here than coffee groves, and grocery stores from Kaua'i to the Big Island would stock shelves with Marmite jars instead of Spam cans. If only things were so simple. Beryl would mate one of her corgis with the Queen's. Hank would be well. Stevie would know what to do with the rest of her life.

"This part of the flag wasn't enough for Mother," Stevie says. "She needed the real thing."

"Uh-huh," Lila agrees. "Especially after her parents died."

"Dad doesn't even want her to know he's sick. Did he tell you?"

"I got the idea. Me? I'm buddies with both my ex-husbands. Just outgrew 'em, that's all. No foul, no harm. But not everybody's built for that kind of deal."

"I heard what you said in there, Lila. About Dad wanting me to come. But the reason he called me was so I'd talk to his lawyer."

Lila sighs and drills her with a look that's part amusement, part exasperation. "Let me ask you something, Stevie. How long have you known your father?"

"Funny. Almost his exact words yesterday, when he said something that upset me. I just thought that meant he wasn't going to apologize."

"Or that you shouldn't expect him to change. How else was he gonna get you on that airplane? He's not gonna say, 'Sweetheart, my time is short, I want you with me more than anybody else on this earth.' "

"Why not? I know how he thinks about lots of other stuff that's important to him."

"Big difference between thinks and feels, yeah? Easier to say he wants you talking with the man who does what Hank tells him to after he's gone—get you out here like that. He's gonna try and stay in charge of things, like always."

"You sound as if that's all right."

"Just how it is. He's not used to leaning on anybody else for what he needs, doing what anybody else tells him. You don't know what it took to get him to keep the oxygen here, and tonight's the first time he's used it. We had a deal—once we uncork that tank, no more cigarettes."

"You took them?"

Lila nods. "He wouldn't want you to see. It's not like he was smoking many—three or four a day, maybe, and that's just since he quit the chemo in Seattle, so he probably won't be too cranky. But here's what you hold on to, Stevie. He's not on morphine yet. He's still counting out his own pills. Still driving, too. If he had his way, that man would drive himself to the cemetery. And I wouldn't advise you trying to take the keys away—he'll fight you too hard. Everything's gotta be *his* idea."

"Well, what *can* I do? I can't just sit here and watch him die." A notion so awful that Stevie clutches the counter until alternative actions spring to mind. In a flash, she can see herself ordering a small satellite dish to pull in every game the Cubs play for the rest of the season—and, God willing, the postseason, too. That's not all. She'll buy a flat-screen television—not one of those behemoths that devour entire rooms, but something big enough so Hank can scrutinize pitches and argue with umpires. Things, just things, like the monster FDR biography, far more think than feel, and none filled up with any of the spirit—any of the *breath*—she wishes might flow between them. But once she articulates what she has in mind, even Lila agrees that such things might go a long way toward keeping her father tied to this life so that maybe, just maybe, they'll get the kind of timeless time she needs.

"Keep talking story with him, too." Lila says. "Like you were about Bittersweet Place."

Stevie nods. In the islands, talking story—swapping tales, or listening with an open heart to somebody else's—was what let you know you'd really made a connection.

"Going back to the beginning," Lila continues. "It's a real comfort at the end. One of the first things you learn, doing the work I do." Then she presses an old wet kitchen cloth to the quilt, and when she lifts it, the bloodstain is gone.

Chapter 5

It wasn't so long ago that sleeping straight through the night was something Japhy Hungerford took for granted. Alana used to say that he slept so well it was a shame he couldn't be paid to do it. But then Alana's regular bouts of insomnia, during which she read in bed with a book light, gave her plenty of opportunities to observe every salient characteristic of Japhy's rapid-eye-movement slumber, which she declared almost as entertaining in its quirks—riddled with chuckles, sighs, urgent mumbled words—as their dog's, and so deep that even when she flushed the toilet after getting up to pee, it didn't disturb him. Now he's like her. Now it takes nothing at all to wake him in the middle of the night, and always at three thirty in the morning. The devil's hour. This time it's a finely tuned motorcycle gearing down to turn on the grass drive that runs past the house he's renting. At the foot of his bed, Rainier raises her big, black head with a soft, perfunctory woof.

Japhy considers getting up to take a couple of Benadryl, the strongest sleep aid he'll allow himself since weaning off the prescription stuff. But then he'd be sleepy still for his early-morning Sunday trip to Hanale'i, on the opposite side of the island. That, on top of his hangover, would be awful. Strange, feeling this way from only two drinks. Christine, his office manager, must have gone overboard with the mango mojitos, just like she did in deciding to throw a surprise party in his honor.

He had hoped his birthday would go unnoticed this year, that he wouldn't have to try and be cheerful about it for other people's sake, but when he got home from the beach, there everybody was, lying in wait for him. Everybody had included Sharon, a woman whose cat he'd treated for a respiratory virus. She was also Christine's yoga teacher, and had clearly been invited for Japhy. Which turned out to be awkward. At least it wasn't personal. At least it wasn't about him.

After misjudging her capacity for mojitos, Sharon took off her shirt to demonstrate how she could scrunch up her shoulders and hollow out her already flat belly so that it looked vacuumed up into her rib cage, then roll her abdominal muscles from one side to the other. A bizarre maneuver better suited for an ashram, performed by some turbaned mystic whose name begins with "Baba." Maybe if Sharon had been like everyone else and sopped up all the alcohol with heavy-duty food—buttery baked potatoes, barbecued steaks, chicken teriyaki—she wouldn't have gotten so smashed. But Sharon was a vegan; bits of the brown rice salad that she'd brought to the party were the only food that passed her lips. Japhy can't judge her on that score, since he's cycled in and out of being vegetarian a few times himself—for reasons most people assumed were obvious, given his profession. But never once has he been smitten by a woman with serious dietary restrictions. In fact, given a *third* drink last night, he might have confessed to Sharon a pronounced preference for enthusiastic omnivores.

"We have so much in common," she had insisted after gluing herself to Japhy's side. "I mean, we're both taking the path of healers."

"Christine says you're a terrific yoga teacher."

"It's not just yoga. I have a doctorate in healthology."

A doctorate in healthology? Who knew such a thing even existed? As a relatively straight arrow, Japhy has never been quite sure how to process such slices from the wigglier side of island life. On Kaua'i, there weren't so many opportunities for him to become adept as there would be on Mau'i, the island that, with its booming New Age and personal-enlightenment market, might as well be made of Jell-O. Still, Sharon would not be the first to consult Japhy or hear him on the radio and assume that his emphasis on whole foods and natural remedies constituted a much broader kinship; it is almost as common as people mis-hearing his name as "Jeffrey." "That's great" was all he could think to tell her.

"I would like to worship you with my body," Sharon informed him.

"As opposed to your mind?" When she looked hurt by this crack, Japhy hastened to add, "No, really—I'm flattered." Which happened to be true. And let's be honest: he was tempted, too. Who wouldn't be? Sharon was incredible-looking—a lithe, henna-haired sprite with guileless, myopic eyes and an adorable overbite. He liked her scent—exotic, floral. He liked her smile. He even liked that she'd named her six-toed tabby Fred, for Fred Astaire. But while he found it exciting to imagine what amazing muscular feats Sharon might be moved to perform in the throes of passion, it was also a bit frightening. Especially when he could picture her jumping up in the middle of foreplay to run off and puke, and how lousy he'd feel about himself then.

Is it possible for a guileless woman to beguile him? Is he beguileable at all? Probably not. But maybe it's a healthy thing that the questions even occur.

Now, proceeding on the principle that rest is the next best thing to sleep, Japhy forces himself to wooze around in bed with his eyes closed for another hour and a half. When the motorcycle passes by again, going in the opposite direction, he surrenders to wakefulness, getting up to shower, shave, and start the coffee. While it brews, he plays his new CD of Hawaiian chant and drum music. A real ear-opener—he'd never realized drumming could be so nuanced.

After drinking half a cup, Japhy loads the bed of his white Ford pickup with bags of recyclable party trash. At the exact hour and minute that he breathed his very first breath, he decides to resurrect an old birthday habit and call his mother in Seattle. It's not that he's *forgotten* to do it. It's just been difficult, recapturing all the gratitude for his existence that had once made the call such an effortless gesture.

"Hello, dear," Kate says, answering with a froggy voice in the middle of the first ring.

"This," he tells her, "would be your number one son."

"No kidding. Who else would have the nerve to phone at eight-oh-twelve on this fine Sunday morning?"

"What day of the week was it thirty-five years ago?"

"Can't remember. But I do seem to recall screaming for drugs."

"Did I wake you?"

"When you were born?"

"Ha-ha."

"No, I'm having tea."

Japhy pictures Kate in the cozy clutter of her Cowan Park house—wrapped in her old mauve flannel kimono, lemoned Earl Grey in her cup, with Shanghai Lil, her youngest cat, regally composed in a towel-lined basket atop the cherry-wood dining table. *The New York Times* would be spread out by the basket, with the Seattle paper, still folded, awaiting its turn. The certainty with which he can see all this brings unexpected comfort and the smallest twinge of homesickness. "Happy birthday, Mom," he says. "Thanks for having me."

"Oh, happy birthday yourself! Good Lord, Japhy, it's early your time. What are you doing up at this hour?"

"Same as you. Getting ready for church." His mother always says that while she's never met a sophisticated religious symbol she didn't like, she draws the line at human sacrifice. But she's no regular churchgoer. Which is pretty much what you might expect from a polymath who named her firstborn child for a major character in a minor Kerouac novel. The best answer he ever got out of her as to why she had done this was that during her freshman year at Berkeley, she developed a massive crush on Gary Snyder, whose poems about the Northwest had led her to graduate school in Seattle.

"Then why couldn't you just name me Gary?" he'd asked. What a solid, easy name *that* would have been to take through life. But no, a sometime poet herself, Kate preferred the softer, dreamier sound of

"Japhy," the name Kerouac had given his Snyder character in *The Dharma Bums.* While Japhy still pretends to be aggrieved with her on this score, he stopped minding when girls who'd never heard of Kerouac *or* Snyder let him know they thought his name was not just appealing, but sexy. "There actually *is* a church on the island that you'd like," he tells his mother now. "Everything's in Hawaiian, even the hymns. This cool harmonic thing happens that just blows me away."

"It's such a musical language. The Welsh got all the consonants, but Hawaiians got a better deal with all the vowels. There's melody just in all those repetitious sounds. Speaking of which, is that a rooster I hear?"

"More than one, as a matter of fact."

"Oh—before I forget. We need a plan for the holidays. They'll be on us before you know it. If you'd rather not come to Seattle, we could all go there. It's nearly a year since you left, and we miss you."

With that, the last trace of homesickness evaporates. "Holidays are tough, Mom. And it's hard on everyone else, having me around."

"How can you say such a thing, honey? Everyone loves you so much."

"I wish that made it easier."

A long sigh on the other end of the line. "And I wish I could shut my big mouth and have faith that you're putting a good life together for yourself, that you know better than any of us what you need. You always did before. But an island! And such a quiet one—apart from the roosters, that is. I know how much you loved *visiting* Kauaʻi. I'm just afraid you're *living* out there like some kind of hermit."

"Hermits don't renovate houses, Mom. Hermits don't start up new practices. Hermits don't have radio shows and parties."

"You had a party? How wonderful! I'm so glad you told me. That helps me feel a whole lot better."

If she can get this excited about a party, she'd probably be ecstatic if she knew he might still be in bed having sex with a contortionist. Not that he's the sort of son who would bring up such a thing, or that she's the sort of mother who would think it any of her business. Kate has simply fallen into the habit of worrying about him far too much. Which is a minor reason why leaving Seattle for Kauaʻi had seemed such a good move.

"Because of course you need friends," his mother is saying. "People who know what you've been through."

"I had that in Seattle. After a certain point, it's just not all that helpful."

As the old agony creeps over him again, Japhy regrets making this call. He takes a slow breath. "This is the right way for me to go."

Saying so feels like good practice. For exactly what, he's not sure. Maybe for a night he can sleep straight through.

Chapter 6

Before returning to bed, Stevie brought a clock radio out to the lanai, and when she first stirs beneath the pineapple quilt at dawn, roused by one of the roosters that have wandered the island since the last big hurricane, the illuminated dial reads 6:00 a.m. As though suffering from some avian posttraumatic stress syndrome, the birds crow compulsively throughout the day, which is why the Realtor who leases Hank's house to tourists has stocked the bathrooms with wax earplugs. But for Stevie, accustomed to New York's morning cacophonies of garbage trucks and car alarms, the rooster is a happy reminder of where she is. She turns onto her side, falls back to sleep, and doesn't open her eyes again until seven thirty, when this time she's jolted into consciousness by a loud, twangy, raucous song that seems to be all in favor of humans consuming dog food—fricasseed or deep-fried.

Gentle, melodic Hawaiian music—that's what Stevie remembered this station playing on Sunday mornings. That's what she'd expected when she set the radio to go off, not this silly hillbilly stuff.

"Flip it on over, cook it any way.
Eat along with Rover, three times a day."

Heedlessly leaping off the futon, Stevie stubs her toe and reels into a cedar chest that bangs her shin. While she winces and rubs her leg, the song gives way to some guy speaking with the sort of low, lazy voice that must be standard issue on noncommercial stations. "You're tuned to listener-supported KKCR on the garden isle of Kaua'i," he rumbles. "If you just joined us, that was the Austin Lounge Lizards with a little something for our canine friends. I'm tempted to play their next cut for you: 'Why Couldn't We Blow Up Saddam?' But this is the *Paradise for Pets* program, I'm a vet, and we're not here for politics today, soooo . . . guess we'll stick to relevant topics. Before I take your calls, let me tell you a little something about using melatonin for animals. . . ."

The Divine Deejay who spun "Ain't No Grave" out of Chicago's thin air must not have traced Stevie to Kōloa yet. She snaps off the radio, goes to the kitchen, and grinds enough beans for a full, strong pot of Hank's favorite Kona peaberry.

Lila gave Stevie enough information last night about Hank's vital signs, medications, and daily rhythms so that she's confident her father will indeed awaken this morning, but not soon. Ten a.m. at the earliest, by which time the Cubs game in Milwaukee will be under way.

There's no half-and-half in the refrigerator, stocked mainly with sugar-sweetened bottles of tea and carry-out grocery store containers of barbecued ribs, fried chicken, potato salad, mac and cheese. The kind of rich, fatty foods an ill person who believes he's playing with house money eats—though not very much, judging by the purchase dates and how full the containers still are. Eyes bigger than his stomach, probably. Stevie scribbles a shopping list with plenty of greens, fruits, juices, and yogurt. Then she changes into the running clothes she wore yesterday—they want washing, but there's nothing else to wear apart from sweats or something too dressy—and takes a cup of dark, buttery brew outside to drink straight up.

Heavy-bottomed clouds hover above the rolling peaks of Haʻupu Range, blowing inland to weep over waterfalls. Low sun slices the shoreline sky. Only a trace of nighttime fragrance rides the trades this morning, heady now with eucalyptus and plumeria. For a while, as Stevie sips coffee on the steps where Hank fell, she feels more centered. Then the image of him lying helpless on the ground returns, and the shot of adrenaline from that is stronger than any caffeine surge.

If anything, her resistance to letting Hank go has grown stronger. It's almost as though she's afraid of slipping away herself in his wake, untethered by marriage or children of her own. Maybe she requires Hank's demanding existence to define hers, and what can she do about *that* except figure out some way of turning into him herself? Which isn't an option. Not an appealing one, anyway. She has to stop future-tripping. She has to stay on track in the present, where the most frightening possibility is that she'll be a disaster as a daughter. That, on top of her disasters with Brian and the garden, would do her in. End her turn at bat, send her to the showers, demote her to the farm team. Could Hank grasp her situation if she explained it to him like that, with stupid sports metaphors? She doubts it. Her anguish feels much too female for her father to comprehend.

Stevie flashes on a long-ago stormy Sunday when Hank was supposed to be watching her here at the Kōloa house. Instead, he was watching a baseball game, and when he checked at last on Stevie—four years old at the time, trapped indoors by the weather—he found her sitting at Beryl's vanity, her face a mess of lipstick, blusher, powder, and mascara. Right away, just from the look of him, Stevie knew she was in trouble, and began wailing well before he lifted her off the satin-skirted chair to smack her bottom and haul her into the bathroom, where he rubbed off all that makeup with a solution of cold cream and tears.

What had kept him from laughing? What had kept him from pulling out a camera, memorializing the mess she'd made? What had kept him from kindness? She might have a clue if she knew something significant about what his own family was like—information deeper down than the cursory facts her parents had supplied, a broad-stroke sketch of distant people who couldn't be relied on to love him, or even to stay alive. Which doesn't quite jibe with Margo's home movies. Well, no better place from which to go looking for information about ancestors than Hawai'i. Every schoolchild here learns how human antecedents were once so sacred that people introduced themselves by chanting their genealogy, doing this according to rules so strict that screwing up meant being put to death. Wealth mattered, of course, but not nearly so much as lineage, and at this very moment, there might be an e-mail from Margo, illuminating the paternal side of Stevie's. Just the thought touches off a ripple of anticipation.

Although the dial-up connection at Hank's house is Stone Age compared to the high-speed cable hookups that Stevie's used to, the Internet radio feed works just fine. With the WGN site set for the Cubs broadcast, Stevie opens her e-mail program, and now the computer starts a slow-motion crawl through cyberspace, taking forever to let her know she has ninety-three messages waiting. Most of which are certain to be distressing. Brian wondering when she'll get her things out of his place, or when he can pick up his stuff at hers. Radioactive fallout from Chicago—other clients frantic about her messing up *their* projects or, worse, canceling contracts. The first message must be enormous with office-sent drawings or photographs; after five minutes, it's still loading. Stevie has neither the heart nor the patience to wait. Wishing there were a way to block out everything but word from Margo, she closes the program, finds her flip-flops, grabs a basket, and goes outside again to pick mangoes for breakfast.

An itinerant hen, wings flapping, comes squawking across the yard, herding five chicks to hide under red oleander beside the carport. Close behind comes a sturdy-looking little dog whose chest hits the grass in a play bow, its tail a comic dervish. "What do you think you're after?" Stevie says. "Food or toys?"

The creature cocks its head, shakes it hard, paws at a floppy ear, and bounces over to stand at her feet. She stoops down to assess: saucer eyes, bearded muzzle, licorice nose, and light brown fur tipped with a deeper shade along the shoulders. A border terrier mix, unless she's mistaken, and she's probably not, given how her post-ectopic-pregnancy depression had morphed into puppy lust, the kind that compels you to buy pricey illustrated books about dog breeds and training manuals written by monks who raise German shepherds. The dogs she most wanted all had beards and big, soulful-looking eyes. It was ludicrous, of course. She travels too much to take on a puppy.

The terrier sits on request and then, after Stevie sets her basket aside, seems eager to be picked up for closer examination. There's male equipment here, a dark strip of fur marking the penis. He doesn't wear a collar or tags. One ear flops over at a point higher than the other, the way her father described his dog Pepper's ears. Is this little guy a dog or a puppy? She can't be sure. His paws look big for the rest of his body, but he has an adult's self-possession, giving her hand a decorous lick instead of gnawing on it. Opening his mouth with a finger, she's surprised to see a few gummy gaps where adult teeth are beginning to push through; the rest are all sharp and tiny. Definitely a puppy. As he scampers a few feet away to bat a *kukui* nut between his paws, Stevie laughs. "Aren't you a pip?" Pip—the perfect name for him. As in not just pipsqueak, an accurate description size-wise, but Pip, the orphan in *Great Expectations,* because she can't imagine a puppy so wonderful as this wandering around without a collar if he didn't need a new home.

Mrs. Linn from across the way thinks so, too. "Never saw him before," she tells Stevie. "You don't see a puppy without tags on the loose in this neighborhood unless somebody wants to get rid of it."

I manifested Pip, Stevie thinks as the puppy trails her to the rear of Mrs. Linn's property and back through the monkeypod trees and mango grove edging her father's. *I should keep him for Hank. Another terrier like the one he loved as a kid—as good an anchor as the Cubs and that FDR biography. Maybe better.* Then her sensible self comes butting in. *Who will take him after Hank dies? You'll be too overwhelmed, even more of a mess than you are now. No, it's a bad idea, a selfish idea, more for yourself than for your father. Do the right thing and make sure this puppy ends up with people who won't ditch him again.*

"Hi, Stephanie," the radio vet says when he comes on the line. "I understand you have a problem for us to solve here. Let's see if I can read my engineer's handwriting—a lost terrier-mix puppy in Kōloa with brown fur and no I.D. Is that right?"

"Are we on the air now?" Stevie asks. The puppy is beside her on the steps, snarfing Cheerios from her hand, stopping only to shake his head and lap water.

"Uh-huh, you're my last caller. How can I help?"

Odd, how this person she found so annoying a short while ago is now so reassuring. Maybe the Divine Deejay has a bead on her after all.

"Well," Stevie says, "I don't think he's lost. I think he's abandoned." She hopes nobody else caught the break in her voice. Clearing her throat, stalling for composure time, she notices the underside of her right arm, dotted with tiny, itchy welts. "He's so well-behaved—I didn't think he was a puppy until I looked at his teeth. He might have fleas, but really, that is the *only* thing wrong with him. He's smart. Sits when you say so. Playful, but not hyper. I'd keep him if I could. If my situation weren't so, well, complicated." She takes a raspy breath, unable to hide the ridiculous fact that she's crying. "I just feel so bad for him. On account of being abandoned, I mean. And now I'm abandoning him, too." She laughs at how pitiful that sounds, but the laugh comes out more like a honking snort. "He's going to have trust issues, don't you think?"

That gets the chuckle that she wanted. "He's lucky someone like you found him. And he sounds pretty resilient. I'd say it's time to be practical."

"That's why I called," Stevie declares. "I have to be practical."

"I'm guessing this is an older puppy. He's intact, right?"

"Intact?"

"Not neutered?"

"Let me check." Stevie wedges the phone against her shoulder to pick the puppy up for another underside scope. "Uh-oh. He's only got one. Shouldn't he have two to be intact?"

"Ah," the vet says. "Cryptorchidism."

"That sounds awful."

"It's actually a common occurrence with terriers, and anyone out there with a male ought to listen up. *Crypt* means hidden, and *orchis* is testis, if I'm remembering my Greek right, so it's the failure of one or both testicles to descend into the scrotum. Always wise to neuter when this happens, because the testicle is meant to be at a lower temperature. With cryptorchid dogs, the testicle's kept inside the body, at a higher temperature, and over time, that increases the risk of cancer."

The pup scrambles onto Stevie's lap, shakes his head again, and paws at his ear. When she reaches to lift the flap and see what's bothering him, he trembles and emits a shrill yelp, nipping the air by her hand.

"I think we all heard that," the vet says.

"There must be some problem with his ear. He won't let me look inside it."

"Probably an infection. The Humane Society shelter is where you want to take him. It's the only public shelter on the island, so everybody who loses an animal checks there first thing. They'll treat the ear, give him his shots, and if you're right about his being abandoned, they'll put him up for adoption."

Stevie claws at the welts on her arm. "What if nobody wants him? They won't kill him, will they?"

"No worries, Stephanie. Older dogs are the ones they sometimes have trouble finding homes for, but—"

"If I go there, will I see those older dogs that they kill? Because I don't think I could handle seeing them. I don't even like *thinking* about seeing them. They shouldn't have to die just because they're older!"

"I know what you mean, but you won't have to see any dogs you don't want to see, and as I was about to say, you've got a puppy on your hands there. Everybody's crazy for puppies. Puppies go to new homes in no time at all."

"Will they make sure whoever gets him knows about that crypto-stuff?"

"They do a terrific job. Don't let this wreck your vacation."

Stevie has a pretty good idea what he means. She's not laid-back enough to be local. She reeks of mainland neuroses. She doesn't want the hassle of bringing a puppy back to the States. If there were genuine *aloha* in her heart, she wouldn't be talking like this. She wouldn't be calling at all. "Who said I was on vacation?"

"You're from here?"

"I was born here. Wilcox Memorial Hospital, Dr. Moore attending. At least, that's what it says on my birth certificate." It's not like her, being so oppositional with a stranger. It is, however, very much like Hank. Oh, God, she's turning into him already.

"Well, I just assumed," the radio vet says. "Never a good idea, right? We're running out of time, Stephanie. But I can tell you that if *I* found a puppy I couldn't keep, the shelter is where I'd take him."

A glimpse of her snoring father and a quick call to Lila bolster Stevie's resolve; she most likely has time enough to get to the shelter and then shop on the way back before Hank awakens, and even if she runs a little late, he'll be fine on his own for a while.

The shelter is on Kaumuali'i Highway, the island's main thoroughfare, just outside Līhu'e. With the puppy snoozing on her lap, she drives the Mustang top-down beneath an arch of giant eucalyptus trees almost a mile long, heading *mauka* out of Kōloa. Cloud shadows fall in the Lawai Valley, where dewdrop diamonds stud jungly roadside ferns. Farther on, the sky spits out sprinkles—a little blessing, the locals call such sparse downfalls, not worth putting up the top for.

It's people I have to accommodate now, not dogs, Stevie tells herself. And her silent chant all the way to Līhu'e, fortifying her intention, goes like this: *Fleas, infections, neutering, housebreaking, training.*

When Stevie walks into the shelter, the ponytailed young woman who's working the front desk calls out to someone in the corridor behind her, "She's here. You owe me." Then, eyes fixed on the puppy in Stevie's arms: "We bet on whether or not you'd bring him in. Oh, he's sure got a great big sense of himself, doesn't he? Hi, there, Mr. Adorable. How ya doin', Mr. Handsome?"

"You heard me on the radio?" Stevie asks.

"Yep." The woman, whose name tag reads "Leilani Chong," comes around from behind the desk and scratches under the puppy's muzzle. "Some upset-sounding dude called here right after the show. Wouldn't give his name, but from what I could make out, he left this puppy in a box at Dr. Japhy's place. Must have been a pretty flimsy box, yeah? Oh, and he said he left a note, too, about how the pup can walk on his hind legs for treats and answers to 'Laki.' "

"He answers to 'Pip,' too. Who's Dr. Japhy?"

"The vet you talked to. Four other people, including my mom, called about coming here to see the puppy. That must make you feel good."

It should. But it doesn't.

A dark-haired *haole* guy wearing board shorts and a close-fitting cobalt-colored T-shirt walks in. One of the island's legion of twenty-something construction-workers-cum-surfers, judging by his build. The same irresponsible jerk who dumped Pip, she guesses, wanting to reclaim him now. He doesn't look overcome with remorse—he's probably not deep enough for that—but there *is* something sort of regretful about him, maybe even sad. Stevie imagines he got the puppy as girlfriend-bait. Which, as she knows from personal experience, is a killer technique. Why is it that a single woman with a dog is so often suspected of deficient intraspecies skills, while a man gets credit for the nurturing gene? "Hey," this one says to Leilani. "Would've been here sooner, but there was a backup on the bridge."

Then he turns to Stevie, going for Pip with a tight-lipped grin that dots the parentheses around his mouth with deep dimples. Well, charm isn't going to work—not on her, not today. "Even if you *didn't* try to get rid of him once already," she says, "being negligent enough to let him have fleas and an ear infection disqualifies you from dog ownership."

Leilani hoots.

"What?" Stevie doesn't get the joke.

"Remind me what your name is, I'll introduce you to Dr. Japhy."

Stevie's not so much embarrassed as surprised; if he's a vet, he's got to be older than he looks. "I'm Stevie Pollack," she tells him.

"Japhy Hungerford." He holds out his hand for the puppy to sniff. "I wondered if you'd be here."

Now she can hear that timbre from the radio in his voice, and something else, too—a touch of amusement, as though he was in on the bet about the head-case caller. "Sorry," she says. "I just didn't expect you to be, well, you."

"I volunteer here on Sundays, but I don't like to broadcast the fact. Why don't we go to the examining room? I'll check him out."

❋

Stevie holds Pip still on a metal table while the vet coos praise, patting Pip's chest with one hand and using the other to aim a rectal thermometer. After the requisite time, he removes it to read. "Looks good," he says. Then, after checking Pip's teeth: "Which ear's the problem?" As though following orders, Pip does his shake-and-scratch demo. The vet takes him from Stevie. "Okay, pup, we'll see what's bugging you, all right?"

He runs his long, narrow hands over flanks and belly while looking off into space, creating enough rapport that Pip melts into a submissive trance, offering just the faintest of whimpers as the ear examination begins. "Well, no wonder," the vet says, then reaches into a drawer for a pair of long-nosed forceps.

Stevie realizes that she's holding her breath—not out of fear or anxiety, but because she's mesmerized by the dark hair on the vet's arms. How it lies along muscle, sleek and swirling. Its just-right density—not furry, not sparse. The elegant way it tapers off at the wrist. Weird. She's never paid so much attention to *anybody's* arm hair before, and now she's a connoisseur. Still, she can't come close to capturing what's compelling about his. It's so physical, so visceral. Must be hormonal, or maybe molecular. She can remember, when she first saw this person, thinking he was attractive in a general, distant, abstract way, not dwelling on any particular characteristic apart from dimples, which on other men have always struck her as being somehow rubbery or doughy or downright dopey, even. But one close look at his arms and it's like she fell down a mine shaft. Nothing remotely similar has ever happened to her, and it's no less thrilling than scary. A queasy combination for Stevie, who, preferring thrills and scares straight up, would never fling her hands in the air on a roller-coaster ride. Good thing, then, that she presents as a whacked-out city woman with dirty hair, squished jog-bra breasts, and grubby clothes. That ought to keep her from turning into a bigger fool than she's been already.

Another soft whimper from Pip and the forceps emerge from his ear, grasping a small pod with sticky-looking, arrow-quill serrations. "Grass seed," the vet says. "Lucky we got it early. These things are nasty. They eventually migrate all the way into the ear canal, and when they puncture the ear drum, you've got major trouble—not only internal infection but balance problems and vertigo."

Stevie nods, staring at the grass seed, but doing this keeps the vet's arms in view, sends the belly-swarming butterflies swooping down to her pelvis, so she forces her gaze to the wall, where there's a chart of Hawaiian names suitable for pets. Aka means laughter. Ola means alive. And Laki means lucky. An apt name for this puppy, though not enough to make her forget about Pip. Now she's sensible enough to speak. "Is there any danger of over-vaccinating him?"

"You've done some homework."

"My mother breeds show dogs."

"I don't like generalities," the vet says, "but generally, mixed breeds have healthier immune systems than purebreds."

"Wouldn't it be great if that applied to humans?"

The dimples appear again, this time with a glimpse of teeth, and it's a nice-enough smile, less guarded and warmer than the closed-lip version—intrigued, maybe, but not quite inviting, so the butterflies stay still. "I'm not sure what you mean by that," he says.

"Me, neither." No point in explaining that she's thinking about photographs of her *hapa* Hawaiian great-grandmother, in high-necked *holokū* as well as low-cut Worth gowns from Paris. She's thinking about Lila, voted Miss Cosmopolitan by her Līhu'e high school classmates, an honor bestowed on girls from more than two different cultures. She's thinking about herself, leaving footprints in so many places that she's lost her own trail. "So the shots won't be a problem?"

"I talked to Leilani after the show. The guy who called here said he'd never seen a vet."

"Minimum dosages, right?"

"Standard protocol for me. Listen, it's okay if you have to get going, I can take it from here."

"Oh. All right." That's it, then. The little dog will be fine. Stevie's free to go. But she can't. "I changed my mind," she says as if announcing an astonishing event. "I'm keeping Pip."

After Pip's vaccinated, Leilani bathes him in a big steel sink. Stevie writes a check, making a generous donation in addition to the shelter's standard fees, then heads back to Kōloa equipped with kibble, leash, collar, and a small crate. Only when she's miles away from that man and his arm hair does it occur to her that if Pip was left at his house, he must live in Kōloa, too.

❁

Stevie races around the kitchen, unloading the groceries she got at Sueoka's Market along with two full bags from the produce stand, where every piece of fruit and every vegetable bore a sticker indicating which farmer grew it, and Treeny, the proprietress, penciled her purchases into a ledger, item by item. Treeny had refused to let Stevie leave without a bagful of *māmaki* leaves from the Hanapēpē Valley to brew into medicinal tea for her father. "Make him drink," she'd said, wagging an arthritic brown finger. "You be the boss." But as Stevie chops and tosses into the blender chunks of pineapple, mango, papaya, and apple banana—half the size of a standard Chiquita, and twice as sweet—she figures she'll have more success getting something healthy into Hank if she's not quite so transparent. A smoothie at least has the consistency of a milk shake, and if a dollop of butter pecan ice cream helps it down her father's throat, well, why not?

Hank had managed in her absence to shower, shave, and dress in the tropical version of his usual uniform—short-sleeved chambray shirt and pressed khaki shorts. He's on the lanai with his coffee, seated on a densely woven rattan armchair that's as old as Stevie but fitted out with new pale blue canvas cushions. Hank has a good eye for design, but except for clothes, he's no shopper; it's Estelle, the real estate agent, who keeps the place up for him. His cane hooks onto the back of the chair and his bruised leg, which Stevie had rubbed with menthol cream and wrapped in a heating pad, rests atop a pillow on the matching ottoman. She'd ministered to him in a brisk, taking-care-of-business fashion, suspecting he'd balk at more tender treatment. Still, his allowing her to care for him at all showed how things were shifting.

"The game, Stevie," he says now. "What about the game?"

She brings their breakfast drinks, flips open her computer, and cranks up the volume. It's the bottom of the third inning, with the Cubs ahead two to nothing.

"A good start," Stevie says.

"Milwaukee can hit, too," Hank says. "They were on a tear before the Cubs came to town. Everything depends on pitching."

"Well, they've got Kerry Wood today. Isn't he their ace? The guy with the ninety-five-mile-an-hour fastball?"

"Ninety-seven. Haven't you been watching this season? We can't count on him, Stevie—he hasn't won a game for a month now."

"So he's due."

"Not only do the Cubs have to win for this game to make a difference, but Houston has to lose."

"You keep throwing me curveballs, Dad."

"Have to hit those if you want to play in the big leagues."

As an experiment, Stevie tries agreeing with him. "You're right. The Cubs have a lot going against them."

"Doesn't mean they won't pull it off. They've yet to lose a game in Miller Park this season. And one of the Brewers starters is out with an injury—that's a plus."

So if she's negative, he's positive? Interesting.

"I'll be back in a sec," Stevie says, then goes to the carport for Pip, curled into a ball atop her sweatshirt inside the crate. She offers him water, lets him scurry and sniff around long enough to pee a few times, then carries him to the lanai. "You probably won't like him, Dad," she says. "But this is Pip. I thought he might run the bases with you."

"Very funny." Hank's grin is broad enough for Stevie to catch a glimmer not just of how she first knew him, but of the man her mother married, the one in Margo's home movies, and past all that to the child he must once have been. On a birthday, maybe. Or when the Cubs won the pennant. He was born in a pennant year—1932, on November 2. All Souls Day, the Day of the Dead. Not that her father ever celebrated. No, his Church of the Resurrection is Wrigley Field, and he's got to be thinking it's his last chance to see his team in postseason play, his last chance to see them go the distance.

Stevie puts Pip on the floor, holds a piece of kibble above his nose, and as the puppy walks across the lanai to Hank on his hind legs, Randall Simon belts a three-run homer, putting the Cubs ahead by five.

Hank is quicker than the broadcasters to anticipate pitches, plays, and lineup changes. Which makes this game more interesting to Stevie than most she's seen in person, much less on TV. Pip shuttles between their laps for a while, then he's on the floor, gnawing a rag Stevie knotted for him. His hind legs aren't tucked beneath him, in the way most dogs rest, but stretched straight out behind. "Must be a terrier trait," Hank says. "Pepper did that, too."

Hank lifts Pip onto the ottoman and needs just three pieces of kibble to teach him how to shake. "He's smart," Hank says.

"Smart as Pepper?"

"Could be. We'll see."

Good, Stevie thinks. *He's invested.*

Milwaukee scores on a double in the fourth, and once more with a home run in the sixth. During the seventh-inning stretch, Stevie mixes drinks and cuts sliced-chicken sandwiches into quarters to tempt Hank, who told her he wasn't hungry. Rather than set places for them at the oilcloth-covered lanai dining table, she puts the food within easy reach of Hank's chair. After drinking half his mai tai, he nibbles his way through a plateful.

"Mr. Wood doesn't have too many pitches left," Hank says. "The Cubs better sew this one up."

They do, in short order, scoring three men. "Your wish is their command," Stevie tells him.

"Ah," Hank sighs. "If only."

Wood leaves the game after pitching in the seventh, and Milwaukee can't do a thing against his reliever.

"Streak, streak!" Stevie cries as the last Brewers batter goes down. "The Cubs are on fire! Dr. Longball's on the main line for Chicago, and he's saying, look out Houston, look out!"

"Look out yourself, kiddo." Hank points at Pip, who's raised a leg against the coffee table, and reaches for the editorial section of the Sunday *Honolulu Advertiser.*

As he rolls up the paper for a swat, Stevie lunges to pick up Pip. "Hitting's old-school, Dad," she says. "So is rubbing his nose in it. Praising him when he does it right works better."

Now she has to walk her talk—with Hank watching from the lanai. Pip gives her several opportunities to launch into loud, preposterous raptures of approval. When she returns with him and his crate, her father sits frowning on the edge of his chair, hands folded over the top of his cane.

"I have a question," he says.

"If it's Pip, that was my fault, he just needs to get out every few hours.

I think he's almost house-trained, but the crate will help. Plus, if I clean up where he went with vinegar and give him something to eat in that same spot, he won't mark it again."

"That's not it."

"Oh. Then what?"

"Once, when you were little," Hank says, "after you were down for the night, you called out for water. So I got out of bed and brought you a glass, but when you kept calling for more, I could tell it wasn't the water. You just wanted attention."

"Maybe I had a nightmare."

"You weren't crying."

"Well, what did you do?"

"You don't remember?"

Stevie shakes her head. "Nope."

"Good. That's a load off my mind." He transfers the cane to his left hand, grips the chair arm with his right, and starts to rise.

"Wait, wait—why? What happened?"

"I spanked you. I'm glad you forgot."

Stevie's not sure if what's transpired here is tragic, or the funniest thing that's occurred since she got to Kaua'i. Maybe it's both. She puts Pip in his crate and follows her father across the living room. "Let me see if I've got this right. So long as I don't remember you doing some lousy thing, then it's fine? Then it didn't affect me and you get your ticket to heaven punched?"

"You know I don't believe in heaven."

"You've never said why."

"Delusions don't interest me, that's why. Anyway, we're judged enough on earth."

"Want to know my idea of heaven, Dad? It's not where you're judged. It's where you're finally just *understood.*"

"That would be another world, all right."

"Maybe what happens when you die isn't comprehensible. I mean, rationality goes only so far."

"I only wish it went further."

"Okay, forget about heaven."

"Gladly."

"Why do you think you spanked me?"

"Christ, I don't know, Stevie."

"For one crazy second there, I thought you were going to apologize."

"Look, you're a grown woman. I can't change the past."

"You're the one who brought it up."

"And now I'm sorry I did!"

Well, there's an apology—of sorts. Only it doesn't quite count because it's to himself. What was it Margo said in the park yesterday? *They'd all rather die than apologize.* Why would you join a club like that if you didn't, on some level, have it figured out that being wrong might kill you? But Stevie isn't ready to barrel into *this* subject without a little more research. Anyway, it's not a matter of preference for Hank anymore; according to him and the hospice people, he *is* dying, and it looks as though the surest route to daughter disaster is to hammer away at paternal shortcomings. Especially now, when a few curt, retaliatory words are all it takes to awaken within her that attention-thirsty child from the night she can't even remember. All Hank wants in the world, she's guessing, is to not leave it feeling like a failure. And where is the room there for what *she* wants?

From his crate, Pip lets loose with high, mournful howls. Poor thing. He needs to bond. He needs to be held. Stevie goes to get him, and when she returns to Hank, he's settling onto his bed. "Just remember," he says, "it was your idea to come here, not mine."

"Dad, please. I don't want to spoil the day."

"You think I do?"

As explosions go with Hank, this one is nothing, a mere puff of smoke. No yelling, nobody crying but the dog. Differences made possible by death and Prozac.

Still carrying Pip, Stevie retrieves the FDR biography from her briefcase and takes it to Hank, who's got his nose in a paperback spy novel opened to a page near the end. "I know you've read a lot of books about Roosevelt," she tells him, "but this one is supposed to be definitive."

"It's big enough," he says, peering over his reading glasses. Then, turning back to his novel: "Put it on the nightstand. I'll get to it after this hugger-mugger."

"Should I shut your door?"

"No, the breeze is nice."

“Anything else I can get you?”

“A glass of water?” Those ultramarine eyes of his stay glued to the page. If Hank is kidding, Stevie can’t tell.

When she brings the water, he has one more request. “Why don’t you leave Pip here with me.”

Chapter 7

Stevie's e-mail program has plenty of time to retrieve messages while she does lunch dishes, wipes down counters, damp-mops the floors, starts a small load of laundry in the utility room, and takes a shower. Another flurry of activity to help her feel as though she has a real purpose here.

Wet hair wrapped in a towel, she slathers on lotion and dresses in her good bra, last clean pair of panties, and the cheongsam she wore to the garden ceremony. Then she pads barefoot back to her computer. The ninth new message in her e-mail queue is from Brian, but the one she clicks on is the third, from mgaynor@windycity.com.

how are we related? you ask. . . . that is exactly what i was dying to tell you in the park. here i am, stevie, your long-lost cousin margo, but don't worry.

i don't need any money.

i don't need any organs.

i don't need any BLOOD!!!

you don't know anything about your father's sister, do you? that's my mother, evelyn, fifteen months older than hank. the one in the wedding dress, the one whose house you came to as a baby. mother died almost two years ago from the worst cancer there is, pancreatic, and if i tell you that dead as she is, i can still be caught arguing with her, will you even want to know me?!?! i could give you evelyn's side of why she stopped speaking to hank, but that's all it is—her side. what's for sure is how she was still so angry at the end she didn't want her brother to know she was dying. i wonder if someone else told him. i wanted to at the time, but still too many strings attached? then i tried but couldn't find him. okay, i'll cut to the chase.

people just don't carry around so much anger, so much hurt, unless they don't also feel need (big-time need). probably even love. no, definitely love—ABSOLUTELY love. otherwise, you just wouldn't care, would you? i'd bet every cent i have that hank still cares, too, that's how sure i am of being right, and you know how important being right is to a pollack, don't you?! wow, it just hit me that evelyn DID actually speak to hank at the end—the very end. she was in a morphine haze and once again i only heard her side, but she wasn't angry. actually, she could have been nine years old because i caught something in there about PEPPER—hank's wonder dog with the magic paws. ohmygod, how do you like that?! my brain's such a sieve from perimenopause that i couldn't tell you what i had for lunch, but i remember hearing about some dog that died before i was even born. well, my point? i do have one. it's that hank's still here, and it doesn't have to be for him like it was with evelyn. if he wanted to air HIS side of things, i could listen, and it might do him good, especially seeing as how i happen to be the only other person still alive who ever fought with her tooth and nail the way he once did.

of course, she never stopped speaking to me for more than a few months, and with hank the cut was final. i might have landed in his camp, though, if i hadn't had children. evelyn wanted to be a grandmother so badly that i could use them to make her behave, which i did, because when she was good, she was very, very good.

one reason i tracked you down yesterday is that i have to write a family history for school (yes, i'm the oldest in my class, argggh). my joke title is "waste management," and my theme is that all their garbage got handed down for us to recycle somehow, and to do it right you have to separate the PAPER from the PLASTIC!

evelyn might quit yelling at me if i can find a way to pull off what she never could—speak with her brother again in reality, instead of in a hallucination. they say the loss you don't grieve turns into grievance, and i can just hear hank crying bullshit at me. i mean, he's such a bear and his generation doesn't talk about emotions, but i have a hunch that since you grew up with him, you're with me on this. or am i as big a nutbag as you thought i was in the park? this sounds like all i want from you is to be my facilitator, when the truth is, i would dearly love to know my cousin, who amazes me with her ability to turn a poisoned place into a garden. FORGET ABOUT THAT CRITIC! as my mother always used to say, there are more horses' asses than there are horses, and if your work brings you back here again, please stay with me? i'll round up my kids and you can meet everyone.

omg again, this is getting loooong for an e-mail. which reminds me, does hank do e-mail? i seem to recall him being a pretty fair two-finger typist once upon a time, and hey, he must be soooo happy about his precious cubs. i never pass wrigley field without thinking of him. have you told him you met me? don't for a second think you have to respond at length like this. answer as short as you like but do answer. DO!!!!!!

Omg is right.

How to respond? *Family* Fan Stevie wants to run straight for Margo's outstretched arms. Her Own Person Stevie is inclined to triple-lock the door. Island Girl Stevie is strangely silent. And the Uber Stevie hosting these other selves just sits at the computer with her cursor hovering over the "reply" button, unable to click because she has no idea what to say. Being reminded by Margo about the critic's review sends every rotten word flooding back through her head. But that's just the gravy, not the ever-more-evident meat of the matter. Here she is,

Stephanie Anne Pollack, the woman who doesn't know how to fit people into her designs, holding a jumble of human jigsaw puzzle pieces, and as if that weren't hard enough, somebody threw away the box with the picture that shows what it's supposed to look like when you put them all together. This must be a free-form job she has to figure out how to do. By touch, maybe. With eyes closed, perhaps. Or not. She could pack up Pip, go back to Pineapple Street, and stay away until Hank makes it clear, very clear, that he wants her around. Then, of course, she'd never know if Margo might have made a difference. To him, to her, to them. It would be too late.

Before Stevie can reach any conclusion, a blue Camry pulls into the drive. Just what she needs—more people pieces. Lila emerges from the back seat, not wearing motorcycle leathers today but a coral-colored muumuu and matching hibiscus blossom in her hair. With her is a small entourage. Everyone looks festive, especially the beautiful doll-like little girl in a bright red hula skirt and orchid lei who's further adorned with a modest crop of ferns woven into headpiece, anklets, and wristlets.

Lila waves and motions for Stevie to come outside. "Just a second," Stevie calls. A second is all it takes to read Brian's message.

Hey, babe.

Sorry about Chicago.

It's the kind of thing that gets worse before it gets better.

Like us? Maybe. I don't know.

Where the hell are you?

After Margo's headlong rush of emotion, Brian's words seem all the more cryptic, parsimonious, noncommittal. Stevie suspects that if she hadn't been blasted for her garden, he wouldn't have written at all. To him, she knows exactly how to respond:

I'm in my comfort zone.

She sends the message, closes her computer, takes the towel off her head, and goes outside.

❁

"This is Carly," Lila says, introducing the little girl. "My brother Calvin's granddaughter." The older gentleman in the starched cotton *aloha* shirt and feather-banded *lauhala* hat is Calvin. "I remember you," he says, and kisses Stevie's cheek, which is all the prompting Carly and her parents require to do the same.

"Carly's dancing her first big hula today," Lila says. "At the high school festival."

"Wow," Stevie says. "Congratulations, Carly. Break a lei." And when the little girl's forehead puckers: "Never mind, sweetie, that was just a silly joke. What I meant to say is, good luck and have a wonderful time."

"You all go on," Lila tells her brother. "We'll meet you there."

"I don't know if I should, Lila," Stevie says.

"Well, I do. You need to get out. So does Hank."

"I don't think he's strong enough, do you?"

"We'll see."

As the Camry pulls away, the women head for Hank's room. He's still reading, holding his book with his left hand while Pip sleeps in the curve of his right arm. "Looks like a fit to me," Lila says.

"That's Pip," Stevie says. "If I go, he goes."

"Goes where?" Hank asks. After hearing their plan he says, "Give me a few minutes, I'll join you."

Waiting with Lila on the lanai, Stevie shakes her head. "If it had been my idea, he never would have wanted to come."

"Or maybe goes more like this—*you* wouldn't risk *asking.*"

"No, he's doing it for *you,* Lila. Why is that?"

Lila shrugs. "I'm not blood. I don't get under his skin."

Trailed by Pip, Hank appears in a pair of his long khakis. Since shorts and swim trunks expose his withered leg, he'll wear them only at home or on the beach. Although he's barely limping now, Lila insists that he bring his cane, and as if bargaining, Hank insists on driving. They're almost like an old married couple, one where both parties are too overridingly fond of each other to be annoyed by little things. Never in her life has Stevie lived with—or been part of—a couple like that.

"Oh, for crying out loud," Hank shouts as they wait in a long, pokey line of cars entering the high school parking lot, and as he swings around to drive over the grass on a route of his own invention, Stevie's pulse races the way it always does whenever he's short-tempered. She would ask him to stop so she could get out and walk if it weren't for Lila, who just rolls her eyes at Hank, saying he's lucky that the cop directing traffic is her cousin, especially since Hank almost ran over his foot. Then she whips a white-and-blue handicapped card out of her canvas bag and slaps it onto the dash with a practiced air.

Hank parks in a designated spot close to the athletic field, where a portable stage, picnic tables, and festival booths are set up, with students hawking beverages and food. It's late afternoon and the air smells of grilling *hulihuli* chicken, steamed *laulau,* and frying *malasadas*—the Portuguese pastries ubiquitous at community events. Though creaky getting out of the car, Hank regroups enough to walk across a corner of the field to where Lila's family sits. He moves along with an almost sprightly air, wagging his cane in greeting to some of the people he knows, stopping to embrace others who once worked with him at the Coco Grove Hotel—the people who made up what Beryl always contended was his *real* family, the people who saw him only in the roles of genial host or generous employer and still held him in high, uncomplicated regard.

Stevie lags behind with the leashed puppy, who insists on meeting other dogs—a shih tzu entranced by Pip's butt, a Pomeranian intent on mounting him, a neutered pug clearly threatened by that lone cryptorchid ball of his. But even from a distance she can tell that Hank is performing, and she doesn't put it past Lila to have calculated how making this extra effort for an audience would do him good.

Lila's mother, Mrs. Wei, the matriarch of this Hawaiian-Chinese-Portuguese clan, wears a muumuu and hibiscus identical to Lila's. She's a vivid preview of how Lila herself will age, retaining not only stately height but plumped, dewy skin and a pronounced delicacy to her features. Lila's son Johnny, once the slender boy Stevie shared her first kiss with while perched on a monkeypod branch, is now a hearty, barrel-chested man. "Sistah!" he cries while hugging Stevie. " 'Bout time you got yourself back here."

Johnny's seventeen-year-old daughter Nola carries a teething baby on her hip. "This is Sean," Lila says, hoisting the baby into Stevie's arms, "my first great-grandbaby."

"And the whole entire reason," Johnny says, "why Momma went *lolo,* buying that damn motorcycle. A great-*tūtū* at fifty-nine? She couldn't deal."

"Shows how much you know," sniffs Johnny's wife, Amy. "That Nighthawk *is* how she deals!"

"Face it, Johnny." Lila grabs a chunk of his cheek in a playful pinch. "Your momma's wild, and the thing about wild women—they *nevah* ride behind."

Stevie takes her time with the baby before giving him back to Nola, and as she breathes in the sweet, soapy smell of his wispy dark hair and looks into his bright, inquisitive eyes, she's conscious of how being allowed to hold him is an honor, bestowed because she qualifies as extended family. Giving birth at an early age is not unusual for island girls. Maybe it's got to do with how soft the air is, how little needs to be worn in its warmth, how effortlessly all other things rooted here propagate. If anyone is an oddity, it's Stevie. She can practically read the minds of Carly and the other children Lila introduces—*Where are her kids?*

She stands out in other ways, too. Just about every person here besides herself and Hank somehow traces back to sugar, the tall cane that the name Kōloa comes from, the cane you can still see growing, though the fields no longer burn at night for harvest and the town's once-thriving mill wears a forlorn, abandoned air.

Stevie takes a place at the picnic table opposite her father. Maybe in the midst of Lila's family, he might be more amenable to discussing his own. But Johnny, who coaches the high school baseball team, gets Hank talking about the pennant race, and all she can do is wait for them to exhaust the subject.

On the stage where dancers and musicians will perform, a man with long, wavy hair bustles around setting things up. Stevie wonders whether he's contemplating a sex-change operation. Not because of his hair, or the ti-leaf head lei he's wearing, or the *kukui*-nut lei around his neck, or his toga-like robe in royal Hawaiian colors, red and yellow. Even macho men in the hula world do some of their fiercest warrior dances while wearing outfits that resemble gigantic taffeta hair bows. No, what makes her suspect imminent gender reassignment are his eyebrows, which from this distance appear plucked down to nothing.

Lila is the first to catch Stevie's curiosity. "Our hula teacher," she says in her that-explains-everything tone. Then the man himself notices. He puts his hands on his hips, hunches his shoulders, and squints. "Stevie?" he calls out.

From that characteristic gesture, she recognizes Kiko, who was every bit as dramatic as a kid, always blaming the *menehune,* Hawai'i's version of devilish elves, whenever he lost his homework or arrived late for school. Even more impressive was that Kiko had seen the Night Marchers, something he confessed to Stevie at recess one day in hushed, terrified tones, but only after she swore she'd never tell. (Discussing ghosts, spirits, or people having more than one soul—common enough topics in families like Kiko's—was considered inappropriate for school and understood to be forbidden, *kapu.*) Kiko was convinced he'd survived this encounter for just one reason: he remembered to take off all his clothes and lie facedown, flat on the ground. Otherwise the Night Marchers would have killed him for being in their path (also *kapu*). Sharing such a spooky secret was so thrilling that Stevie had spilled her Pele beans, conjuring up the singed hem, the bare feet, the smoldering ashes. She wonders if he remembers.

The last time she'd seen Kiko, he weighed a good deal less, had short hair, and was doing the Samoan fire dance in a Princeville hotel's kitschy luau show. Maybe he'd *burned* his eyebrows off.

"So, Kiko," Stevie says as he hops down from the stage to wrap his arms around her. "You're a *kumu hula* now, yeah?" Already she's falling into island speech patterns.

"Uh-huh, and *you* should come to my class." Kiko holds her at arm's length for a moment's assessment. "Cute dress, that." He pulls her in again and whispers by her ear. "Nevah go back, evah. Stay, stay, stay."

Then he gets busy lining up Carly and her classmates, a group that includes four adorable little boys in white shirts, red cummerbunds, and black pants. As they file onstage, Kiko goes to the microphone and speaks in a soft, singsong voice. *"Aloha nui loa,"* he says. "That's maximum *aloha,* everybody, so spread it around. Today, our *keiki* do a dance for Pele." No wonder Carly's dress is flame red. Stevie steals a look at Lila, who gives a nod that says, *Yeah, that's why I dragged you here.*

"Pele made our island first of all," Kiko continues, "after a big *huhū* with her daddy. We reverence Madame Pele today, yeah? She who shaped the sacred land. But back then? Never won any popularity contests. Got kicked out everywhere she went till she hopped over to the Big Island. Such a temper, so intense. Lucky for us, though. No *huhū*, no island, and we wouldn't be here today."

Having read Margo's e-mail, Stevie hears a link to Hank's story, to his sister, Evelyn. "Remind you of anyone?" she asks, but he's so intent on picking at the plate of *laulau* Lila brought him that all he does is chew and frown as if she's not making sense.

"As some of us here know well," Kiko is saying now, "Pele has a real soft spot for her firstborn, so every now and then, she comes back to Kaua'i. Today we tell about one of those visits, a very long time ago, and how she fell in love with a handsome young chief she danced a beautiful hula for, calling the winds."

Two young women come onstage to sit beside Kiko. He lifts an *ipu*—a gourd he beats like a drum, chanting a Hawaiian *mele* hula—while the women strike out a strong rhythm with pairs of peeled guava-wood sticks and the children start to move. This is not the *hapa haole* hula Stevie learned in her own *keiki* class, but a more nuanced, bent-kneed, authentic sort of dance, gestures mated to Kiko's chant. What comes across isn't so much the bad-girl goddess Kiko described, but a bold enchantress confident of her powers. It's easy for Stevie to imagine the woman she met on the beach so long ago performing these moves. She catches the meaning of only a few words here and there, but they're enough to convey everything Pele asks of the winds that she's calling, what she wants them to stir up in that young chief of hers. Carly is especially expressive, fingertips floating from her heart to her lips and into the air, and Lila, who must have coached her, does a small, contained version of all the gestures above her lap.

"Let's hear it for our babies," Kiko says when the dance ends, and the crowd erupts into applause. "And now I'd like to invite some of our beautiful wahine up here to join us."

Lila and Mrs. Wei take the stage with four other older women in identical muumuus, including Miss Nishimura, Stevie's third-grade teacher, now Mrs. Tanimoto. "Beautiful" seems just the right word—not just for their appearance, but for how glad everyone is to pay them attention. As they fall into line behind the children, Kiko pulls out his ukulele to play "Little Grass Shack." It's the corniest of corny *hapa haole* hula, but the steps and gestures are known to all, so when the song ends and Kiko asks anyone who'd like to dance to come onstage for an encore, he has lots of takers. Including Stevie, who can't keep from grinning the whole while, laughing when Kiko cries out, "Dance like you *invented* it! Everybody bucka*loose*!" It's such a relief, forgetting herself this way. No, not forgetting. Remembering.

As they finish, Stevie spots the radio vet standing off to the side, a large black mixed-breed dog lying at his feet. He obviously recognizes this cleaned-up, dressed-up version of Stevie, because when she comes offstage, he's there waiting.

"Looked like you were having fun," he says. "You were good, too."

"Oh no, I was barely keeping up. Who's this?" she asks, nodding at the dog.

"Rainier."

"As in the mountain?"

"Yeah. She and I come from Seattle, too."

Stevie leans down to pat Rainier's big, noble head, creased above her chocolate-colored eyes. It's probably just a trait from a touch of shar-pei, whereas the rest of her looks more like Lab mixed with setter. Still, the expression is easy to read as concerned, maybe sad. Not unlike her human's. "I've been to Seattle a lot," she says, "but I'm not *from* there."

"Right," Japhy says. "I remember your saying that you were born here, and it's not that I didn't believe you. But, well, families are complicated these days, aren't they?"

"Yes," she says. "They certainly are."

"It's just that I saw you sitting with Hank, and I knew he had a daughter, and *he* lives most of the year in Seattle." He stops to smile one of those closed-lipped, sociable, dimple-inducing smiles.

"I live in New York now. You know my father?"

"I'm renting his cottage while the house I bought gets fixed up."

"You're kidding!"

"It's a small island."

"So that was you having a party last night?"

"The party kind of had me. Word got out it was my birthday, and I was more or less forced into celebrating."

"Seems like you prefer animals to people."

"I do seem to spend most of my time with them. Listen, about your puppy—"

"I think he's turning out to be my father's puppy," Stevie says, gesturing toward where Hank sits holding Pip.

"Ah." The way Japhy says the word is just the way he said it earlier today, on his radio show, when she told him about Pip's testicular equipment, and she no longer feels any need to explain why she was so whacked-out then. He gets it. Which is compelling, but nowhere near so dangerous as the arm hair she refuses to let herself gaze upon. Besides, he's not the only one absorbing information. A rebound affair with yet another divorced, messed-up man—that's what Stevie's early-warning system is alerting her against. And as someone trained by both parents to leave the islands in order to excel, she has more than a little bit of built-in disdain for someone her age who throws in the towel to live here full-time. Restless now, eager to get back to Hank, she smiles and nods in a way meant to say "so long." But when she turns to leave, Japhy falls in step beside her.

"About the puppy," he says. "The box he came in was on my lanai. A couple of toys in there worth keeping. I'd give you the treats they packed, but the brand is one of those that're loaded with gluten." Then, at her puzzled look: "Overly processed grain."

"So much for eating along with Rover," Stevie says.

"That reminds me. How did you happen to be listening this morning?"

"By mistake."

At the sight of Pip, Rainier hunkers down as though trying to shrink herself into an approachable playmate size, and while they inspect each other, Hank shakes Japhy's hand. "I'm ready to go," Hank tells Stevie.

"I'll go with you," she says.

"That's not necessary. Maybe Japhy here can give you a lift."

Before Stevie can protest, Japhy says, "I'd be happy to," and she can't decide if her father is avoiding her, being considerate, or matchmaking.

As Hank leaves alone and Lila greets Japhy in a familiar way, music begins for the next bunch of dancers who have taken the stage, a troupe that performs a revue at the Sheraton much like the one Stevie saw Kiko in. Their show is pure entertainment—"a Polynesian tour," as the troupe's announcer promises—and it starts off with flashy Tahitian hip shaking. Then comes the Samoan fire dance, executed by someone who must be new on the job because he drops the flaming baton four times.

"Next stop," the announcer says, "the Cook Islands!"

Six young women in headdresses and mini-length bark skirts twirl long cords with fluorescent *poi* balls attached. Stevie hopes their coconut bras and bare, undulating bellies will keep Japhy glued to his seat. "I'll just walk home," she tells him. "Pip could use the exercise."

He shakes his head and points at the puppy, her little canine Quisling, asleep between Rainier's paws.

Japhy's pickup has a jump seat in the cab big enough for both dogs to squeeze onto. "I'm surprised they put something like that on the program," Stevie says as he steers out of the parking lot. "Something so touristy."

"Well," Japhy says, "it's not the kind of thing that locals would ever pay to see, so it's nice when they can get it for free."

"They didn't used to have shows like that here."

"You mean in your small-kid time?"

She smiles at his use of the lingo. "Yeah, but that was before the big jets started landing. Back then, people didn't talk so much about tourists. What we had were visitors." They ride in silence for a while before Stevie speaks again. "So—melatonin. I take it for jet lag. I missed what you were saying on the radio about using it for animals. What's the deal?"

"Well," Japhy says, "the evidence is more anecdotal than scientific at this point, but when animals have cancer, it seems melatonin might lengthen their lives."

"What about humans?"

"I'm a vet."

"I know that, I was just wondering."

"Because of Hank?" He turns to catch her nod. "I thought so. He's looking better, though. Better than when he got here last week, anyway."

"He was having chemo in Seattle," Stevie says. "It must have been so awful, he decided to stop."

"It can take real courage."

"Well, he's always had *that.*"

"I meant it can take courage to refuse the treatment. Sometimes it's a wash. If not in terms of how much longer someone might live, then quality of life."

"That's a tough concept for me—especially when someone is my father. You're probably more familiar with death than I am."

"Could be."

"I meant in your work."

"Right."

"Did I say something wrong?"

"No, not at all. Guess I'm more tired than I realized. Staying up late with the party, getting up early for the radio show."

"I'll just hop out at your place," Stevie says as he turns onto the grass drive that leads to his cottage and winds its way to Hank's house.

"Are you sure?"

"Positive."

"Okay," he says, "but wait here a minute." He jogs over to the lanai and returns with two squeaky toys, one of which is a hedgehog that Stevie, saying "Thanks," waves over her shoulder to him as she leaves.

Walking home, Stevie grows more certain with each step that what Japhy has just done was blow her off. Which isn't so much insulting as irritating, since that's exactly what she'd wanted to do to him back at the high school. But she's not in high school anymore—why get miffed over being beaten to the punch?

It's inky dark now. Around the curve, her father's house comes into view. With only a single lamp on the lanai giving light, the stars and waning moon shine all the more brightly. Crossing the lawn, she expects Hank to be in bed. But he surprises her by speaking from one of the white Adirondack chairs arranged around a small outdoor table. "In my day, a fellow always saw the girl all the way to the door."

"I bet. Especially when her dad recruited him for the job."

"I didn't twist his arm."

"Yes you did. Out here for the stars?"

"Mostly just mulling things over. Considering my regrets. Shall I tell you what my biggest one is?"

Stevie puts Pip on the ground with his toys. "Sure."

"When the sword of Damocles is dangling over your head, you think about all the chances you didn't take, all the times being afraid stopped you. This is good advice, by the way. I hope you're paying attention."

"So what's your biggest regret?"

"That I didn't believe more in myself when I was younger."

Well, what was she expecting? That his biggest regret would have been spanking her? Not that she didn't suspect it might be somewhere on the list, if it was on his mind enough today to mention. No, what she'd anticipated hearing was something about his marriage, or the failure thereof. Though having little faith in himself might have been a factor there, too, if an extra amount would have made him feel more lovable, and therefore more loving. She tries to formulate all this into a coherent sentence, but only manages to say, "I think I know what you mean."

"Nothing to cry over, kiddo. It's no tragedy when a child outlives the parent. That's the natural order of things. Meanwhile, I'm still around, and there's good news, too—a little sweet to go with the bitter. Houston lost, the Cubs are half a game ahead. And now that I don't have to worry about wrecking my liver anymore, how about a little nightcap to celebrate?"

In the kitchen, while mixing the rum, lime juice, rock candy syrup, and curaçao for another round of mai tais, Stevie wonders how she's going to tell Hank about Margo's e-mail. Small hope of civil discourse about a family feud when she can't even have a nice conversation with him about heaven. Maybe if she doesn't act like it's such a big deal to her, he'll respond in kind. It's not as if Evelyn is going to materialize in their midst. What Margo wrote is just a letter, after all.

Just a letter.

The phrase crackles in Stevie's head with live-wire intensity until she remembers the red wool letter "P" that she found in her Chicago hotel room. The sixth floor—that's where Hank said he'd lived at 201 East Delaware. She flashes on herself in the Raphael Hotel elevator, punching the number 6. So much has happened since then. That must be why she's only now piecing it together, but piecing it together she is, and what's more, she's doing it with the same odd certainty that first struck her on Michigan Avenue in Roosevelt Jefferson Jr.'s taxicab.

Stevie puts the drinks on a tray along with a battery-powered lantern, and stops for the wool letter on her way back outside.

After she and Hank have both had a few sips, she picks up the letter and holds it in front of the lantern's yellow glow. "Look familiar?" she asks Hank.

He handles the piece of wool much as Stevie did when she found it—running his fingers over its contours, inhaling its aroma, turning it this way and that. When at last he speaks, his voice is rough with emotion. "Where did you get this?"

"Chicago, in my sixth-floor hotel room on East Delaware—under a floorboard, by the fireplace. Was it really yours?"

"I think so," Hank says, nodding, and for a second, Stevie thinks *he* might weep.

"What's the 'P' for?" she asks.

"The Pearson School. I earned it on the swim team. It was something you were supposed to treasure—they didn't issue replacements. People wore the letters sewn onto sweaters, you know. But mine disappeared the day after I got it, before I could even buy my sweater. I thought it was gone forever. She said she burned it."

"Evelyn?"

"Who else?"

"And you believed her?"

"Oh, you bet. There was no telling what Evelyn would do when she was angry."

For a while, the only sounds come from mating pond frogs and Pip, who's discovered the hedgehog's squeaker and seems to be using it to send Morse code messages. Then Hank turns to Stevie with a stare that pierces the dim light.

"Who told you about my sister?"

Chapter 8

Surely it would soften things between them, presenting her father with that old, wooly letter he had earned and cherished and thought destroyed. He would see her as the anti-Evelyn, the wonder daughter with the magnetic soul, the one human on the planet who might mend his heart. That was Stevie's thinking, anyway, the reason why she had let her guard down. Instead, it's like he's spring-loaded to the pissed-off position. No sooner does she mention Margo's name than Hank sweeps aside her discovery so fast that it might be no more remarkable than locating a lost sock. "Why didn't you tell me you met Margo?" he demands.

Sweet anticipation sours into gut-searing disappointment. She'll never get a grip on his approval. "What was I supposed to do, Dad? Break the news when you called me in Chicago? 'Gee, sorry you're dying, and oh, by the way, I just met your niece. You know, my cousin? The one I never knew I had?' "

"I meant after you got here," Hank says, grabbing his drink for a thin-lipped sip. "Obviously."

"I had no idea you used to live at 201 East Delaware, Dad, none. But I made a reservation there anyway, and ended up staying right where you used to live."

"So?"

"So I don't think it was an accident. I think I was *supposed* to stay there. Because of you."

"Now you sound like your grandfather," Hank says.

"That doesn't bother me. I loved him."

"So did I. But he lived in a dream world, and let me tell you something. The kind of thing you're talking about is the kind of thing I would not believe in even if it existed. Anyway, that's no excuse for not mentioning Margo."

"Well, you won't believe this, either, but there wasn't any good opportunity before."

"What did she want?"

When I'm negative he's positive, Stevie reminds herself. How best to strap him into another double-downbeat bind so he'll be squirming to escape for some brighter place? Mindlessly clawing the fleabites on her arm, it comes to her. "You'd get a pretty good idea of what she wants if you read the e-mail I got from Margo today. But if I were you, I wouldn't do that."

"Why not?" He still sounds suspicious, but at least the volume's down to an almost peaceable level.

"Because she's so, I don't know, oversharing."

"What do you mean?"

"There's too much information in that e-mail of hers."

"About what?"

"Personal stuff," Stevie says. "Family stuff. You're practically strangers, aren't you? And the way she writes, it seems like you used to be really close."

"Well, we were. Once. Though God only knows what lies about me Evelyn's told her. Did she say anything about that?"

"Not much. Mostly she goes on about how she wants to reconnect with you, with me. How it's such a waste that she lost us. How she wishes she told you when Evelyn died but—"

"Evelyn's dead?"

"You didn't know?"

"When did she die?"

"Two years ago, I think."

"From what?"

"Cancer—pancreatic."

Hank sets aside his drink and leans forward, shoulders quaking, to put his face in his hands. The sight is astonishing for Stevie. She once saw a lone tear slide down her father's cheek, but that was a long time ago, the day she left for England with Beryl. Never before has she seen him weep. As Hank snorts back mucus and tears, she moves to put her arms around him, but before she can reach him he's on his feet, turned away from her, so plainly embarrassed by his emotion and so resistant to being touched that all she can do is land a few feeble pats on his back.

Hank grabs his cane and cracks it against the chair. "Goddamn her," he says. Then he stalks off to the house, letting the screen door slam behind him.

Stevie's blood pounds as though she's just run a minute mile. Whatever her father's going through, he's not going to let her help. The only thing she can do is wait. She hates to wait. *I'd rather die than wait* is how she used to put it, back when death seemed a distant reality, before it was the air she breathed.

While Stevie considers jumping into the Mustang to prowl the island for a pack of American Spirits, Pip whines and plants the whole of his quivery, vulnerable little body on top of her left foot. Such a simple statement of his requirements: *Don't make a move before you tend to me.* Well, he's entitled. In canine terms, Pip's had a day as tough as they come—not just abandoned, injected, every orifice inspected, but suddenly at the mercy of new humans whose smells and ways he must learn in order to survive. She lifts him to her chest and kisses the gully between his fringed eyebrows that might as well be designed for that purpose. "It's all right," she says. "Nobody's upset with you."

❋

Stevie's in the kitchen washing out glasses when Hank comes in, his usual take-charge attitude belied by red-rimmed eyes. "I'd like to read that e-mail," he says. There's a resentful crease in his voice, as if he knows he's been manipulated and doesn't intend to go down easy.

She brings her laptop to the dining room table, clicks to open Margo's e-mail, and turns the computer over to Hank, who immediately starts crabbing. "The print's too small, can't you make it bigger?" Then, after she obliges, it's the screen contrast that requires heightening. And why does she have to own a Mac when what he's used to is a PC?

As Hank settles down and starts reading, Stevie watches his face soften. At one point, it seems he might cry again. At another, he harrumphs. Several times, he chuckles.

Hank closes the laptop lid and shouts Stevie's name. He must be in such a time melt that he doesn't realize she's still close by in the kitchen. "Right here, Dad." She sets aside her pot of brewing māmaki tea to sit with him at the koa-wood table.

"I suppose I should respond to this," he says.

"I could e-mail your phone number here to Margo, have her call you."

"No, no. I'd rather write."

Stevie imagines that this preference has something to do with the pride Hank has always taken in crafting business letters, observing all the rules of proper grammar and composition. His style couldn't be more different not just from Margo's e-mail, but from all the professional e-mails Stevie receives and writes herself. The blunders Hank takes pains to avoid are practically a point of pride—as if the correspondent is too damn brilliant and busy to be bothered with persnickety details. Also, it's easier to control written correspondence than a conversation, two-way by definition. "Tell me when you're ready, Dad, and I'll get you going."

"I don't want to tie up your computer."

"Where's yours?"

"In Seattle."

"Okay, I'll get you another. A PC, like you're used to."

Hank shakes his head. "I might not be alive long enough to justify the expense."

Never mind that he expects to be contradicted. Letting that statement stand would hurt her more than Hank. "Of course you will. That's the last thing you should be worrying about."

Stevie takes Pip outside once more, just to be on the safe side, and when she returns with the puppy in her arms, Hank is in bed reading the FDR biography, the door to his room open. She had planned on crating Pip for the night, the way Beryl always does with her corgi puppies until they prove housebroken, but now the notion strikes her as mean. Pip's all emptied out, and besides, like everybody else in this house, the safer he feels, the better he'll behave.

"You pick where you'll sleep," she whispers to Pip, then sets him down and starts walking back to the lanai, glancing over her shoulder to see if he goes to Hank or follows her.

Pip paces the hall as if on patrol, up one side and down the other, before stopping to sit. As he yawns, his front legs slide out beneath him until he's lying flat. As though making a third, unexpected choice—to guard the house from there—Pip puts his head on his forepaws. But then he's on his feet again, ambling into Hank's room.

How did Pip decide? Stevie wonders. On the basis of whom he preferred? She doesn't think so. In fact, she's pretty sure he chose exactly the way she had wanted him to. On the basis of who needed him most.

Chapter 9

More than a week passes and not once does Stevie set foot on a beach, not once does she step into the ocean.

Usually nothing short of a hurricane can keep her from swimming within hours of arrival. Immersed in salty, floaty, amniotic waters, she's more in her element even than when walking land that's hers to sculpt, to plant, to dream on. This time, though, the sea is her incentive, her reward for handling Hank and charging through a myriad of tasks, the sort she always delegates to Claudia, who's a whiz at making anything electronic function the way it should. Somehow, in just over a day, Stevie managed to install a flat-screen TV and satellite hookup, with only a little help from Johnny in securing the dish. Then she set about having the house wired into high-speed Internet service, purchased a laptop for Hank that she sweated over to make user-friendly, and sorted through another mass of cords and installation manuals to create a makeshift office for herself in one of the guest bedrooms. By now, she could probably qualify as a clerk at RadioShack, or a computer tech in Bangalore (like the young woman she cajoled a family recipe for coconut chutney out of during long waits for the new laptop to shut down and power up again).

Results were quick to come.

A flurry of e-mails flew between Margo and Hank.

Perfect reception sailed out over the Pacific into the lanai, where Stevie and her father watched the Cubs drop two out of three games to Montreal, then win two out of three against Cincinnati.

Lila, with her island genius for cross-cultural improvisation, served the coconut chutney with chicken baked in ti leaves. Everyone at this family dinner, including Hank, pronounced the dish sublime.

And finally, Stevie forced herself to shift into a problem-solving mind-set for her poor, maligned garden.

No doubt about it, what she's got on her hands is a full-blown public design calamity. Not so bad as windows blowing out of the John Hancock Tower, maybe, but worse than anything experienced by any other LA at her firm, where the founding partner, Arthur Stewart, is pressing her to fly back to Chicago and do some damage control at a community forum next week. "I'll see how things go with my father," Stevie told him, giving herself a mental kick for cowering behind Hank's illness. Even when projects go well, the idea of public speaking makes her stomach do backflips.

Stevie's fountain now resembles a crime scene, drained and cordoned off with yellow caution tape. Claudia e-mailed photos, and painful as looking at them is, Stevie knows these measures had to be taken. Otherwise, the leaking pump, which must be replaced, would have turned the surrounding area into a swamp. And since the weather has remained warm, people would have just kept climbing into the fountain and falling down. There were three more accidents after opening day, with the *Tribune* reporting serious sprains and bruises, so Stevie's under the gun to devise a plan to make the fountain's granite surfaces less slippery. Meanwhile, she's having Claudia remove damaged lawn on the fountain's perimeter, then lay in swaths of sturdier—and more regionally appropriate—prairie rye.

Enough for now. Stevie is exhausted—not in her body, but her short-circuiting brain. With her father's biggest regret in mind, she decides to at least try and *behave* as if she believes in herself. What would she do on this warm, sun-dappled early Monday morning if she weren't afraid of anything? The answer is clear: claim her reward.

Leaving Hank with a pitcher of minty iced māmaki tea and the Roosevelt biography that he's already several hundred pages into, she walks to Kōloa and buys herself a black bikini (minimal maybe, but with a flattering cut that conceals a couple of dimpled scars—the first from an appendix that burst a long time ago, the second marking her lost right ovary's more recent exit route). She also purchases a pale pink, tissue-thin T-shirt and a red fringed pareo imprinted with sea turtles. Once the tags are snipped, she wears all of it out of the store, the pareo folded and tied into a short skirt.

Back at Hank's house, she opens the carport utility closet to pull out first a silver-trimmed trail bike, then a snorkel, mask, and fins, all of which she stuffs into a canary yellow canvas backpack. The next layer includes bottled water, bike lock, a tube of the sunscreen now coating her body, cell phone, wallet, Pip's blue retractable leash, a Baggie filled with kibble, a collapsible bowl, and the nearly gnawed-to-death hedgehog that Pip now fetches by name (which, for some inexplicable reason, is Ralph). Then Stevie puts on her sunglasses, shoulders the backpack, lifts Pip into the cushioned bike basket, and rides off *makai,* toward the sea.

As she breezes toward Po'ipū, her thoughts are all with Hank. He adjusted, not without grumbling, to Margo's wild punctuation and e. e. cummings style, and to celebrate their reconnection, Margo FedExed a bubble-wrapped six-pack of Old Style beer (a brand sold at Wrigley Field) and a CD of the sound track to *Oh Brother, Where Art Thou?* None of which Hank found so hilarious as Stevie did, but never mind. Now he seems almost as jazzed about receiving Margo's reply to his third message as he is about watching the Cubs play the Mets later this morning. It's no mystery what they're writing about; they both copy Stevie on everything. They've touched on Evelyn's death and Hank's illness, but only lightly. Most of what they've traded are pleasant, polite memories. Stevie wonders when family shit is going to hit the fan, and if they'll be eager then to copy her on *that*.

Hank is using his cane just when outside the house now. He seems to be gaining strength. Maybe it's from writing Margo, or the rebound effect from stopping chemo. Or maybe it's the *māmaki* tea.

"He's drinking it," Stevie calls out as she slows by the produce stand to wave at Treeny, arms full of fern shoots and crimson rambutan pom-poms.

"You the boss," Treeny hollers.

Hardly. What she's done is crumble up Treeny's *māmaki* leaves and shake them into a Twinings tin so that if Hank sees her brewing, he won't suspect. He likes the taste. It bothers her a little, being so sly about it. But presenting the tea as medicinal without a prescription from a traditional physician, preferably male, would be the kiss of death. Bad phrase. That kiss is what she's doing her damnedest to stave off.

Lila filled Stevie in on everything that, according to Hawaiian folk remedies, *māmaki* tea is good for. Not just liver problems, but cleansing the body of toxins, aiding digestion, lowering blood pressure, even relaxing women's muscles for childbirth. That last effect doesn't apply to Hank, of course, but interesting information nevertheless. Doubtful the stuff ever passed Beryl's lips, especially considering how Stevie, poised to enter the world feetfirst, had to be delivered by cesarean. Yet chances are that some of her other maternal ancestors gulped it by the gallon.

As salt air hits Stevie's lungs, she picks up enough speed that Pip's beard and eyebrows are blown backwards. No reason to dawdle through this dull commercial stretch of fast-food stands, tour-package places, and diving equipment. Turning onto Po'ipū Road, sailing past all the resorts and condos lining the shore, she catches glimpses of a gently roiling sea. At the end of Ainako Street, she leashes up Pip and locks the bike to a banana tree. Stevie didn't bring binoculars today, but she sees no evidence of spinner dolphins beyond the half-dozen surfers on Keoneloa Bay, where waters are too treacherous for swimming.

Leaving her flip-flops in the bike basket, she crosses Shipwreck

Beach with Pip in tow. They climb a craggy, scrub-covered lithified sand dune and walk along an elevated coastal trail, Pip cocking his head and barking at the loud, peculiar pops and cracks from waves below washing over lava rock. Island music to Stevie's ears—an operatic argument between Pele and her sister Namakaokaha'i, who's not only goddess of the sea but the tough cookie who booted Pele off Kaua'i. Funny how Hank fled his own difficult sister for a place where sibling quarrels are mythic. Not that she expects *him* ever to see the situation in such a light. With just the little Hank's told her of Evelyn, his anger and resentment were so evident that Stevie felt she could grab them, and she doubts Margo will be fooled by his attempt to inject the Evelyn topic with embalming fluid in his last e-mail:

> It is such a happy surprise to be in contact with you again that I don't wish to jeopardize our correspondence with disturbing information pertaining to your mother. It was never an intention of mine that our differences would terminate relations between other family members.

But Hank is eager to discover how Margo will respond.

In the distance farther along, Stevie spots a stable where half a dozen horses are being saddled—for visitors, for tourists, for people who have paid good money to enjoy a scenic trail ride and who represent what, for better and worse, is the island's main industry now. A state of affairs that Hank, being in the business, predicted well before the first big jets landed and the last sugar mill shut down. But alone on these limestone cliffs, Stevie feels as if she's in her own private nature preserve. The beauty of *this* exquisitely scalloped shoreline, unlike Chicago's, owes zip to ordinary mortals.

After a mile, when Pip wearies, she carries him to where the trail ends at Māhā'ulepū's first pristine stretch of golden sand. While Pip splashes in a freshwater stream, Stevie scans the area. Behind the beach is a sinkhole she discovered the hidden entry to as a child; now archeologists sift through mud there for the bones of birds washed up by a tsunami thousands of years ago. If studying tropical plants stateside hadn't always made her so homesick, she'd know the name of every native species sprigging the sinkhole rim. Still, she can make out a rare Pritchardia palm and the fragrant green-leaf maile that hula dancers prize for lei.

A few windsurfers are out on the open water. Stevie takes their stately pace as a sign that snorkeling will be good; can't see much with the sand stirred up. She walks ahead, around another curve, to even calmer surf surrounded by coral shelves. No one else is around, but an enormous monk seal snoozes yards above the waterline, gray body coated with sand, and there are footprints left by the state wildlife employee who marked off the surrounding area with yellow caution tape and planted a sign ordering humans to respect this endangered creature's space. How reassuring, to see something so amazing as a monk seal taped off in the same way as her fountain.

Stevie calls Pip, running free now, to a cozy spot high on the beach shaded by ironwood trees and edged with wild purple morning glories. Then she strips down to her bikini, unpacks her snorkeling gear, and leaves Pip leashed to a low-hanging bough, gnawing on Ralph.

Hawaiian defogger—that's what locals call the spit they rub into snorkel masks before rinsing with salt water, and that's the method Stevie uses today. Next she pulls on fins and offers a whispered supplication to Namakaokaha'i—which, thanks to Lila, is second nature, even after all this time—asking permission to swim. Superstitious maybe, but being by herself, there's a practical side to the ritual, too—a reminder of how often drownings occur on this island. You don't want to get so spaced-out chasing the electric colors of a dragon wrasse that a rip current catches you and slams your head into a hunk of coral. Calm as conditions seem, Stevie takes the precaution of tossing a few sticks of driftwood into the water and watching for a while, making sure they aren't carried far.

Finally, walking backwards with flippered feet, she splashes into the warming crystalline water and shrieks from the sheer joy of it. Then she's on her way, fins fluttering, hands glued to her sides so as not to disturb the grazing fish below.

Even the common convict tangs and yellowfin goatfish are gorgeous. Farther out, she spots some of her favorite rarities—an orangeband surgeonfish, a sergeant major damselfish, a compact squared-off black fish with white polka dots that she doesn't know the name of but resembles a purse she had as a child. All this would be enough for a peak experience, but she crosses the boundary into bliss when a juvenile sea turtle washes over the reef and swims alongside her with dark eyes at once curious and shy. It's not the first time swimming with a sea turtle for Stevie. This *honu,* with its large, heart-shaped shell and speckled skin, has a male's longer tail. She minimizes her motion, aware that stress could short-circuit his capacity to stay underwater for hours and cause him to drown within minutes. Otherwise, barring disease or ecological calamity, her swimming companion could easily live for over eighty years.

Never before has a *honu* stuck with Stevie for so long before changing direction, and she realizes this is the omen she had come here hoping to find. Every Hawaiian family possesses its own *'aumakua,* an animal acting as a guardian, a protector. Because Stevie fell too far from the tree (as Grandpa would say) to know what her great-great-tūtū's family *'aumakua* was, she had long ago settled on the armored, tender-bellied sea turtle as her personal one. Which is why she bought that *honu*-imprinted pareo to wear. Better yet, island *honu* are symbols of longevity—the very thing she's trying to conjure for Hank.

Swimming back toward shore, Stevie lingers above a mushroom-shaped coral formation where a pig-snouted Picasso triggerfish—the famously tongue-twisting *humuhumu-nukunuku-āpua'a*—drifts around like a neon piscine blimp. But something distracts her. A pair of somethings, actually. Two churning black objects she catches with peripheral vision then turns, pulse quickening, to see them whiz her way. Once they're in focus, she feels like a dunce for being spooked.

Dog legs, that's all they are—furry black dog-paddling dog legs. Stevie doesn't need to read a collar tag to know whose dog this is. Treading water, she pushes back her mask and pats Rainier's dignified, furrowed head, then breaststrokes over to a shallow spot, where she perches on a grooved slab of lithified sand, grabs one of the driftwood sticks she'd tossed in earlier, and hurls it for the dog. She looks around, searching the beach for Japhy, but he's nowhere in sight.

Stevie leans down to remove her fins while Rainier swims out to retrieve the stick. It's in the next moments, keeping her balance barefoot on the rock even as she holds the fins in one hand, even as she tosses the stick again with the other, even as breaking waves slap at her knees, that it hits Stevie. The solution for people falling down in her fountain is at her feet—literally. If a stonemason cuts grooves in the fountain's slick granite to mimic the channeled rock of lithified sand she's standing on, *nobody* could climb in and fall down, not unless they were drunk, and drunks don't get written up in the *Trib* when they take a tumble. The last thing left to worry about is how much this fix will cost, but not now. Now she's nearly drunk herself, reeling from the sense of fate intervening on her behalf.

Rainier paddles back again and Stevie falls on her neck with kisses. "Oh, good doggie good doggie good doggie, oh, thank you thank you thank you."

As Pip lets loose with one of his poor-neglected-me wails, Rainier shakes water over Stevie and kicks up sand bounding to the ironwood trees. Stevie follows, unhooking Pip so they can play.

When Rainier, with Pip at her hip, leaves for where the windsurfers are, Stevie puts on her sunglasses and brings up the rear. She guesses that they're headed for Japhy, whom she soon spots coming ashore, tacking back and forth in a lazy Z.

Stevie couldn't resist tuning in to his radio show yesterday morning, but just for a few minutes while she brewed coffee. Still, that was long enough to hear him dedicate Taj Mahal's bluesy version of "Little Brown Dog" to Pip, "the lost puppy who found a fine home with last week's caller." Another goofy dog song—only this was the kind you'd play for a very young child.

"Oh I buyed myself a little dog and its color it was brown. . . .
His legs they were fourteen yards long, his ears they were broad.
Round the world in half a day on him I could ride. . . ."

Hearing it, Stevie had felt a little goofy herself—for dodging Japhy all week. And now, buoyant and unguarded after her swim, she can't even remember why she'd wanted to.

Hauling his gear out of the water, Japhy calls out a hello that brings both dogs barreling into the surf. Stevie runs to catch Pip before he's caught in a wave, but Japhy beats her to it, and as he hands the puppy over, their fingers touch. Her heart flops in her chest. Now she remembers. Is she really covered in chicken skin from head to foot, nipples poking out her bikini top, or does it only feel that way? She's too self-conscious to check. It's a good thing he can't see her eyes, how much effort it takes to train them on his.

"So," Stevie says as they walk ashore, "you're a beach bum today, too."

"Monday's my one day off."

"That's the trouble with living in paradise. A lot of people work two or three jobs just to survive."

"That's not exactly my situation."

"Oh." Something knotted in his tone suggests a change of subject. She nods toward the ocean. "Kind of slow out there today."

"I don't mind going slow."

"As a general principle, or just in the water?"

"Both. What are you up to?"

"Nothing much. Snorkeling."

"Yeah? What did you see?"

"Lots. Everything from the *honu* I swam with to your dog."

It doesn't matter that the wind and water have slapped the hair on Japhy's head into an absurd-looking Sno-Kone formation, a style that might be worn by a Teletubby or some nerdy comic character. She's still in trouble. The hair on his arms is infinitely more dangerous wet than dry, and since he's bare-chested, there's *that* nicely tufted territory to consider, too. Even his dimples strike her as enticing now. When Japhy says, "I'm starving," Stevie takes a long, deep, nerve-gathering breath and tries to summon a casual tone. "How do you feel about saimin?" she asks.

"At Hamura's?"

"Where else?"

A week on the island without a meal at Hamura's—another record for Stevie. Her stomach rumbles at the thought. It's just lunch, she tells herself. Lunch with a crowd of hungry people sitting at a counter, elbow to elbow. No risk there. Nothing intimate about it. Japhy will have to put a shirt on—that will help. And if he disdains chopsticks, or slurps his saimin noodles in a disgusting way, or says disparaging things about his ex, all the better. Bargaining with desire, that's what she's doing. And never having done it before, she thinks she's being sensible, redirecting all the buzz between her legs to some safer, more cerebral place.

Alone at the ironwood tree, packing up her things to leave, she calls Hank. "Just a second," he says instead of hello. She hears the baseball game in the background. Then Hank erupts. "Hah! Error by the Mets! Wigginton can't throw out the garbage, and the Cubs score again—four to nothing!"

"It's me, Dad."

"I figured."

"What inning is it?"

"Fourth."

"Only the fourth? And you were worried about Clement pitching hurt."

"He *is* pitching hurt. That strained groin bothers him, no question. But he's incredible anyway."

There's a pang at not being with him in her usual game-time armchair—part regret, part guilt, part wanting him to say he hoped she was enjoying herself, but it wasn't as much fun watching without her. "I hope you're listening to yourself," she tells him.

"I don't *listen to myself,* Stevie. But I do remember what I've said, in case you think my brain's gone soft."

"You're way off base, Dad. All I meant was Clement's a good role model for you."

"I don't need a role model."

"If you say so. There's some gazpacho in the fridge."

"Fine."

"Okay, okay—you can get off the phone now. See you for the recap after lunch."

There's no comb, no lip gloss, no blusher, no anything to pretty herself up with in the knapsack. Just as well. Look at where her coming on tough and sexy had led with Brian. A strong, independent professional—that's what he thought he was getting. The antithesis of his ex-wife. Then, surprise! Stevie turned out to have dependent needs. Nothing spineless or bizarre, like requiring Brian to manage her finances or spank her to orgasms. Just fairly ordinary longings for comfort, tenderness, attention. But because Stevie hadn't advertised them up front, he must have thought she came with some sort of no-need guarantee, violation of which constituted bait-and-switch tactics in his book. No wonder he thought she didn't have a comfort zone.

After brushing sand off her chest and torso, Stevie clips her hair into a ponytail, slips on her T-shirt, ties the pareo around her waist, then trots back to where Japhy and the dogs wait. What if it turns out dogs are all they have in common? Oh well, that's enough to get them through lunch.

Stevie follows Japhy up a steep dune, through an ironwood grove, then down again to the end of a red-dirt cane road where his pickup is parked. There are just five other cars nearby, and out of those, only two look like rentals. "I wonder how long it'll stay this quiet out here," Japhy says as he loads his gear into the truck bed. "Developers are itching to build another resort."

"I worry, too. It *is* all privately owned." A few years ago, when a massive hunk of real estate encompassing Māhā'ulepū changed hands, Stevie read all the reports. No longer the property of sugar-rich missionary descendants, the land now belongs to an island-born *haole,* an information-age captain of industry. Lately, though, she's been too busy to keep track. "I wonder why something hasn't happened already."

"Endangered blind wolf spiders," Japhy says. "That's why."

"Lava tube spiders are blind?"

"Yep. And they feed on a sand flea species—also endangered, also blind."

"The blind eating the blind."

That's when she hears Japhy laugh, really laugh, for the first time. It's a nice laugh, not all honked-out and nasal, like hers, but deep and melodic. He reaches into the truck cab to pull on a worn gray T-shirt and squashes his Sno-Kone hairdo with a navy blue Mariners cap. Then he removes a Baggie full of almonds from the glove compartment and offers some to Stevie, who declines, before popping a handful into his mouth and herding the dogs onto the jump seat. "If this place turns out to be a critical habitat for the spider and the flea," he says, munching, "then the whole shore is conservation land—can't be developed."

"God, I hope that's the verdict. It would be such a neat historical rhyme."

Japhy starts the engine and looks over his shoulder while backing up. "Yeah? How so?"

"Kaua'i is the one island Kamehameha the Great never invaded and conquered—it got ceded over to him. The only time he dared attack was in 1796, when he sent ten thousand warriors to Māhā'ulepū. But before his men got here, most drowned in a terrible storm, and Kaua'i's king, Kaumuali'i, was ready for the ones who made it. His warriors finished them off."

"Impressive," Japhy says. They're headed *mauka* now. A fat midday cloud hovers over the peak of Ha'upu Range, a doily threatening to land on Queen Victoria's head. "You're telling me stuff I didn't know."

"Just your basic Kōloa Grammar School history, but it happens to be true. I kind of like the idea that Māhā'ulepū isn't there for the taking."

"Me, too. Locals already act like it belongs to them. There's a group restoring native plants, getting rid of invasive vegetation. That's your line of work, isn't it?"

"Not really," Stevie says. "Plants are just a piece of what I do. I'm not so much a gardener as a designer."

"Sounds pretty conceptual."

"It is."

"Your father sure is proud of you."

"So I've heard."

"According to Hank, you're famous in your field."

At that, Stevie snorts. "Infamous is probably more like it these days."

"How come?"

"Oh, it's a long, boring story."

"Not to me, I bet. I was just thinking about a hunk of old mill property up in the hills outside Līhu'e —bought up by a local consortium to save from development. All the clearing and cleanup's done. There's a fantastic ocean view, and a flume cutting through—the kind that used to run water from the hills to the cane fields."

"Lila broke her wrist sliding down one of those flumes. It was totally against the law, but so much fun. All the kids around here used to sneak in on hot days when nobody was looking."

"Must've been quite a ride."

"Yeah, and now tourists pay to do it in those little tube boats."

"This place is slated for a public park with gardens. They're taking bids. Not a huge budget, but decent. Probably too bush-league for someone at your level, though."

"The firm I'm with goes for high-profile, big-ticket projects," she tells him. "But I'd be glad to look at the site, make some suggestions. Know anyone who's involved?"

"Sure. It's a small island, remember?"

The pickup bounces as they hit a deep pothole on the old cane road. Japhy swerves around more ruts, a job requiring such undivided attention that there's no further talk until they hit smooth pavement and Stevie tells him where to pull over for her bike.

She gets out, undoes the lock, and as she wheels the bike away from the banana tree, back to Japhy's pickup, she notices something in the basket that wasn't there before. A box of strike-anywhere matches with its trademark blue diamond.

Chapter 10

Ever since Margo started e-mailing Hank, the interior territory occupied by her dead mother has grown vaster. So vast that it no longer consists of only badlands and barren, precipitous cliffs, but actually contains a few meadow-like pockets of peace. Now, for instance, Margo can recall many more wonderful shared moments than she could when Evelyn was alive.

Like Evelyn reading Mrs. Piggle-Wiggle stories aloud at bedtime, using a different voice for every character and happy to endlessly reread Margo's favorite, about how Mrs. Piggle-Wiggle cures Melanie the Crybaby with a magic potion that turns her tears into a force of nature capable of flooding basements and potentially drowning the stray kitten Melanie saves and gets to keep—the *real* cure for her crying. Like going to see *The Music Man* at a fancy downtown theater, just the two of them, and singing "Seventy-Six Trombones" and "Shipoopi" in the car all the way home. Like the way Evelyn would scratch Margo's back to soothe an asthma attack, then kiss the top of her head, saying, "Nighty-night, my little Margo May, sleep tight, sugarplum," and leave her nodding off in a cozy mentholated cloud. Doing lovely things for Margo that, come to think of it, her own mother would have been constitutionally incapable of doing for her.

This is the *only* Evelyn known to Margo's daughter, Cammie—the grandmother whose sole purpose in appearing was to enchant, to coddle, to indulge. Cammie never had to contend with Evelyn the Terrible—not like her little brother, Ben, did.

I wish you wouldn't refer to me like that. Your son's manners were atrocious. Somebody had to teach him how to behave.

"Go ahead, Mother, blame me. That's your answer for everything."

People would like you better if you were nicer. No wonder you don't have much of a social life.

"Your definition of a social life doesn't interest me."

That's right, I forgot. You're so social you're going to be a social worker.

"Wrong again. The degree is in MFT—marital and family therapy."

I can't believe that's what you really want to do with your life.

"Oh, you'd be surprised how many therapists had mothers like you."

That's no excuse for whining about private matters with a stranger the way you do every week. What must your husband think?

"As if you're really concerned about Kenny!"

I thought we were remembering the good times. I can think of lots more than you can. Are you ready for my list?

"I was making my own. Stuff yours."

Despite the resurfacing of sweeter recollections, exchanges with Evelyn have grown so fractious Margo has taken to jotting them down for Grace Kiriakades, the therapist she sees as part of her training. Grace has an office close to campus. Today, as Grace emerges from the hall to summon Margo, she wears one of her flowing, ethnic tunics and looks like a cross between Meryl Streep and Anouk Aimée, of an age somewhere in between. In Grace's plant-filled consultation room, there's a wall full of books, which are heavily underlined and freely loaned, plus a pair of Scandinavian-style chairs and ottomans facing each other, with a box of tissues next to the one Margo settles into, kicking off her Dansko clogs and stretching her long, blue-jeaned legs out in front of her.

Instead of considering Margo a raving loon for having arguments with her dead mother, Grace treats their tiffs like special deliveries from Margo's subconscious, fragile packages meant to be carefully unwrapped and marveled over. To deliver the latest, Margo pushes up the sleeves of her loose, pale green linen sweater and reaches for her notebook.

"Well, that was your mother's MO," Grace says when she finishes. "Lashing out at you for what she denied in herself."

"And controlling me when she couldn't control herself."

"No wonder she's upsetting to you still."

"But maybe Mother has a point. I hardly talk about my kids' best qualities, or how good Kenny is to me, considering what a pain in the ass I can be. All I ever talk about here is the bad stuff."

"Would you rather we start with you telling me what felt best about your week?"

"Nah. Let's go straight to the bad stuff."

And oh, is there ever an abundance of the bad stuff, an endless supply, much of it spilling from Evelyn's family dinners at the big house on Deere Park Drive, which always started out being so nice, with tantalizing smells of garlic-sprigged prime rib roasting in one oven and a nutty, cinnamon aroma from Nana's schnecken baking in the other. Hank was no longer in attendance by then, but Evelyn's aunts and uncles and their descendants would all come, every time, as if they didn't know that, before the meal's end, someone (often Evelyn) would not be speaking to someone else (often Nana), or that another person (often Margo) would leave the table bathed in hot, humiliated tears, or that at any moment in the midst of all this, with everyone pretending not to notice any disagreements except the ones they were having over politics, Jeremy, the teenage autistic savant, would break his silence of the previous few hours by going to the piano to play "Sometimes I Feel Like a Motherless Child," singing as if some psychic surgeon had transplanted Billie Holiday's larynx into his throat.

So many dinners, all the same—it's impossible to keep them straight. But there must have been one when Hank returned to Chicago with his new wife and Baby Stevie. Maybe that's what drove them back to Hawai'i so fast—who can say? Then Nana died and, soon after, Hank got polio. "Maybe that's not a coincidence," Margo had written to him in one of her e-mails.

"I don't see the connection" was his reply.

Well. At least he still steps up to the plate. To use a phrase Hank *would* understand.

Margo's father—also dead, for nearly a decade now—had always accommodated Evelyn's fits of temper. He never once dared to take his daughter's side when Margo and her mother quarreled. If Evelyn wasn't speaking to Margo, he froze her out, too. Maybe that's why Margo remains so attached to her memories of Hank. While her father was off playing golf, it was Hank who made sure she got to go to baseball games and the zoo, and he never hesitated to stick up for Margo if he thought her mother was being unfair. Which only added fuel to Evelyn's fires, but Hank had fire enough of his own not to mind.

Today, Margo re-creates for Grace the time Evelyn gave away the cocker spaniel puppy that had been a birthday present from Uncle Hank. "There wasn't any warning. I just came back from camp and Ginger was gone. It was awful, but I can see how I was too young for the responsibility of a dog. Mother got a Westie puppy for me herself when I was eleven. And she didn't give Buddy away until I left for college."

"That's totally normal," Grace tells her.

"What? Getting rid of your children's pets?"

"Wanting to let your mother off the hook. Making excuses for her hurtful behavior. But to forgive, *really* forgive, you have to face the anger head on. That's how you get to a place of mature compassion without betraying yourself. When you've worked through honoring the memory of the child in you who wasn't properly cared for in the past, then—and only then—are you equipped to honor people who exhibit that same need in the present."

Pretty formal language for Grace. Usually she refers to Margo's childlike self as "your little cookie," a term that Margo actually prefers. "How does your inner child respond to this memory?" sounds heaps ickier to her than "What's your little cookie got to say about that?" Or maybe Margo's just a sucker for baby talk.

Truth be told, she'd all but forgotten about Ginger until she and Hank began corresponding. Her feelings around losing the dog must have gotten all balled up with losing him.

At the end of her session with Grace, Margo closes her eyes to discover her body's response to everything she's talked about. As usual, her busy little monkey mind rebels, wanting to dwell on all the day's tasks—outlining the paper she has to write on family systems, inviting Cammie out for a movie, mailing Ben the first-edition copy of a collection of Hemingway short stories she's bought for his birthday, planning tonight's dinner, and oh, don't forget to pick up the dry cleaning. After this chatter ends, the fist of tension behind her breastbone dissolves, the last trace of Evelyn leaves her head, and she starts to weep—not a Melanie-like flood but a long, quiet stream that ends precisely when her hour is up, and instead of walking out of Grace's office exhausted from her emotion, she's actually energized.

In the campus student union where Margo goes to grab a snack, a crowd of euphoric, mostly male students are gathered around a television set, shouting the words to "Take Me Out to the Ball Game" for the seventh-inning stretch at Wrigley Field. When she steps closer to join them, they make room for her to sit with the good-boy manners they reserve for older women. Easy enough to remember, though, how these are the same sort of guys who were once so quick to flatter and flirt in her undergraduate days, caught by Margo's wide smile, short skirts, and the contrast between her ice blue eyes and her long, thick curtain of ebony hair (which she tortured into straightness then). Thank God her husband still pays attention. Not only does Kenny still surprise her with flowers and remember their anniversary in thoughtful, inventive ways, but she's managed to convince him that lanky, flat-chested, gray-haired women in Dansko clogs are sexy. If she ever appeared in Evelyn's sable coat, wearing one of Evelyn's Valentino suits underneath, face coated with the powder Evelyn thought essential to camouflaging Margo's slight—very slight—sprinkling of acne scars, Kenny would think it was Halloween. Not that Margo would ever pull such a stunt. She gave Evelyn's clothes away months ago. In fact, by now all those

Valentinos and Adolfos and Blasses have most likely been torn apart at the seams and reassembled by some hip young designer who'd plucked them up for peanuts at the annual Pearson School rummage sale.

It's a dazzling, sunstruck day in Chicago, with a gentle breeze off Lake Michigan rippling Wrigley Field's flags. While everyone is singing, a camera roams the bleachers, finding a little girl atop a man's shoulders, and suddenly Margo is six again, perched on her uncle's shoulders for the stretch, joyously tapping out "one, two, three strikes you're out" on his head. Her eyes fill with tears. She's tempted to grab her cell phone and call Hank in Hawai'i, where he's sure to be watching, too. Instead, she takes her blueberry yogurt and coffee downstairs to the tech center, where she finds a computer and writes him an e-mail. It comes out very differently from all her others of the past week, those sweet, cajoling efforts designed to relax Hank's business-letter formality. In this e-mail, what she calls up from inside isn't good stuff or bad stuff, but the deep-down stuff of essence, the kind that doesn't ever really change. She hopes he'll be able to see that. But what if he can't?

You'll be sorry, Evelyn hollers, *that's what. You'll wish you'd listened to me!*

"Too late, Mother. I already sent it."

Chapter 11

Leaving the dogs leashed outside with kibble and water, Stevie and Japhy enter Hamura's through a screen door that thwacks behind them. It's only half past eleven, but already the diner is so crowded that they take the last pair of side-by-side stools at the orange, serpentine counter. The counter's built low to the floor for people much shorter than Japhy, whose knees fit underneath only if he splays them, putting the left one into a relationship with Stevie's right thigh that is not only companionable but alarmingly thrilling.

Steam rises from enormous pots of broth and freshly made noodles. Grilling teriyaki meat fills the air with sweet, smoky smells. Little has changed here since Stevie was a child; even faces behind the counter seem familiar, although that could be more a trick of genetics than memory, since everyone belongs to the same family. Stevie imagines how miserable Brian would be if she'd insisted on bringing him to Hamura's. He doesn't go in for hole-in-the-wall places. He'd hate the plastic water glasses, cheap plates, canned soft drinks. He'd ponder the menu with a serious expression, needing to decide for himself rather than trust her recommendations, and would probably insist on leaving the second he saw that one of his culinary options was Spam saimin. *You don't like it,* haole *boy? Well, you know where you come from.* That's what a tough local woman would tell him. That's what Stevie wishes *she'd* told him, only not about Spam saimin.

Japhy declines the offered menu, as does Stevie. When she says, "I'll have the special and a Diet Coke, please," he echoes her order and adds a couple of grilled chicken skewers to share.

"You're a Mariners fan," Stevie says.

"You mean the cap?" He hands it over for inspection. "No adjustable band, see? The real McCoy, custom made for Dan Wilson."

"*The* Dan Wilson?"

"Uh-huh. We have the same size head."

Stevie reaches up to put the cap on him backwards, the way a catcher like Wilson wears it behind the plate. Japhy's thick hair is smashed flat on top now, and she can feel its saltwater stickiness, see how it's dried into distressingly endearing waves above his neck, behind his ears. "How'd you figure that out?" she asks. "Are you a groupie?"

"I took care of the family dog. After I mentioned how I'd always wanted a genuine Major League player's cap, Dan had me try on one of his, and it was a perfect fit. He's a regular neighborhood guy—great wife, sweet kids, lots of heart. Not one of those celebrity-style athletes with a mansion on the lake."

"He's also an excellent catcher. I admire excellent catchers."

"That was my position in high school."

Stevie turns this over in her mind, picturing a younger Japhy crouched in catcher's armor, legs wide and flexed, arms tight with the tension of play, flashing signals to the pitcher, tagging a player out at home plate, flipping back his face mask to chase down a pop fly, throwing the ball at least as many times as anybody else in the game. It counted for a lot in baseball, being a smart catcher, but it wasn't a glamorous position, not like shortstop or third base. Stevie must have said as much aloud without realizing, because Japhy is nodding his agreement as he swivels the cap right side around.

"That was my big advantage. Going out for catcher, you aren't competing with all the hotshots. None of them wants to spend the whole game in a crouch. Same-o in the majors, according to Dan. But to answer your question—yeah, I'm a fan. I love baseball. I just don't understand when people say it's boring."

Stevie notices that his eyes change color like a chameleon. At the shelter, she'd thought them to be dusky blue, but in this light they almost look sea green. "Anybody who says baseball is boring ought to watch a game with my father."

"Wouldn't mind doing that myself." He takes a long drink of water. "Glad you were free today."

"Me, too."

"You were being brave, weren't you, coming out for lunch like this?"

"Brave," she says, feeling her face redden. God, is she really so transparent? "That wasn't brave. I like being spontaneous—I'm just usually too scheduled."

"My life in Seattle was kind of like that."

"Is that why you left?"

"No." He slips his chopsticks out of their paper wrap, snaps them apart, and rubs them together to smooth the edges. "How long do you plan to stay, this trip?"

So he doesn't want to discuss why he moved here. Fine, she'll keep things light. "Not sure. Until it's time to leave." Mentally, she gives Japhy points for the chopsticks, for how he ordered. But she also jots down her first official entry on his deficit list: come-here-go-away behavior. Easy enough to recognize, since it was one of Brian's specialties. No sooner does she fault Japhy, though, than she doubts her judgment. If she could poll all the women in her father's life, they'd probably say that, in the matter of "come here, go away," she'd been born to a master. Maybe she's conditioned to bring it out in men, getting the worst of them because she doesn't know how to ask for the best. Stevie pops open her Diet Coke and shakes off the notion with a small shudder.

"Cold?" Japhy asks.

"No, I'm fine."

Little scraps of pidgin fly through the air: "You know da kine. . . ." "Eh, no make like dat, sistah. . . ." "So I wen turn da corner, dere dat babooze." It's talk that's quick and fluid, the lilt soothing Stevie's jitters for being so familiar, so missed. It's talk as complex and flavorful as the saimin special that the fast-moving waitress puts down in front of her and Japhy—communal bowls filled with pieces from just about every nationality that ever worked the cane. Chinese wontons, Korean mustard cabbage, Portuguese sausage, with noodles inspired by Filipino *pancit* and Japanese ramen, but fattened with eggs from Hawaiian chickens. As for Spam on the menu, there's history there, too—the legacy of U.S. Army rations. Just its presence means the lack of anything British in the mix can't be chalked up solely to good taste.

Without a word, Japhy passes Stevie a bottle of shoyu sauce to season her saimin, shakes out some chili sauce into his own, and as they trade, his hand lingers on hers for a moment, purposeful this time. "Save room for the *liliko'i* pie," he advises. "It's so great here."

"Lila's is even better," she says. "More lemon, I think that's why."

Japhy is adept at the two-handed maneuvers of chopsticks and spoon required to consume the saimin's broth along with everything else, and it's Stevie, not Japhy, who noisily slurps up the ends of curly noodles dangling past her chin. Not that he seems to notice. He's too busy eating and telling her about how lucky he was to be able to take over the practice of a retiring vet here in Līhu'e, which means he's one of the few on the island who perform surgeries.

"So," Stevie says. "Sounds like *you'll* be the one cutting off Pip's balls. When does that happen?"

"I'm guessing he's lost more puppy teeth since you got him?"

"Yeah, he's down to his last few."

"Then he really ought to be neutered soon—no later than a month from now."

"I wish you'd tell my father why that has to be done. He won't believe me."

"There's a traditional male for you."

"Meaning you're not one?"

"Well," he says, extending the syllable into a low, two-note song, "my mother would feel she'd failed if anybody told her I was."

"Your *name* isn't traditional."

"It's from a Kerouac book."

"Your mother was a beatnik?"

"More of a bohemian, really. Although Alana used to say Mom defies description."

"Alana?"

"She was my wife."

"Now *you're* the brave one," Stevie says, but her playful smile fades as his ocean eyes turn to the waitress, sliding a plate of teriyaki skewers between them.

Japhy picks up one of the skewers, then replaces it without taking a bite. "I don't want to talk about her," he says, voice curt. But when he speaks again, it's as if he's rewound their conversation to an earlier point. "Must be good for your father, having Pip around."

Stevie's confused. On the one hand, she's miffed with him for being so brusque. On the other, she wouldn't think much of Japhy for joking about his marriage if it ended badly—not at such an early stage. It's like they're playing poker. No sooner does he lay a personal card on the table than he freaks and covers it with the puppy. Okay, she'll play the puppy. "That was the main reason why I wanted Pip. Dad had a terrier he was crazy about as a kid."

Instead of waiting to see what he'll do—pick up or draw another—she's compelled to set some sort of example by flipping out even *more* personal cards, describing all her other life-prolonging strategies for Hank—the Cubs, the Roosevelt biography, her brand-new cousin, the *māmaki* tea. Japhy's slice of *liliko'i* pie arrives, and he cuts it in half for them to share. *Liliko'i*—the Hawaiian name for passion fruit! Must be why she can't shut up, telling him about the problem with her fountain in Chicago, and how she owes the solution for it to Rainier. "She's such a fine dog. I love how thoughtful she always looks, even when she's just playing around. How old is she?"

"Seven in November."

"Isn't it a hassle bringing a dog to the islands?"

"Yeah, she had to be in quarantine for a month. But I visited every day, and even though I felt terrible doing that to her, I couldn't move here without Rainier. We've been through too much together. And she didn't seem to hold it against me afterwards. Well, you know about dogs. Buddhas in fur suits. I mean, look what Rainier did for you and your fountain."

She's startled to detect so much emotion behind these words. But then, he *is* a vet.

When the waitress slaps down their check, Stevie grabs it and pulls her wallet out of the knapsack to pay. Japhy reaches for his own wallet and holds out a handful of bills. She waves them away, saying, "No, no—this was my idea."

"That's cool," Japhy says. "But I get it next time."

Maybe he's just being polite. No talk is cheaper than what passes for social lubrication, and Japhy might actually prefer the prospect of biting bullets to eating with her again. It's no use telling herself these things, though, because she's already wondering when next time might be. She's already lost her bargain with desire.

Chapter 12

After dropping Stevie off at her father's place, Japhy drives west past acres of coffee trees, headed for the house he's renovating in Waimea. As he follows the curving road, it occurs to him that the biggest advantage of living among people who are, as Japhy's mother puts it, "aware of what you've been through," is simple: you don't often find yourself in the position of having to explain. Japhy purposely left behind such comfort. And it *had* been a comfort. Once. Until, without any warning, it became a burden.

Moving to Kaua'i was the closest he had come in years to acting with the certainty he'd once so easily applied to everything. *Everything.*

"You know what I admire most about you?" Alana had said when they were just beginning to fall in love.

"No," he told her. "But I can't wait to hear."

"How well you seem to know yourself."

In those days, being a big believer in full disclosure, Japhy had insisted on giving Alana a thorough rundown of all his pluses and minuses: While he seldom lost his temper, he did tend to hold a grudge. When hurt, he clammed up. He loved cooking, hated shopping. His only addictions, relatively benign, were salted nuts and coffee—the dark, expensive kind, French roasted. He grew irritable when hungry—a low-blood-sugar thing that meant he always had a stash of almonds handy. His family could be overwhelming, consisting as it did of voluble, opinionated parents and stepparents, one full-blooded sibling, and a handful of steps and halves who were starting to have children of their own. Since he was just out of vet school with student loans to pay off, it might be a while before he was established enough to afford a house, much less a child, but he wanted a dog right away. He even dropped his pants, standing in the middle of Alana's brightly lit kitchen to point out the slightly bowed legs and knee-surgery scars that she might have failed to notice. By which time Alana was laughing.

"You are out of your mind," she said when he finished, "if you expect a performance like that from me."

"Meaning what? You don't know yourself so well?"

"Meaning I leave *my* pants on till I know you better."

"It's not about sex."

"I prefer to preserve my mystery."

"Don't worry about your mystery," he said. "You have mystery to burn."

"Right now, I can only tell you this. I feel more like who I am when I'm with you than anybody else."

If he were capable of formulating a statement like that, Japhy could have kept *his* pants on, too—for a while longer, anyway, until the more romantic moment Alana was waiting for arrived. But this was her gift: boiling down his actions into words that mirrored the emotional complexity behind them. A gift he had learned how to give, too. And maybe it's a gift of time that he can think of it this way instead of feeling shredded and enraged, as he used to. Maybe he can learn to give again.

A big maybe. Since now he is not only rusty at disclosure but wary of it, too. There's no other explanation for how he could sit next to Stevie at Hamura's, close enough to relish the fresh, spicy scent of her sun-drenched skin, and be incapable of revealing what she wanted to hear. He'd like to let himself off the hook with the excuse that the restaurant was too crowded, too hectic, too noisy. But alone in his pickup hadn't felt right, either.

What's the proper length of time that ought to pass before you divulge difficult information about yourself? He can't remember ever needing to know such a rule from his earlier life as a single person, when everything was so much simpler. Anyway, Stevie has enough difficulties of her own with her father's impending death, and he can tell she's still in that early phase, with hope feeding on hope. It surprises Japhy to realize his silence has another motive, too—one not nearly so considerate or noble. He's afraid of scaring her away.

Before he had a radio show to host on Sunday mornings, Japhy used to come to Waimea town so he could slide into a back pew at the Hawaiian-language church and hear the hymns, celestial-sounding from Hawaiian throats. No wonder few of the early missionaries ever sailed back to New England. The stuff they sang there wouldn't sound anywhere near as spiritual.

As Japhy drives past the church now, Rainier sticks her head out the window and barks, poised to run for the beach when they reach the house he's bought. The house is nothing fancy, just another old plantation cottage—two rooms larger than the one he rents from Hank and, because of its weathered, rooted look, the only sort of house he'd wanted to live in. Built to survive hurricanes. Which, he'd learned, didn't mean heavy and solid. Just fixable after being blown apart.

Since the property included beachfront land, it was pricier than he could have afforded without dipping into money he'd set aside for other purposes. He kept looking at less-expensive places with their own seductive features. Fruit groves, mountain views, established gardens. But in the end he couldn't resist being so close to the sea.

After exchanging "howzits" with the two-man crew installing solar panels in the roof, Japhy puts on the pair of work gloves he keeps here, grabs some two-by-fours leaning against the side of the house, and goes out back, where his project for the day is to finish the decking beneath an outdoor shower and tub. The tub is nothing fancy, either. It's older than he is, as old as the house itself, and large enough for a tall person like him to soak in at night with only his head in the air, listening to the surf and watching the stars.

There are more clear nights per annum on this dry, desert side than anywhere else on the island, and sunsets are spectacular, skies streaked with fiery light as the yolk-like globe, shimmering, slips below the sea. Japhy likes hanging out at the town pier, where locals talk story and fish for whatever's running. He enjoys catching movies at the Waimea Theater, where it's worth arriving early to snag one of the cushioned armchairs in the middle rows. Like much else around here, his favorite supermarket dates back to plantation days. All major factors, along with the scarcity of resort development, in Waimea's appeal for him.

Most tourists want sugary white-sand beaches and swimmable water; Waimea's beach is torn by riptides, stained brown from river sediment, glittering with mica. The tourists that do come generally stop only for shave ice at JoJo's—renowned for all its different blends of powdery ice, ice cream, and syrup—or a quick visit to the underwhelming Captain Cook monument on the tiny town square.

The modesty of Cook's statue strikes Japhy as fitting. A reflection of local chagrin over natives' mistaking the explorer for a god, plus reluctance to glorify his 1778 first Hawaiian landing in Waimea as a "discovery," seeing as how it occurred centuries after Polynesians had arrived in their double-hulled canoes. The preferred term for Cook's landing is "first contact." Which makes the British seaman and his crew sound less like gods than invading extra-terrestrials. In a way, of course, they were.

For all the time Japhy's put into this house, he's never shown the place to anyone who wasn't working on it. Why not invite Stevie, though? She might have some landscaping ideas. It's Japhy's understanding that after the last hurricane hit, in 1990—another September 11 disaster—the previous absentee owners were too tapped out from repairing the place to bother with restoring their garden, modest to begin with. Given the aridity, he'd like to emphasize plants that don't require much water. But he couldn't choose them on his own. What little gardening he'd done had been in wet Seattle, and even then, Alana was always the one who came home from nurseries with flats of plants.

Okay, so gardening is not the most pressing reason he wants Stevie out here. It's not the most pressing topic he ought to discuss with her, either. Before things heat up any further, he'll have to decide how.

Done with the deck, Japhy moves the tub into place. Its faucet isn't at the head of the tub but in the middle, so someone besides him, facing in the opposite direction, could fit in without having to dodge the spigot. He hadn't thought of that before.

Now he pictures Stevie's high-calved, slender legs, so long for a woman who's petite, but not so long that she could sit comfortably in such a big tub without somebody else there to brace her feet against. His next project ought to be a low lattice wall around the tub. Something to ensure a little extra privacy for the scene unspooling in his head.

Chapter 13

Hank's house is quiet when Stevie returns, sun sloping into westward-facing windows, warm afternoon air spiked with plumeria and stirred by the soft whirr of ceiling fans. Pip's toenails click on the bamboo floor as he follows Stevie to Hank's room. Poking her head in, she sees her father propped against pillows, opening the lid to his laptop computer. "Hi," she says. "How'd the game go?"

"Terrific. The Cubs beat your team."

"My team?"

"You're a New Yorker now, aren't you? Isn't that why you went to the beach, so you wouldn't have to root against them?"

"Oh, stop." As she lifts Pip onto the quilted orange bedspread and then sits by Hank's feet, he closes the computer, setting it aside so that Pip can have his lap. "Tell me all about it," she says. "What was the final score?"

"Four to one."

"So the Mets eked out a run against Clement."

"Barely," Hank says, flipping Pip over for a belly rub. "It was unearned, on a wild pitch. The climax to a pathetic fifth-inning rally that started when Clement couldn't field a bunt fast enough."

"His injury, huh?"

"Probably. The beautiful thing was how the Cubs knocked themselves out to give Clement such a big early lead because they knew he wasn't a hundred percent, and Clement just kept giving everything he had to deserve it. You can't buy team spirit like that. For all their vaunted star power, the Mets were hamstrung."

"Call me crazy, but I have a feeling the Cubs are going to make it to the playoffs."

"They're one and a half games behind Houston again."

"I don't care what you say—it's still a race and I'm going to be optimistic."

"Looks like you got some color out there."

"Feels like, too. You could use a swim yourself, Dad. Next day the Cubs aren't playing, let's go to Puolo Point. We can drive right up to the beach. You can practically step out of the car into the water."

"If I'm up to it."

She plans to tell him about bumping into Japhy, how that was what delayed her, but before she can, Hank sets Pip aside to open the computer again, and this time, he powers it up. "I was just going to check my e-mail."

"Oh. Okay." Stevie fetches Hank's lunch dishes from the lanai and carries them to the kitchen. She considers going to her own computer and sending her solution for the slippery fountain to New York, but she'd rather savor it privately for a while. Once she sets the wheels in motion, all the island sweetness of her discovery will give way to Chicago costs, client concerns, schedules. Besides, she needs to shower off salt, sand, and sweat.

Stevie closes the bathroom door behind her, strips, and unclips her hair. Instead of turning on the shower, she just stands there, regarding herself in the mirror. Her cheeks and shoulders are not so much pinked by the sun as burnished to a coppery color, with the boundaries of her new bikini clearly visible. But for a few strips of cloth, she had been this naked with Japhy at Māhā'ulepū. Maybe it was a Freudian slip on his part, saying he was starving. A thought that sends heat bubbling up from her belly to the crown of her head and touches off another surge of chicken skin, only this time she can watch how her nipples snap to, along with every other bit of visible flesh. Agitated erectile tissue in a cupless bikini top. Not so obvious as a hard-on for a guy in board shorts—which she had been too busy being embarrassed to even consider, much less check for. But still, it would have been difficult to miss. If, that is, Japhy had been looking at her chest. Not just looking, but wanting to touch.

That's her fantasy, anyway. She steps into the shower thinking how it will remain nothing more than a fantasy if whatever kept Japhy from talking about his ex keeps him from falling down a mine shaft of his own. Her mind runs a hamster wheel of possibilities. Did they split up back in Seattle, or here, on Kaua'i, and is *that* what he's hiding? It could be they're only separated, not divorced at all. Somebody else might already be in the picture. Each explanation worse than the last. But she'd feel silly, hopping off to bunnyland for some sunnier story, and she knows all too well that the complications behind what difficult men conceal are endless. Is Japhy difficult? Maybe after "next time" she'll know. If he's not, they might laugh together over all her terrible scenarios. Hop, hop, hop.

When Stevie emerges from the bathroom in her Johnny's T-shirt and running shorts—she really needs to have some more practical garments sent from Pineapple Street—Hank's bedroom door is closed and Pip sits outside whimpering. "Shhh," Stevie says, thinking her father is asleep. Then she catches a whiff of cigarette smoke and knocks. "Dad? Are you all right?"

"Fit as a fucking fiddle."

She cracks open the door and Pip makes a run for the bed. It's surprising when he manages to land next to Hank, leaping a height so much greater than his own. But Hank, brow furrowed and intent on his freshly lit cigarette, ignores Pip.

"Looks like you're having a relapse," Stevie says, working to sound calm. "Still had a pack hidden somewhere, huh?"

As she draws closer, Hank reaches for the laptop beside him and shuts the lid with more force than necessary. "What's it matter?" he says. "I'm dying anyway."

"You gave Lila your word!"

Hank starts to put the cigarette out in the ramekin he's using as an ashtray, then takes another drag instead, his face paling as he makes an evident effort not to cough. "I told her I'd stop when I had to be on oxygen. I meant when I had to be on oxygen *all* the time. Haven't had any for a week, not since I fell."

"Come on, Dad. One second you're dying, the next you're not that sick? Can't have it both ways." Then it dawns on her. "You heard from Margo, didn't you?"

"Don't talk to me about Margo. She's crazy. Crazy like her mother."

"I don't know what she could have written, but—"

"That's right, you don't." He's yelling now.

"Whatever it was, I'm sure she didn't mean to upset you like this."

"Don't argue with me."

"I'm not arguing. I'm being reasonable."

"Close the door. And take the dog. I'm in no mood right now for either one of you."

"No problem." Stevie goes to his bed to pick up Pip and snatches a Marlboro Light out of the half-empty pack that's on the antique tansu Hank uses as his dresser. Looking him in the eye, she flicks on the lighter, inhales, and blows a stream of smoke in his direction before she leaves.

Stevie clicks her own computer back to life to see if Margo copied her on whatever she wrote to Hank. She didn't. She just left Stevie holding the bag. And instead of handing it back to her, back to Hank, Stevie is sitting here sucking down big lungfuls of smoke, being just as self-destructive as her father. Oh, he can sing paeans for the Cubs, how they rally behind some pitcher with a pulled muscle in his groin, but what does she get for playing so hard on his team? Banished with the dog.

Stevie marches back into Hank's room, stubs her cigarette out in his ramekin, and extends it toward him. "Your turn."

Hank just stares at his smoke, as if calculating how many more drags are left before he's down to the filter, then tips in the ash and brings it to his mouth again.

"Now," she says.

"Don't be so damn bossy," he shouts.

Stevie slams the ramekin down on Hank's bedside table. "You want to kill yourself? Fine, go ahead. I just wish you cared a little about how watching you do it makes me feel." She's shouting herself, matching his volume and then some. "You're forgetting a whole lot of important things here. You're forgetting how much better you've been feeling. You're forgetting how damn happy you were to have your niece back. How I made it so you could write each other, so you could watch your games, so you could have a housebroken puppy to play with."

"Now *you* sound like Evelyn."

"And who the hell is Evelyn? I never knew her, thanks to you."

"Aloha!" It's Lila's voice, coming from the lanai. "Sounds like you two could use a referee."

"Oh, hell," Hank says.

At the sight of Lila in her motorcycle leathers and nurse's blue cottons, duty bag in hand, Stevie bursts into tears. Hank takes a final drag and puts out the butt with an exasperated sigh. "*You* talk to him," Stevie says. "He can't hear me."

Lila grabs her by the shoulders as she storms past, steering her to the lanai and onto the couch. "Tell, tell, tell," Lila says, stroking Stevie's hair as she sobs onto her cushiony shoulder.

"There's nothing *to* tell. I lost it. I yelled at him."

"Sometimes he needs to be yelled at. Sometimes if you don't, he just rolls right over you."

Stevie raises her head and swipes at her eyes. "But he's hurting."

"You, too, seems like."

"No, I'm bad. I'm selfish. My career's a mess, Brian dumped me, and I've been out there thinking about getting laid while my father's dying."

A big sigh from Lila. "I run out of fingers, counting all the babies in my family who come into this world nine months after funerals."

"Is that supposed to make me feel better?"

"It's supposed to make you feel human."

"Everything's terrible, and I'm only making it worse. I'm no good at this. I should leave. He'd be happier with strangers here taking care of him." With that, another wave of anger builds, bringing another surge of tears, and Stevie trembles with the effort of battling them both into submission.

Lila takes Stevie's hands and squeezes hard. *"Ku'u pua laha 'ole,"* she says. My beloved person. And because it was one of Grandpa's endearments, too, Stevie also knows the literal translation from Hawaiian: my rare, choice flower. As tears win out, Lila's grip softens. "Whoever decided the world's gonna end if Stevie lets loose with a little lava? She needs a whole new story 'bout that. One where she waits, lets the lava cool all the way to hard, sees how it turns to new land she walks on. Besides, her father's not dead yet, and right this minute, he's feeling like a stupid old fut for smoking and yelling at *her,* I bet. That's how this whole thing started, yeah?"

One last, long, rib-rocking breath and Stevie's cried out. She kisses Lila's cheek. "I love you for that."

"I love you, though."

It's an old game between them, going back to Stevie's childhood. The next line is hers. "Oh yeah?" she says with a sniff. "Who says?"

"I says, that's who."

"Okay, you win."

"No, you win."

"But I insist."

"And I love *you,*" Lila says, "for that."

When Stevie was little, this could go on and on and on while Lila cooked, or bathed her, or as they sat together tailing string beans. But now, Stevie ends it with a shake of her head. "He's my father, I have to put up with him. Why do *you*?"

"Oh, he's always had his qualities."

"You mean he's handsome for a *haole*?"

"Plus, I wouldn't be a nurse if it weren't for Hank. I wanted to hire on at the Coco Grove kitchen after you left with your mother, but he wouldn't take me."

"You decided to be a nurse because he wouldn't give you a job? I mean, I'm glad you went back to school, but that's terrible!"

"Take off those stink-ears, Stevie. That hotel job was dead-end. I went to nursing school 'cause he convinced me. Helped me do it, too."

"How?"

"Oh, this and that. Scholarship money he knew how to snag, a loan he never let me repay. Still, tough for me at the start. My boyfriends at Līhu'e High mattered more than studying. Had to learn how practically from scratch. But plenty better pay in the end."

"Geez. Thanks for finally telling me."

"Hank wanted it quiet, no food for da kine talk that sorta thing makes 'round here, 'specially when all he was doing then was looking out for me. But I don't see harm in it now."

Stevie frowns, once again suspecting more between Lila and her father than she can bring herself to ask about, so she chews at her bottom lip until a different question comes to mind. "Do you think he did it so you'd be the one looking out for him when something like this happened?"

"Well"—Lila shrugs, stepping out of her leathers—"the man does like to plan ahead, doesn't he?"

While Lila tends to Hank, Stevie goes out to the papaya grove with a basket to clear windfall and shears to trim back leaves. She has a pretty good idea of what Lila has just done for her, because it's what Lila always does: provide a snug pocket of appreciation for her to slip into. But really, it's more. It's Lila's refusal to let her abandon herself—something Stevie always does, at least when emotions run high and fears kick in. But can anyone else ever save her from that?

Before long, her basket is full and she has a pile of leaves stacked for later hauling. This is as demanding as most gardening gets at Hank's place, where flowers and fruit trees thrive on their own and need only be gathered, trimmed, or propped up after a storm. The earth is so fertile that if a faucet drips, a patch of wild mint sprouts in the wet spot. Lilies, torch ginger, and oleander may all be separated out one from another, blooming in their designated beds close by the house, but that's only because it was Stevie who planted them on earlier visits.

Elsewhere, epiphytic orchids hang from monkeypod branches over a local-style mix of pastel-colored wildflowers, purple bougainvillea, all kinds of heliconia, hibiscus, and giant anthuriums that look like erotic valentines, with floppy yellow phalluses popping out of crimson hearts. Essentially the same hodgepodge it's been ever since she can remember. By comparison, the gardens and public places that Stevie designs are strikingly formal. "Modern reinterpretations of Versailles elegance," according to one admiring European critic. And it's true. Stevie fell in love with the order of Versailles when she first set eyes on it during her junior year abroad. But would Versailles have been so entrancing if being pulled up by the roots here hadn't stirred up so much chaos, if that chaos didn't require the calm of clean, tidy, uncluttered external structures? It's not the first time she's wondered. But she's never before been so inclined to think that the answer is yes. To design an entire island landscape with *mauka* and *makai* as her only important orientations—now *that* might prove something.

Finished in the grove, Stevie bags the windfall and tucks it into one of Lila's roomy motorcycle pouches; there's always something that someone in her enormous family can use an extra batch of papayas for. Then, having worked up enough of a sweat to require another shower, Stevie plops down in Hank's shaded Adirondack chair. The view from here is the one most often available to him these days. It bothers Stevie. What could be a gorgeous, sweeping panorama of the Ha'upu Range is cut off by a wall of bougainvillea clinging to a high old ornamental fence. The bougainvillea is pretty enough, especially when flowering, as now. Must be why it's been left there so long. Then, too, it would be a pain to dig up and remove the thorn-laden vine and fence. But designwise, the fence adds nothing; subtracting it would include so much more. Most people limit gardens by confining what's seen to what's owned, as if a proprietary view is more valuable, or makes them feel more secure. Always a limiting idea, in Stevie's opinion, but especially so in Kaua'i.

Hank might not appreciate an expanded vista any more than he has anything else she's been knocking herself out to do for him. But that wouldn't be the nature of the gift, not if she gave it in the right way—with *kahiau*, from the heart, without expectation of any return. And out here in her element, she can't help being curious enough to put on a pair of gardening gloves and go poking around at the base of the fence with a shovel to determine what removing it would involve.

Pulling vines aside, she finds an orb of smooth brown lava rock. Stevie's been collecting lava rocks like this on her walks with Pip the last few days, using them to encircle an old flower bed by a trio of *kukui* trees out near the cottage that Japhy rents. But when she tries to remove this particular rock, she can't; it extends too deeply into the earth. To wedge it out, she uses a shovel and lots of muscle.

Panting, Stevie sets the shovel aside. Far from being a simple sphere like the others, this weighty chunk of stone is contoured, with an almost seat-like shape. Running her hands over it, Stevie wonders what it could have once been. Part of an early Polynesian dining suite? A piece of someone's throne? One day she may find out. Meanwhile, this rock's place of honor—after she figures out how to move it—will be by the *kukui* trees, at the wildflower bed's center. Maybe there the stone's spiritual power—what Hawaiians call *mana*—will become evident.

Stevie fills her basket with cut flowers before going back inside, and as she stands in the kitchen arranging them, Lila brings her up to date on Hank. He's holding steady. No big changes. The kind of news that earlier would have prompted a rush of gratitude and relief. But with Margo backfiring, Stevie's little house of hope-cards for Hank has tumbled. "What happens when there *are* big changes?" Stevie asks. She can't bring herself to use hospice language and put the question in terms of what happens when Hank is closer to *actively dying*.

"We'll use a service to bring in aides," Lila says. "He has good insurance, it's all covered. Meanwhile, if you want to leave—"

"I don't, not now."

"I'm just saying. You might need to take care of that messy career of yours, or deal with the dump chump, or hit the stores in Honolulu so you'll have something hot to wear with whoever made you think about getting laid, and I have a pretty good idea about *that*."

"Forget what I said about getting laid. That was only an example of how screwed up I am."

"Just know you're not chained to this house. If you need time away, I can spend nights here, and we'll start breaking somebody else in during the day, getting 'em used to your daddy's sweet disposition."

Pulling Hank's pack of Marlboros from her pocket, Lila snaps them into the trash one by one.

"This time," Lila says, "I made sure to get them all."

After Lila leaves, Stevie goes to Hank's room with her most artful arrangement: red torch ginger sprigged with ferns in a delicate blue glass vase.

Reading glasses rest on Hank's nose, but his eyes are closed and his hands folded beneath the FDR book on his chest, rising and falling with his rhythmic, whistling breath. The laptop's open beside him, screen filled with floating geometric shapes. Stevie sets her flowers on the tansu and worries about the computer. It shouldn't be left sitting on the bedspread. The fabric will block fan vents on the bottom, and that, as she knows from bitter experience, can cause a system crash. She moves the computer with the lid still open, and on contact with the tansu, the screen saver disappears and up pops Margo's e-mail. After a backward glance at her father, Stevie reads.

hiya uncle hank,

i'm going to break with our brief tradition here and make this e-mail just between you and me on account of how it's going to be a little more personal this time, though if you want to show stevie what i've written it is totally your call, and i doubt that by now ANYTHING i have to say is going to surprise HER!

you must have busted quite a few buttons over that article about stevie in the trib, which I saw only by accident, and thank god i did, since that's how i ended up being the crazy lady who cornered her in the park. crazy on account of how she had not a clue who i was. which brings me to an interesting (in my humble opinion) observation that i'm sure WON'T make you smile, so just grin and bear it best you can. despite all your differences with my mother/your sister, you're a lot like her as a parent because for whatever reason (i'm being trained not to assign motives, can you tell?) neither one of you, when it came to family stuff, gave your daughter a full deck to play with. anyway, the trib article quoted stevie saying how much she can't stand FAKE NATURE, places that aren't true to their roots, and i think she's absolutely spot on there, so enough beating around the familial shrubbery, gotta show MY roots here. if i write back to you as though your last e-mail didn't send an impossible-to-miss message of how painful your feelings for evelyn still are, i'll never forgive myself and what's worse, all we're ever gonna have between us before you die is FAKE NICE, and where is that going to get us? NO PLACE! when i WANT to get guess where?

THERE

in hawaii

with YOU!!!!!

i've all but bought my ticket and honest to god, I am not about to cross three time zones just to be miss polite, even though that's how you probably THINK you want me to be, and that's how evelyn went loco forcing me to be (she actually slapped my face once when i was in college for being so ill-mannered as to say DAMN—not even the f word—in front of one of her fancy fucking friends).

different as stevie and i are, we're neither one of us shallow breathers. probably because we're both pollack daughters—and unc, being a pollack daughter is one tough row to hoe, specially since in our family, love is so COMPLETELY knotted up with anger, which even a guy like you would have to admit if you'd been born twenty years later and forced to take advanced psych courses. at least guys get to vent!!! and venting, let's not forget, is something miss polites are never ever supposed to do, on peril of finding themselves labeled hysterics, harpies, shrews, witches, bitches, and on and on. i bet it isn't easy for you to see that even being a pollack SON was no picnic, given not just the mix of blood and business in our line, but the impossibility of pleasing your mother and the way she set her children against each other, competing for her favor. (is that why you had only one child yourself? i think it's why evelyn did.) at least nana wasn't YOUR gender, and you could probably kid yourself more about how much she loved you, since people with penises were automatically superior in her book.

in a way stevie was spared, never having to deal with such an uncuddly grandmother, though I have to say, nana baked wonderful schnecken, and i'm not talking about the dumbed-down commercial sticky bun version of her schnecken, which I'm pretty sure helped bring everything to the boiling point with you and mother, getting all twisted up with nana in the little margo may business. but whatever your opinion on THAT, you've got to agree with me that those packaged cinnamon rolls, with all the lard and preservatives and that insipid little margo may logo girl who taunted me from billboards and grocery store cases, didn't hold a candle to nana's

REAL schnecken. i can taste them now!!! we still had tons in the freezer after nana died, and they were the main reason why i plumped up in junior high. oh, those buttery buns of brown sugar and whole-wheat flour—the stuff i self-medicated with during fits of angst and acne. until, that is, evelyn put a padlock on the freezer door after deciding i was going to wear a size eight dress for my confirmation if it killed us both, and believe me, IT ALMOST DID!!!

so what does she want from me? you're asking yourself, and i'll tell you. i want what i never got to have with nana or evelyn before they left the planet. i want your REAL nature because when it comes to FAKE nature, stevie's right—why bother?

your loving (believe it or not) niece,

margo

Never mind that Stevie has no clear idea what Margo meant by mentioning a full family deck, much less schnecken. (And was her cousin named for the girl on the coffee-cake-company logo, or was it the other way around?) After speed-reading this, she feels as though she has a magical mirror-image big sister, shaped by so many of the same invisible forces it's almost like sharing a private language, the sort of shorthand she'd always envied when she watched her best friends with their siblings. How much easier it would be to shrug off a parent's weirdness when you weren't the only one who had to absorb it. "Mom's organizing the junk drawer again," you'd say, "she must be p.m.s.-ing." Or, "Steer clear of Dad, he's slipped into one of his psychotic pockets." And you wouldn't just be talking to yourself.

What did Margo write, though, that Hank found so upsetting? She'll have to read through the e-mail again more slowly, keeping in mind his hypersensitivity to criticism—so much, come to think of it, like her own.

Stevie forwards Margo's e-mail to herself, then clicks into Hank's list of sent e-mails to delete her sneaky trail. But when she goes to her desk to bring up the letter on her own computer, there's another copy that Hank himself forwarded to her half an hour ago. Above the text of Margo's message, he wrote the following:

Stevie,

The anger stops here. I love you. Let's get that straight.

Chapter 14

Stevie and Hank talk of more than just baseball as they watch the next Cubs game. Last night, at his request, she'd Googled up that first *Tribune* article about her—the nice one—and now, with Hank muting the sound during long commercial breaks, they discuss not only her new garden and why she'd kept it a secret, hoping to dazzle him with it next spring, but her terrible review, how it hit all the harder because of breaking up with Brian. Hank listens without interrupting and—even more surprising—without giving any advice. Until, that is, she mentions the community forum in Chicago next week, the face-saving exercise that Arthur is lobbying for her to attend.

"He's right," Hank says. "You should go. It's a smart move."

She grimaces. "Not for me. I'm a terrible public speaker."

"Then don't give a speech. Answer questions, stand up for your work."

"You don't get it, Dad. This isn't like a normal business, where if you work hard, you get rewarded. In my line, you can work your ass off and if someone important says it sucks, you're sunk."

"Oh, I get it, all right. Everything that critic wrote will be thrown in your face again, and that critic hurt your feelings."

"My feelings? Geez. I'm not a little girl anymore."

"Okay, not your feelings. Your ego. What's the difference? All you have to do is absorb the attack. Then you can define your own terms."

"Is that what you tried to do with your family?"

"Apples and oranges, Stevie."

"From what I can tell, pineapples and schnecken is probably more like it."

As this latest batch of commercials ends, Hank grabs the remote devices in his lap to turn up the sound, sharpen the contrast, and fine-tune the color, wielding them with staccato movements, like some ambidextrous video gunslinger firing off rounds. He's always been crazy for gadgets, and these that Stevie's brought into the house are marvelous new toys. When she touches one to demonstrate a particular function or feature, it's all he can do to contain his impatience until he's got it in his grip again. If there were a button to put their conversation on hold, he'd have punched that one, too. It's the ninth inning, the Mets have two men on base, and they're within a run of tying the score. The game must be watched; silence must be observed. Even Pip seems to get the message, pausing from his efforts to extract Ralph's squeaker from the seam he's ripped apart.

After the Mets' last-gasp rally fizzles, Hank grins with a player's air of hard-earned fatigue. "Two down, one to go."

Maybe it's only because Stevie has gotten used to all the weight he's lost, along with all the extra hours of sleep and rest he requires, but her hopes have bounced her back to a place where she can almost convince herself that reining in his anger has quelled the cancer, too.

Hank clicks off the TV, refills his glass of iced tea, and hefts his Roosevelt book. On his way outside, Pip at his heels, he pauses at the lanai door to cut his eyes at Stevie. "You always got back on the bike," he says.

It's a familiar observation. In fact, if Hank could design a greeting card to send her, that would be the sentiment he'd want it to express. He's never been one for sending cards, though, not even when they were continents apart; what she got from him then were telephone calls and occasional letters. But now, watching her father cross the lawn, carefully fold himself into the hammock, and reach down for Pip, she might as well be riding that first two-wheeler of hers, with him doing his best to run despite his bad left leg, his right hand gripping the seat, keeping her on his strong side, saying, "You've got it now, Stevie!" when she finds her balance, then letting go with a forceful shove.

But this time she *doesn't* have it, not by a long shot. How can she, when she's headed for unknown territory, with Hank slated to disappear from his familiar station somewhere behind her? With her still wanting to go back and heal him. And him still trying to launch her forward. Talk about "come here, go away." No wonder she's wobbling all over the place. And yet, and yet. There's something different in this particular shove of Hank's, something she can't quite define. A lack of concern around the outcome, perhaps. Or a faith apart from pride. Neither of which she'd ever before felt was hers to command.

Stevie goes to her desk, steady enough now for sending her fountain fix off to New York, booking a return trip to Chicago, and arranging to stay with Margo.

"You should come with me," Stevie tells Hank during the next day's game, with Kerry Wood pitching and the Cubs ahead at the stretch three to nothing. "We could go to your favorite haunts, watch the Cubs clinch their division at Wrigley Field, meet up with Margo for dinner."

"Don't count your chickens, kiddo. Anyway, you're leaving on Monday and they don't play in Chicago again until the weekend."

"So? That's when they'll clinch their division, I just know it. We could stay over—the Drake, for old times' sake. Or the Raphael—that hotel where you used to live. Come on, Dad. Don't you want to see the Cubs while they're sewing it up and everybody's so excited?"

"Before they blow it, you mean?"

"I'll pretend you didn't say that. I could hire a driver," Stevie says, remembering her blessings from Roosevelt Jefferson Jr. "We'll make it so you won't have to walk any far distances."

"Well, I do love that ballpark. Want to know *my* idea of heaven? It's going to Wrigley Field for the first game of the season. Seeing that first glimpse of ivy against the redbrick wall. Hearing that first crack of batting practice. Smelling that first whiff of cut grass, hot dogs, and beer."

"That does it, we're going."

"Hey, not so fast. All I have to do to get there is close my eyes and remember. Which is a hell of a lot easier than flying these days."

"It's not so bad first-class. If there ever was a time to splurge, it's now."

"No, no—too long a trip for me, and that's final. I'll be more comfortable right here. I can see the pitches on this TV of yours even better than from a box seat. And don't forget, Margo wants to visit. She could fly back with you."

"Yeah, I thought of that, too. But Dad, are you sure? I mean, would that be nice for you, having her here?"

"Would it be nice? No. It would be a goddamn miracle."

"If you believed in miracles, you mean."

"Smartass."

While Stevie slices tomatoes for their lunch, she considers how having Hank eager for Margo's visit, along with her own return, is all the more incentive for him to stay alive. And for her, that's a lot like buying travel insurance. Still, her throat constricts. If she can't get her father to Chicago for the Cubs next week, how will she ever get him there for her garden next spring?

As Stevie emerges from the kitchen, Hank slaps the arm of his chair. "How do you like that? Wood's going to bat here in the eighth."

"So he'll pitch the ninth."

"Right you are."

"Cool. They're letting him go for his shut-out." Wood gets it, too, throwing a perfect ninth inning. "Three in a row," Stevie crows. "I *told* you they'd sweep the Mets!"

Much as Stevie enjoys sleeping on the lanai, the privacy of having her own room has become more important. Still, she leaves the door cracked open so that she can hear Hank, should he call for her through his own partially opened door (he hasn't), and so that Pip can get in (he stays with Hank every night and then barks by her bed to go outside at dawn). If she minded that Pip couldn't hold his bladder longer, she'd cut off his water supply shortly after his dinner, like all the puppy-training books advise. But she likes getting out with him for this time of low, luminous light. She likes having the next four or five hours all to herself.

On this particular morning—the morning after the Cubs sweep—she brings out the cushion for Hank's Adirondack chair and sits with her coffee while Pip chases chicks around the yard. When she returns from Chicago, she'll tear down that fence. A more generous view will be right in keeping with the space that seems to be freeing up inside her father. But what she needs to mull over now is the dream that Pip's yips awakened her from.

In her dream, she was back in Brooklyn but dressed for the beach, wearing her black bikini, and showing Japhy around her Pineapple Street apartment. Not much territory to cover there. Living room, Pullman kitchen, bathroom with a half-size tub—so dinky that someone as tall as Japhy would have to soak with knees up around his chin—and her bedroom, big enough to hold a desk and drawing board for the work she does at home.

This dream Japhy of Stevie's was most interested in the small number of personal mementos she's allowed into her carefully edited, uncluttered surroundings. A photograph of her as a biscuit-haired, sun-kissed child. The silver bracelet with her secret name engraved on the inside. An old music box in her bedroom, with a hula girl and palm tree on top. "Grandpa gave that to me," she told Japhy in the dream. And though in real life the music box mechanism is broken—she'd played it to death years ago—when Japhy wound it up, the hula girl twirled and out came the tinkly, familiar version of "Lovely Hula Hands." But instead of being happy that the music box worked again, she yelled at him to put it down before it broke again. And she was so mad at herself for yelling that she woke up right away, before she could apologize and stop him from leaving.

What could this mean? No "aha" interpretation clicks into place. But it feels like a Big Dream, the kind she never has to write down to remember. The kind that will reveal itself over time.

❁

Today is a travel day for the Cubs—no game. Finished with her coffee, Stevie herds Pip inside to feed him and blends up a smoothie for herself with a frozen apple banana. After showering, she dresses in her running clothes (again), and goes straight to her desk, tucking away the last tendrils of her dream to make a string of calls to the mainland and finish up preliminary CAD drawings for the fountain's resurfacing. Then she'll be free to take Hank swimming at Puolo Point.

Invested as she is in the curative powers of FDR and baseball, it's nevertheless troubling to her that Hank's been so absorbed in ball games and the Roosevelt biography that the only time he's left the house in a week was for a haircut in Līhu'e. She worries about him becoming disconnected from his body. Isn't that how old people slip further and further away? If Hank's going to remain on the island, she wants the island to be doing all it can to lengthen his life. She wants her *honu* looking out for him. He seems to have forgotten how much he loves being in the water. He needs that, too.

Apart from how accessible the beach is at Puolo Point, there's something else spurring her to go there with Hank. She wants to score some salt. Local salt, stained pink from red volcanic soil. Flavorful salt, rich with minerals. Sacred salt, too, called *'alaea* by the Hawaiians who harvest it, people whose families were culling and trading salt hundreds of years ago. The only problem is, as much as she'd like to have this salt, she can't buy it. Nobody can. A gift from the *'aina,* it may only be given or traded. But with luck and animal cunning, maybe she'll bring some home with her today.

As Stevie hangs up from speaking with Frank Acosta, the stonecutter from Indiana she'll be working with on the fountain, a FedEx truck pulls up in front of the house. The driver has her sign for two separate items, an envelope and a large box.

She takes them to the kitchen to open. The envelope contains her airline tickets, along with an information sheet about the community-forum meeting. The good news is that Enrico and Larry will be on the panel with her; they're so eloquent and supportive, maybe a little of their public élan will rub off. The awful news is that the forum moderator will be Christopher Caldwell, the *Tribune* critic who trashed her. *No!* she tells herself. *He didn't trash you, he trashed your garden.* There is, after all, a difference.

Lorna sent the box. After popping apart its seals with a carving knife, Stevie can see all the sundresses, shorts, shirts, summer-weight sweaters, swimsuits, and underwear she'd asked Lorna to collect for her, along with spiffier apparel for Chicago. A plastic bag holds Stevie's birth control supplies, which she *hadn't* asked for, though she did, come to think of it, laughingly mention her recent arm-hair infatuation when she and Lorna spoke on the phone. Digging down deeper into the box, Stevie finds more unexpected extras. Bubble bath from Kiehl's. Bagels from Zabar's. Middle Eastern spices from Sahadi's grocery on Atlantic Avenue, along with a jar of preserved lemons. For Hank there's an airtight container holding a slice of Junior's cheesecake. For Pip, a variety pack from a Madison Avenue dog bakery. Such a New York care package! But that's not all. Lorna's last surprise for Stevie is a smaller carton packed with tissue paper and excelsior, with the music box she'd dreamed of last night nestled in the center.

As Stevie's former college roommate, Lorna knows all too well that before the music box broke, Stevie could not, *would not,* go to sleep without first winding it up. Maybe Lorna found someone to fix the mechanism, as Stevie herself had once tried and failed to do. Her heart takes a little hop, but no—the winding key still won't budge. Even so, she's touched to tears that Lorna thought to send the music box along with the rest, that a Big Dream had hinted at its arrival.

Hank turns the Defender's keys over to Stevie for their drive to Puolo Point. He's never asked to be driven anywhere before. For her, it's another uneasy passage, particularly since he insists on giving directions at every turn, even when she's made a big show of switching on the blinker well in advance to prove she knows where she's going. Otherwise, he seems happy to be chauffeured, pointing out along the way all the houses that were damaged by the last hurricane—some looking nicer than ever, some with tarps still hanging over their roofs—and reading aloud the occasional bumper sticker. "Aloha Means Hello AND Goodbye," advises one. "Probably a warning to tourists," Hank says.

"Yeah. 'Have fun, but don't forget to go home'—that kind of thing."

While the Hank of old could have done thirty minutes easy on all the social and economic complexities lurking behind such an attitude, the Hank of today merely sighs. "If the driver were my age, it might be more of a philosophical statement. Life is short. We no sooner arrive than we're gone. Come in weak as a baby, go out the same way. *That* kind of thing."

When they reach the outskirts of Hanapēpē town, Stevie pulls into the Ace Hardware parking lot. "I just have a quick errand to run," she tells Hank, then dashes inside to purchase a Razor ripsaw sharp enough to cut through *kiawe,* the tough Hawaiian mesquite ubiquitous at barbecues.

Next stop is the Hanapēpē Pūpū Factory, where Stevie buys *ahi poke* for lunch on the beach. There are three different types for sale, and Stevie chooses the "original style"—sashimi-grade tuna seasoned only with seaweed, sesame oil, green onions, and a little salt, just the way Lila always made it. The salt's not Puolo Point salt; it's from the Big Island. Not as savory, but the next best thing.

Then it's on to the Point, where the paved road ends just beyond a *kiawe* forest, near the Chinese Cemetery and a small landing strip. Stevie turns onto red dirt tracks running by the salt ponds, ringed by boulders to keep cars—and people—away. More than a dozen rectangular ponds line up side by side, bulging with salt that glitters in the sun. This is just how Stevie hoped to find the ponds—full and dry and ready for harvest. The trouble is, no one's there to tend them. She can't just *take* salt. Even if there were a god or goddess of salt ponds to petition for permission to do such a thing—and as far as she knows, there isn't—she'd still feel like a thief, never mind the absence of a sign warning *"Kapu."*

Muttering "damn," she pulls the Rover up close to a sand dune. When Hank leans heavily on her arm to climb it, she feels a stab of tenderness touched with apprehension. Maybe he's too weak for this trip after all.

A couple of young men stand atop the reef flinging their net. Inside the reef, where the water is calm, several snorkelers swim. It's an unassuming place, pretty but not spectacular, crowded only on weekends, when local families come to spend the day at the other end of this curving beach, where there's a lifeguard stand, a grove of tall palms, and picnic facilities. Stevie leaves Hank on firmer sand, still damp from high tide, to carry in their food, towels, cooler, beach mats, folding chairs, magazines, and an umbrella, since there are no palms here. She anchors the beach mats with rocks to keep them flat against the trades.

"Want to go in now?" she asks when everything's set up, and at Hank's nod, she unties her *honu* pareo, worn today over an old red Speedo that Lorna sent. When Hank takes off his shirt, stripping down to his black swim shorts, she notices that they're almost too big for him, despite how tightly the drawstring is pulled.

He declines her offer of sunscreen—"Skin cancer is the least of my worries now"—but she's relieved at how much steadier he is, managing on his own the short stretch of straw-colored sand between them and the sea. "Ah," he says as they step into small, rippling waves. "This feels so good." He takes her arm again to walk in deeper, where the bottom grows uneven. Immersed to his thighs, Hank lets go of Stevie, holds his breath, and flops in backwards. How wonderful it must be, flinging himself like that without any danger of damage, trusting the ocean to cradle him. The water's so bathtub-warm and salty, floating takes no effort, and there isn't any current. They both stay in for a long time, lying on their backs to survey the cloudscape—pillowy poufs clustered over the sea, dense gray clumps curled around mountains—stroking aimlessly, moving in all directions. When Pip barks from the water's edge, bored after reducing Ralph to a plush husk, Stevie coaxes him into the shallows and he has a paddle, too.

After lunch, Stevie spots Lila's granddaughter, Nola, arriving with her mother, Amy, and baby son, Sean. After exchanging hellos, Nola removes Sean's diaper, tucks it into her bag, and puts the baby on her shoulder. Then the two women wade into the water. From long childhood days at local beaches, Stevie has a pretty good idea what they're up to. Sure enough, when Nola's in waist deep, she starts to sway in a gentle, rocking motion mimicking the waves and shifts Sean to dip his feet. Then Nola and Amy pass the baby back and forth, dipping him in deeper, again and again, until he's in almost up to his chin. Sean throws back his head to laugh.

It must be this trio's second or third afternoon here. Tomorrow, Nola will float Sean on his belly, her hands beneath him, wetting his face and eyes. The next day, she'll let go long enough for Sean to automatically start paddling, the way Pip just did. And the day after that, with his mother and grandmother standing about a yard apart, Sean will churn on his own through the water between them. By the end of the week, the distance will be even greater, and Sean will be swimming.

"Babies learn early here," Hank lazily observes.

"They do in New York, too. Remember my friend Lorna? She took her son to a baby swimming class at the Y. He didn't get to be naked like Sean, but same idea."

"Only not so practical," Hank says. "A New York toddler doesn't have so much chance of wandering off where he might drown."

"True."

"You were out of diapers when you learned, but just barely."

"Yeah. Lessons at the hotel pool. I remember." What she remembers better is swimming in that pool with Hank, arms around his neck and riding his back. Reveling in the rare chance to be that close, that playful with him.

"I was a lot older before I could swim. In fact, one reason I wanted you to learn so young was something that happened to me. When I was six, I waded off a ledge in Lake Michigan. Would have drowned if Evelyn hadn't been there to pull me out."

"Wow. If it weren't for Evelyn saving you, we wouldn't be here."

"Well, that's going a little far. In fact, she got into trouble for not going in when I did to keep an eye on me. She was older, she already knew how to swim."

"Still. It's the best thing I've heard you say about her."

"Oh, we were still close then. She used to call me her little sugarplum. My mother would pack sandwiches for us to take to the park, and when we had the mumps at the same time, she stuffed kerchiefs with cold compresses and tied them up on top of our heads."

"Really? I've only ever seen that in cartoons."

"I shared a room with Evelyn until I was nine, so whenever one of us got sick, it was practically guaranteed the other one would, too."

"That's old to be sharing a bedroom with your sister."

"The Depression was on, my grandmother was living with us. Anyway, children then didn't all have rooms of their own, not in that neighborhood. My father kept his desk and a safe between our beds, and I remember my mother coming in at night, when we were supposed to be asleep, to sneak out money she wanted for us kids. Piano lessons, school clothes—things like that."

"Your father sounds pretty controlling."

"Tyrannical would be closer to the mark."

"Did your mother ever get caught?"

Hank shrugs. "All I know is, they were always fighting about money, right up until the day he died."

"What did he die of?"

"A heart attack."

"How old were you then?"

"December 1945, so I would have just turned thirteen."

"Oh," Stevie says. "The same year the Cubs won the pennant. The same year Roosevelt died. Talk about taking the bitter with the sweet."

"Even now, I can remember how the world just stopped for me."

"It must have been hard, losing a father that young."

"I meant when I heard Roosevelt died."

"You were more upset about the President than your father?"

"Oh, yes. He'd been president ever since I could remember. It didn't seem possible that he was gone. In fact, my clearest early memory is of seeing him."

"You actually *saw* Roosevelt?"

"Right before my fifth birthday, when he came to Chicago to open the Outerlink Drive Bridge. My mother idolized him, and she took us all bundled up at the crack of dawn to get a spot near the bridge to watch the parade that came up Michigan Avenue. It was incredible, just incredible. There was a covered wagon, horse-drawn carriages, a locomotive with tires, all kinds of people marching—firemen, policemen, soldiers, veterans. And cowboys, too—Hawaiian cowboys. They were my favorite."

"*Paniolo* in Chicago?"

"Must have been a big rodeo in town. But what everybody had come for was Roosevelt, and finally, when it was time for him to speak, my mother held me up so I could see him."

How different their first recollections are. Hank's so large and public, lifted into the air to revere a president. Hers so small and private, walking for a father with his hero's affliction. "No wonder the memory stuck," she says.

"Of course, history's taught me that Roosevelt wasn't quite so perfect as I'd believed in my boyhood. He might have done more for refugees fleeing Hitler. He underestimated Stalin. And he made a terrible mistake interning Japanese Americans. If the threat had been real, you can bet the same thing would have gone on in Hawai'i, too. Pearl Harbor happened here, after all. It was U.S. territory, and proportionally there were a hell of a lot more people of Japanese descent on these islands than on the mainland Pacific Coast."

"But you can't judge just by everything we know today," Stevie offers.

"My point. He pulled the country through a terrible time, achieved so many other difficult things. I was right to cry for him, and boy, did I ever. But I didn't shed a tear for my own father."

"That's sad."

"Well, he wasn't much of a father. He did leave my mother with a business that was doing well—the economy was better by then. And once she held the reins, she moved the three of us away from Bittersweet Place as fast as she could."

Though these last can't be pleasant memories, Hank relates them in the same easy tone as the nicer ones, as if they'd never been too disturbing for him to tell. As if they were a father and daughter who had *always* discussed such things. Lila would be pleased to know they've been talking story, as she advised. But it stops with the end of Sean's swimming lesson. At Hank's invitation, Nola and Amy lay their mats on the beach nearby, then proceed to sit and dry off.

Crawling around, Sean just can't keep his hands off Pip. And Stevie just can't keep her hands off Sean, though as she holds him this time her stomach clenches a little. Probably just cramps starting up. Now that she's down to a single ovary, her periods, always suceptible to stress, have turned more erratic than ever. Her last was almost seven weeks ago, and the one before that showed up after a similar hiatus. No reason to suspect herself pregnant, either. The first of those two periods came well after Brian had taken to wearing a condom as backup for her cervical cap—which she hadn't been wearing on the fateful night they'd gotten sloshed and excused themselves from a boring dinner party to have sex against a bathroom door. "Better to err on caution's side," he'd said to justify the condom. "Especially after what you've been through." Even then, she'd guessed that he wasn't protecting her so much as himself. No guy likes wearing condoms, and Brian had wanted her to go on the pill. But she hated how she felt on hormones, and really, by then they could not agree on anything. Since her last period, they hadn't made love at all—because of conflicting travel schedules, and spatting when together. The Chicago trip he'd bailed out of was supposed to get their sex life back on track.

Another factor disrupting her cycle might be all the weight she'd lost, running so much and eating so little since her troubles with Brian began. Possible, her gynecologist allowed, but the reason could just as easily be a real problem—emphasis on "real"—and Stevie's freaked not just by that word, but by the very idea of going through the tests that would rule out or confirm some ominous cause. The tests that would require her to first drink two quarts of water, then endure some stranger driving a robot-like camera all around her vagina, taking pelvic pictures for half an hour. No thanks. She'd need incentive to put herself through something like that, especially since she's convinced having a baby just isn't in the cards for her. She's already been warned to proceed with enormous care if results from that damn test show it's okay for her to try again, because even if she managed to conceive without in vitro assistance—which from her doctor's tone sounded unlikely—so many women are prone to repeated ectopic pregnancies. How could she possibly handle another when she still hasn't fully dealt with fallout from the last?

Anyway, her top priority as Her Own Person Stevie is to be fine whichever way her life turns out, whether she becomes a mother or doesn't become a mother, because, God knows, she's certainly seen her share of friends who were determined to have a baby no matter what, and ended up with babies, all right, but also nightmare marriages—nightmare divorces, too, and she'd hate to inflict one of those on a child of her own. The bigger miracle, she tells herself, would be not giving birth, but getting the imaginary diploma she longs for, the one that graduates her from chasing after love from impossible men. Which, suddenly and inexplicably, considering all the day's pleasures, seems farther out of reach than ever.

Stevie and Hank take a second, shorter swim when they're alone again. Helping him ashore, she looks beyond the dunes' rim of pale green pickle grass to see someone with a bucket, rinsing salt crystals in well water from an ocean-fed aquifer. A muscular man with short, thick graying hair, wearing a faded armless work shirt, knee-length cutoff jeans, and flip-flops. A beautiful old hat made of sugar cane tassel shades his face. She wouldn't be surprised if he descended from a chiefly line. He has that kind of bearing.

"I'll be back in just a few," Stevie says when Hank's settled into his chair with a copy of *Newsweek*. She puts on her sunglasses and unfolds the pareo to tie it over her shoulder into something resembling a dress—not so much to be modest as respectful—then goes to the Defender, takes the Razor ripsaw from its bag, and walks barefoot toward the salt ponds. She waits beside one of the bordering boulders until the man notices her and speaks. "Nice saw." The beckoning motion of his head lets her know it's all right to enter the area.

"I just bought it," she tells him, drawing closer. "But then I found out I don't need a new saw. My father already has one at home."

He peers in Hank's direction. "Your father?" Then, at her nod: "Saw you walking with him."

"It's really lifted his spirits, coming here."

"He's going home to spirit soon enough."

Oh, God—can this man discern something she can't? "Not too soon, I hope."

"You shouldn't worry. Ancestors aren't made of smoke. They don't just disappear. My name is Robert. Robert Kapahana."

"Nice to meet you, Robert. I'm Makalani. Makalani Pollack." She feels a little funny, shopping her secret Hawaiian name for salt, especially since she's never told it to anyone before—not even Lila. But what compels her is an old fear born of an old pain: being shunned and excluded as the "fish-belly howl-ee" girl, with not enough native blood to matter.

"Makalani, eh?" He waits for noise from a landing tourist helicopter to subside. "Then you know what I mean when I say that I am a person called a *papa kanaka kahuna.*" He pauses for a moment, then smiles and nods and turns to drain his bucket.

Stevie realizes she's just failed a test, and though she's not sure what the correct answer is to his unasked question, she takes a stab. "You communicate with messengers to the spirit world."

"I have *direct* spiritual connection with my ancestors." There's no hint of irritation in his voice, and she's pleased when he faces her again. "My ancestors are not at rest."

"Oh. I'm sorry. What are they upset about?"

"The land here. They don't want this part of the Point turned into a park. They don't want playing fields, septic systems, more traffic, more dust. Some people even think it's smart to build a Go-Kart track—as if those helicopters so close aren't bad enough. All that would hurt the fish, the wildlife. Not to mention the *kiawe* forest back there, and these salt pans right here. Hurt them bad."

"I worry about those things, too. I hope we can stop them. In fact," she adds impulsively, "I wish I could throw up yellow tape all around all my favorite island places, like they do with monk seals, just to remind everybody how precious and fragile it all is."

"Except for being impossible, not such a bad idea."

Something tells Stevie to shove up her sunglasses so he can see her eyes. "Is your salt here really as healthy as everybody says?"

"Oh yeah. Would do your father good. Lots of hematite—helps with pain, blood flow—plus a bunch of other minerals most people take vitamins to get. No chemical preservatives, either. Plenty better than that pours-when-it-rains store-bought stuff. Stronger taste, so you don't need near as much—good for you that way, too. And it finishes real sweet."

"Salt's good for a lot of things, but it's not so good when salt air gets to saws. Rusts 'em right out. Maybe you know somebody who could use one like this. Somebody who likes to cut wood from that forest. Grilling with *kiawe*'s so tasty—even more, I bet, with special salt like yours."

"Maybe I do know somebody like that." Robert motions for her to follow him to his truck, where he reaches into the cab for a clear plastic bag of pink salt that looks to weigh at least two pounds. "It's a funny color," he says. "You might not want it."

"I think the color's beautiful."

"Government says it's not food-grade. Government says you can't sell salt extracted outside. Wants it done behind closed doors, under roofs."

"That's a silly rule."

"Not rule—law. Law made by the same government that illegally overthrew the kingdom of Hawai'i. Me, I fought in Vietnam for that government. Signed up to do it, too—wasn't even drafted. Warrior blood still runs strong, I guess. Doesn't mean I approve of what that government's done, though. Especially not here."

Stevie takes a jagged breath, surprised at how deeply she'd like to say something worthwhile, something more meaningful than a bumper sticker sentiment. A bit of wisdom to match the name she pitched to Robert, that's what she wants to convey. Eyes of Heaven words.

"Annexation . . . ," she begins, slow and careful, but the rest comes tumbling out. "Power-hungry people never understand how to embrace the culture they colonize. But that's where they'll find the medicine they *really* need. My grandfather taught me this. He talked to spirits, too. I know the salt is safe. I mean, I've heard stories about people who died from eating hot dogs roasted on oleander sticks."

"Everybody local tells those stories. Folks from Peoria don't know about the poison in oleander. They say a whole family died on a beach in Waimea, right after their hot-dog picnic."

"What I heard is that they were were swimming when the poison hit, so the official cause of death was drowning. Gruesome, yeah? But who's ever heard of anyone killed by island salt?" Stevie leans into the cab to lay the ripsaw on the floor. "I'm so glad we met," she tells him as he extends the bag of salt to her.

"Malama pono," he says. Take good care.

Stevie's at her desk Friday night, catching up on her e-mail. Pip's at her feet, chewing on ears belonging to Ralph II. Hank went to bed with his book an hour ago. When the phone rings, she picks up right away in case he's fallen asleep. It's Japhy. "Remember how I said I'd get the check when we went out again?" he begins.

"Changed your mind?"

"Noooo. But 'check' implies *restaurant.* What do you say we go out for a sunset picnic instead?"

Okay, here comes next time. Stevie draws a breath, bewildered not just by how some small animal part of herself loses all tension at the sound of his voice, no longer on alert for when they'll connect again, but by the amount of oxygen required before she can figure out what to say. "Where do you want to go?"

"Well, someone like me can't take someone like you anywhere you've never been before, not on this island. But I don't care, the location's a secret."

"Are you providing the picnic?"

"Something better than hot dogs, I promise. Did you ever hear that horror story about hot dogs and oleander sticks?"

"Oh, yes. It's a big one."

"But do you suppose anybody ever really died that way?"

"I don't know how you'd find out for sure. But stories like that are a lot like all the local superstitions. Something solid is usually behind them."

"Yeah? Hit me with one of those superstitions."

"Well, my personal favorite is, 'No ocean swimming when the red wiliwili bloom.' "

"Sounds silly."

"Doesn't it? But red wiliwili trees flower at the same time young seabirds fledge, so sharks come close to shore then to feed on the fledglings. It all just got boiled down to something simple that a child could remember."

"Hmm. I like what I'm learning from you."

Stevie feels a slow flush of pleasure spread from her scalp to the palms of her hands. "I'll be gone next week," she says. "I'm leaving early Monday morning to spend a few days in Chicago."

"Then how about tomorrow? Kind of short notice for date night number two. Is it cool anymore to refer to Saturday night that way? I'm a little rusty."

"To tell you the truth," Stevie says, "I don't think it was ever cool. But it is kind of cute."

Chapter 15

It's five thirty when Stevie and Japhy set out the next evening, with their dogs on the jump seat of Japhy's pickup and a cooler at Stevie's feet. She lifts the lid. Before Japhy can notice and finish saying, "Hey, no peeking," she's caught a glimpse of roast chicken, slaw, sesame noodles, and a bottle of pinot noir. No plastic carry-out containers, either—all the food's homemade. Stevie's known enough men who fancy themselves chefs not to be overimpressed. Usually they're in it for the applause. Unless she's mistaken, though, what Japhy's done is something more caring, and to fully appreciate it, she almost needs a rewired brain. No obsessing tonight, that's the key. Not about Hank's health, not about her career, and not about the wife Japhy mentioned. When the kinks between her shoulders loosen, it feels as if her body's in agreement.

Japhy's mahogany-colored hair, still wet from his shower, dampens the collar of a white linen shirt that sets off his tan and appears freshly ironed. His cotton slacks are black. Since Stevie's wearing a black tank top and white linen pants, they look like a couple that's date-dressed. She had wanted to run back inside and change, but considering how keen she'd been to see him—and to learn where he's taking her—being horrified that other people might think they'd done this on purpose was sillier by far than date-dressing. They must also have been on the same schedule getting ready; if Stevie hadn't waved a hair dryer around for ten minutes, her head, too, would still be wet. The only tropical colors between them are her red pareo and the sky blue blanket that Japhy brought, each folded by a cooler on the floorboard. Even with the windows open, the mingling mint and citrus scents of their shampoos fill the pickup cab.

"Haven't kept up with the Cubs since they went to Pittsburgh," Japhy says. "How are they doing?"

"Split a double header yesterday, lost today. But Mark Prior's pitching tomorrow, so they might pick up another."

"Gonna be watching?"

"Oh yes—and early, too. Pittsburgh's an hour ahead of Chicago, so six hours ahead of us. But I have baseball coming out my ears right now, and a ton of stuff to do before I leave, so this is really a treat—my first beach sunset since I got here. We *are* going to a beach, aren't we?"

Japhy nods. "Guess I can tell you that much."

"Good. I brought binoculars. I haven't seen any spinner dolphins for so long. Spinner dolphins and sea turtles—they're my favorites."

"I'm partial to mammals, but those turtles get to me, too. Swimming the way they do, all on their own in the sea. So vulnerable when they wash ashore."

"Did I mention that I swam with a *honu* at Māhā'ulepū the other day?"

"Yeah, you mentioned it."

Of course she mentioned it. Though Stevie's not considered loquacious by anyone who knows her well, she all but babbles when Japhy's around. Not that he seems to mind. "Ever swim with spinner dolphins?" he asks.

"Never been that far out. Anyway, sometimes you can spot them late in the day, so I thought I'd do some serious looking. Does that interfere with any of your plans?" Something a touch ponderous in his expression made her ask.

"Nope. Not so long as we leave time for some serious talking." Is he teasing or announcing the discussion she's hoping for, about what brought him here? From his tone it could be either. Before she figures out how to respond, he pulls into the parking lot at Sueoka's Market, saying, "We need some ice."

While Japhy heads inside, Stevie clips Pip's leash onto his collar and takes him to a nearby tree for a quick pee; she's not sure how long the trip ahead is, and she'd forgotten to let him out before leaving home. Mature as Pip's behavior is, it's easy to forget he's still a puppy, and a universal trait of puppies is converting every trickle of water consumed into vast puddles.

"Stevie," someone calls, and she swivels around to see an old brown Toyota wagon with Kiko at the wheel, driving slowly by with a thumb-and-pinky-finger shaka wave. "When you gonna come to class?" he hollers. A rhetorical question, since he doesn't stop for an answer, and he probably wouldn't be able to hear her even if he did because of the cranked up Hawaiian *mele* he's playing and the two small yellow dogs in the back seat, barking their heads off at the sight of Pip. Then, as Kiko picks up speed again, one dog jumps out the window. The dog's leash, still attached to its harness, catches on something inside the car.

Stevie screams Kiko's name as the car behind his swerves to a stop and its driver sounds the brief, hesitant toot of islanders so unaccustomed to honking that they often can't find their horns. Kiko slams on the brakes, but not before his dog's been dragged for twenty feet or so, its front legs rigid to keep from flipping over.

"Oh, my God," Kiko cries as he jumps out of the car. "Jerry!" He runs over to the howling dog, then sobs at the sight of horribly torn, bleeding forepaws.

"We have to get out of the road," Stevie says. She puts Kiko and the dogs into the back seat, so rattled that she nearly slams the door on her fingers.

It's been a while since she's driven a clutch. Being so light-headed and wobble-limbed makes steering Kiko's car into the parking lot by Japhy's pickup an especially lurchy procedure.

"I killed him," Kiko wails. Stevie starts crying, too. Mainly because she's not certain Jerry will survive his injuries, but a bit because she can't seem to escape dealing with death and disaster.

"We need you here," she calls out to Japhy as he crosses the parking lot with his bag of ice.

Japhy's ice came in handy for first aid. After injecting Jerry with painkiller from a kit in his truck, Japhy grabbed an old beach towel from the back of Kiko's car, put it under the bag of ice on Kiko's lap, and told him to hold the dog's forepaws, which look barely attached, against the bag firmly enough to stanch the flow of blood. Jerry's hind paws, bleeding too, hadn't taken the drag's brunt and were still intact.

That all took less than five minutes, and now, as Stevie drives Kiko's car to Līhu'e, following Japhy, she keeps up a running litany, telling Kiko how if something awful like this had to happen, it couldn't have occurred at a better time or place, because Japhy's the only private-practice vet who does surgery on this side of the island. Kiko's other dog and Pip are both quiet, as if they realize the situation's gravity from Jerry's whimpering. "I'm guessing your dogs are littermates," Stevie says.

"They are. Fourteen months old."

"Right. I heard you telling Japhy. And he said Jerry's old enough so infection's not such a threat. Jerry's got a good chance of bouncing back. What's his buddy's name?"

"Elaine—my poor little Lainey. They're so bonded, I hate to think what losing Jerry would do to her. I hear dogs really don't get a brain till they're two, but I'm the one who's an idiot. How could I let this happen? Stupid, stupid, stupid."

"It was an accident, Kiko. At least they were wearing harnesses. A leash clipped to a collar would've snapped his neck. Japhy's going to do everything he can, I know he will. He's taken care of our dog, and he's not some by-the-numbers kind of vet. He's really skilled, the kind dogs totally trust, and that's got to be a plus when an animal's traumatized." Stevie looks in the rearview mirror and sees tears streaming down Kiko's face. She's tempted to stop and find a Kleenex so he can wipe his eyes and puff his nose, but she can tell he's not going to let go of Jerry for a second. Anyway, it's more important to reach Līhu'e soon; Japhy said time could make all the difference.

Japhy turns on his blinker, parks alongside a small one-story building with a sign that reads "Līhu'e Animal Hospital," and jumps out to unlock the front door. Inside, he throws on a surgical smock before taking Jerry from Kiko. "Do everything you can," Kiko tells him. "No worries for cost."

"I need X-rays to make sure nothing's broken," Japhy says. "Then I'll prep him and put him under. Use the phone if you need to, eat if you're hungry—there's food in that basket. If you're not, there's a fridge down the hall." Then he shoulders through a swinging door and is gone.

The front of Kiko's vintage *aloha* shirt is splattered with blood. His face looks pinched and pale. "I couldn't touch food now," he says.

Looking at him, Stevie fights down a wave of queasiness. "Me neither."

Kiko goes to dump the ice bag and wash up, then sinks into a waiting room chair. *"Mahalo,"* he says. Thank you. Stevie has pretty much taken to avoiding the word since it's become such a tourist-industry staple, always on the lips of airline attendants. But Kiko's *mahalo* is a gift in itself, rich with emotion. *"Mahalo,"* he repeats, "for being with me how I'd want to be for you."

"No need mention," Stevie says, slipping unconsciously into pidgin. "Japhy got the hard part, yeah?" She fills a cup at the water cooler and brings it to him.

"I bet you two were going somewhere special," Kiko says between sips. "Sorry for messing that up. Heard from Lila how your father's sick. You could've used the break."

Well, yes. But she waits for her own twinge of regret to subside before replying. "This never would happen if I'm not standing there on the corner with Pip. And my dad's doing so much better since I came. Ease up on yourself, okay? Waiting's tough enough."

As she settles into the chair beside him, he reaches over to take her hand. "I'm just calling on the universe for the best possible outcome."

Stevie nods. "I'm with you there."

"I meant your father and you—not just Jerry."

She lifts their hands and kisses Kiko's lightly. In the silence that follows, it dawns on her why his dogs' names sound so familiar. "Jerry and Elaine? Don't tell me you named them for the Seinfeld characters."

"What? You think just 'cause I'm traditional I don't keep up with my popular culture?"

"Well, knowing you, I am kind of surprised they don't have Hawaiian names."

"My *kids* have Hawaiian names," he says. "Keola and Lehua."

"You have children?"

"Yeah, four and six years old. It's not polite to be so surprised, Stevie."

"Sorry—I just assumed. Nevah smart, right?" Time's felt so elongated since she landed on Kaua'i, it doesn't seem possible that Japhy had made a wrong assumption about *her* only two weeks ago, when she was on the air with him and he took her for a tourist.

"Better get someone to teach my *keiki* class tonight," Kiko says, flipping out his cell phone

After Kiko has made his arrangements, Stevie peppers him with questions to distract them both from Jerry's plight. She learns that he gave up performing at hotels years ago—and yes, he *did* burn his eyebrows off doing the torch dance. These days, he works four different jobs. Apart from running the hula studio he inherited from his aunty Lovey, he keeps books for a handful of small businesses in Kapa'a, and choreographs for luau performance troupes. Having children makes all those jobs a necessity; island cost of living is high, and he's diligent about saving for their future.

"I know 'Keola' means life," Stevie says, "and 'Lehua' is a flower, right?"

"Yeah, the flower on *'ohi'a* trees."

"Pretty."

"My little girl danced before she walked, and that's no lie. She was the youngest one onstage at the high school. I'm gonna make a hula just for her someday, all about when Pele turned herself into a beautiful young woman and—"

"She's always turning herself into a beautiful young woman, isn't she?"

"Nope. Shows up an old lady just as much. That's who my great-*tūtū* saw once—Pele the Crone. But in this story I'm talking about, Pele skews young on account of how hot she is for 'Ohi'a. Pele just has to have him. But 'Ohi'a, he stays faithful to his sweetheart Lehua, so Pele turns him into a gnarly old tree. And Lehua, so she can be with 'Ohi'a always, changes into a flower to grow on his branches."

It would be nice, Stevie thinks, if ordinary people could change so dramatically at will. But then, look at Kiko—more transformed than she ever could have guessed. "That'll be some hula," she says.

"Figured you'd chime to the Pele part. But I know what you're *really* wondering. How'd a *mahū* like him end up with kids?"

"Kiko! I would never call you that."

"In old times, *mahū* was no slur—not like when we were on the playground, yeah? Meant you were special in lots of good ways. Nobody judged. Always like that in my family. My momma was happy how I turned out. No daughters, and plenty pig-hunting, pig-headed surfer-type sons in the house already. Nice having one interested in *her* things—'specially the hula, looking after the littler kids, talking story with her all the time."

It makes Stevie feel calmer, hearing more about the man Kiko's grown up to be, seeing how those pieces fit with the lively little boy she knew so well. The boy who'd once protected her on that same playground he'd mentioned. She remembers a day in fourth grade when he cornered Ricky Fujimoto. "Lay offa Stevie," Kiko had commanded. "No more dat '*haole*' stuff."

"You don't like what I say 'bout *haole*?" Ricky spat back. "You sure not gonna like what I say 'bout *mahū*."

Kiko was big for his age and had no trouble pinning Ricky to the dirt. "Shows what you know. Stevie got blood so old, she can go Kamehameha school if she want. Top that, banana boy."

Kiko was no bully. But call his best friend "*haole*" enough to make her cry? Better get ready to be slapped down and branded with whatever nasty name existed for being whatever *you* were. And unless you were among the minority who happened to be pure, one-hundred-percent-hetero Hawaiian, there was bound to be *something*. Like, for instance, "banana," a term guaranteed to gall Japanese-descended kids; yellow on the outside, white on the inside. Not so bad as "*haole*," maybe, but just about.

Kiko's claim for Stevie that day was true. She could meet the elite Kamehameha High School's most essential entrance requirement: bona fide possession of an island ancestor who existed at the time of first contact. In fact, going to Kamehameha with Kiko was another dream crushed by her parents' divorce. It may have even been something Beryl wished to prevent by taking Stevie to England. What mattered even more, though—then *and* now—was how Kiko had accepted her, and all her mismatched parts, just as unquestioningly as his own family did him.

"Has the racial stuff here changed much?" Stevie asks.

"Some. Not a lot. My kids are *hapa,* and little as they are, they already know what that means."

"Well, I hope it's easier for them than it was in our day."

"I hope so, too. I feel in my heart it will be."

His children's birth mother, Kiko tells Stevie, is a golf pro at a fancy Princeville resort, and her partner a woman who manages an island beef ranch. Kiko lives in an attached apartment at their house. "They could have paid for a sperm donor, but they wanted the *keiki* to really know their daddy." His eyes glitter again. "If Jerry doesn't make it, it'll tear everybody up pretty bad." Then he sighs and reprimands himself. "That kinda worry won't help. Nothing but praying for what you don't want."

Kiko jumps up at the sight of Japhy coming through the swinging door.

"I wasn't sure we could save the paw pads until I got Jerry on the table," Japhy says. "Then I saw a way to clean out the dead tissue and sew everything back together. The big thing now is to monitor him for pain, but I think if we keep him comfortable he'll pull through all right. It'll be a long recovery, and he can't go home for a while yet. My plan is—"

But Kiko's hugging him so hard that Japhy has to wait to tell the rest.

If Stevie gave Kiko a glowing description of Japhy before, it pales alongside how Kiko enthuses while driving her back to Kōloa from the clinic. "I just knew he was going to come out and tell me he ought to put Jerry down—a quality-of-life thing. Either that, or he'd ask if I *wanted* to put him down because of the bill. That's what your by-the-numbers vet would do, and you were right, he ain't one of those. Goes by touch and feel, not just protocol. Gets inside animals to heal them. I can tell these things. Icing on the cake, how he's easy on the eyes. I know what got to you, sistah—the dimples, right?"

"Geez, Kiko. Pip's the one he's on intimate terms with."

"I can keep secrets. This one's just between us girls in the powder room."

"Okay. I've never liked dimples."

"C'mon."

"Actually, it was arm hair. Don't ask. I can't explain."

"That's how it always goes—till pheromones wear off, anyway. And they always do, after a few years. Then you gotta dig deeper for pay dirt. Been there 'nough to know."

Before they left the clinic, Japhy had said he planned to watch Jerry for a few more hours to make certain the pain was under control; then he'd take him to the shelter, where a tech assistant would check on him through the night. "I could keep you company," Stevie had offered.

"Thanks," he said, "but the bigger favor's taking Rainier home. If you could let her out in the yard for a while, take her inside for some fresh water and a carrot from the fridge, she'll be good till I get there."

"Of course," she'd told him, hoping her disappointment didn't show.

As Kiko pulls into Japhy's drive, he turns to Stevie. "Mind if I hang here? The kids'll get all wound up if I tell 'em 'bout Jerry before bedtime. Plus, not quite ready to let you go."

"Sure."

Kiko kills the engine. The trades have slowed to a lazy breeze, and the setting sun stains jagged magenta streaks across a dusky pink sky. Leaving the little dogs in Kiko's car, Stevie lets Rainier out for a yard tour, then calls her to the cottage. She's a little leery about what she'll see inside, having mentally minimized more than one guy's potential as boyfriend material for living in surroundings she found tacky, generic, or just plain thoughtless—especially since good design is so cheap these days. Being judgmental about somebody else's domestic taste is not, she realizes, one of her lovelier qualities. But when Kiko says "Nice place," he's right. Everything's clean and simple, from the hand-painted landscape pictures on the wall to the khaki-covered settee and streamlined shelves filled with books and music.

"I don't know how much longer he'll be here," Stevie offers. "Japhy's renovating a house of his own."

The kitchen's more of a mess, but it's the kind of mess she likes. Roasting pan soaking in the sink, spice jars on the counter alongside mixing bowls, garlic press, herb snippers, and cutting boards still sprinkled with bits of chopped vegetables. Evidence of the meal he'd made for them to share. While Stevie deals with Rainier, Kiko reports from the living room. "No books-for-looks; he actually reads, you can tell from the spines. Mostly science things and novels—serious kind. Poetry, too." Then Kiko's on to the CDs. "Big on jazz, instrumentals, soulful boy singers. Jeff Buckley, Dave Matthews, Eddie Vedder—people like that. Pretty eclectic. There's folk, bluegrass, country-and-western, some whacky Dr. Demento-ish stuff, too. Not much Hawaiian, though. I could give him a hand there."

"You're such a terrible snoop," Stevie says as Kiko joins her in the kitchen, opening cabinets now.

"It's not like I'm reading his mail. This one's definitely your type, Stevie. Jars of beans and rice and nuts all labeled and lined up so neat."

"What makes you think I'm so crazy for neat?"

Kiko just rolls his eyes and takes off for the bedroom, but Stevie follows and grabs his arm as he enters. "Enough," she says. "This isn't '*Mahū* Eye for the Straight Guy.' I'm not going to stand here while you analyze the bed linens." But Stevie lingers in spite of herself, catching sight of what look to be family photographs on the dresser. There's an older woman with Japhy's dimples—his mother?—and a younger woman with a baby in her arms. A sister, maybe. Perhaps a friend. There she goes, hopping off to bunnyland again. Most likely it's Japhy's ex and their child. Stevie wonders if Hank ever displayed such a photo of her and Beryl after his divorce. Doubtful. She flashes on Brian's adolescent daughter, who always treated Stevie with exaggerated politeness, a bridled version of her mother's outright hostility. At least Brian didn't live with a photo of the woman. Not a good sign, that. Who comes with heavier baggage, the man who despises his ex, or the man who's pining away for her? And what woman in her right mind would knowingly choose either?

"Let's go get Pip and Lainey," Stevie tells Kiko. "I want to show you something while there's still light."

Throwing her pareo shawl-like around her shoulders, Stevie leads Kiko across Japhy's yard and around the wedges of banana trees and bromeliads that screen the far end of Hank's. When they reach the trio of *kukui* trees, she points out the seat-shaped lava rock she found. "I dug that out from beneath a fence the other day."

"Funny you put it here by *kukui* trees. In old times, they planted them for chiefs killed in battle."

"Funny how? What do you think it is?"

"*Was,* you mean." He stoops down at the edge of the flower bed for a closer look, feeling the shape just as Stevie had. Then he stands, folds his arms, and turns back to her with one of his hunch-shouldered little smiles. "How's your tummy?" he asks.

"Fine," she says, but that's a lie. Her stomach is rumbling with hunger and contracting, too—from the ominous tone in Kiko's voice, probably. "Why?"

" 'Cause it might be a birthing stone, the kind you see at sacred sites. Only this stone's littler, so I'm not positive."

"Women sat on this thing to give birth?"

"It's possible. But not just any old women. Only ones of high rank—royal, chiefly."

"Must have been pretty uncomfortable."

"What, because it's not all plush and poufy? I got news for you—worst way in the world to labor is flat on your back. Just doesn't make sense. None of *my* mommas lie down till *after* they pop. Anyhow, plenty women say they cramp up when they get near birthing stones. Sympathy pains. And it's cool how you've got lava rocks all around this one, 'cause they'd bury the *piko*—the umbilical cord—in lava rocks. If rats ate the *piko,* meant that baby would grow up rotten, a disgrace. You should see your face! Am I weirding you out?"

Stevie draws the pareo around her shoulders more tightly. "Nope," she says. "It had to be something like that."

The next morning, Stevie makes a point of listening to Japhy's entire radio show. He fields questions from listeners on everything from homeopathic pet remedies (he's for them, used judiciously) to declawing (against) to raw-food diets (depends on the animal's metabolism). Then he finishes up with something of a sermon for his listeners.

"I'm not such a safety nut that I'm going to tell you to get special seats and belts for your dogs for when they're riding around with you," Japhy says. "But you know what? Way too many dogs on this island die from jumping out of cars and trucks. It's not always the injuries that kill, either. Sometimes they're euthanized because the cost of saving them is prohibitive for their owners. So here's what I urge you to do: Keep windows up high enough so your dog can't clear them. Don't leave leashes on—they can cause additional damage in an accident. And never, ever let a dog ride in an open truck bed unless she's inside a kennel. 'Nuff said. Tune in next week, when I promise we'll spend the whole hour on cats. For now, I'll leave you with a poem. It's called 'Love Dogs,' by Rumi." After taking an audible breath, Japhy begins to read.

"The grief you cry out from
draws you toward union."

Stevie turns up the volume, leans in closer to the radio, and closes her eyes to listen to the rest.

"Your pure sadness
that wants help
is the secret cup.

Listen to the moan of a dog for its master.
That whining is the connection.

There are love dogs
no one knows the names of.

Give your life
to be one of them."

When Stevie opens her eyes again, her cheeks are wet.

"I loved that poem you read," Stevie tells Japhy when he stops by later with Rainier. She's stepped outside to talk, but they can still hear the television—and Hank, too.

"Ramirez homered!" Hank calls out.

"Great!" she hollers, then turns back to Japhy. "Now the Cubs are ahead of the Pirates three to nothing, top of the third inning. You're not on at the shelter today?"

"Nope," he says, "they just hired another full-time vet. But I did stop by to check on Jerry. Thought you'd like to know he had a pretty good night. I'll switch him over to my place tomorrow, probably send him home in another day or two, then have him in to change his bandages. That'll require anesthesia until the stitches come out."

"Kiko must be relieved."

"He sounded pleased. Especially when I told him he gets the family rate—for not even thinking about putting his dog down."

The sound of commercials comes from the lanai; if Stevie's not there, Hank doesn't bother to mute them. She jams her hands into the pockets of an old sundress made of turquoise *palaka* cloth, smocked across her chest into such a tight, stretchy texture she doesn't have to bother with a bra. "It's so nice out today, you might not want to be indoors. But if you're interested in watching baseball . . ."

"I was hoping you'd ask."

She probably shouldn't have—not after seeing that photo in Japhy's bedroom. Plus, nothing could be further from the romance of last night's picnic plans than the two of them sitting together in front of a television screen with her terminally ill father. Not that Hank *looks* terminally ill today, with his tan darkened from their Puolo Point swim, his mood light with game-time excitement. Still, she might not be able to hide her irritation—or, just as bad, her hurt—should Hank revert to his old antagonistic self. Especially since she's way behind on getting ready to leave for Chicago, and so nervous already that she has to consciously unclench her jaw at regular intervals because, if she doesn't, she'll barely be able to open her mouth when the time comes to defend her fountain.

So why the thrill thrumming through her head? It's startling to realize she can't attribute this to the proximity of Japhy's arm hair, not anymore; he's becoming too dimensional for her to categorize in body parts. Which means she's more exposed than she was in her bikini. More vulnerable, too. And *that* sets off almost as many backflips in her belly as the prospect of public speaking.

Stevie puts a water bowl outside for the dogs, then goes to the kitchen for macadamia nuts, mango salsa, corn chips, chilled glasses, and the last of the Old Style beers that Margo sent. "I know it's still early here," she explains to Japhy, who helps carry everything back to the lanai, "but it's past three o'clock in Pittsburgh."

"I get it," he tells her. "Certain rituals must be observed."

It soon becomes clear that Japhy enjoys a skilled pitcher's duel with a hot hitter every bit as much as Hank. "Uh-oh," Japhy says when a Pirate who's been on a streak since the All-Star break comes to bat. "You don't want to walk this guy—he's a threat to steal second every time he gets on."

Hank nods. "Let's see how Prior pitches him."

None of them speaks again until seven pitches later, when the play-by-play announcer says, "And he's out on a routine ground ball."

"Routine ground ball," Hank snorts. "For cry-eye."

"Nothing routine about it," Japhy agrees. "First a fastball up and in, a couple of sliders away, and he comes back with a split-finger change-up and a curve that drops right off the table."

"Right," Hank says. "Then he rattles him with an off-speed pitch so he can jam him up high and tight with that fastball again, just the way he started. That's not routine. That's poetry."

Listening to them, it occurs to Stevie what a limited baseball buddy she is compared to Japhy. "Japhy was a catcher," she tells Hank. "That's why he knows so much about pitching."

"Oh yeah? High school?"

"College, too," Japhy tells him. "Until I popped a ligament skiing."

"What do you think of the Cubs' chances?"

"Pretty good. They're almost leading their division, right?"

"If they win today and St. Louis beats Houston, they're just a half game away."

"Boston's hot, too. Kind of unbelievable, isn't it, that the Cubs and Red Sox might play in the same World Series? The two cursed teams. What would happen then?"

"The world as we know it," Hank intones, "would come to an end. If you believe in curses, that is."

"I'm guessing *you* don't," Japhy says.

"Oh boy," Stevie mutters. "Are you ever going to get an earful."

Either Hank doesn't hear, or chooses to ignore her. "Do I look like someone stupid enough to believe in curses? Why would Babe Ruth curse Boston for trading him to the Yankees? What would be the motive? He was better off with New York. And the Cubs are supposedly cursed because that nut job couldn't watch the game with his smelly goddamn goat? Even more ridiculous. Why should a barnyard animal be allowed into a ballpark? Anyway, I say wait your turn, Boston. The Red Sox haven't been denied a World Series shot for as long as the Cubs. Besides, I don't like Red Sox fans. They're whiners. Bad losers. Bullies, even."

From Japhy's easy grin and the lift of his eyebrows, Stevie gets the impression that while he doesn't agree with her father, he's accustomed enough to tetchy, opinionated older people to get a kick out of him. Which makes it easier for *her* to see Hank in that light, too. "Seems like the biggest thing against the Cubs," Japhy says, "is how Wrigley Field's a hitter's park."

Hank's eyes narrow and that cleft chin of his juts forward. "What do you mean?"

"Powerful right-handed hitters have such an edge there. When the Cubs traded Fergie Jenkins to the Rangers, he said that's why Wrigley's a bad ballpark. Too many easy home runs."

Another snort from Hank. "And you believed him?"

"Well," Japhy says, "I'd love to watch a game from the bleachers, I bet it's a gas. But they do cut off the power alley. And if I'm not mistaken, stats show more left-center homers in Wrigley than in other ballparks."

"I could refute your arguments one by one," Hank says. "But since I need to conserve my energy, I'd rather let my darling daughter do it. You tell him, Stevie."

Stevie picks up the remote on the arm of Hank's chair, mutes the TV, and turns to Japhy. "Okay, here's what my dad would say if he weren't on Prozac. Remember, this isn't me disputing you, it's him." She takes a long inhale and lets fly. "Bullshit! Fergie Jenkins can gripe about Wrigley Field all he wants, but he had a penchant for giving up home runs—he gave 'em up everywhere he pitched. The bleachers shorten Wrigley's power alley, I'll grant you that. But the left and right field walls are unusually long, so if a ball's hit down right or left field, it's not an easy home run—it's a very difficult home run. Plus, everything depends on which way the wind blows. If it's blowing in off the lake, it's a pitcher's park. If it's blowing out, it's a hitter's park. Anyway, if you apply Jenkins's logic, Ebbets Field and Yankee Stadium are bad ballparks, too. Ted Williams had a short porch in right field playing for Boston, and Babe Ruth had a short porch in right playing for New York. The power alleys might be deeper, sure. But if you're a leftie and can pull the ball a little like Williams and Ruth, you get home runs that would be outs anywhere else."

As Japhy laughs, throwing up his hands in mock surrender, Stevie reaches over to give Hank's arm a gentle jab. "How'd I do?"

"Pretty good. Except you forgot to mention one thing. No ballpark anywhere is as beautiful as Wrigley Field."

When the game ends with a Cubs win, Stevie postpones her travel preparations even further to throw together an impromptu lunch with Japhy, who offers up what's left of his roast chicken—all but the leg and thigh he dined on last night—for a salad. After slicing the meat, he watches her concoct a vinaigrette. "Pink salt?" he says as she whisks a pinch into the dressing. Stevie lowers her voice so it won't carry back to Hank, reading on the lanai now, and explains where the salt came from, why she'd wanted it, then pours some into a quart-size Ziploc bag for Japhy to take home, just as she had for Lila, all the while wondering whether she'd want him hanging around in such a chummy way if their picnic last night had gone off as planned.

They've yet to be truly alone for any length of time. They've yet to have a truly serious talk, too—and isn't that what he'd wanted? Then again, might it be a step forward that he's sought her out here, in a context more personal, more unpredictable? Who knows. Her head's nowhere near clear enough to follow such questions through to rational conclusions.

Soon after they sit down with Hank at the lanai table, Lila arrives in a mud-splattered Civic driven by Melveen, the young but decidedly maternal-looking nursing aide who will be coming to the house for part of each day that Stevie is away. "I'll give the tour while you finish lunch," Lila says. Charming as Hank was when Lila introduced him to Melveen—it doesn't hurt that she's attractive in a vigorous, big-boned way—as soon as the women are out of earshot, he grumbles about being fine on his own.

"It's just for a few days, Dad," Stevie reassures, but the mere mention of time in this context seems to extinguish his appetite. She can almost see Hank's sword of Damocles dangling over his shrunken yet still leonine profile, can almost hear his unexpressed thoughts. How many more weeks? How many more months? Even so, she might just be projecting. He might just be filled up on nuts and chips.

"You've almost converted me into a Cubs fan, Hank," Japhy says as he leaves. "I'll check the schedule, see if I can work it out to catch a game or two this week. If you don't mind my coming here, that is."

"No, no," Hank says. "I'd be delighted."

"I'm not asking myself over just because your TV's way sharper than mine. But I can't deny it's a factor."

Stevie wants to hug Japhy for that, and she does. But only after he departs without remembering his salt, and she runs outside to give him the bag.

It's a quick hug. Friendly, nothing sexual about it. At least not on the surface—the current crackling down her spine can't be seen. As Stevie releases Japhy and turns away, he scoops her back and leans down to brush her lips with a kiss that lands lightly, lasting only a second, but his lips as they soften on hers are sweet, and the warm pressure of his hand on her shoulder is something so solid she can conjure the feel of it all through the day and into the night.

It's past eleven when Stevie goes to bed, and she's beat—from tasks that included conferring with Lila and Melveen, polishing up her Chicago presentation, e-mailing, phone-calling, and, while still in the thick of packing, telling Hank not just good night but goodbye. She'll be gone long before he awakens in the morning. Exhausted though her body is, her mind will not rest, dipping into one well of anxiety after another and then, bored with itself, re-creating the sensations of Japhy's kiss—more pleasant, yes, but hardly calming. She takes her pillow and pineapple quilt to the futon on the lanai, but sleep won't come there, either. A light flicks on in the hallway and she sees Lila, already moved into the other guest bedroom, walking barefoot to the bathroom. When Lila comes to the kitchen for a glass of water, Stevie's there, too, pulling a bottle of vodka from the freezer to pour herself a shot.

Undone from its braid, Lila's hair spills all around her shoulders, waves grazing the top of her long, cream-colored batiste nightgown. "Nerves?" she asks, filling her glass.

"Big-time."

"Well, that stuff won't put you to sleep—not for long, anyway. The sugar'll kick in and wake you up again."

"Yeah, you're right." Stevie replaces the bottle. "I'm just desperate to get some rest."

Finishing her water, Lila reaches into the freezer herself, past the boxes of fruit-juice sweetened cherry Popsicles that Stevie buys for Hank, and behind those, old cartons of frozen vegetables left behind by renters. What Lila pulls out is a Baggie, filled with a big handful of what looks to be marijuana buds. "This might help," Lila says. "Brought it for your father when he first got here, so nauseous from the chemo he couldn't eat."

"I'm amazed he had the strength to travel," Stevie says.

"Nothing stops that man when he's determined. Your father's daughter there, yeah? Meant that as a compliment—why pull a face?"

Stevie shoos the question away with a wave of her hand. It doesn't seem worth mentioning that her mother never, ever meant it as a compliment when she compared Stevie to Hank. As Beryl often did, whenever she perceived some action of Stevie's as the least bit willful or short-tempered or inconsiderate. "Did the marijuana work?"

"Oh yeah, made all the difference."

"I'm so glad. But you and my dad smoking *pakalolo*? That's flat-out strange."

"Who said *I* was smoking *pakalolo*? I'm the nurse, remember?"

"Did it come from a lab, or from some old hippie's secret patch up in the hills?"

"Doesn't matter where, only why. Therapeutic either way, and I got more patients than Hank needing it, you know."

"It's just tough for me to imagine my father toking, much less breaking the law."

"Well, I'm not saying it made him favor Bob Marley over Frank Sinatra. But he did wonder what all the damn fuss was about."

Stevie takes the Baggie from Lila and frowns, considering. "It's been so long, I barely remember what this stuff does to me. Guess it couldn't hurt, though."

"Up to you, my girl." Lila produces a lighter and small pipe from her duty kit and lays them on the counter. "Medicinal grade, remember. All you need is a puff or two." Although they'd said good night earlier, she lays a hand on Stevie's cheek and then folds her into another long hug before going back to bed.

Stevie's so wound up that she forgets Lila's instruction and instead of one or two puffs, ends up taking four or five, after which she's so relaxed that going back to bed doesn't seem anywhere near so wonderful an idea as polishing off a cherry Popsicle, then hauling her pillow and a sleeping bag out to the clearing by the *kukui* trees. This way, she'll at least have a cloudless, diamond-studded sky to look at if she can't fall asleep. And if she does? No problem. The roosters will wake her in plenty of time to make her flight. Anyway, falling asleep no longer feels like the most important thing in the world. Soon enough she'll be stuck in a plane for hours on end; she can catch up then.

Lying inside the bag, Stevie folds her hands behind her head and scans the sky, locating the few constellations she knows the names of and concocting others of her own design. A ship's sail. A guitar that Picasso might have shaped in his Cubist period. A dog's head, not unlike Pip's, stealing Stevie's breath away when one of its eyes turns into a shooting star. She prefers to wish on shooting stars, not on first stars seen, and there's no dearth of things to wish for now. Remission for Hank, a Cubs victory in the World Series, her damn diploma—and that's just for starters. But the wish she finally settles on surprises her for being so much simpler, not nearly so specific. It's almost as though the fallen star blazed some new trail in her heart, because what she wants most is to appreciate not just her own life but the life of everybody touching it. Whether known or unknown. Whether past, present, or future. Whatever that takes. No sooner does this wish form than she falls asleep, not stirring again until hours later, when she hears the sound of a drum.

No, it's the sound of *many* drums.

Flutes, too.

Also chanting.

Barking dogs as well.

Maybe she's dreaming, because try as she may, she can't seem to open her eyes, not even as the earth beneath her starts to shake, and the vibrations seem to come not just from drums, but distant footsteps, too—*many* footsteps, drawing closer. Her pulse hammers, her skin feels on fire, and then it comes to her, the realization of what these sounds signify. Night Marchers. She's in their path. They're coming close, headed for the shore, and she doesn't need to open her eyes to see their robes and spears, or to understand that this is not their usual route. Why have they come? The birthing stone—that has to be what drew them. They entered this world as their mothers pushed against it, squatted over it, and each *piko* of theirs, cut by priests with bamboo knives, must have eluded rats or they never would have marched at all.

Do they want to thank her for unearthing the stone? Possible, she supposes, though she's never before heard of *friendly* Night Marchers. They're warriors, returning to old battlegrounds. This procession must be headed for Māhā'ulepū, where the last of King Kamehameha's invaders were slain, and she longs to see faces, to verify not just the Night Marchers' presence but their very existence. To look on Night Marchers, though, is *kapu.* To look on Night Marchers is to have your soul taken. To look on Night Marchers is to die. *That* must be why she can't open her eyes—her body knows better than to let her. Stevie remembers Kiko's encounter, his contention that the only reason he survived was because he took off all his clothes and lay facedown on the ground.

Eyes still sealed shut, she wriggles out of her filmy cotton pants and T-shirt. The Night Marchers won't be able to tell that she's naked if she's inside the sleeping bag, so she crawls out, sprawls on top of it, and lies as still as she can for what seems a long while, waiting for them to pass. When all is quiet once more, it's as though some internal camera exits her body and flies up to satellite height, zooming in to track the Night Marchers' progress from above. As they snake their way closer to the ocean, she sees the flares of their torches, the tops of their heads. But everything goes dark again when the camera's tether snaps. She catches the perfume of nighttime blooms as the trades brush by, rattling banana tree leaves at the clearing's edge. Chill seeps into Stevie's limbs and she starts to stir. Surely it's safe by now to wriggle back into her sleeping bag, if not to open her eyes.

Just as she rises to her knees, though, a hand lands on her shoulder. Stevie recoils with a scream at the whispered sound of her name. Now her eyes are open, all right. And what she sees is Japhy, arms wound around her shivering, naked self.

"I couldn't sleep," Stevie manages, face buried in his neck.

"Me neither."

Keeping an arm around her waist, he unzips the sleeping bag and then they're inside it together, limbs entwined, and she's tasting the comfort of his kiss again. But this time the kiss lasts long enough for him to shape it into something more intense, for her to turn it toward imperative. As panic leaves Stevie's throat, the only other sensation that matters is Japhy's healing hands on her neck, her spine, discovering the trail of incisions on her belly. Amazing, how the way he lingers on those scars makes her feel not damaged and ugly but sexy and alive. He's not just reacting to her desire, either. He's releasing it from all her usual defenses, an intricate creature he might read with his fingertips to understand what she needs. And what she needs is to go on like this, without another word, until he's every bit as naked as she is.

Which most certainly is not what Japhy came out here looking for, much less wanting. But it most certainly is what he needs, too. That's what Stevie's senses tell her. *All* of her senses, not just the ones aware of his accelerating heartbeat, his eyes lifting to fix laser-like on hers, the warm, honeyed scent of skin so similar to the taste of him. She believes what her senses say. Otherwise this wouldn't be happening with such abandon. Effortless as the milky half-moon slipping past the mountains. Fluid as silver-bottomed *kukui* leaves fluttering overhead. Thrilling as stars wheeling in the sky. Didn't old-fashioned movies cut to such images when actors made love? Stevie nearly laughs at the thought. How impossible it is, separating these surroundings from the core of warmth pulsing to his touch, her burgeoning pleasure.

The ground they lie on is hard, and it can't be easy for a long-legged man like Japhy to undress within the confines of a sleeping bag. But the earth cushions them as they roll more tightly into each other, and it's as if her hand—traveling slowly down from his breastbone to slip beneath the waistband of frayed, softened jeans settled low on his hips—is magically possessed. No sooner does she clasp his erection than it seems the pants are gone—dematerialized, just spirited away. Jeans were all he'd been wearing. No shirt and nothing underneath. Maybe he'd thrown them on because he heard the Night Marchers, too. Maybe that's why they don't speak, when just a few days before they had so much left to say. Entire histories to exchange. Characteristics to compare, contrast. All the normal preludes.

But there's nothing normal about this. Oh, she's awakened to make love before, but only indoors, with someone who was there when she'd fallen asleep, someone she was already intimate with. A woozy, quick, almost proprietary operation that in no way resembles the hyperawareness of locking into Japhy, of Japhy locking into her, the escalating fever spread by their lips. She tosses back the unzipped top of the sleeping bag so soft night air can cool their skin, then wraps her legs tight around his waist as he raises her up to sit across his thighs, their connection holding, quickening. Her climax comes in long, delicious waves, lasting so long it laps over his.

They lie back on her pillow, still cinched close. Japhy exhales her name, but before he can say anything else, Stevie strokes his cheek and whispers into his ear. "Bumbye." Her favorite piece of pidgin—a much sweeter sound than "later," which is what it means. Somehow she's sure that the words he almost uttered hold such weight that she can't possibly take them with her to Chicago, not when there's so much weight already in what they've just done. He nods, turning his head to slip her fingers into his mouth, and soon they're kissing again, making love again.

Afterward, his hand tangled in her hair, Stevie feels Japhy's breath lengthen with the rise and fall of his chest beneath her head. *Now he can sleep,* she thinks. Now she can, too.

❁

As the flight from Līhuʻe lifts off, Stevie finds herself wondering if any of it had really happened.

As for the Night Marchers, she has nothing more concrete than intuition to go on. What puzzles her most is not so much why they came, but what life-or-death battle they might portend. Her father's? The one she's about to fight for her career in Chicago? Or something entirely unforeseen?

As for Japhy, well, that's simpler. At least she's certain he was there last night; she can still feel him inside her. A fact that lets loose a flood of so many other sensations that one second she's dipping her head and crossing her legs with a small private smile, and the next she's hunched forward in her seat to gnaw on all they've left unsaid. She had run back to the house when roosters awakened them. Jolted into travel mode, she'd had no time for discussion.

If everything hadn't been so surreal, if it had been first-time sex with any other man on the planet at this point in her life, she would have been more cautious. But Japhy doesn't strike her as reckless, not at all, and he hadn't hesitated, either. Why? Because they'd read each other right and neither one was worried? So it seems. Though she's really too jazzed by the prolonged afterglow and groggy from lack of sleep to tell for sure.

Stevie sits up to gaze down on the canyon, cliffs, and shorelines of Kauaʻi as the plane gains altitude. From here, it looks like an island you could put your arms around.

Chapter 16

Striving for perfection, Margo learned as Evelyn's daughter, is the enemy of a good time. One reason why Evelyn's family dinners were always so fraught was that before any of her guests even arrived, she had so frazzled herself seeing to the just-rightness of every last detail that it took nothing at all to make her snap. Once, as a joke, Margo's second cousin Frankie set a piece of plastic molded to resemble puke on Evelyn's precious white flokati rug and Evelyn shot off into the stratosphere, unable to calm herself even as Frankie peeled the thing off and stood there waving it like a flag, his face squinched in astonishment.

That was not amusing.

"But it was silly. I guess nobody in charge ever let you just be silly, huh?"

Well, I can't say it was ever encouraged.

While only a few weeks ago Margo would have reproached Evelyn for raising her in precisely the same shitty way, now she thinks what a shame that is. Or, rather, was. Where did all Evelyn's unquenchable rage come from but a whole lifetime of never feeling fully loved or embraced? A problem never solved by perfectionism. It's no excuse, of course. But it is a reason. Not that Evelyn appreciates Margo's generosity in acknowledging it.

I hate to think where that flokati ended up. Gracing the floor of some starving artist's filthy garret, knowing you.

"Garrets are in operas, Mother."

Hovel, then. A nicer term than "rat hole," anyway. You should have kept it for your children. Flokatis are back in style now.

"What I should have done was give the frigging flokati to Frankie."

That actually gets a laugh out of Evelyn. It's so much easier lately, defusing her dead mother's snits.

With Evelyn's penchant for wrecking family occasions in mind, Margo's kept her planning for Stevie's visit to a minimum. It's such an unexpected opportunity, reconnecting while Hank's still alive, when it can do everyone the most good; she doesn't want to blow it by wearing herself out before Stevie even steps off the plane. Besides, Stevie's bound to be a wreck, from the awful double whammy of her father's illness and the prospect of that jerk from the *Trib* moderating her panel tomorrow. Margo's never had a high-profile career, but having lost both parents, she can readily imagine what her cousin is facing with Hank, and her only real agenda for the next few days, before they fly to Kaua'i together, is to help Stevie do whatever she feels like in whatever downtime she has, whatever that means—museum hopping, shopping, or reading trashy magazines on the couch in her bathrobe.

Funny, how protective she feels toward Stevie. Not maternal but sisterly. Neither of them has ever known what it's like to be a sister, much less have one, and somehow Margo doubts there's a relative in England who could come as close as she herself might to filling that bill for her cousin—not if the rest of Stevie's maternal relations are as clipped and self-contained as Margo remembers Beryl being.

Still, there were preparations Margo had to make. A raft of course work to finish in advance so that taking time off to visit Hank won't put her off track in school. She stocked the fridge and made sure that there were clean linens and fresh flowers in the guest room. She also lined her kids up to come over and join them tonight for a late dinner, in deference to Stevie's jet lag. And finally, she insisted on driving to O'Hare for Stevie rather than let her take a cab. That's what Margo's ready to do now, sitting in her old silver Saab near the airport, waiting for Stevie's call to come pick her up at the curb outside baggage claim. What did people do before cell phones? She can remember using a pen to write parking lot locations on the back of her hand, then setting off on long hikes to the terminal and even longer ones to the gate, waiting with all the other people poised to hug arriving passengers. Nostalgic as she is for the sweetness of that pre-9/11 part, she doesn't miss the rest.

Her cell phone rings. Stevie's name and number pop up on the display panel. Before even answering, Margo is on her way.

At first, Margo looks right past Stevie. She expects someone who resembles the sophisticated, troubled person she met in the park. Stevie has to wave both arms in the air before Margo realizes that her cousin is this glowing woman with loose wavy hair and a big smile who's dressed like a kid—*looks* like a kid—in jeans and a cropped T-shirt. "It's like you were the 'before' version of Stevie last time I saw you," Margo says once they've hugged and stowed Stevie's stuff. "And now you're the 'after.' I am *not* talking about clothes, either. What's with the makeover?"

"It's the tan," Stevie says. "I can't stand lying out in the sun, it's so boring. But on Kaua'i I'm dark before I know it, without even trying. Dad used to say all I had to do was *look* at the sun and boom, I got color."

"He's the same way. So's my Ben. And me? I'm allergic to the sun. Thank God for broad-spectrum sunscreens or I'd have to be a shut-in in Hawai'i. Are you tired?"

"Ought to be. Haven't slept much lately. Guess I'm running on adrenaline."

"The good news there is you'll be ready for bed on Central Daylight Time."

"I'm glad you found me," Stevie says, reaching over the gearshift to lay a hand on Margo's shoulder. "I'm glad to be here."

Would the two of them ever be friends if they weren't related? Margo wonders as she responds to Stevie's emotion. An impossible question, really. But she hopes the answer turns out to be yes.

Maybe she's glad to get away from her father, too.

"Leave it to you, Mother, to invent a reason like that."

When Stevie speaks again, it's almost as though she's heard this phantom exchange. "It's pretty crazy, how all over the map I am these days. Some of the worst things are happening at the same time as some of the best."

Margo's not sure if the mysteries of blood are what's at work or a vulcanian mind-meld, but whatever it is seems to be flowing both ways, because glancing over at Stevie, she's compelled to say, "We can swing by Bittersweet Place on the way home. That's what you were thinking, isn't it? 'You have to take the bitter with the sweet'—the family motto. If they ever said it with even an iota of irony, it could have been a joke on their old address."

"I *was* thinking about that. Yes, let's do it."

Margo exits the expressway and works her way toward Clarendon, turning east onto Bittersweet. "The street's only one block long," Margo says, "and wouldn't you know? It's one-way. I can never remember—is it yin that's masculine and yang that's feminine?"

"Opposite," Stevie says.

"Okay, then. Yang up the yin-yang—that's Bittersweet Place. We're close to the lake now, and the park where Evelyn and Hank would have their liverwurst-sandwich picnics." She pulls over to the curb by an old four-story brick building that sits atop a grassy slope. "This is where their apartment was. The three-bedroom place with the famous safe between their beds. I'm sure the building's gone condo by now, but everybody rented then."

"Wait," Stevie says, a pinch of panic in her voice. "I have no idea where I am. Which way is the lake? The river? The Loop?"

"Well," Margo begins, "we're just east of—"

"I don't do directions. You'll have to point."

So Margo does and Stevie swivels around in her seat, sticking her right hand out toward the lake and her left toward the river, resembling nothing so much as a flight attendant indicating exit rows. Then her face relaxes again and she says, "Okay, got it."

Stevie stares at the building with such intensity that Margo can almost see it anew herself. Bay windows, old-fashioned sleeping porches, and fire escapes extend from an L-shaped structure, with an elevated entrance that's somewhere between a portico and a stoop. An ordinary building that somehow emanates an air of resolve, an echo of the people who'd once lived there.

"I've seen this place before," Stevie says. "Once, when I was snooping in Dad's desk, I found an old black-and-white photograph and I knew it had to be him when he was little—sitting on a pony, with a girl behind him. I used to look at it a lot. Then one day it disappeared and I could never find it again. Anyway, this building was in the background, I think."

"It was!" Margo exclaims. "Nana rented that Shetland pony for Hank's eighth birthday. My mother was the girl with her arms around his waist. All of her best family memories were here—when she and Hank were still close, and they had lots of relatives around."

"I still don't get what came between them," Stevie says. "Back then, or later, even."

"The way I figure, it goes back to Nana. She couldn't be happy. You never met a more critical woman. Her own mother died in childbirth, like a lot of immigrants did then, and Nana had to quit school to work in a factory, rolling cigars. But she was smart and strong, and damned if her children weren't going to live someplace better and go to private school for the best education she could buy. She was the whole world to them. They might as well not have had a father, for all he was around. I only just found out what killed him—a heart attack in his mistress's bed. Funny, the stuff I've learned asking questions for my family history paper. Nana certainly never told anybody."

"So how did she wreck things?"

"Putting wedges between her kids when they got older."

"Why?"

"Well," Margo says, "I happen to have a brand-new theory about that. Would you care to hear?"

"Oh, you bet."

"So they'd turn to her instead of each other. So she'd be the one they kept needing most. I mean, what if they teamed up against her and she lost her children, too? So she played the martyr, always sacrificing for their sake. Which kept her center stage, smelling like a rose, while she planted stinky grievances between them. And it worked so well that when Nana's bakery got in trouble, everybody dived in to save her by switching over to a wholesale operation, inventing the Little Margo May business."

"Named for you, or vice versa?"

"For me," Margo hoots. "Which was bad enough. I'd never forgive them for the other way around. They were all in on it, you know. Mother, Daddy, and Hank, too. He must have just finished his Army stint."

"Sounds like they got along *then.*"

"They were at their best in a crisis, and building a business together, they had a real esprit. I have to guess about what went wrong, though. Has Hank mentioned anything about it?"

Stevie shakes her head.

"I've tried to bring it up in e-mails."

"Maybe," Stevie says, "he's waiting for when you get there."

At Margo and Kenny's Lincoln Park apartment building, they take the elevator up from the garage. It stops on the lobby floor and there's Margo's firstborn, just arrived by train from school in Champaign. "Ben!" Margo cries, and no sooner are the words "Hi, Mom" out of his mouth than Stevie's saying, "Wow. You've got Dad's cleft chin."

"That's not all," Margo says, tousling Ben's thick, dark hair. "He's got the wave."

"Come on, Mom." Ben bats her hand away with a self-conscious grin. "Behave yourself."

"He's annoyed," Margo informs Stevie, "because he uses gel and a blow dryer to keep that wave from lying all flat and silly on the middle of his forehead, and here I am messing it up. My hair's so short now, I don't have to worry about it anymore. Evelyn had helmet hair—that was her solution."

"What I do," Stevie says, "is layer the wave and put my part right in the middle of it. Got that trick from the guy who cut Dad's hair in Seattle."

Margo thinks it's neat, what her cousin just did—bringing the wave gene back around to a male thing for Ben's sake, throwing an arm around his shoulder to confide, looking happy to be sharing a quirk that's so personal yet ultimately so inconsequential. Margo's not surprised. Brief as all Stevie's e-mails and phone calls from Hawai'i have been, her longing for connection bled through.

If only other family traits could be subdued as easily as the wave. Like that Pollack temper. Ben had emerged from the womb after a fifteen-hour labor with the dial on *his* Pollack temper turned up full blast, incensed at being squeezed and yanked and forced to swallow air. Once, when he was almost three, Ben threw a tantrum at the Jewel, flinging himself to the floor while Margo ordered meat from the butcher. "Oh, what an adorable little boy," an older woman said, leaning down to pat his cheek. "What's your name?"

"Benjie," he'd cried. (He didn't insist on "Ben" till much later.) Then adorable little Benjie stopped his wailing long enough to look the woman in the eye and bite her hand.

It's long after dinner when Margo tells Stevie this story—so mortifying at the time, such a crack-up now that Ben's made it to college without killing anybody. Not that Margo ever for a second thought he might. Evelyn had been the one who believed Ben was a budding terrorist. Wouldn't you know.

By themselves at the kitchen table, Stevie and Margo share a pot of orange-ginger-mint tea while the dishwasher hums. Stevie has already devoured with her eyes every ancestral item in the cabinet Margo reserves for such material, including duplicates of that black-and-white birthday photo taken on Bittersweet Place. Evelyn's copy had a cut-out hole where Hank's head ought to have been. Nana's was complete, hand-tinted, and framed; Stevie's rain-cloud-colored eyes filled with tears when Margo gave it to her.

Remembering how Hank and Evelyn and all the other relatives would stay up late after dinner smoking cigarettes and drinking coffee, shouting one another down as they argued politics, Margo's especially pleased with the way her and Stevie's voices stay at a low, companionable murmur, broken only by complicitous hoots. How far they've evolved from those dominating, domineering Pollack parents of theirs, from reacting to those destructive family patterns, from embodying all those temperamental twitches Margo is chronicling in her family history paper. The paper in which Hank is the major missing link.

"What do you do with *your* fire?" Margo asks Stevie.

Her cousin shrugs. "Water it down, turn it to steam."

"That's my daughter's way. Even though I swear I did everything I could to contradict what Evelyn taught me, that anger unsexes a woman. Evelyn, of all people!"

"Oh," Stevie says, "sometimes I think that one comes in Cheerios."

"Hope you didn't mind, Cammie showing you her slides tonight."

"Of course not. She's starting to make some interesting sculptures."

"It's so exciting for her, getting a new relative who has the design gene. Makes her feel less like an alien, I think."

Margo's husband, Kenny, walks in from the den, where he's been watching the eleven o'clock news. "This is funny," he says. "Three Cubs fans flew to Texas and took a billy goat to the Astros' ballpark."

Margo squints, tilting her head. "Are you telling a joke?"

"No, it was on TV. Security wouldn't let these guys into the park with the goat, so they stood outside the stadium and performed a ceremony to transfer the billy goat curse to Houston."

Stevie lets loose with one of her goose-like laughs—such an endearing counterpoint to her outward grace. But Margo, a casual fan, doesn't see the humor. "Will someone please explain?"

"Back in '45," Stevie says, "the last time the Cubs played in a World Series, this guy put a curse on the team because he and his billy goat got thrown out of the fourth game at Wrigley Field. Hence the billy goat curse."

"They lost that game to Detroit," Kenny says, "and lost the Series, too, and haven't won a pennant since. But now, if Houston loses their next few games, the Cubs will be sitting pretty for the division lead. Then they're into postseason play, with another shot at the Series." Kenny clasps his hands prayerfully, brings them to his chest, and bows his head; then he reaches for the table to knock wood. Odd behavior for a man who got completely creeped out the one time he overheard his wife talking to her dead mother. But then, no small part of why Margo married Kenny was his warm levelheadedness. In their early years especially, she could be likened to a jumpy Thoroughbred who raced better for being stabled with a placid piebald. If Margo had an attention deficit disorder, as Grace Kiriakades has hinted more than once, well, Kenny was her human Ritalin. Still, there are times when she yearns for a man with mystical inclinations—not to sleep with, to talk with. Such men do exist, of that Margo is certain. But so far, she's encountered them only in books.

"Not that I believe in curses," Kenny's telling Stevie now. "Do you?"

"I believe in their power. But then, I'm from Hawai'i. Myths, blessings, curses—they're everywhere. Contagious, too. Every year tourists mail back tons of lava rocks they brought home as souvenirs. They claim their luck's gone bad because the volcano goddess is upset with them for stealing what's hers. My father thinks it's all too silly for words."

"Rationalists have no patience with magical thinking," Margo says, giving Kenny a pointed look. "But me? I hope what those guys did with the goat works."

Kenny just grins at her. He's halfway out of the room before he stops to say "Oh, I forgot to mention, Margo. I'll be in Cincinnati for the game tomorrow. A client gave me a ticket."

"Kenny! How are you ever going to make it back in time for Stevie's event?"

Stevie's hand covers her mouth for a yawn that ends up sounding more like a moan. "Not a problem. I hope *nobody* comes. I only wish that I could go to the game, too."

"Well, you've got the outfit," Kenny observes.

He's referring to the T-shirt and cap that Margo gave Stevie over dessert. The T-shirt is a feminine, fitted style bearing the Cubs logo and the number 34 across the back and chest—Kerry Wood's number. The cap is player style, from 1933—the closest Margo could come to the year of Hank's birth. It's far darker than the current bright blue version, almost black, and the lone letter "C" is in a more elegant typeface. It fits Stevie perfectly.

Late the next morning, she shows up for breakfast wearing both.

Stevie had spoken to her father and Lila before crawling into bed, and by then her eyes were reddened with fatigue. Not a good time for calling Japhy—she'd only yawn in his ear. How strange to start the day outside with island roosters' crows, and end it with muted elephant trumpetings from Lincoln Park Zoo. A thought that ignites a whole chain of other comparisons. From Night Marchers to the billy goat curse. From an island where few buildings stood taller than a palm tree to Lake Shore Drive, with its towering Mies van der Rohe masterpiece of glass and steel. From the place where her father wished to die to the one where he was born. From having no close kin but her parents to having a fresh batch of cousins. From being held in a lover's arms to aching for that to happen again. Then she fell into a deep, dreamless sleep that lasted for ten and a half hours.

In the morning, Margo insists on following Stevie's lead. "I'm up for anything you feel like," she says.

So they leave after coffee and yogurt for a long, brisk walk along the shore, then return to shower and change before setting off in Margo's Saab for a late lunch downtown, at a restaurant in Water Tower Place. The Saab's trunk is packed with everything Stevie needs for her presentation, including the suit from agnès b. that she's worn to countless nerve-wracking events over the last few years. Well-cut taupe gabardine that might as well be chain mail, for all the protective power she hopes it bestows.

Stevie had wanted to head south after lunch to check in with her garden, though there's little for her to do there until tomorrow, when Frank Acosta arrives with his stonecutting equipment. But digging away at an enormous chef's salad, Stevie discovers that her favorite pieces at the Art Institute are among Margo's as well, after which nothing will do for them but to soak in Rothko's visceral washes of color, then marvel over Caillebot's Parisian light and the intricacies of Cornell's boxed constructions. Everything Stevie fell in love with on her first visit to Chicago, when Hank dropped her off at the Institute. Only now she has someone to share it with.

Together they explore other parts of the Institute, too—the sculpture hall, and a traveling show of Japanese conceptual pieces. Stevie's so caught up in it all that she forgets to be nervous about her presentation.

Over tea in the cafeteria, though, it feels as though her stomach is limbering up for backflips. "I better head over to the auditorium," she tells Margo.

"Really?" Margo checks her watch. "We've got two hours."

"I know, but I'd like to go over my notes before I change and throw on some makeup. What I should do is take a cab from here and meet up with you back at your place when it's over and done with. You really don't need to come to this thing, honest."

"Oh, no," Margo says. "Forget it. I'm not letting you walk into that lion's den all by yourself."

After buckling herself into Margo's car, Stevie mentally checks out to review her slides, her talking points, her responses should Christopher Caldwell repeat any of the nastier sentiments from his review. But when Margo swerves to avoid a cop cruiser that nearly sideswipes the Saab, Stevie's jolted back into the moment. "Can you believe that?" Margo says. "I tell you—I do *not* think of cops as my friends. If I were in trouble, I would *never* go to a cop for help. Would you?"

"Yes," Stevie says. "But I didn't have a Pollack mother."

"You're right—let's blame Evelyn! I'm sure she's why I have such a problem with authority. And it *was* different for you, Stevie. If you'd grown up tangling with Hank on a daily basis, it might be another story."

Interesting, what Margo just said, and without a shred of judgment in her voice. But what's odd is how Stevie's belly stops in mid-flip to settle down. It's not unlike what happened yesterday, when she realized that the apartment building on Bittersweet was the backdrop for the photograph of her father as a boy—the disappeared photograph that had inspired her long-ago time-traveling dream of finding him at that age. And now, thanks to Margo, she has her own copy to keep. A small thing, but it makes her feel more anchored somehow. Maybe instead of studying her notes, arming herself to the teeth against Christopher Caldwell, what she ought to do is go out with Margo for a glass of wine. That might relax her even more. She'll suggest it when they get to the auditorium. Now Margo's distracted by the traffic on Ontario.

"Damn," Margo says. "I shouldn't have come this way." She grows more visibly annoyed waiting through three changes of the same red light. Hers is the last car to cross on the fourth, and this puts them within a block of Michigan Avenue. A few more light changes and they're alongside a taxi stand at the Allerton Hotel. A police cruiser sits parked at the corner, and as Margo's car approaches, a muscular, red-haired cop strides out into the street, directly in front of the Saab, to have what looks to be a friendly discussion with a gray-haired taxi diver. "The same cop who nearly hit us, I bet," Margo grumbles. She switches on her right-turn blinker as if hoping the cop will notice. But the cop doesn't look like he cares that the light has changed again, or that he's holding up a long line of cars, or that Margo is performing a full-tilt, would-you-please-let-me-pass pantomime. Then Margo's expression changes. Tension tugs the corners of her mouth, pulling her neck muscles taut. Stevie's seen this transformation in Hank too many times not to recognize the signs. Margo is about to erupt.

Margo lays into the horn—a sharp, angry come-on-asshole blast. *Shit*. This is worse—so much worse—than what Stevie had anticipated. She sits in stunned silence, almost doubling over when a spear of stage fright stabs her gut. On top of that, there's a wave of nausea. If her stomach doesn't settle down pretty soon, she'll be puking into her Cubs cap. She'll reach the auditorium fried, incoherent, doomed by her gene pool. Provided she gets there at all.

The cop swivels around to look at Margo, his eyes wide with astonishment, then narrowing into outrage. Stevie's no lip reader, but she thinks he's hollering, "What the hell is *wrong* with you, lady?" The same question Stevie would ask if she could make her mouth move. She considers jumping out to climb into the nearest cab at the taxi stand, the one whose driver was talking to the cop before Margo lost her mind. From this angle, he looks like Roosevelt Jefferson Jr., the man who took her to O'Hare a few weeks ago. No, that can't be right—there are too many taxis in Chicago for that to be right. She's so upset she's hallucinating. But why, then, does the cabbie turn, look her dead in the eye, and smile?

"Oh, for heaven's sake," Margo cries at the cop. "Can't you just move?"

The car windows are closed; he can't hear her. But he can sure tell she's yelling back at him, and Stevie can sure tell that Margo's opinion of law enforcement officials has fulfilled itself. This one is never, ever going to be her friend. He thumps on the Saab's hood so hard that it's surprising his fist doesn't leave an imprint. Stevie would know what to do if it all weren't happening so fast, if she could be her grown-up self.

She'd tell Margo, calm down, don't play into his power trip, there is no way you can win here.

Too late.

As the light goes green again, there's an opening in the next lane and Margo cuts her wheels to the left. Stevie gasps. The cop's standing so close to Margo's fender—does she really think she can go anywhere without clipping him? But the Saab's turning radius is tight enough that Margo gets away clean, swinging sharply onto Michigan.

Then what's bound to happen seems to hit her. "He's going to follow me," Margo says. "He's going to give me a ticket. Goddamn it, that bastard's going to follow me and give me a ticket. Right? Right?"

Stevie shrugs and swallows around the knob in her throat, not sure if she's more frightened of Margo or of the cop. And not just any cop, either. A *Chicago* cop. A pissed-off Chicago cop. And is there anyone familiar with the city's history who doesn't equate pissed-off Chicago cop with trouble?

Sure enough, the cruiser comes screaming after them, the cop's voice over the loudspeaker commanding Margo to pull over.

Stevie unhooks her seat belt to reach into the back for Margo's purse, knowing she'll need her driver's license. Margo lowers her window as the cop approaches. "We were stuck in traffic for so long," she says. "I was frustrated and—"

"One more word, lady, and you're arrested. I'm going to write you two tickets." The cop notices Stevie clipping her seat belt back together. "*Three* tickets," he says, nodding at her, "that last one for your passenger not wearing a seat belt."

Finally, Stevie speaks. "I just took it off to—"

"Another word," he warns again. Then he disappears into his cruiser with Margo's license and registration papers.

Margo turns to Stevie with a smile that really ought to be more remorseful. "Well," she says, "did that remind you of anyone?"

The cop is back before Stevie can answer. She wipes damp palms across her blue-jeaned thighs, expecting more of the worst. But Margo evidently doesn't tangle with the police often enough to have a record, because instead of clapping her into handcuffs, the cop orders her to drive to the station on Larrabee Street to get her tickets, with him behind her all the way. Oh, why didn't Stevie say something sooner? Why didn't she run while she could? Why did she ever e-mail Margo to begin with? But Stevie's question for the cop is, "Could you please give her the tickets now?"

"Like I said, she gets them at the station."

"All right," Margo says, "but can I at least let my cousin out here?"

Great. Now the cop has an excuse to be suspicious about Stevie. "No." He comes around to Stevie's side of the car. "I.D., please."

"My cousin is a very well-known landscape architect," Margo informs him as he takes Stevie's license hostage. "She needs to—"

"Just drive where I say, lady."

Barking instructions over his loudspeaker, the cop herds Margo from Michigan Avenue splendor through housing project squalor, directing her to turn into a parking lot behind the police station, then walk around to the front entrance. Then he leaves his cruiser, without a backward look at them, and heads for the building's rear entrance. He must figure they're a safe bet not to flee. Stevie checks her watch. A little more than an hour until the forum is scheduled to begin. She can just imagine the field day Caldwell would have if word got out that she was a no-show on account of cooling her heels in a police station. Then those benches he hates really would be tombstones—for her career.

"I am so sorry," Margo says. "I—"

"Let's just get this over with."

Blue and white helium balloons are tethered to railings and a banner above the doors proclaims Police Appreciation Day. A jovial officer stationed at the entry nods as they walk in. "Are you here to appreciate the police today?" he inquires. Sounds of speeches and applause come from a meeting room off the lobby.

"We're here to get a ticket," Stevie says.

"*Three* tickets," Margo corrects.

The desk sergeant tells them to take a seat, and as they do, Margo pats Stevie's arm. "I bet you wish you got that cab back at the Institute."

"Don't remind me." But snapping at Margo makes her feel not just trapped but snarly, too. "What I mostly wish," she says with a sigh, "is that I'd told you all the right things so we wouldn't be sitting here now."

"Me, too."

Stevie shoots Margo a look that's not so much snarly as goggle-eyed with disbelief.

"Not that I'm blaming *you*!" Margo rushes to add. "And not that he wasn't a jerk, conducting business out in the street like that instead of on the curb. But I shouldn't have lost my head. That mistake was all mine. I should have caught it quicker, dropped it faster."

Well, at least she's got *that* right.

Stevie had brought her satchel along so she could look over her notes, but she's too panicked about making it to the auditorium in time to concentrate on anything except the cop who stopped them. He's behind a counter at the far end of the station. After consulting with another officer, he pulls out his ticket book and sits at a computer. "He's playing with us," Stevie tells Margo. "When we came along, I bet it was coming up on the end of his shift and he hadn't met his ticket quota yet. You punched the clock for him. Now he's teaching us a lesson for being in such a hurry, making us wait for him to finish all his paperwork."

"It's me he's punishing." Margo pulls out her cell phone. "I'm calling a cab for you."

But at that moment, Stevie wouldn't trust Margo to call a coin toss. "No, *I* will." She searches her wallet for the receipt on which Roosevelt Jefferson Jr. wrote "Blessings on your journey home," then pops open her own cell to punch in the phone number stamped at the top.

"Hi," she says when Roosevelt Jefferson, Jr., answers. "Was that you at the Allerton Hotel a little while ago?"

"Yes indeedy," he says, not bothering to ask who she is. Because he knows already? That's what it feels like.

"Great! I'm at the Larrabee Street station. Can you take me across town? I've got a very important meeting, and I'm desperate to get there as soon as possible."

"I'd like to help you out, but seeing as how I just caught a fare to O'Hare, well, I can't get there anytime soon."

Damn! She'd been so sure that he would save the day. "Okay, I'll call for another car."

"Drivers don't much like pickups at cop shops in rough neighborhoods. That guy on your case—he's not so bad, once you get him talking. Think you can?"

"I don't know. Maybe."

And then he's gone.

Stevie closes her phone and holds up a hand to keep Margo quiet until she's on her feet with a plan. "What are you going to do?" Margo wants to know.

"See if I can spread a little *aloha.*"

The cop by the door gives Stevie permission to step outside and untie three balloons. Then she pastes the most sincere, contrite, police-appreciating smile on her face that she can manage and strolls over to the counter, balloons bobbing overhead. "Officer," she says, "I know it's been a tough day, but maybe you've got someone at home who'd like to play with these?"

"What were you and Officer Krupke gabbing about for so long?" Margo asks as they leave the station, dashing to her car.

"Officer *Horgan.* His two-year-old son and the Cubs, mostly. They won today—six to nothing. We talked about Kaua'i, too. He went there with his wife. In the end, he decided against the seat belt thing. Just two tickets." Stevie hands them to Margo. "Reckless driving, and assault with intent. Court date's November 18. A good lawyer should be able to save your license."

"Assault with intent," Margo scoffs. "If I'd *intended* to hit him, I *would* have."

What Stevie hears is unadulterated, bullheaded Pollack bravado. "For God's sake, Margo. You can't tell that to the judge!" Then she begins to laugh despite herself, and the laugh gains such momentum that in no time at all, she's helpless to stop. As they get into the car, she doesn't feel like she's Margo's only passenger. It's as if the Saab is a ghostly conveyance, and every intense, confrontational, rebellious member of her father's family is in it with them.

"What'll you say if you have to testify?" Margo asks.

"Testify?" Instantly, Stevie sobers up. "How am I going to testify to anything other than the fact that my cousin acted like a lunatic?"

"Don't worry. We'll think of something."

Chapter 17

The forum is already in progress when Stevie and Margo arrive at the auditorium. Stevie's still wearing her flared jeans and Cubs T-shirt and cap, but she did manage to slap on some lipstick and slip into her agnès b. jacket. No time for nerves now. She has to help a backstage techie hook her laptop into the auditorium display system, then signal the coordinator when she's ready to join everybody else onstage, and wait for a break to be introduced. Done with the computer, Stevie pulls off her cap and hands it to Margo. "Leave it on," Margo hisses. "But take off the jacket."

"No way!"

"It's good P.R., trust me. And you're so feminine the baseball stuff looks zippy instead of butch."

"Not disrespectful?"

"Pretend you're Bill Murray, or Vince Vaughan. They'd eat dinner at the Pump Room wearing Cubs caps and shirts."

Who knows why *that* should dragoon her into putting the cap back on and handing Margo her jacket, but it does. Margo wets a finger to tame Stevie's right eyebrow. "Now you're ready."

The incredible thing is that she does feel ready. And maybe Margo isn't so crazy after all, because this outfit goes even further than the cheongsam did to belie Christopher Caldwell's typecasting of Stevie as a New York minimalist. A description he must be enamored of, because he repeats it in his introduction: "Ms. Stephanie Pollack, the well-known young New York minimalist."

As Stevie walks onstage, Margo applauds enthusiastically from the wings, but hardly anyone in the audience claps. Stevie nods to Caldwell, standing tall and professorial-looking at the podium in a suit and striped tie. Larry and Enrico rise to kiss her cheek. "Relax," Larry whispers. "Go get him," Enrico advises. And there you have it: the difference between the metaphysical master plantsman and the balls-out famous architect. But what she needs to do is something else, a third thing she can only sense her way toward. Stevie slides into her chair. "Sorry I'm late," she breathes into her mic. "Got caught up in some gnarly traffic."

"It's no secret I have certain issues with your garden, Ms. Pollack," Caldwell says. "As do many of those here tonight. As a lifelong Cubs fan, however, I have to say, I approve of your attire."

"Well, I'm glad for the chance to address those issues, Mr. Caldwell. I'm a fan, too—thanks to my father. He's Chicago born and bred, and we've been watching games from his house in Hawai'i. It's such good medicine for him." She switches her gaze from Caldwell to the audience. For this sort of thing, it's a big turnout. "I'd planned on dressing up for you all, honest, but there just wasn't time, and anyway, I like wearing Kerry Wood's number on the same day he pitched a shutout."

Stevie perceives a shift. Did everybody in the hall just loosen up, or is it only her? She can't tell. But there's a healthy smattering of laughter—even some applause—and by the time she steps to the podium for her presentation, it does seem less like she's been defensive than doing what her father had advised: absorbing the attack. Now she gets to take a crack at defining her own terms.

As the hall goes dark, Stevie begins with drawings and manipulated images that progress all her garden's plantings to maturity. "I especially wanted to show you these," she says, "because we put in so many ornamental grasses that haven't yet reached full breadth and height." She uncaps a laser light and points it to the Shadow Plate projected on the overhead screen. "Here you can see just how much they do to soften this section's shape, but accentuate it at the same time. I call it the Shadow Plate because, for me, it represents the dark histories so many people who came here hoped to leave behind. It's also a shade garden within the bigger garden, and as you can see, when all the foliage matures, these benches won't look nearly so much like the tombstones Mr. Caldwell compared them to. They might even grow on him."

"Pun intended, I trust," Caldwell chimes in.

"Nope, sorry. My puns are always accidental." The truth is, she had indeed thought of memorial stones when she first conceived those benches. It seemed appropriate, considering her immigration theme. But then she'd gotten lost—in pure design, in the more complicated fountain—and she's not ready to admit that now she doesn't know *what* to make of the benches. Best to keep things breezy, move on. "And here are all the tall blooms that we won't start to see on the Light Plate until next spring. Basically the same idea—softening and lifting, only with color, because the Light Plate is a brighter, more expansive space. But maybe the biggest difference of all will be the Shoulder Hedge, when it grows out to conceal and mold to the metal forms that are still so visible and cold-looking. Then the hedge will resemble the series of waves you see here—a tribute to all the different waves of immigrants who built the big-shouldered city."

So far, so good. "It's always hard to open a place when you know the public will see just a fraction of everything you've planned to be there." She clicks onto a photograph from opening day, of the Frisbee-throwing guy falling down in her fountain. "But here's one thing I did *not* plan on, and I'd really like to apologize for that mistake. I underestimated the fountain's attraction as an interactive place, and overestimated it as a meditative one, where people would be drawn to just *watch* the water, all the dips and turns it takes. So. I had to find a solution. Something to make the granite less slippery for everybody who wades into the fountain, without compromising the design." Stevie clicks onward to photos she took at Māhā'ulepū, showing grooved lithified rocks. "The solutions," she says, "are always in nature."

It's no cakewalk from there. Stevie can't tell Caldwell what the costs will be—not just for grooving the granite, but for replacing the fountain's faulty drains and repairing its innovative, ecologically correct, and wildly dysfunctional recirculating water pump. She doesn't yet know. Those figures change daily, with each new job estimate.

People in the audience raise other issues she can't address with precision. How the price of repairs will be split between her firm, the city, and donor-raised funds. When the fountain will be full and flowing again. Whether dogs will be allowed to drink from the fountain then, let alone jump into it. But none of that matters nearly so much as her certainty that she's delivered her best presentation ever. And better yet is the comment Caldwell makes before moving on to Larry's portion of the program.

"Artists have to dream," he says. "And if they make an error in bringing a dream to fruition, they ought to be given a second chance. After listening to Ms. Pollack tonight, I'm starting to rethink my position on her mistakes. While it remains true that those mistakes created the situation that's such a nuisance now, I predict that in the end they'll represent a moment of controversy in the long life of a good public place. However, I don't believe I'll ever care much for her benches."

There's a backstage reception afterward, but before a crowd has time to gather, Stevie slips off to call Japhy, trotting past tables set up for drinks and pupus. *No, canapés,* she reminds herself. *This is Chicago, remember?*

Now Stevie feels sure of how big a part making love with Japhy played in holding her together out there. Now she's ready to tell him how glad she is it happened. Now she'd like to hear whatever it was he'd wanted to let her know out by the *kukui* trees, which probably amounts to the same thing.

"I've been feeling bad since you left," he says.

"Don't feel bad. I'll be back soon."

"No, it's not that."

"Then what?"

"You were pretty upset when I found you. Plus you were naked, and I don't know—it just seems like I took advantage."

"Is that all? Don't worry, there's an explanation. I was just too shaken up to tell you then."

"That's what I mean. I shouldn't have rushed things. I should have waited."

"You weren't the only one involved, Japhy."

"Okay. *We* should have waited."

"I'm not good at waiting."

And then, as if to give her some much-needed practice, he says, "Hold on, Stevie." Nothing but seconds of silence on his end until he clears his throat and returns to her with a heavy sigh. "I want to tell you more—just not on the phone. When do you get here?"

"Thursday."

"We'll talk then."

We should have waited. Just a gentleman's way of saying "I wish I hadn't fucked you." Stevie can't consider mingling yet, not before ordering a drink to help restore her sense of triumph. As the bartender hands over a vodka martini, Enrico shows up at her elbow. "From the look on your face," he says, "I guess you already know."

"So what's my line here?" Stevie takes a swallow that goes straight to her head. Except for the fact that she's drinking vodka instead of champagne, it's the garden opening all over again, with her once more dumped—or almost, anyway, from the sound of it—and behind the curve. "Could you please just cut to the chase?"

"The chase indeed. Call me romantic, Stevie, but I thought you'd be *glad* to see him here."

Her eyes follow Enrico's gaze to where Christopher Caldwell stands, engrossed in conversation with a man whose back is turned to her. She can't see the man's face, but she can tell who it is from the slope of his shoulders, from the elegant cut of his fine, sandy hair, from the Italian cordovan jacket she gave him for his birthday. Stevie puts her drink aside to grab a handful of nuts. In a situation like this, protein's better than alcohol. "What's Brian doing here?"

"He says a project brought him to town. I think her name is Stevie. Don't tell me you're surprised."

"But I am!"

"Didn't you see him out there, leading the applause?"

"No." Stevie flashes on one of Kiko's pronouncements, about how pheromones always wear off after a few years. And when they do, well, look out. Fantasy kicks in and before you know it, you're having moonlit sex in a sleeping bag with some guy you barely know. Nothing more than a little fling—certainly nothing to get whacked out over, not on a night when she ought to be proud of herself. If it weren't for Hank's illness and her own career catastrophe knocking her so far off-kilter, she might never have gone blind as a wolf spider, ignoring all her doubts. There's still time ahead with Hank, and her reputation's not so sullied she has to hide out in Hawai'i for the rest of her life the way Grandpa did. Not after tonight.

Stevie starts moving through the throng in Brian's direction, but before she's taken three steps, Margo sails over with the garden's major private donor in tow. "Mrs. Levanthal," Stevie stops to say, "how nice to see you again." Margo and Elizabeth Schaeffer Levanthal—what an odd couple. Margo so exuberant and obviously her age, Mrs. Levanthal so reserved and well-preserved that she might as well be frozen at forty. Although Mrs. Levanthal married into a family fortune built on home-hair-dye kits—the kind that eventually turn women's hair into parched, uniformly colored manes of straw—her chic pageboy is a lustrous salon marvel of ginger laced with coppery highlights.

"I was just having the most delightful chat with Liz here," Margo says. *Liz?* Stevie cuts her eyes at Margo, pleading with her to be quiet or, better yet, just go away, but her cousin babbles on, oblivious. "Of course, to Liz, I was only ever the sweet little cinnamon roll girl—hey, score an accidental pun for me, too. But she and Mother worked together on all sorts of charity bashes."

"Fund-raising events, Margo," Mrs. Levanthal chides.

The last Stevie heard from New York, La Levanthal, as she's known in the office, was "most unhappy" with all the snafus in *her* garden—which it officially is, since her name is the one appearing on the entrance plaque. But now her expression comes the closest to animated that Stevie has seen. "I had no idea," Mrs. Leventhal tells her, "that you were Evelyn's niece."

"Neither did I."

"You didn't?"

And while Stevie fumbles for an explanation, Margo laughs and pats her back in a maternal way, as if Stevie's gaucheness might be resolved with a single hearty burp. "Don't worry, you were eloquent when it counted." Then, to Mrs. Levanthal: "What Stevie means is she didn't know that you and Mother were friendly. I can't think why I didn't tell her sooner."

"Yes," Mrs. Levanthal says, "we had many common interests. Well, Stephanie, the important thing is, we're on track again. You'll want to seriously consider backrests for those benches. Otherwise, stick to your guns and don't worry about the financing. Financing is where I excel."

It's so crowded that Stevie doesn't notice Brian standing nearby until Mrs. Levanthal turns to speak with someone else. "And eavesdropping is where *I* excel," Brian says. "When a client tells you 'Don't worry about the financing,' it's time to go out and celebrate. That's where I come in." Brian leans close to kiss Stevie's cheek. "I was half expecting you to be a wreck up there," he whispers, a hint of gin and olive on his breath. "But you were *great.* You looked great, too. Congratulations."

"Thanks for coming. That means a lot to me."

"I know what a shit-storm this project's been ever since it opened. At least, that's the word. And I heard about your father. What a load to deal with all at once, and on top of what happened with us. You really hid it well."

"That's funny," she tells him. "I felt pretty naked up there."

"Naked, eh?"

It's been so long since Brian's flirted with her, it takes a moment to realize that's what he's doing. But honesty compels her to clarify. "It didn't feel like I was hiding anything."

Brian's idea for celebrating, it turns out, is taking Stevie to one of the city's finest restaurants, and he seems especially pleased when he learns she's never been there before. Then, giving her sporty clothes a measuring look, he says, "I guess you could go like that." But there's no question that the outfit she'd planned to wear in the first place would be more appropriate, so she arranges to meet him outside the auditorium after a trip to Margo's car.

"This Brian," Margo says as she and Stevie take the elevator down to the garage. "He's an architect, isn't he?"

"Yep. How could you tell?"

"The Rado watch was a clue, but his glasses were the dead giveaway. Deconstructed Philip Johnson."

Stevie laughs. "Very good."

"You don't spend your life in Chicago without learning *something* about architects." Margo unlocks the Saab's trunk. "They look the part, usually. You'd never take one for an accountant. So is this a business dinner?"

"That's not why I'd like to be alone with him." Stevie stows her computer, satchel, and Cubs cap, then opens the front door and stands behind it to wriggle out of her jeans and T-shirt and into her agnès b. slacks, blouse, and jacket, with Margo flanking to ensure that if anybody comes along, they won't be able to catch much of her quick-change act. "Actually," Stevie continues, "it's more like an unfinished-business dinner. We were a couple for almost three years. He broke off with me the day before I met you."

"Now I get it. He wants you back."

Stevie tucks her blouse and zips her pants. "Maybe."

"You're not still mad about the cop, are you?"

"Everything turned out fine, don't worry about the cop." Stevie returns to the trunk for her heels. "In fact," she adds as Margo hands over a spare apartment key, "don't worry about anything. That's *my* plan for the evening."

Stevie and Brian take a taxi to St. Clair Street, where they enter an impeccably finished loft-like space. Talk about minimal. If this place weren't a restaurant, if there were sculptures on the floor and massive paintings on the bright white walls, it could easily be one of the SoHo art galleries where she and Brian sometimes attended openings.

It's late enough on an ordinary weeknight that they're able to get a table after a short wait, and no sooner are they seated than a team of skilled servers in designer suits starts attending to them. Clearly, dining here is no casual enterprise. It's a theatrical event. An impression only furthered when the appetizer Brian ordered appears on a glass spiral staircase, an ascending arrangement of crème fraiche, capers, diced onion, and chopped hard-boiled egg, plus four different sturgeon caviars in four different colors—black, green, orange, and yellow.

Brian raises his champagne flute for Stevie to clink with hers. After she does, he shakes his head and keeps her from sipping with a hand on her wrist. "No, no," he says. "When you clink, you have to look the other person in the eye. Otherwise you get seven years of bad sex."

Which only reminds Stevie of her most recent sex, how excellent it was. Not just technically adept but tender, too. Real intimacy, not fake. Or so she'd thought. No point getting all twisted up there, though, not with her partner in that enterprise regretting that it ever even happened. She must respond to what Brian's saying before her body starts remembering another man's, before desire beckons her down that mine shaft again and she dives in headfirst like some stupid moony teenager. "Is it me who'd get the seven years of bad sex, or both of us?"

"Sorry, babe. Just you."

Stevie smiles, gluing her eyes to Brian's as they clink again. "Nobody," she says, "deserves that kind of punishment."

"I sure wouldn't want it starting up tonight."

He leans over their shared corner of the table to give her a kiss that's brief, but dense with implications. This dinner will be not just foreplay but full-fledged gastro porn. It will be the sort of sensual urban adventure Brian's so great at creating, a huge part of his charm, and tonight it's all for her. She could have fallen on her face onstage at the forum, and then he would have brought her here to lift her spirits. As it is, he's showing that he can be on her side when she's riding high. Especially nice, considering how poorly Brian took it when Stevie ended up receiving far more recognition for the symphony hall in Pittsburgh they'd collaborated on than he did. Was that the *real* start of their troubles?

"I'm glad you're with me," Brian says as they build caviar and fixings onto toast points.

"Me, too. This is really special."

"I would never have ordered it just for myself."

Tiny bubbles of caviar pop between Stevie's teeth, hitting the taste bud equivalent of the G-spot. Brian's right. Food so exquisite as this is meant to be shared. Consuming it alone would be not a little like masturbation.

"What you want to do now," Brian says, "is make your donor happy with those benches. Then your next best move? Get your work published. Ask Caldwell to write the introduction. That'll *really* shove him all the way into your corner and neutralize the situation."

"Good idea."

"And if you put everything you've got into snaring another major project before the cost of fixing this one leaks out, then Chicago is history."

"I'm sure you're right."

As black truffle lobster risotto appears on marble tiles, Stevie feels an urge to mention that small-time project in Līhu'e—the one Japhy told her about—as an alternative to the course of action Brian's suggesting. How perverse. Brian's advice is politically astute. She's just so far from being ready to act on it that he might as well be telling her to circumnavigate the universe and, while she's at it, bring back some lunar dust. Her problem, not his. He cares. That's the important thing.

"You know," Brian muses, "what Caldwell said tonight about your garden could apply to us. We messed up, no question. But maybe someday we'll look back on the mess as just a bad patch we pulled ourselves through."

"How do you see us doing that?"

"Forgiving and forgetting. Starting fresh." His leg brushes against hers as he leans in closer. "Learning from our mistakes, not repeating them." Then his head swivels to watch their servers return, wheeling a cart up to the table. "Look, they're going to finish the roast duck here."

Stevie appreciates his excitement. The tastes and textures of these delicacies are so intoxicating that their past problems seem like a wilted, dreary side dish. Brian has dropped everything to be here. He's trying to make a nice new memory for them to share. All she has to do is enjoy. "I wonder," Stevie says, "what kind of vinegar they're deglazing with."

❁

After chocolate soufflés with thyme ice cream and decaf espressos, Stevie suggests a walk.

Brian ushers her outside with a hand at the small of her back—possibly the most suggestive place a man can touch a woman wearing clothes, yet she feels nothing rise up in response beyond a certain flat familiarity. She's defended herself too well against Brian—that's the problem. She doesn't remember what it's like to be in love with him. Her mind reels back to pre-ectopic times, before sex became so fraught, when she could get lost in their kisses, the rhythms of their quickening breath. That restores fizz to his touch.

It's a beautiful late-September night, clear and cool, with a gentle wind blowing in off the lake. As they reach the broad sidewalk of Michigan Avenue, adorned with flower beds and crowded even at this late hour, Brian says, "Let's head north." Then, because he knows all about her directional deficiency, he takes Stevie by the shoulders to turn her the right way. "I'm staying at the Drake," he informs her as they pass Brooks Brothers display windows.

"Is that where we're headed?"

"Well, we are walking in that direction."

"The Drake is my father's favorite hotel."

"Really?"

"I told you about staying there with him on my very first trip to Chicago. That's how I got to know the city. Remember?"

"Now I do."

"And when he was in college, Dad worked at the Drake as a night clerk. We talked about that the night we had dinner with him."

"I knew he was in hotels. I only got into the Drake because they had a last-minute cancellation. We're lucky some visiting Cubs fan didn't beat me to it—Chicago's crawling with them."

"Not surprising," Stevie says. "Their next few home games are big ones."

"My first choice was the Raphael Hotel. If you go down Mies van der Rohe Way from the Drake and turn the corner, there it is."

"Yes. 201 East Delaware Place. I know it."

She closes her eyes for a moment, willing him to confess that he's teasing her, that this urge of his to stay at the Raphael had sprung from his heart because that was where *they* were supposed to spend a romantic night before the garden opening—before their breakup fight, which started over his cancelling on her at the last minute. She wants to be touched by Brian doing something as sentimental and loving—as corny, even—as that. When he doesn't bring it up, there seems no point in reminding him when she'd been at the Raphael, much less sharing the treasure of her story about Hank once living in the very same rooms where she'd stayed, risking a smudge of disappointment should Brian fail to find it remarkable.

The kind of magic he embraces is just so different. It's the meal they shared tonight. It's having a home he designed featured in *Architectural Digest* someday. It's Mies van der Rohe—far too minimalist even for Stevie's taste, but one of Brian's idols. Brian's poor memory isn't any crime, either; like a lot of people in design, he retains visual information far better than verbal. And unlike her, he's also had quite a lot to drink. Still, in their time together, she'd opened up to him in ways she seldom did with anyone. That it left such a small impression makes her feel . . . what? Ignored? No. Erased. Forgiveness is one thing, but how much else of what matters to her so deeply has he already forgotten, or will he forget in the future, and can she live with that?

God is in the details.

Brian would recognize the quote, since it's from Mies himself.

Well, love is in the details, too.

And when Brian again expresses concern about her father—"It must be hard," he says, "what's going on in Hawai'i"—she can't bring herself to discuss why spending her time with Hank is more imperative by far than kissing La Levanthal's derriere, or buttering up Caldwell, or chasing after a new commission. Not that Brian wouldn't listen. If he really wants her back he might even remember. But somehow she's certain that none of what she has to say would mean nearly so much to him as she'd like. Especially when it came to harder-to-explain things—like Pele, Pip, Puolo Point salt, the Cubs' clinch, and how unaccountably guilty and distraught she feels being away from Hank for a few days, considering that she left with his blessing and he seems to be holding steady. What's more, there's dirt on her heart from the mere thought of sleeping with Brian again and not saying a word about Japhy. Why should that be? It doesn't make sense. If she's willing to give Brian another chance, such a confession would be not only a tactical error, but unkind to boot. Also stupid. She hadn't been unfaithful.

Brian takes her hand, his grip slackening after an initial squeeze. She notices his palms, how smooth and dry they are. Tempting to loosen her wrist, just to see if he'd catch her hand before it dropped away. As they walk along—slowing to inspect windows at Marshall Field, pausing to scope the John Hancock Tower's X-braced exterior—it comes to Stevie that, in a way, they're here together under false pretenses. The woman he'd applauded tonight was the confident, radiant, fresh-from-lovemaking Stevie, the island girl full of her own nature and already doing everything possible to work things out with a difficult man—her father. It doesn't matter what happened, or might happen, with Japhy. She can't be that woman with Brian.

As they reach the Drake, she lets her wrist go limp and watches, as though observing a lab experiment, while her hand falls out of Brian's. When he steps ahead to hold the door open, Stevie stops and touches his arm. "I'm sorry," she says. "I thought I could do this, I honestly did. But it's not what I need."

Stevie lets herself into Margo's apartment and finds her cousin in the living room, wrapped in a coral-colored terry-cloth robe with pen in hand and a yellow legal pad on her lap. "I wasn't sure I'd see you tonight," she says, "so I was just writing you a note about my e-mail from Hank. He was anxious to hear how your presentation went."

Stevie flops down beside Margo on the velvety purple couch strewn with kilim-covered pillows. Her cousin's face shines with moisture, and she smells soothingly of lavender swirled with rose and clove. Funny, how Margo speaks of Evelyn as being such a knockout, when for Stevie, Margo's the real stunner. Not that she's without flaws. An aristocratic nose that extends a touch beyond what a plastic surgeon would pronounce perfect. Bottom teeth a bit snaggled. Porcelain skin marked with faint traces of long-ago acne. But somehow, the sum is greater for the glitches, and without them, Margo's beauty wouldn't be so much more inviting than Evelyn's. "I called Dad on the way over. He said you sent him a full report. Thanks."

"I didn't say a word about the police, or your stalker, either."

"Stalker?"

"That's what *I* call a guy who only wants you when he thinks maybe he can't have you. What's so funny?"

"That day in the park, Margo, I thought *you* were a stalker. But it's just as well you didn't mention Brian to Dad."

"No point worrying him, I thought. Only I really ought to own that projection. *I'm* the one who hoped you wouldn't end up spending the night with Brian. That's what you were planning, isn't it?"

"Not planning, considering."

Over another pot of orange-ginger-mint tea, Stevie tells Margo about her time on the island with Japhy, their deflating phone conversation before the reception, how seeing Brian had jolted her back into reality. But what Margo keeps asking about is her breakup with Brian, the troubles that preceded it. After spitting all that out, Stevie sighs. "Let's change the subject. He's history now. My friend Lorna thinks the first significant thing you can remember a man saying tells the whole story. With Brian, the gist was, 'Here's what works for me.' "

"Hmm," Margo responds. "Maybe your friend is on to something there. Kenny's first words were, 'Let's go someplace we can talk,' and he had to shout because we were at a Led Zeppelin concert. It really stuck for some reason—probably for being such a refreshing change from 'Let's go someplace we can screw.' Not that he wasn't up for that, too. But once we started talking, I just felt so, I don't know, cared for. But I still don't get how come you rolled the dice again with Mr. Here's What Works for Me. After how he hurt your heart, why did you even *imagine* you could work things out with him?"

"Weren't you listening? I just said he's history, didn't I? If I didn't know better, I'd think he dumped me all over again. But *I'm* the one who walked away."

"Thank God. Since you're the one who betrayed herself tonight going out with him in the first place."

"Whoa! Stop right there. What you just said—that is *not* how I see it."

"No," Margo says, patting Stevie's shoulder. "No, of course not. I've got a lot of nerve, pounding away at you like this, and I wouldn't be, I swear, if we weren't family. I mean, what if a withholding man punches all *your* buttons just like a cop does mine?"

Stevie moans as she pinches the bridge of her nose, then presses palms into her cheeks. "I've had enough psychology tonight," she says, starting to stand. "I'm going to bed."

"I'm sorry." As Margo pats the place beside her on the couch, her voice takes an irresistible cajoling turn. "Stay a little longer, please?"

Stevie falls back against the pillows, arms folded tight across her chest. "You make me sound desperate to be married, like that's my only ambition, and it isn't. I've never been traditional. I'm not like you, Margo."

"No, not a traditional female."

"What's that supposed to mean?"

"Nothing critical, I promise. Someone with your talent *ought* to be ambitious."

"If you're talking about my career, I prefer to be considered daring."

"How about audacious?"

Stevie laughs. "That works for me."

"Call me a yenta, Stevie, but I'd like to see you in a great relationship with a man who's just deep-down good to you."

"So would I! But it's not like I think I'm worthless without a man. I'm not a woman like that. I can't even stand the *idea* of being a woman like that. I was just looking at what was in front of me. Brian there to celebrate and this other guy pushing me away, wanting to undo something I thought was pretty special."

"But *you're* the one coming up with all the crummy reasons for why Whosis said what he did on the phone."

"Japhy."

"What's that, a family name?"

"No, from a Kerouac novel. I looked it up online. Japhy Ryder—he's the character in *The Dharma Bums.* Japhy Hungerford—he's the vet in Kaua'i."

"You just did it again."

"What?"

"Every time you say his name, you touch your chest. Not like you're feeling yourself up or anything, but right above your breast. The heart chakra, according to the woo-woo crowd. And believe it or not, I would have been a card-carrying member once upon a time except for the fact that I could *not* stop eating meat. So how good was it with him?"

"I don't know how to answer that." Stevie kicks off her shoes and tucks her legs beneath her, too stirred up for sleep now. "Ever made love after you saw a shooting star and Night Marchers walked on your back and your head was full of night-blooming jasmine and nobody said a word even though it happened like something you'd always hoped would happen but never even knew you did?"

"I can tell you this with absolute certainty. No, I have not."

"Well, it's not easy to describe."

"It did happen, though. Which probably means it's serious. Japhy doesn't sound like the one-night-stand type."

"If you've got better explanations than mine for what he said, I'd like to hear them."

Lips pursed, Margo slowly shakes her head. "I have no idea what's eating him. Neither do you, though, and that's my point."

It's an interesting point, Stevie thinks later, as she sinks into bed. It had made her twitchy, the headlong way Margo raced to conclusions, but maybe she was on to something after all. *I'm so geared to rejection I assume it's there even when it's not, and when it is, what do I do? Act like Pip—wriggle all over and walk on my hind legs to change it. I can't see acceptance when it's staring me in the face. No wonder I've trusted men I shouldn't, mistrusted ones I should.*

How differently might she carry her conversation with Japhy if she were as convinced as Margo that whatever was going on with him didn't mean anything awful about her? She comforts herself to sleep with the question.

But her dreams that night are not peaceful. They play out like a movie edited by someone cranked up on speed, one jagged jump cut after another. In one frame she's boarding a jet with a Night Marcher painted on its tail, and in the next, she's bouncing in her seat while the engines turn into missiles that fire off one by one. She strains to see what's below, but the next cut takes her to a landing strip suspended on clouds where passengers are greeted with fragrant tuberose lei. "Are we dead?" she asks the pilot, who turns out to be Japhy. "No," he says, "we're not dead. We're in Kaua'i."

Such a nonsensical bunch of fragments that, on awakening, she can only write them off to travel anxiety and concern for Hank. Anyway, there are more pressing things to do this morning than analyze her dreams. She has to get herself to the garden.

Frank Acosta plows grooves into the emptied fountain's surface with a diamond-bladed saw housed in an apparatus resembling a lawn mower. Since the saw's gas engine roars louder than a mower, both Frank and Stevie wear ear protectors in addition to their safety glasses, face masks, and work boots. Water pours out of an attached hose to cool the blade and wet down the machine's trail of granite particles. It's evident how in sync Frank is with Stevie's specs, steering expert cuts so that the fountain, when it's filled again, will drain efficiently. Before long, she feels superfluous. It's not rocket science, this method she's chosen for making the granite less slippery. Still, the fountain's her baby and she's so riveted by the process that she doesn't take her eyes from the job until it's time to break for lunch.

As Frank switches off the saw, Stevie pulls down her mask and sets aside the safety glasses and ear protectors. Looking beyond the newly laid ryegrass, the ring of yellow caution tape still surrounding the fountain, she feels her breath catch at what she sees. Every single bench within view is occupied—by students, seniors, mothers and small children, dog walkers, bicyclists, and a few brown-baggers obviously on their own lunchtime breaks. One wears a UPS uniform; another's in a three-piece suit. And while some sit facing the fountain, many more are turned elsewhere—toward the lake, toward the Light Plate's meadow, toward the Shadow Plate's trees.

"Look," Stevie tells Frank. "People!"

He gives her a quizzical smile. "You were expecting some other species?"

"I wasn't expecting *anybody*—not on the benches."

"Well, it's a beautiful day."

"I'll say!"

Stevie would scare these people away if she abandoned her turkey sandwich to run around doing what she feels like doing, which is hug them all in gratitude. Not just for coming here today, but for demonstrating exactly why her benches are fine just as they are. The benches don't need backrests. Backrests would dictate which direction to face, what everyone ought to be looking at. But without backrests, they're free to decide for themselves.

Stevie hadn't imagined this freedom when she'd designed the benches. What made them turn out like they did stemmed from her flaw—her trouble distinguishing north from south, east from west. She couldn't decide which direction to favor over the rest, and so her decision was no decision. Which she now sees as a marvelous accident, maybe even the best thing about her garden. Not so grand as the fountain, maybe, but more human, somehow. She had it wrong in her presentation. It isn't plants that will keep the benches from looking like tombstones. It's people.

When Stevie finishes with the fountain, Roosevelt Jefferson Jr. picks her up and drives his immaculate Crown Victoria all the way out on Cicero Avenue so she can shop at George's Music Room—the best place in all the city for buying blues. She had confessed to Mr. Jefferson her urge—no, compulsion—to own a copy of "Ain't No Grave," the exact version she'd heard on the radio during their first trip together. An eyes-of-heaven song for sure. The trouble is, neither of them knows the artist's name.

While Mr. Jefferson waits in the cab with his crossword puzzle, Stevie runs inside George's and describes to a clerk the rendition she's looking for: "A capella, a woman singing her guts out and stamping her feet so that even if you didn't understand a word of English, you'd get the song, how it's about spirit surviving death. Definitely gospel-tinged, but with this power that reminds me of Hawaiian chants. Maybe that's just because I'm from Hawai'i. The thing is, I'm going back soon and I *have* to have it."

What an outpouring. But the clerk nods as if people speak to him this way all the time. Then he goes straight to a bin labeled "B" and pulls out a CD with a striking brunette on the cover. "I think this is what you're looking for," he says.

Just as Stevie had suspected, the singer who so eerily conveyed the essence of an elderly black man is not black herself. Rory Block—another *haole* girl with a guy's name, the souls of ancients rumbling around inside.

It was a huge detour, going to George's, and heading back to Lincoln Park, they crawl along Lake Shore Drive, still clogged with rush hour traffic. But for reasons Stevie can't explain, that particular song, sung by that particular person, is a necessary companion to whatever lies ahead in Kaua'i. It's also somehow essential to whatever shot she still has at becoming Her Own Person Stevie.

Chapter 18

Stevie on the phone turned Japhy into an idiot. He couldn't help it. When she called it was nighttime in Chicago but afternoon in Kaua'i, with him still at work. If he went any deeper, what cracked open inside might be more than he could handle. He didn't want to risk that, not with surgeries to evaluate, stitches to remove, conditions to diagnose. Besides, while they spoke, Christine had walked into his office, delivering charts he wouldn't need for another day. A flimsy pretext for the chance to overhear him on the phone with the woman whose call she'd just transferred. If Christine were a dog her ears would have pricked when she caught him saying, "We should have waited."

To tell Stevie what he must, he needed them to be close. So he could see the intensity in those smoky, feline eyes of hers. So they could touch. So he could say, *Before this goes any further, there's something you should know.* That's the statement he'd taken pains to devise and memorize for their picnic, the sentence Jerry's accident had forced him to file away for later. But every word had flown from his head the moment he found Stevie in the dark, naked and screaming.

What does he tell her instead? *I should have waited.* Not only bogus, but starchy, stupid, mainland-*haole* sounding—like those buttoned-up old-time missionaries he's read about, so obsessed with quashing Hawaiian sexuality that they passed laws against "rascally sleeping." Truth is, there's nothing Japhy regrets. Mystifying—that's what his lovemaking with Stevie was. Not rascally. The only shame would have been if it never happened. And it never would have if he hadn't bolted up awake again at three thirty in the morning.

That night, he'd given up on going back to sleep, knowing for a fact he'd already had as much as he would get. Might as well chase those devil-hour demons, he figured. Might as well get something useful done. And so he slipped on his jeans, made a pot of coffee, and went to work in the living room, boxing up things for the move to Waimea. The CD of Hawaiian chant and drum music kept him busy to the beat. No lingering. No rereading inscriptions in books he and Alana had given each other. No flipping through photo albums she'd put together. Which was exactly what he'd done the last time he moved. Impossible to avoid remembering, but he wasn't ready for a repeat of that drawn-out process. Wasn't ready to discover whether doing it again would rip him raw as before, or be easier to bear. Either way held its own kind of pain.

He hadn't gotten far—only one box half-full of fiction, with authors Agee to Irving—when Rainier bolted out from the bedroom, pawed at the front door, and barked her sharp, insistent bark. Bizarre behavior, unless she was sick. But with Rainier, sick meant dashing to the nearest tree to relieve herself, and when Japhy opened the door, she skidded to a stop at the edge of the lanai, refusing to go any farther. Then she threw her nose in the air, sniffed, and jumped back on all fours as if threatened by what she'd smelled. Skittering over to Japhy's side, she raised her head and howled.

Good thing none of Japhy's neighbors lived close by—they'd *all* be awake. He went back indoors, turned off the stereo, grabbed a flashlight, and tried to coax Rainier off the lanai. No dice, even though he shined the flashlight everywhere to prove that whatever wandering creature her nose saw—and a dog's nose *did* work like vision—was no longer around. At least she stopped howling. Now she just panted, whined, and looked at him with imploring eyes. He'd never known of a dog as old as Rainier going through a fear phase, but that's how he decided to treat the cause of whatever was bugging her.

"Come," he called. When she didn't respond, he walked beyond the foliage and trees at the far border of Hank's broad yard, flashlight trained ahead so he wouldn't step barefoot on *kukui* nuts or *kiawe* thorns. Once Rainier lost sight of him, she loped over. Still, her hackles were raised.

As Japhy turned back for the cottage he froze, feeling a tremor beneath his feet. It lasted only a few seconds. A fleeting temblor—not unusual here. Well, that explained it. Animals were sensitive to even mild quakes, often sounding advance alarms. "It's okay," he told Rainier. "All over." That's when he spotted Stevie, sprawled on her stomach by a stand of *kukui* trees.

Japhy ran over in a state of heart-chilled terror, thinking her dead after some terrible attack. When he reached her side she stirred, rising to her knees. Breath left his body all at once, like from a gut-punch, while he bent down to touch the cool, moist skin on her shoulder. As if wakened from a nightmare, Stevie jumped, screamed, then curled shivering into his arms.

Rainier was too discreet a dog to linger.

Japhy could have said his piece, could have let Stevie know what she was getting into, if only she hadn't hushed him and rushed off so soon after waking. As it is, he hopes to rectify his phone-call idiocy by meeting her plane.

When he calls Hank's house first thing after breakfast, still sitting at the kitchen table, Lila gives him all of Stevie's flight information. She also offers to leave keys to Hank's wheels under the driver's seat, because it's supposed to rain and this way, Japhy won't have to tarp luggage in the back of his pickup. "Was she planning to rent a car?" Japhy asks.

"Hank won't hear of her doing that again," Lila says. "I offered to get them myself, but Stevie, well, *she* wouldn't hear of *that.* Said not to bother, they'd take a taxi. Should we let her know you'll be waiting, or do you want to surprise her?"

"Let's keep it a surprise." There's a sensible reason for his preference. What if an animal emergency comes up at the last minute? He wouldn't want to disappoint Stevie yet again. But his bigger reason is something deeper. Apart from all her competence and accomplishments, Stevie strikes him as someone who's been shortchanged when it comes to happy surprises. She needs more, especially these days. That's his hunch, anyway. Look at the thrill she got from keeping Pip, from their impromptu lunch at Hamura's, from their picnic's secret destination—not to mention their powerful, unexpected lovemaking. He wants to see that look of unguarded pleasure on her face again, knowing that he put it there. In fact, he can't wait.

But he'll have to wait—all day long. Stevie's plane doesn't get in until eight ten tonight.

Japhy parks a pencil behind his ear, fetches the phone book, and sits again to check on her flights. According to the information Lila gave him, Stevie should still be in the air on the first leg of her journey, from Chicago to Los Angeles. But after he punches in the flight number, the automated airline information service transfers him to a human being, a woman who tells him that Stevie's flight from Chicago was cancelled due to equipment failure. At the words "equipment failure," the cheese toast Japhy had for breakfast rises in his throat. *Don't overreact,* he admonishes himself. They'd caught *this* equipment failure on the ground, not in the air. The way they were supposed to. Fortunately, he'd asked Lila for Stevie's confirmation number, which the clerk needs in order to tell him that Stevie was rerouted to Seattle, where she would catch another plane to Los Angeles.

"There's an airline change from Seattle to L.A.," the clerk is saying now. "For that leg of the trip she'll be flying on— Wait a minute, my computer went down."

Japhy coils in on himself, rapping his thigh with the flat of his palm, already so certain of which airline Stevie will be on that when the clerk finally utters its name, he leaps to his feet. "Those motherfucking asshole sons of bitches!"

"Sir!" the clerk says. "There's no need to get belligerent."

Japhy chokes back his rage. She's right, of course. How was she to know? Los Angeles—where Flight 261 from Puerto Vallarta was supposed to make an emergency landing. Seattle—where he'd been waiting for Alana to arrive with their baby. And the same carrier, too.

"I'm sorry," he says. "My wife and daughter . . ." But the line's gone dead.

His stomach lurches again from imagining Stevie aboard one of those jets with the smiling Eskimo's face painted on the tail. The face that had never failed to show up in Japhy's time of nightmares. The mascot's smile added a surreal dimension to the horror, mutated from the calm, pleasant expression that it was into a satanic smirk, mocking Flight 261's hurtling descent into the sea.

After the news broke that inadequate maintenance had caused the crash, countless people told Japhy they could never bring themselves to fly that airline again—correctly assuming he wouldn't be able to, either. But as time passed, it became clear that far more people he'd never met felt otherwise. There's a reason, he's learned. Something known as post-tragedy vigilance. Airlines are thought to double down on safety after a crash. Anyway, he can't justify calling Stevie's cell with a demand to change her flight to L.A. All he can do is deal with the fear, with the razor-sharp shards of grief unearthed by his fury.

Japhy supposes that if Stevie had been curious enough, if she'd been wary enough of him, if she'd had time enough to burn, she would already know what he hasn't told her yet. She would have found out the same way that Christine, his officer manager, did—by performing one of those Google searches, the stealth mode of finding out about other people. He's glad Stevie hasn't gone that route. It had been weird, walking into the clinic and being confronted with Christine's tearful embrace, him rushing to comfort and make whatever was upsetting her easier somehow, wanting to fill that role, to expand into the space for others that had opened up again, only to be told, "No, *I'm* okay—it's *you* I'm feeling bad for."

He didn't like how stodgy he'd sounded to himself after she said that. "I would prefer that you not discuss my situation with anyone else." As if Alana and Megan's deaths could ever be defined as a "situation." As if he'd caught Christine stealing instead of snooping. Though maybe "fishing" is a better description for what she'd done, throwing out the line of his unusual name and the city of Seattle, expecting to reel in only evidence of his expertise, the professional organizations he's joined, maybe a hobby or two. Not the sort of information that makes you cry. Whatever her reasons, it seems Christine kept her word. At least he hasn't been ambushed by a pitying hug from anybody else. Hasn't taken any hits to the solar plexus lately, either, the kind that used to land when the stray person who barely knew him felt entitled to say strange things, usually variations on "Well, I guess *your* number wasn't up yet."

It wasn't Japhy's plan to make a mystery of his loss when he moved to Kaua'i. What he wanted to avoid was being defined by it, as he'd come to be in Seattle. When at last he'd been ready to work again, this had hampered tending to his clients. Whom he considered to be the animals he cared for no less than the humans whom he advised, educated, and consoled when necessary. The animals forced him into the present moment, then into his knowledge, then into his skills—the internal rising tide that must flow out again. The animals were true, full of their own individual natures. Even when aggressive, their intentions were easy to read, never convoluted or hidden. But the animals' humans always brought up the crash, if only with questions in their eyes. *Is he really ready to work again? Should I say something about it? Do I want to know more than I already do?* Studying him as if he were the one who required help.

Which, of course, he did. He got it, too. Not only from family and friends standing by to help carry the terrible weight of those first few years, but from the people *he* paid.

From Sunitra, his physician, who prescribed aids for his appetite, his anxiety, his sleep.

From Rachel, his therapist, who believed so fervently in healing through what she called "the dark emotions" that he kept coming back, hoping a little of her faith might rub off.

From Jenny, the operator of Super Happy Fun Dog Care Company, who picked up Rainier every morning in an old school bus, took her to one of Seattle's off-leash parks, and brought her home to Queen Anne

Hill exhausted, leaving behind a note that detailed her activities. *"Rainier's starting to perk up,"* Jenny would write. *"She had a blast in the lake today, and her new best friend is Murphy the standard schnauz, another ball-aholic. I might be their alpha bitch, but I'm also their enabler, and when they get into a twelve-step program, me and my arm expect apologies."* He was glad for Jenny's sense of humor, for how she kept Rainier active and healthy when he didn't have the heart to. But after a while he crumpled her notes without reading them. They reminded him too much of all the glowing progress reports that would never be written for Megan.

Japhy had to hire an attorney, too—for the court case stemming from the crash, wrongful-death lawsuits filed by surviving relatives. He forced himself to attend the federal hearing in Washington, D.C., getting on a plane for the first time since Alana and Megan plunged into the Pacific. Rationally, he knew all the heightened airport security precautions and inspections were because of 9/11. But watching footage of the fiery crashes had only heightened his anguish, and now, set loose again in this altered world, he couldn't help feeling that all the extra care resulted from the other crash. The earlier, accidental crash with eighty-eight victims. The watery crash. His crash.

At the hearing, with his mother, Kate, and Alana's parents seated close by, he'd found it easier to handle his outrage at corporate lies and obfuscation than all the emotions stirred by reading transcripts from the cockpit recorder. It had been difficult enough before, knowing precisely how long Flight 261's first nosedive lasted, how long the fatal second one lasted. Eighty seconds, then ninety. That was the stuff of his waking nightmares. Impossible to keep from picturing Alana holding Megan in the seat he had booked for her, Alana's prolonged terror as she clung to their baby. Impossible not to always be wishing time backwards, a feat he could manage only in his dreams, where he was with them in Mexico instead of awaiting them in Seattle, and he could avert their deaths by changing flights at the last minute, or losing their passports, or even breaching security to run outside and make sure the jackscrew that had caused the catastrophe was properly greased, with a functioning fail-safe device in place. Japhy had loved sci-fi books as a kid, and in his favorites, a familiar dilemma was whether the time-traveling hero should destroy some monster like Hitler or Stalin, thereby saving millions, or prevent a bad thing from happening to someone he loved. Like making sure Grandpa never climbed that ladder he fell from, or Dad dodged that bullet in Vietnam. Japhy used to think he'd be in the kill-Hitler-or-Stalin camp. Not anymore.

The cockpit recorder transcript gave him reality—the reality of words. Words spoken by the pilot after pulling out of the first dive. Words that those on board would have wanted to hear, would have wanted to believe. Words that were familiar and unaffected enough to be convincing. "Folks, we have a flight control problem up front here and we're working on it. That's Los Angeles off to the right there. That's where we are intending to go. . . . I don't anticipate any big problems once we get a couple of subsystems on line. But we will be going into LAX, and I'd anticipate us parking there in about twenty to thirty minutes." Twelve minutes later, the plane pitched and rolled and the pilot was fighting to fly again, speaking only to his copilot. "Push, push, push—push the blue side up." Without being told, Japhy knew "blue side" must be jargon for the sky. But the plane kept flying blue side down. Speed brakes failed to slow its descent. And all the captain could say then was, "Ah, here we go."

"It's better to understand what happened," Kate told Japhy afterwards, on the ride back to their hotel. He wasn't sure. Now there was so much more nightmare material to process.

Alana had just been hired as environmental reporter at *Seattle Weekly* when they met. Several years later, after they moved into their modest bungalow on Queen Anne Hill and Alana became pregnant with Megan, she'd switched to freelance assignments written from home. Their January trip to Mexico was their first vacation since Megan was born, and they were to share a house with her parents and her sister's family, who were flying in from Maryland. Japhy had looked forward to hanging out with Megan, an active, joyful baby who seldom cried unless she was hungry or had a full diaper, and was just starting to pull herself to her feet. Though he could only be there for half the month, Alana would stay on, her family helping with Megan during the hours she planned to work. She was hammering out the proposal for a book she wanted to write, about the long-term health and environmental consequences of a Washington State nuclear site. In Mexico, she'd have time to focus and finish it up.

On the day of Japhy's departure, Megan took her first steps, leveraging off a table on the terra-cotta patio, rolling on her feet, reaching for her father's hands. Alana caught it all on her sister's video camera. "Your goodbye present," she said.

Japhy arrived in Seattle that night on the same flight from Puerto Vallarta that his wife and baby were due to take two weeks later. Walking through the concourse, he stopped to stare at an enormous mural that he must have been too preoccupied to notice last time through, when he and Alana were juggling baby and bags and stroller, along with their preflight coffees. The mural was made up of eleven contiguous panels, painted in an airbrushed, photo-realistic style, full of rich reds, purples, and blues, and much too large to view all at once.

The first panels showed a magician wearing a black cape and top hat who, with the help of his assistant, was putting a saucy-looking lady into a box on wheels. If you viewed the panels from left to right, as Japhy did walking slowly by, the box twirled around and then, hocus-pocus, opened up empty. But the trick worked both ways. When Japhy retraced his steps, starting with the empty box, the magic was that the lady materialized.

The paintings seemed wonderfully right for an airport, where people appeared out of thin air, as he just had. Or disappeared into it. Doing what they were never meant to do. Flying. Just as Stevie is right now.

Japhy calls again from work, without any outbursts this time, for Stevie's Seattle-to-L.A. flight information. Then he calls repeatedly, until he can be sure that the plane has landed safely in Los Angeles and she's back in the air, on her way to Lihu'e.

The cabin lights are still turned off when Stevie awakens with a blow-up travel pillow wrapped around her neck. Margo, asleep in the next seat, wears an identical pillow—she'd brought them both from home—plus an eye mask, noise-canceling headphones, and a pair of slippers because her feet swell on long flights. For all Margo's jazzy energy, she's surprisingly well organized. Stevie unbuckles her seat belt and heads for the lavatory to brush her teeth with bottled water. On her way back, she asks a flight attendant with a hibiscus blossom tucked into her hair for two containers of POG—the mixture of passion fruit, orange, and guava juices always served on flights to the islands.

Such a long, disjointed trip. And it had started out so smoothly, with Roosevelt Jefferson Jr. picking her and Margo up and getting them to O'Hare with plenty of time to spare. Which they needed, because their flight had been cancelled and their trip had to be rescheduled. A pain in the ass, of course, only amplified by how stressed so many of the people around them were, whipping out a cell phone or thumbing a BlackBerry with an edge that Stevie recognized all too well from when things went wrong on her own business trips. But she and Margo were first in line for rescheduling, and as it turned out, if they ran to catch a flight to Seattle, they could get from Seattle to Los Angeles in time for their originally scheduled flight to Līhu'e.

Waiting to board in Seattle, Stevie looked out a window at their jet and had a time-freezing sense of familiarity, almost a déjà vu. Painted onto the tail was a noble, masculine face—not a Hawaiian Night Marcher, as in her dream, but an Alaskan Inuit. What could *that* portend? By then, though, she was too eager to reach their final destination to get worked up about it. Oh, she'd remembered about this airline's crash. Such things stuck in your mind when you logged miles at her level. But that was years ago, and anyway, it couldn't be any worse than flying for the first time after 9/11.

She'd been right not to worry. The trip to L.A. could not have been more routine. On the ground again, traveling with Margo from one terminal to another, Stevie had checked her cell phone. There was only one personal message, and that was from Hank. He sounded tired, very tired, but his words were warm. "Hi, Stevie. The Cubs got rained out, so you're not missing anything. You and Margo are my big excitement for the day. Can't tell you how glad I'll be to see you both." Nothing from Brian, which was a relief. Nothing from Japhy, either. No surprise there. He wasn't any good at discussing personal matters on the phone—she could see that now.

Stevie returns to her seat beside Margo, still sleeping, and tears the foil cover from one of the POG containers. It strikes her as almost amusing, how Japhy could be so clumsy at *conveying* intimate information when he clearly had such a talent for *acquiring* it. Which she could tell not just from her own babbling in his attentive presence, but from watching him examine Pip and Jerry, reading them with his hands. He'd read her that way, too, out by the *kukui* trees. As juice slips down Stevie's throat, a rush of damp heat pulses from her core, delectable but disconcerting, too. Where Japhy's concerned, she reminds herself, the operative loss-minimization plan is to have no expectations. None. Not for seeing him, not for talking to him, and especially not for making love with him.

Margo stirs as the pilot announces the weather in Līhu'e—rainy, sixty-five degrees—and their expected arrival in less than an hour. Cabin lights come on, along with soft slack-key guitar music, as the plane begins its descent.

"Will they greet us with leis and kisses?" Margo inquires in a husky voice. She's taken off the headphones, but her eyes are still masked.

"*Lei* and kisses," Stevie says. "There aren't plurals in Hawaiian. And no, you've watched too many old movies. They don't do that anymore."

After they land, though, Japhy makes a liar out of her. Exiting the small airport's secured arrival area, Stevie spots him waiting with strung flowers dangling from his arm. There's a tense, tight set to his lips. No sign of dimples, even as he catches sight of her and waves. If she's not mistaken, he doesn't look happy to see her so much as relieved.

"*Aloha,*" he says, looping the first of his narrow, delicate lei over Margo's head and kissing her cheek. Tuberose, as in Stevie's dream. *We're not dead,* she remembers her dream pilot Japhy saying, *we're in Kaua'i.* Oh, we are indeed.

Margo raises the lei to her nose, inhaling deeply. "Good lord. Talk about aromatherapy."

When Japhy turns to Stevie, she stands true to her no expectations rule, stock-still and fighting the impulse to hold out her arms. What if he only intends a cheek peck for her, too? But after settling the lei on her shoulders, he pulls her into a long, full-on, blossom-crushing kiss. Her fingers fly out to roost along his spine as she inhales traces of tropical air on his skin.

"Thanks for coming," she says after catching her breath. "What a wonderful surprise."

"I was hoping you'd feel that way. It's raining."

"It is?"

"The pilot's weather report." Margo nudges. "Remember?"

"Oh, right."

"So I brought Hank's wheels," Japhy says. He's got Stevie firmly by the hand now. "Let's pick up your bags."

"Wait. I forgot to introduce you."

At that, Japhy's dimples become evident. "Didn't I just hang a lei on your cousin Margo?"

"That's me," Margo tells him. "And you can only be Japhy. You've already kissed us, so I guess we're good to go? I'm asking because this is my first trip to Hawai'i. There might be some part of the ritual I don't know."

"Let's see," Japhy says. "Have you set your watch back five hours?"

"Uh-huh. Now what?"

"Take it off."

Japhy stands by Stevie at the baggage carousel with one arm tight around her waist, letting go only to grab luggage. As they step outside the airport, sheets of rain slant through the air, the thumping tail end of a wet Kona wind. Japhy leaves them at the covered curb to make a dash for Hank's car, and when he's a safe distance away, Margo turns to Stevie with a grin. "That sure didn't look to me like somebody who said 'We should have waited.' "

But Stevie, feeling light-headed, barely hears. "What?"

"You want to know what? I'll tell you what." Margo executes a hip-swiveling dance at Stevie's side, churning arms overhead while she chants, "I told you so, I told you so, I told you so."

"Okay, okay," Stevie laughs. "I guess he's glad to see me."

"Glad? What an understatement. I'm thinking of a line from an old Bette Midler song—'*Auwe*, come on, I wanna lei ya.' "

"Well," Stevie says, "Bette Midler *is* from Hawai'i."

Japhy's full of questions once they hit the Kaumuali'i Highway, asking about their trip, Stevie's presentation, the fountain resurfacing. All the while, he steers with one arm, holding Stevie's hand on his thigh—another reason to be glad for the old Defender's automatic transmission. But as they approach the eucalyptus tree tunnel, she can think of nothing but her father, and what effect Margo in person will have on him.

Although Stevie herself had laid the makings for this ancestral fire, she can't predict what will happen when match is touched to kindling. After so many years, it might be too damp to blaze into something meaningful; she could be fanning embers for the duration of Margo's stay, unable to remember why reeling in a relative for Hank's sake had seemed like such a great idea. Her concern isn't all on her father's behalf, though. She doesn't want to be the only one left behind whose feelings for him run blood-deep and strong.

The rain lets up and Stevie, verging on a tuberose headache, rolls down the window for a long, lung-filling breath. As they approach the turn to Kōloa, she glances at Margo. "We're almost there."

"I'm pretty nervous," Margo confesses.

"You haven't seen Hank in how long?" Japhy asks.

"Ages—please don't make me do the math. My gray hair's going to be a shocker for him."

"The last time you saw Dad," Stevie says, "he had two good legs, didn't he?"

Margo nods, swiping at her eyes. "I've got to stop with the crying over that. He was such an athlete—it kills me every time I think about it."

"After a certain age," Japhy says, "everybody plays hurt."

Margo leans over to pat his shoulder. "How true. Thanks for saying so."

Japhy pulls the Defender alongside Hank's house. Shades are up on the wide windows that span each side of the lanai. Light shines out from the kitchen, where Lila stands in jeans and tank top, wiping down the counters, and from the living room, where Hank sits reading, Pip balled up for a snooze against his thigh. Stevie feels a flush of homecoming pleasure, then alarm—at how drawn her father looks, at how he's wearing a sweater and has a blanket over his legs on a night so warm as this.

"Hi, kids," Hank calls after car doors slam. "I'd come and greet you, but this thing is really slowing me down."

Stevie can tell what it cost her father to admit that. "It's okay, Dad." She steps out of her shoes while Japhy does the same before hauling luggage into the lanai. "We'll come to you."

A yelping Pip races out to ricochet against Stevie's legs, whimpering until she stoops down to his level. Before she can greet Lila, sweeping into the lanai, or introduce Margo, still unbuckling her sandals, Japhy kisses her again, lightly this time. "Hank got enough of me," he says, "watching the Cubs beat Cincinnati."

"You took off from work?"

"No, he slept in, so Lila recorded the game and we all watched later. I brought pizza, it was fun."

"Was this after I called you?"

He nods. "You're the ones he's waiting for. We'll talk later."

"Yes," Stevie says, fingertips grazing his cheek. "We definitely will."

As Stevie and Margo walk into the living room, Hank tosses aside his blanket and leverages himself off the armrest to stand. "I'm not much to look at these days," he says, "but I'm still breathing."

Giving him a quick, fierce hug, Stevie kisses his cheek, then steps aside to watch as Margo and Hank embrace. "Oh, just look at *us,* Uncle Hank!" Margo exclaims. "Every single one of us—you, Stevie, Lila, and me. Look at what we all made happen. I'm so happy to be here. Right now *everybody* looks wonderful to me."

Lila hooks an arm through Stevie's and murmurs, "Family for sure, those two, yeah?"

Stevie nods, wondering how this could have escaped her notice until now. They're the ones who *look* related, both of them so tall, with the same startling Baltic blue eyes, high-bridged nose, and widow's-peak hairline. They even have the same jutting chin, though Margo's is without a cleft. The more they talk, the more they sound alike, too, with Margo's Chicago accent teasing out tendrils of Hank's. It's obvious what a pleasure this reunion is for them. Even Pip seems affected, repeatedly flinging a bedraggled Ralph II into the air, seized by a canine fit of joy. Stevie's earlier doubts dissolve. Still, another pang of trepidation comes when she glances at the Roosevelt biography, noticing Hank's place marked so much closer to the end.

Lila leaves, rumbling off on her Nighthawk, and Margo goes diving into her suitcase to emerge with a fruitcake tin and box of chocolate mint candy. "I brought you these," she tells Hank, "so you can take the sweet with the sweet for a change. Frangos and schnecken."

Hank's face breaks into a broad grin. "Marshall Field's Frangos?"

"Of course."

"And you made schnecken—real schnecken?"

"Uh-huh." Margo removes the lid to reveal layers of fat, glazed coiled buns separated by sheets of wax paper. "Yesterday, for the first time in I don't know how long, while Stevie was at her garden."

"Why's it called schnecken?" Stevie asks.

"*Schnecken*'s German for snail," Margo says. "Must be from how the dough's rolled up with all the filling before it's sliced."

"The Hawaiian word for snail," Stevie says, "is *pūpū*. Same as for appetizer. Can we have some now? I can't wait to taste it."

"How about you, Uncle Hank?"

"You bet. But just a slice, honey."

While Stevie sets the kettle to boil for some māmaki tea, Margo puts the Frangos in the freezer. "These won't be ready until tomorrow," she tells Stevie. "Frozen Frangos are a Pollack family tradition. Did you know that?"

"No," Stevie says, "but I'm not surprised. I remember being with Dad in Seattle for Christmas, lining up to buy Frangos at Frederick and Nelson. He always had a box in the freezer at his condo. *Has,*" she corrects herself, appalled at her use of the past tense, hoping Hank didn't hear. "But Dad claims Seattle Frangos aren't quite as good as the ones from Marshall Field."

"They aren't," Hank chimes in from the dining room as he pulls out a chair. "Marshall Field got their Frango franchise back in the thirties, when they bought Frederick and Nelson. But I guarantee you, they changed the recipe."

"Either that," Margo says, "or nothing can compare with childhood comfort food."

As Stevie pours their tea, Margo cuts one of her pastries into thirds. "Okay, Uncle Hank," she says. "Mine might not measure up to Nana's, but you tell me."

Stevie and Margo sit on either side of him and then, without another word, they all take big bites and chew slowly with intent, solemn expressions, as though participating not just in the same taste test, but their own improvised version of the Eucharist. Butter, brown sugar, cinnamon, and bits of dark chocolate melt onto Stevie's tongue. So this is schnecken. Nothing like the bland, airy, mass-produced buns named for Margo when she was a child, nothing at all. It's nutty, gooey, creamy, and entirely delicious. Who knows? Maybe Margo baked into these creations of hers an extra-special intangible something to transform the passions that had ripped her family apart. Stevie had never experienced those passions firsthand—not the way Hank and Margo did—but surely she'd grown up shaped by them, by the holes they'd drilled into her father's heart.

"It's great," Hank says. "Even better than Ma's."

Margo smiles over her teacup. "She never passed down her secrets—I had to figure them out for myself. Lots of little things, like shaving the chocolate, mixing sour cream with the milk, and don't handle the dough too much or you get a gut-bomb."

Acts of grace—that's what consecrated food requires. And as they devour every last crumb, Stevie realizes her own act of grace right now should be to leave, to let Margo and Hank be alone for the rest of the evening, rediscovering each other without having to interpret or explain for her sake. Doing so would free Stevie to see Japhy, of course, but the possibilities there only seem to enlarge the grace. "If it's all right with you two," she says, pushing back from the table, "I'll grab a shower and walk Pip." Even with Japhy's lei around her neck, Stevie can detect the stale scent of overcirculated airplane air on her skin, a sour bottom note to the heady tuberose.

After showering, she applies lotion and puts on her smocked turquoise sundress. She's still not counting on Japhy for anything. But with her body twanging to his again, it does seem prudent to fish her cervical cap from the bathroom cupboard.

When she's ready to go, Stevie shows Margo the list of emergency numbers by the phone, to which she adds Japhy's. "I have a feeling this is going to be a *long* walk," Margo says. "Oh, don't worry! I need quality time with my uncle here."

"Don't stay up too late," Stevie says. "Cubs doubleheader in the morning. Who's pitching, Dad?"

"Prior and Clement. In that order."

"Oh, God—they're gonna clinch for sure."

"We'll see," Hank says. "Remember, Stevie. The magic number is three."

"You don't have to tell me what the magic number is."

"Well," Margo says, "*I* could use a little refresher course."

"Not only do they have to win the doubleheader to clinch their division," Hank tells her, "but Houston has to lose. Three games, see? That would put the Cubs into playing postseason for the pennant and then, if they win that, the Series. A tall order, but my daughter is evidently an optimist."

"Well, I'm an optimist, too, Uncle Hank. If we can be in Hawai'i together after all these years, anything can happen."

Stevie takes a shortcut to Japhy's cottage, and as she passes the *kukui* trees, a gentle shower shakes down, the Kona wind's goodbye kiss. She runs the rest of the way as best she can in flip-flops, damp dress clinging to her thighs. Pip races ahead to scramble up the lanai steps, announcing their arrival with a crooning pack bark for Rainier, who's already at the door, nose pressed against the screen. Peering around, Stevie sees Japhy look up from the cardboard box he's sealing with packing tape, BEDROOM written on its side in thick black block letters. "Hey you," she says.

"Hey yourself. Come on in, I'll be with you in a second."

She enters while Japhy, done with the box, pushes it over to the wall, next to a dozen other boxes labeled with their various domestic destinations. Stevie's spirits sink—*So this is what he has to tell me, that he's leaving Kaua'i*—only to buoy up again an instant later, when she recalls the house he's renovating. What a dope, leaping to the worst possible conclusion again. "Packing up already?"

"Yeah. Looking to be out of here by the end of the month."

"That's only a few days off. Wouldn't you know? I finally fall for the boy next door and he moves away."

Japhy's laughter comes quick and easy. "Only to Waimea."

"Waimea, huh? Great place for sunsets." Then it dawns on her. "That's where we were going for the picnic, right?"

"Yep." The kiss he gives her now is very much like their first. Sweetly soft-lipped, brief. But a flicker of tension flashes across his face as he turns off the music on the stereo—one of those soulful guy singers Kiko had remarked upon; Ben Harper, she thinks—then motions for her to join him at the kitchen table in a pool of pale dim light from a shaded overhead fixture.

Japhy studies the tabletop as though to gather his thoughts. For long moments, the only sounds are from a lizard skittering across a window screen, a whisper of wind through chimes outside the kitchen door, and Rainier, who's got Pip between her paws and is noisily licking his ears clean. Well, here it comes—the story of Japhy's divorce. All Stevie has to do is listen, give Japhy the benefit of any doubt, shove aside that earlier worry of hers, the one about him still being in love with his ex. Stevie folds her hands, hooks ankles together, waits with all the patience she can command despite the quiver in her belly.

"Before this goes any further . . ." Japhy begins in that clipped, matter-of-fact way of his she remembers from their lunch at Hamura's. Then he raises his gaze to scoot his chair until their arms are touching. "There's something you should know about me." His voice has turned so low that Stevie tilts her head closer and sweeps hair behind the ear closest to him, as if clearing a path for his words. "My wife and baby girl. Alana. Megan. The plane they were on crashed into the ocean. Everyone died. Alana torn to pieces. Megan so shattered even DNA analysis couldn't identify her."

Stevie, eyes pooling, wraps arms around his shoulders, pulling him closer still. His body softens against hers. She tightens her grip until his breath is warm on her neck.

"You didn't know already," Japhy says, "did you?"

It's all Stevie can do to shake her head in response, even though at some level she *did* know, or she wouldn't have dreamed of Japhy piloting a Night Marcher jet. "That flight from Mexico," she manages, and feels him nodding.

Japhy pulls away to look at her. "Four years ago, almost. You're the first person here I've told. Never really had to tell anyone before. In Seattle, everyone knew."

"That must have helped a little."

"It did. For a while."

"Oh, Japhy. I can only imagine how terrible."

"I wanted to tell you before. Before we . . . got closer."

"The picnic?"

"Later, too. But you didn't want to talk. And on the phone, well, I just couldn't."

"No, of course not."

"It's a lot to take in."

"To say the least. My God."

"I mean for you."

Stevie's startled to realize that his focus is entirely on her, on how she's handling what he's told her. With that, everything shifts. The air between them grows thick—thick enough to choke on, to drown in. Death floods in from every angle, without a drop of transcendent spirit, only dread. She should be the one caring for Japhy, not the other way around. But she can't, not when all she wants to do is to leave, and there's no way to leave without speaking. "It's a long day for me."

"I know this isn't what you were expecting."

No, she wants to scream, *this is not what I was expecting at all! I came here tonight expecting romance. This is so much worse, so much more complicated than what I expected!* Such a horrible confession, and as if that weren't bad enough, she lies: "I'm glad you told me. I'm just too tired to make sense right now. We can talk more later. I better go home, get some rest."

Stars sparkle through gaps between clouds. Moonlight shines off wet banana leaves. Even the soil smells sweet. The only storm now is the inner one propelling Stevie across her father's grounds, past the *kukui* trees, where she stumbles on a broken branch, lands on her butt, and bursts into tears. Pip cocks his head and stares.

Who is she crying for now? If it were for Japhy, for his dead, that would at least be honorable. But really, these tears are for herself, which has got to be shameful. Still, it nags at her, Japhy's not speaking of his tragedy to anyone else on the island. Maybe he doesn't own what happened so much as what happened owns him, and how long will it take to discover for certain if she's got damaged goods on her hands? Will Alana and their baby always be in the middle of any bed he and

Stevie share, and will she always feel the way she does now, like last pick on his team?

From there, her thoughts grow darker. Colder, too. Japhy might have only been attracted to her because death is all that speaks to him, and she's got a dying father; he won't want to hang around when everything's okay, not if mourning lost loved ones has got to be the glue between them. She, on the other hand, might have only been attracted to Japhy in some lemming-like, unconscious way because he felt familiar—a man bereft of wife and daughter, too damaged for any real commitment to another woman. A man much like Brian, much like Hank.

Now that she's named each fear, the fears don't disappear. But they do subside enough so she can remember what makes her so vulnerable. Japhy's kindness, his generosity, his compassion. Not to mention the way he'd made love to her, just a few feet from where she's now sprawled on the ground. He's done more for her than she's done for him, when you come right down to it.

Oh, God. How can she ever be with someone who's deep-down good to her, the way Margo wished, when her nature is so needy, so suspicious? What gives her the right to fault Japhy for things she can only guess at? What makes *her* such a prize? He trusted her enough to reveal what he's told no one else on the island, and what does she do? Run away.

Stevie stands, brushes leaves off her dress, and heads back with Pip to Japhy's cottage.

When she arrives, he's sitting on the lanai. While he doesn't look surprised to see her, she resists the urge to ask if that's true. She doesn't say a word. Instead, she does exactly what she should have done earlier: she takes him by the hand.

Stevie gasps a bit as they enter his bedroom, braced for the photograph of mother and child that she'd glimpsed before on Japhy's dresser, the shock of seeing them again, this time knowing they are dead. A quick glance tells her the dresser's been cleared—all the photographs once there already packed, no doubt. But she decides to take their absence tonight as a sign, a portent of Japhy's readiness for her. Even so, as she leads him toward the bed, she's surprised by the pain of it, this business of fitting in people, actual people—different from any she's experienced. Only now, instead of contracting, a black hole sucking her in, it's more as though the pain is an unseen tool, prying open her chest. There must be some purpose to this procedure. Perhaps the more who arrive—whether living or dead—the more territory there will be for them. And for her, too. It's not territory that might be measured, any more than the spaces between the stitches of her great-*tūtū*'s quilt can be counted and matched to descendants. The intention feels much the same, though. Making room enough for everybody.

If only she can hold on to it.

Japhy stretches out beside Stevie. "Talking about it's still hard," he says. "You don't exactly get over a thing like that. But you do start finding your way. That's where I am, I think. Finding my way."

"Oh, what that must take." Stevie rests her head on his shoulder, her hand cradling his face. Neither of them moves for quite a while, not until Japhy turns so that their glistening eyes can fix on each other's. She can't help but kiss him, first on each cheekbone, then on his lips. There's no reluctance in his response, but compared to the wild driving force of before, when he came to her in the Night Marchers' wake, these kisses and caresses of theirs are like an underwater ballet—deeper, slower, more expressive.

Stevie raises her arms as Japhy lifts the sundress over her head. After setting it aside, he moves toward her again, then hesitates midway. "About last time," he says. "I put things all wrong on the phone. It's not that I didn't want it to happen."

"Good." She begins unbuttoning his shirt in an unhurried crawl from top to bottom, wanting to see every bit of him she can in the glow of light from the living room. "But I already worked that out."

"It's not that I even assumed it would happen. It's more like I had a whole other idea *how* it would happen."

"Really? Based on what?"

"Fantasy. No, instinct. Maybe lust. Could be all of the above. I mean, it's a long time since someone new for me. What's for certain is I bought condoms before we left for the picnic. Just so you know."

"Ah," she says as his shirt falls to the floor. "I'm glad you told me. And just so you know, I'm not involved with anybody else."

"I meant to ask about that, too."

"But you don't have to bother with a condom. I've got the protection base covered."

Japhy plants a line of kisses from the crown of Stevie's head down to her low-cut, lacy red panties, his fingertips lingering once more on her scars. "Appendix?"

"Uh-huh. Ruptured when I was twelve."

"Ouch." He presses his lips along the length of that puckered, horizontal seam before turning his attention to the slanting ridge below. "And this one?"

"Lost ovary."

"Lost how?"

"Bad pregnancy. Ectopic."

Instead of slipping off her panties—as she fervently hopes he will, by this point—he glides up to rest his head on the pillow next to hers, placing a hand on her waist. "I'm sorry," he says.

"It's okay. I'm okay. I mean, it's nothing next to what you've—"

"Don't," he says, his mouth hovering over hers. And then, between kisses: "Don't do that. Ever. Please. All right?"

"All right."

Soon enough, her panties join his shirt on the floor, followed by his jeans and briefs. What's important can no longer be spoken, can only be given through the silent gifts of their bodies. This giving doesn't convince Stevie that she's redeemed herself, that now, after being so bad, she is once again good. She isn't good. At least, she isn't *only* good. Maybe she doesn't have to be. What she's feeling now might be as ephemeral as a kiss, but it's better than good. What she's feeling now is whole.

"There's another thing I need to ask you about," Japhy says, returning from the kitchen with a glass of water to share. "What had you so spooked when I found you outside? The earthquake?"

"What earthquake?"

"There was a quake that night, real minor." He slides back into bed beside her. "Felt it right before I saw you."

"What a shame. If the quake had waited just a few more minutes, we could have said the earth moved the first time we had sex."

"It did anyway."

I love you for that, Stevie almost blurts out. But this is Japhy, not Lila, and earlier worries throw enough shadow still that she confines herself to "What a wonderful thing to say." Japhy sets aside the water glass to spoon around her beneath the white cotton sheet, soft as a newborn's nightshirt. Stevie tucks his hand against her breastbone. "Did you ever have something happen to you that you didn't want to talk about because other people . . . they might think you're gullible, or maybe insane?"

He takes a moment to consider. "When I started practicing, yeah. I'm thinking of a dog I did surgery on for a malignant tumor. A big dog, over a hundred and twenty pounds. Dogs that size usually don't live over ten years, and he was almost that old. Well, I removed most of the tumor, but it wasn't possible to get the entire thing. Everything in all the science said he wouldn't last long—a few weeks, tops. I was cautious with what I told the owner, though, because I had a sense the science was wrong and this dog wouldn't be dying anytime soon."

"Why didn't you say just that?"

"The practice I'd joined in Seattle did vet medicine at the highest level. Their clientele demanded it. I'd have been fired on the spot if my colleagues heard about some feeling I got from being in sync with that dog's life force. It sounds dumb even to me, saying it now."

"Not to me. What happened to the dog?"

"Lived three more years—died when his heart gave out. Had nothing to do with the tumor. The tumor never showed up again."

"You were right, then."

"Yeah, I was right. But since I couldn't give a scientific reason, I never talked about it as anything but a medical anomaly."

"Interesting." Stevie wonders if such an anomaly might still be possible for Hank. In spite of everything, she's still hoping for some kind of miracle.

"Doesn't have much to do with how we wound up in that sleeping bag together, though."

She shrugs against him. "Maybe it was an earthquake. Or maybe it was something else. Ever hear of Night Marchers?"

"Sounds like a Hawaiian thing."

"It is." And so Stevie explains who the Night Marchers are, then relates her experience, telling him how she smoked Hank's medicinal-grade grass, saw the shooting star, heard the drums, the chanting, the barking dogs, then stripped naked so she'd survive this encounter with the Night Marchers, the way Kiko had taught her. She even mentions her idea that the birthing stone had brought them. But her certainty about what happened wavers as Japhy reconstructs his own middle-of-the-night activities—playing his Hawaiian CD full blast, Rainier howling on the lanai before he'd felt the temblor.

"You didn't see them?" Stevie asks.

"Nope. A good thing, too, considering how I wouldn't have known to get naked or not look them in the eye, and then they'd have been forced to kill me."

"Are you making fun of me?"

"Just a little."

"Maybe I dreamed it all. Or do you think I'm crazy now?"

"I think whatever it was, could be something to do with your posterior superior parietal lobe."

"My what?"

He twirls out a lock of hair from the back of her head. "The part of your brain right about here. One of the things it does is orient you in space."

"Could be. I have a hunch mine's pretty weird. Even stone-cold sober in broad daylight, my sense of direction's a joke."

"Want to hear a possible explanation?"

Stevie leans on an elbow and props her head on her hand, stroking his leg with her foot. "Sure."

"When neurons in that part of the brain are quiet, when they're not firing, it's like there's no sense of boundaries." He reaches for her foot and massages the bottom arch with his thumbs. "You don't perceive the world in ways considered normal. Everything's connected—that's the sensation."

"I've had that sensation quite a bit lately. Go on, though, Dr. Japhy, please."

"With your foot or with your brain?"

"Both."

"It's a complex electrical system, the brain. Kind of like a twelve-watt radio receiver. And when it comes to things like ghosts or spirits, well, the conclusions people reach from the research about that—it's almost like a litmus test."

"Mmm," she moans, shifting to give him her other foot for the same delicious treatment. "How so?"

"It's possible to shoot an electrical current through the brain that simulates phantom effects—seeing ghosts, or just feeling their presence. My guess is that it only happens when the posterior superior parietal lobe's in a calm, receptive state. But the point is, you could say the experiment proves spirits don't exist, they're nothing but a biochemical reaction."

"That would be my parents."

"Or you could say it proves that spirits *do* exist, and can only be perceived because they're capable of generating the same sort of current."

"That would be Grandpa."

"Hank's father?"

"No, my mother's. But in his soul, he was more Hawaiian than you'd ever expect a lily-white old English guy like him could be. Way more than his *hapa haole* daughter."

"Which makes you *hapa haole,* too."

"Barely. So tell me, what do *you* say?"

Japhy kisses the top of her foot before releasing it. "I say the answer doesn't depend on science. It depends on how you see the world."

"I mean you, personally, Japhy Hungerford."

"Okay. I, Japhy Hungerford, am personally of the opinion that we're something bigger than a bunch of electrical twitches. Which doesn't mean I'm going to argue against evolution. On the other hand, I'm not going to start playing a didgeridoo, change my name to Jeremy Dreamseed, and move to Mau'i."

As Stevie laughs, a yawn escapes her. "How come you know so much about human brain stuff?"

"I like to read all kinds of research."

Stevie's eyes close as her head comes to rest over Japhy's heart. "And I like what I'm learning from *you.*" She loses the beat beneath her ear to the sound of Japhy's chesty chortle.

Chapter 19

Hawai'i—not a place that a person allergic to the sun ever dreams of going. When Margo lusts for exotic destinations, they are urban, wintry gray, intellectually acute venues, with streets straight out of history books. But once she recovers from being startled awake by the constipated-sounding crowing of a deranged rooster beneath the bedroom window, it's surprising how at home she feels, looking in first thing on her still-slumbering uncle. Exploring his property. Picking ripe, fleshy mangos and papayas and funny little fingerling bananas, too, her toes dipped in dawn-time dew. Slicing fruit and setting coffee to brew. Swaying to an island song on the kitchen radio, sung by a woman with a glottal-stop-studded surname and an eerily high, throaty voice, throbbing with vibrato.

None of this behavior—uncharacteristic, to say the least—raises a single remark from Evelyn. In fact, there hasn't been a word out of her mother for days, not since back in Chicago, when Margo had spied Elizabeth Schaeffer Levanthal after Stevie's presentation, and The Voice of Evelyn went into bellowing mode over Margo's unstyled, uncolored hair, her unmanicured hands, her unfashionable clogs, even the pants she was wearing, an expensive pair of black stretch Cambio jeans. Jeans were jeans to Evelyn, no matter what they cost, no matter how good they looked, and it cut no ice with her that the Cambios flattered Margo's derriere enough to have inspired an unusually frisky bout of before-dinner sex with Kenny when she wore them for the first time.

Please, spare me the details. Do whatever you like in the privacy of your home, but when you're out in public, you ought to remember you're not a kid anymore.

Then, just before Margo headed off in Mrs. Levanthal's direction, her mother's version of a pep talk:

If you're going to drop my name, at least put on some lipstick. And whatever you do, don't kowtow. I don't care how much money she has, you can't buy class. And apart from your clothes, your appearance, your total lack of social stature, you have nothing to be ashamed of with that woman. Shoulders back, chin up, carry on!

It's no doubt due to wishful, deluded, or even demented thinking on Margo's part, but she has an idea Evelyn might actually endorse this trip of hers to Hawai'i. Which makes sense when Margo considers how she'd once been a means of exchange for her mother and uncle, their pint-size, flesh-and-blood redemption coupon. One of them would point a Super 8 movie camera at her little-kid self having a ball somewhere and, already, the bulk of her job was done. All she had to do was remind them of *their* little-kid selves, how happy *they* once were. Easy to imagine that all the validating emotion Hank has manifested toward Margo since her arrival was exactly what her mother had yearned to recapture for herself. Unconditionally, of course. Which, of course, is never possible—not in the real world, anyway. Not with real people living real, uncloistered lives. There are always terms to adult love, always. And always, the trick is the same. It's in how you plant those terms, finding soil rich enough to be a growth medium. Not that Evelyn would ever have understood Margo's analogy; to her, a gardener was someone whom you hired.

It's also possible that Evelyn's been stunned into silence by what Margo and Hank discussed last night, starting with the first thing out of Margo's mouth after Stevie left to see her adorable vet.

"Uncle Hank," she'd said, "I honestly don't care who was right or who was wrong in whatever went on between you, my mother, my father, and your mother, too. You can tell me anything you want about all that, and I promise, I'll listen. Maybe I won't take sides, and maybe that'll piss you off. But I won't be hurt and I won't be offended. I won't argue, either."

From the look on her uncle's face, you'd have thought she'd just levitated off the couch. "How can you do that?"

"I know," she told him. "Sounds crazy to a Pollack, doesn't it?"

"Crazy? No. Difficult, yes."

"Don't give me too much credit. You're one of the first people I ever loved. Plus, it's part of my school assignment, figuring out what went wrong in my family."

"Your 'waste management' paper?"

"Right. We're the only ones who ever went to the mat with Mother, aren't we? We both understand what a dirty fighter she could be."

"Once," Hank said, "she came at me like a cat, claws out and ready to rip."

"How'd that happen?"

"This was on Delaware Place, when I was fifteen. You must realize how your mother liked to keep people waiting. She was always late for everything, including her own wedding."

"Tell me about it. I used to think it was just one more way for her to be in control. But now I wonder if it wasn't something else—how she took forever trying to make everything perfect. Herself, the house, everybody in it. There was always something not quite right enough."

"Punctuality, the courtesy of kings. I've always hated being late. And on the Saturday in question, I'd played baseball all afternoon and needed to shower before my date." Hank paused with a wince, his thin, tan face going ashen gray. "Ah," he said, "don't tell Stevie, but this pain, it's getting worse. I've got a bottle of Loritab on my bathroom counter. Do me a favor, Margo. Bring me one—no, two."

Loritab. Margo recognized the drug's name from the litany of opiates—Vicodan, Darvocet, Loritab, OxyContin—her mother took before advancing to the morphine stage, that netherworld where hallucinations made it impossible to have conversations as lucid as the ones she'd hoped for with Hank. Even with her experienced eye, Margo couldn't gauge what kind of time remained for him. Could be months, weeks, or days. And how much longer would he be able to hang in with her tonight? It didn't look good. But soon after he swallowed his pills, the color returned to Hank's face and he asked, "Where was I?"

"Back in 1947, I think. Ready to shower, so you wouldn't be late for your date."

"Forty-eight, in point of fact. So. We've got just the one bathroom with a shower—the other's a powder room—and Evvie's in there primping for ages already. Ma's begging her to come out, I'm hollering, and what does she do? Locks the damn door. I'm so mad I kick it in."

"Aha. I'm guessing *that's* when she came at you with the claws."

"Yup."

"Well? Did she draw any blood?"

"Not a chance. I was too fast dodging in there to secure the bathroom for myself."

"Was *she* getting ready for a date?"

"Yeah, but that wasn't the problem. She'd been digging at me for days, ever since I earned my swim-team letter. Said I was too full of myself. She was in her senior year by then, for cry-eye! You'd think she'd be too old to care so much about her kid brother's accomplishments. But no, she couldn't stand it, my getting that kind of recognition."

"Mother was always comparing herself to somebody else, and never to the good. She was a terrific swimmer, too. *She* should have been out there competing."

"That wasn't *my* fault. In those days, girls didn't."

"I'm just thinking about how she always needed to be winning at something. Sports would have been a lot healthier than the events she ended up with. You know," she adds, prompted by Hank's mystified expression. "The Olympics of beauty, fashion, wealth, and status."

"I can't speak to that. What I know is, it always killed her, not having the last word. In this case, she stole my letter and told me she burned it. I believed her, too. But she was lying. She hid the letter under a floorboard. That's where Stevie found it."

Margo's turn to be gobsmacked then. "You're kidding!"

"Our building on East Delaware got turned into a hotel—the Raphael. Stevie stayed there, on the same floor where our apartment was. She had no idea I ever lived there. Quite a coincidence, don't you think?"

"If you believe in coincidences."

"What's your explanation?"

"Evelyn helped Stevie find the letter, to clear things up. It sounds like Mother, saying she'd burnt it to hurt you. But knowing her, she would have kept the letter around as a bargaining tool."

"You're too damn smart to believe in ghost stories, Margo. When we're dead, we're dead. Anyway, if Evelyn didn't hide the letter there, who did?"

"Your mother?"

"Come on. Why would Ma do a thing like that?"

"You'll get mad if I tell you."

"No I won't."

"Okay, then. Divide and conquer, that was Nana's way of staying on top. Stirring up trouble instead of trying to resolve it. It was awful of her, considering how much a letterman sweater means to a guy. But it gave her another way to commiserate with her son about how terrible his sister was, then turn around and do the same damn routine with her daughter about the brother. Her misguided idea of bonding with the kids. And it never seemed like that to her. Not to you or Evelyn, either, because she made sure you couldn't trust each other enough to compare notes."

The amazing thing was not Hank's listening to this description of his sainted mother without erupting. Even if he wanted to, it didn't seem as if he had the energy for that. No, the amazing thing was how he looked her in the eye and said, "I'm not agreeing with your theory, Margo. I'm not saying it's wrong, either. But trust sure did play a role in what came between your mother and me."

"How so?"

"No, honey. I don't want to tarnish your memory of your parents."

"I'm a big girl now, Uncle Hank. My memories are my memories—you can't tarnish them. What happened?"

Hank shook his head and gave a short, sharp laugh. "Well, your mother locks herself away again, only this time it's not a bathroom—it's her bedroom, her and your father's bedroom."

"I can't imagine *Dad* ever kicking in the door."

"But he's the reason why she's locked herself up in there. Tom calls me, all upset. 'Evvie thinks I don't love her anymore,' he says. 'She won't talk to me, she won't come out. I'm scared to death about what she might do to herself. Please come over right away, Hank, you're the only one she'll talk to.' That's a shock. If I'm the only one she'll talk to, I figure it must be pretty bad."

"It doesn't surprise *me*. Mother didn't have a single intimate friend, only those social mavens of hers. And you can be sure a Pollack loves you when she fights you tooth and nail, right?" She expected Hank would smile, but he was too impatient to get on with his story. "Where am *I* while this is happening?"

"Summer camp, I think. Your dog's there—Ginger. You're definitely not at home, though. And the thing of it is, your father's put me in a very difficult position. On the one hand, Evelyn's been taking sleeping pills for years, the kind people overdosed on in those days, and she's so emotional, I'm scared myself. On the other, well, remember that little redhead I sat beside in those movies of Evvie's wedding—the ones you gave Stevie?"

"Vaguely."

"She's all grown up by then, married into a fortune—one of those wealthy women Evvie cultivated. Younger than me, but I knew her at the Pearson School. Liz Schaeffer."

"Elizabeth Schaeffer Levanthal? Stevie's garden patron?"

"I noticed that in the newspaper article."

"Liz had no idea Stevie was related to us until I told her at the reception. But what's *she* got to do with Mother locking herself in her bedroom?"

"Hold your horses, I'm getting there. If you're sure I should continue."

"If you stop now, I'll go nuts."

"Well, a while before all this occurs, I'm spending the weekend with friends in Michigan City, and we're at some boathouse dive to grab a bite. Tom was supposed to be out of town on business. But I spot him canoodling with Liz."

"Good Lord. Did they see you?"

"No, they were leaving out the back way. Didn't take much to put it all together, though. Let's just say there'd been other signs." Hank stopped, as if gauging Margo's resistance to what she was hearing.

"I've always wondered why Dad let Mother have the upper hand," Margo said. "If he had an affair, well, that's a big missing piece. Did Mother let you in her bedroom?"

"When I get there, we're just talking through the door. First thing she wants is Tom out of the house, so he leaves. Then she says what's making her crazy is that she's certain Tom's involved with somebody else and he won't admit it. I give her all the usual stuff about working through a bad patch, forgiving and forgetting, taking a little vacation to get things back on track. But she calms down and convinces me she's going to divorce him no matter what, and she'll hire a detective to find out what's really going on if she has to, and the biggest favor I can do is tell her if I know anything. So, like an idiot, I feel sorry for her. I believe her. I tell her."

"Through the bedroom door?"

"Of course not. By then she's let me in."

Margo's head tipped as she pictured Evelyn on the receiving end of Hank's pity. Not a pretty sight. And no wonder Evelyn didn't want her daughter kowtowing to Liz! "Clearly, Mother never divorced Dad. Was that the problem? She lied and you couldn't forgive her?"

"Worse. I gave her the truth and she couldn't forgive me."

"It had to be more complicated than that!"

"You want the gory details? Tom told her *I'm* the one having the affair with Liz, and what I really want is a bigger share of the business before we sell it, so I pinned the affair on him."

"How would that get you a bigger share of the business?"

"Your parents helped finance the start-up for Margo May, and the majority owners were Ma, Evelyn, and Tom, in that order. My piece was small, and it was true that I was asking for more. Hell, I'd earned it by then. But according to Tom, my scheme was to turn Ma and Evelyn against him so they'd bump me way up the ladder and he'd be the one shoved down."

"They had the power to make that happen?"

"Ma made sure they did. Because of my father, probably."

"Were you hoping they'd cut Dad out when you told Mother about the affair?"

"Of course not! It hadn't even occurred to me. The point is, your mother believed her husband."

"Or pretended she did."

"Why would she pretend about a thing like that?"

"My guess? She was humiliated, Uncle Hank. She couldn't deal with all the implications. If she chooses her husband's version, the affair with Liz is kaput. He's boxed himself into a corner, he can't go back to her now, not unless he wants to risk losing everything. And Mother, well, she doesn't have to get a divorce *or* confront Liz. She doesn't have to lose her marital status along with her social status. So she wins out over Dad, Liz, and you, too, by hanging on to more money when the business sells. Don't you see?"

"Money's no excuse for betraying your brother. For swearing you'll never speak again not only to him, but to anybody else who does!"

"Money's never really just about money, is it? What Mother did was terrible. And believe me, I'm not saying you should thank her for it. But it did free you from a family business you had so little interest in—literally *and* figuratively. You'd never worked anywhere but in hotels before Nana's bakery tanked, and now you could finally escape all the family obligations to make your own life. Anyway, Mother *did* speak to you again. I mean, you and Beryl came to Chicago after Stevie was born. I remember how happy I was, seeing you all then."

"Ma was dying. She made us promise to bury the hatchet."

"Interesting," Margo said, "considering that buried letter."

"But Evvie couldn't let it go. She played the martyr, having to take care of Ma, even though Evvie was the one who drove me away. I changed our tickets to fly back here after only two days. I remember Beryl telling me on the plane, 'I'll be happy not to ever again see *those people.*' For me, I told her, they would all die with my mother. But you know, I never really forgave Beryl for that remark." Hank was about to say more, then he shook his head.

"Don't stop for my sake, Uncle Hank."

"No, it's not that. It's that after what you said earlier, I'm thinking, Christ, no wonder. How could I have expected things to be any different?"

There was no longer any anger or bitterness in Hank's words. In fact, Margo could swear she detected a certain sense of wonder, as if he'd just dialed up the combination to some safe he'd been trying to crack his whole life. Perhaps the very safe Nana had always made such a show of breaking into on her children's behalf, proof of their father's neglect. The safe that always reminded them there was never enough, never enough. The safe that was the last thing they saw before they went to sleep, the first thing they saw upon awakening. Hank had also sounded relieved. For Margo that was sweet. Sweeter than all the schnecken in the world. And from there, things went to an even better place.

Which is why now, as coffee begins dripping into the pot, Margo is so glad to see Stevie and Pip appear in the distance, coming across the yard. She's eager to tell her cousin all about it.

Once she and Stevie are settled on the lanai, coffee cups in hand, Margo smiles. "You could be in a painting," she says. " 'Madonna Fresh from Her Lover's Bed.' Aw, you're blushing."

"How's it been with you and Dad?"

"Way to change the subject. Sure you don't want to go first?"

"Yeah. It all still feels pretty private."

"Well! We had a breakthrough last night. A real truth-telling session." Stevie sits back to listen, lapping up every word, from the bathroom fight to the bedroom showdown. Margo can almost hear the click of connections falling into place for her.

"You know what I think is interesting?" Stevie says. "Evelyn's father died with his mistress. Which Nana never told her. But that's when Evelyn stopped getting along with Dad. Then Evelyn catches her own husband in an affair, and she stops speaking with Dad."

"You're right," Margo says. "That part hadn't even occurred to me. I'll have to mention it to Hank. Thank you! I mean, I knew intellectually from my reading how family secrets go underground and affect everybody. But now I *really* understand."

"Do you think talking about it all helped Dad?"

"Oh yes. That's the most important thing I have to tell you. Uncle Hank knows he's dying, and he's okay with that. He's ready."

Stevie's face reddens again, contorting this time. "Well, *I'm* not!"

"Maybe you ought to be. He isn't getting any better."

"He's worse than when I left for Chicago, I can see that. But I'm back now, and I'm not ready for him to die, and I'm not ready for you or anybody else to tell me I should be."

Not the response Margo expected, but before she can think of anything else to say, Stevie's bolted outside, where she disappears into a shed behind the house, emerges with gardening shears and gloves, then goes to work, savagely tearing bougainvillea vines from an ornamental fence.

The hour's so early, the sky so cloud-riddled, that olive-skinned Stevie doesn't have to worry about exposure. But this sun is tropical, and Margo, mindful of her allergy, slaps on a thorough coat of SPF 50 plus a hat before going outside to join her. "I can help," she says. "Got another pair of gloves?"

"In the shed."

Silently, they develop a system for denuding the fence, with Margo pulling out strips that Stevie hacks at either end, until they've got a wheelbarrow stacked full of thorny vines and the fence is bare. Only then does Stevie mention what she's got in mind—giving her father a fuller view from his customary lawn chair.

"Uncle Hank might not believe in heaven," Margo says. "But he's sure got himself a gorgeous slice of it here."

Stevie yanks the vine in her hand with more force than necessary. "Yeah, here. Where he's ready to die."

"I didn't mean to upset you, Stevie."

"It's just that if he's ready to die, I wish he'd told me so himself. It's lousy information to get secondhand."

"He can't talk to you about that, sweetie. You're too dear to him, you're all he's got. Now that I'm in the picture, well, it gives him some peace, handing you off to me. It's not like I'm the only one who's there for you. More like he's sorry we haven't had each other all along."

Then, in the space of a few nods, Stevie's expression shifts from crushed to determined. She might not like riding headlong into battle—Margo's preferred mode of entry—and even a rubber needle could prick her feelings, but Lord, this girl's a fighter.

"He's not dead yet," Stevie says. "There are still things that can happen for him. And for you, too."

"What kind of things?"

"You'll see."

Chapter 20

Stevie makes a dozen different phone calls before Hank appears in his bathrobe for breakfast—slow, bleary-eyed, leaning heavily on his good leg, but focused, too. "If the Cubs are going to clinch today," he says, "I don't want to miss a single pitch."

As he washes down a pain pill with his POG, Stevie notes the time. When he's showered, shaved, dressed, and settled on the lanai, remotes on the portion of lap unoccupied by Pip, Japhy, and Rainier arrive to join them. Stevie's plans are in place. There's nothing to do but watch the game.

Hank's so absorbed that he barely seems to notice when Lila's son Johnny pulls into the drive, hauls an enormous, pot-shaped roaster off the bed of his pickup, and drags it out to the far end of the yard, where he fires it up. Stevie flashes a smile at Margo, ensconced in the rattan armchair across from Hank's, and allows herself a flutter of satisfaction. Hank's definitely not *acting* like a man who's ready to die, and she can't believe it's all a show for her sake.

"Prior won't be pitching any masterpiece," Hank observes early on. "He isn't sharp."

"You're right," Japhy says. "But he's holding Pittsburgh down anyway. That's the sign of a fine pitcher, when he can win without his best stuff."

"Win? I don't want to dampen your enthusiasm, son, but we're a long way from win here."

Son. The very word—and how fondly Hank says it—slaps a seal of approval on the fact of Japhy seated beside her on the couch, arm around her shoulders. Stevie wonders whether Hank thinks of Japhy as someone else, like Margo, whom he can entrust her to, and as she does, it's as if long-asleep senses just ticked to life. Nowhere near enough to make her want to cry *Daddy* or crawl onto her father's lap, but almost. Almost. Never mind how long she's taken care of herself, and how she's now taking care of him in whatever ways he'll allow. Never mind, either, their difficulty in speaking any emotional language besides baseball, or all her battles to toughen up and achieve what winning his love always seemed to require. Hank's still hardwired to consider himself Stevie's protector. Which leaves her wanting to hold him to life tighter than ever.

In the third inning, with the game still scoreless, the trades waft in *kiawe*-spiked smoke so mouthwatering you can almost taste it. Only then does Hank think to question Johnny. "What've you got cooking out there?"

"One big honking porker of a pig, that's what. I'd fix 'er up at home, Unc, but I don't get this channel."

What a whopper. Of course Johnny gets this channel. One reason why Stevie had called on him to help install Hank's satellite dish was that he'd done the same with his own. She watches to see if Hank's suspicious, but all he says is "Smells awful good, that pig. Might have to charge you some slices for the price of admission."

In the eighth inning, with the Cubs ahead four to two, the crowd at Wrigley Field explodes. Hank jumps in his seat, startling Pip off his lap, while Stevie, Japhy, and even Johnny, who's never rooted for the Cubs in his life, exchange gleeful high-fives. Margo spins on them all, hands palm-side-up in some furiously bewildered entreaty to the baseball gods. "I've been so good this whole game," she says. "I've kept my mouth shut, I've watched every pitch, every play, and I *still* don't get what the hell everybody's so excited about. What did I miss? What happened?"

"The scoreboard just flashed the Astros–Brewers score," Stevie cackles. "Houston lost."

"Well, all right then," Margo says. "That's hot. The magic number shrank."

The final inning turns tense, though, when the Cubs' relief pitcher puts on two Pirates. Johnny clutches at his hair. "*Auwē,* get dat babooze off da mound!"

"Shit," Hank says. "Borowski's gonna blow it."

"But Uncle Hank," Margo protests, "all they need's another out and it's over, they've won."

Japhy laughs. "You don't get it yet, Margo. This is the third game I'm watching with your uncle, and I can tell you, he's your fatalistic-type Cubs fan, conditioned by years of disappointment."

"Decades," Hank corrects. "Practically three-quarters of a goddamn century."

"All he can see is the Pirates' tying run on base."

"That's not all," Hank says. "Kendall's up next. One of the Bucs' best hitters."

But Borowski, impervious to such pessimism, gets Kendall to pop up and now the magic number is down from two to just one. If baseball's the only sorcery her father believes in, Stevie thinks, well, bring it on.

Between games, she enlists Margo to help assemble sandwiches for lunch. While they ferry plates and drinks from the kitchen, six of Johnny's high school baseball players arrive with coolers, folding tables, and chairs. Lila blows in, too, carrying bags full of groceries. Melveen, the nursing aide, is on her heels, a rice cooker in each arm. Hank regards the women with a rat-smelling grin. "Something tells me," he says, "you two aren't here to check my vitals."

"Just watch your game," Lila instructs. "Pay us no mind."

"I wonder how many baseball fans I should expect to be cooking their meals over here today?"

"Can we tell him, Stevie?" Melveen asks.

"Sure. He's on to us anyway."

"We're not baseball fans, Hank. We're the luau fairies."

"A luau? What's the occasion?"

Johnny snorts and shakes his head. "The Cubs clinch, man!"

"What if they don't bag the next game?"

"It'll go like it goes." Johnny shrugs. "You know what they say 'round here. If can, can. If no can, *no can.*"

"Johnny, Johnny, Johnny. Is that what you tell those boys out there before a big game?"

"Those boys won their league last year."

"Still. I'm glad Dusty Baker's managing the Cubs and not you."

"To win big ones, gotta know how to hustle *and* hang loose. Besides, long time before that pig's cooked. We'll find plenty reasons to celebrate by then. And that meat? So tender she'll be falling off the bone—gonna broke da mouth, guaranteed."

"Come on you guys," Stevie says. "This is definitely going to be a Cubs Clinch Luau."

As though to prove her right, Sammy Sosa blasts a first-inning home run to center, reaching the top of the bleachers. The Cubs score six more runs in the second, the last on a Moisés Alou homer that gusts out to Waveland Avenue on a strong west wind. Stevie realizes it's been more than four hours since Hank's last pill. Mindful of Lila's caution not to get behind Hank's pain curve, she retrieves the Loritab bottle. Hank holds out his hand for a pill, eyes still on the screen, then washes it down with iced *māmaki* tea.

The house fills with smells of onions frying, rice steaming, *liliko'i* pies baking, potatoes boiling. Clement is pitching so well that Stevie's sure the game is over already, but the crowd on the lanai, grown now to include Johnny's players, strewn like puppies across the floor, stays as riveted as the fans in Wrigley Field, jonesing like them for the delirium of an official victory. Hank feeds this urge even better than the broadcasters, lowering the TV volume to catalog his beloved team's every catastrophic collapse on the road to postseason play.

As the last out's called, Japhy uncorks the bottle of champagne he brought and fills plastic flutes for everyone. Hank, after a few minutes of watching the jubilation in Chicago, picks up his remote to click off the TV. "No," Stevie says, "wait." Someone has just stuck a microphone in Dusty Baker's ecstatic face to ask the inevitable question—how'd he go about managing the Cubs to come this close to breaking their curse?—and she doesn't want to miss what he has to say.

"I just prayed," Baker answers, "and asked the Lord to change the mind-set of these players, of this organization."

Hank groans. "What is it with coaches these days? They've all got a direct pipeline to God."

"At some point," Baker adds, "you have to think about leaving whatever bad has happened in the past."

"Easier said than done," Hank says, flicking off the TV with a sideways look at Stevie. "Although that is a statement with which"—he stops for a rattling cough full of phlegm—"I happen to agree."

Hank spends what's left of the afternoon resting up for the luau, and as the first flurry of people arrives, he walks with his cane out to his lawn chair, wearing not just his customary khakis and chambray shirt, but his white cotton cardigan, too. Sewn to the front pocket is Hank's red woollen letter "P"—a task Margo accomplished while he slept. Stevie had expected her father to say he wasn't fifteen anymore, not by a long shot, and refuse to wear the sweater. Instead, he'd said, "You girls are too much," and put it on along with the Cubs cap that Margo brought for him from Chicago. It gives him a rather snappy air.

Hank accepts a mai tai from Stevie—light on the rum. "What happened to the fence?" he asks.

"Margo and I stripped it, then, a little while ago, Japhy helped me take it down."

"Good idea. Clears up the view." Then Hank shifts his attention to greeting the guests clustering around him. Apart from his age, his illness, and the fact that he's fixed to one spot, he might be back on the job at the Coco Grove Hotel, hosting a luau there. A big part of the reason, actually, why Stevie had wanted to make this happen for him.

For each person invited, a half dozen more show up. Exactly the kind of luau Stevie had wanted. Lila's entire family comes, including all of Johnny's four kids, Carly, baby Sean, both of Lila's ex-husbands, and their current wives. "Talk about a grand slam," Stevie tells her.

"What about you? Didn't even have to shop for anything hot to wear, yeah?" Then, at Stevie's baffled expression: "You know, for our baseball buddy over there. The one who made you think about getting laid."

"No," Stevie says, laughing. "But I did clean up my career mess. I even got to deal with the dump chump. And oh"—she slaps her forehead—"I forgot your present." She runs inside to fetch from her still-unpacked suitcase the garment she'd bought for Lila at a specialty T-shirt store in Chicago, printed across the chest with the legend that Stevie had requested: WILD WOMEN NEVAH RIDE BEHIND.

Kiko comes to the luau with not just Lainey and Jerry—the latter borne like a pasha on a pillow, healing forelegs bandaged—but his children and their two mothers. Kiko's aunty Lovey is also here, fresh from a trip to Tonga to sing at the King's granddaughter's wedding, her ample body draped in orange fabric printed to resemble *kapa* cloth. Since Kiko and Aunty Lovey are in charge of the evening's entertainment, they've provided the sound system that's now playing the late, great Izzie Kamakawiwoʻole, his achingly tender medley of "Somewhere Over the Rainbow" and "What a Wonderful World." And since Aunty Lovey knows Hank from the Coco Grove, where she once performed and taught *hapa* hula to hotel guests, she's drawn others to the luau who once worked with him.

Estelle, Hank's real estate agent, made sure his old Chamber of Commerce and golfing buddies got the word. Johnny's baseball players return to the house, freshly showered, with their girlfriends, lips shiny with gloss and skin glowing from a day at the beach. Japhy's invitation has extended to include other hosts on the island's community radio station, plus Leilani Chong from the animal shelter, and Christine, his office manager, whose husband brings tiki torches.

At six o'clock, when Johnny starts shredding pork and the buffet tables are covered with vases of fresh-cut flowers and platters piled high with *ahi poke,* salads, casseroles, and rice, one last guest arrives. Robert Kapahana. The man Stevie had traded with for salt at Puolo

Point. Robert, Stevie discovers, is another guest invited by Japhy; they both serve on committees trying to save Māhā'ulepū and the Point from mindless development.

"If Japhy'd told me this was Makalani's luau," Robert informs Stevie with a smile, "I would have come here expecting the pleasure of seeing her again."

"Makalani?" Japhy says. "Who's Makalani?"

Stevie removes her silver bracelet and shows the inscription, first to Japhy, then to Robert. "It's the Hawaiian name Grandpa gave me."

"Makalani," Robert tells Japhy, "means Eyes of Heaven."

"Ah," Japhy says. "He got that right."

After Robert relates to Japhy how he and Stevie met, Japhy gives him a generous account of her professional accomplishments. "I told Stevie about the park project out by Līhu'e. After she sees the site, she may have some suggestions for us."

"I know it's a small island," Stevie says, "but you two sure do seem to have your fingers in a lot of pies."

"Got to," Robert says. "The way of life here that attracts people—it's not all hype. It's real. It's worth fighting for. But that takes energy. Watching everything that goes on with the planning commission, the city council. Making sure environmental education gets funded, policies enforced. Then showing up to vote. Not so many newcomers go in for all that. Japhy's just the exception that proves the rule."

"Alana was a journalist," Japhy says in an aside to Stevie. "An eco-reporter. I kind of caught the bug from her."

She likes the way he's spoken, without any catch to his voice, as if it's the most natural thing in the world for him to discuss Alana with her in this context. She's the queasy one, for not being able to imagine the confidence she'd need to bring up his dead wife herself.

"Mostly it's the *kama'āina* community that's vigilant," Robert continues. "People born here understand. Something about the spirit has roots in the land. The customs and lore, the values, the history—that's all passed down so spirit won't die."

"Whoever makes your park," Stevie says, "has a built-in theme there."

Robert frowns. "A theme park? I don't think so. We've got enough stuff for tourists to do around here."

"No, no—what I mean is more subtle than that. More like an overarching idea to inform the design, hold everything together. You don't see it so much as feel it." Stevie hasn't even walked the site, but already she's got a sense of how the park ought to be handled, and it's propelled not by thinking of her career, only of how to help shape a precious piece of reclaimed private land into the best sort of public space. Ideas come to mind—so many that she hopes she'll remember them all to jot down later. "The job's still open, isn't it?" she asks, and when Robert and Japhy nod, she feels a rush of enthusiasm.

When Stevie finally makes it to the buffet table to spear some of Johnny's roasted pork for herself, someone touches her arm. She turns to see a lovely, lithesome young woman wearing a dress that bares an incredibly toned midriff and carrying a plate filled with nothing but lettuce and tomatoes. "Hi," the young woman says, "I'm Sharon. I came with Kealoha." She points across the lawn, indicating a lean, muscular guy in a tank top who looks to be a good physical match for her. "He does the station's contemporary Hawaiian music show. Are you with Japhy tonight?"

"Not at the moment."

"I'm just asking 'cause I saw him kiss you, and I think that's wonderful, so good for his soul, you know? Maybe you can tell him I'm sorry about his birthday party. I sort of threw myself at him, but only because I was drinking, and I don't do alcohol anymore—it toxifies my urine, and that's my health elixir of choice these days."

It's all Stevie can do to stifle a laugh. "Really?"

"Oh yes, but I'd never lay that practice on anybody else. For it to work, you have to be totally committed to your body's natural healing abilities. You have to reverence its beauty. And," she adds, with a baleful glance at Stevie's plate, "you can't eat meat. Anyway, I'm happy with how my path's turning out. Kealoha and I are having *the* most amazing tantric sex. I'm even ejaculating, and that's never happened before."

As Sharon floats away on a cloud of ylang-ylang and geranium, Margo whispers into Stevie's ear, "If that's Sharon sober, I bet she was a riot drunk."

In her gauzy blue halter dress, Margo reminds Stevie of a pale, elegant gazelle.

"Having fun?" Stevie asks.

"I am having a fabulous time. Do you know what a *papa kanaka kahuna* is?"

"Ah, you've met Robert."

"He's amazing. So down-to-earth, but he talks to dead people all the time, and according to Robert, I'm not *pupule.* That's Hawaiian for crazy."

Easy to imagine Margo pouring her heart out to Robert. The sort of man who's strong enough not to be spooked by a bold woman, and nurturing enough not to resist that aspect, either. A rare combination. And her cousin might find Robert all the more intriguing for being impossible to picture wearing a business suit. "Japhy told me Robert's a widower. Maybe he's *pupule* for you."

"Stop. He says the reason my mother's not yelling at me anymore is that she's finally at rest. He thinks *I'm* a messenger for the spirit world, like him. Can you stand it?" Her plate filled now, Margo glides over to where Robert is saving a seat for her.

Widower. A word that applies to Japhy, too, though this occurs to Stevie only as she makes her way back to his side. "Widower" seems such an inadequate description, since he lost a child as well as a wife. Also, he isn't an elder; he's her age, exactly one year and four months younger, as she discovered last night. Still, she finds herself hoping that Robert is someone Japhy will confide in. Robert might be one of the few new people in his life who would know exactly what counsel to give. Might be able to see *him* as broken yet whole. That's her wish, anyway, sharp as sexual desire, and it's startling to realize that she's just defined a portion of what her own heart holds for Japhy, what she already aspires to provide.

When the sun goes down and torches are lit, Aunty Lovey plays her first selection, a slow ukulele version of "My Kind of Town," dedicated to Hank and sung as a sincere, heartfelt paean to Chicago, not swingy and slick the way Sinatra did it. While she warbles in the old-time *ha'i* female falsetto style, Kiko leads Keola and Lehua, his son and daughter, through his idea of a baseball hula, replete with gestures for batting, pitching, and catching.

Aunty Lovey sets her ukulele aside. "I'm gonna talk a little story here," she announces, and the story she tells dates back to the sixties, when Frank Sinatra was in Kaua'i to make a movie, renting a house close to the Coco Grove. One Sunday afternoon, Aunty Lovey says, Sinatra was walking along the shore when the inside wash from a powerful set of waves swept him away. "Hank's new on the job then. Movie-star-handsome in those days, yeah? Plenty more good-looking, if you ask me, than our 'bout-to-drown celebrity. And Hank, he's one of the guys who come to haul Mr. Ring-A-Ding-Ding outta the sea. Bumbye, when Frankie's teeth stop chattering enough for him to thank everybody, he thinks Hank's another visitor, so he asks where he comes from. And what does Hank do? Looks him in the eye, dead-serious-like, to say, 'I'm from your kind of town, Mr. Sinatra.' "

Though Stevie remembers seeing a signed photograph of her father standing with Sinatra—it used to hang in his office and showed both men wearing shirts and slacks, not swimsuits—Lovey's tale is news. Only now does she understand the significance of Sinatra's inscription: *Thanks, Hank, you're a real lifesaver.* She'd always assumed that it meant her father had overseen Sinatra's visit in a genial way, attentive but unobtrusive. Which was, after all, his job. Not exactly Fake Nice, but Professional Nice.

"How come you never told me?" she asks Hank while everybody's still laughing.

"I wasn't the only one who fished him out," he says with a shrug. "And he wasn't the only one who ever got swept away. Most weren't so lucky."

"Yeah, but Dad—Sinatra!"

"He put his pants on one leg at a time, just like everybody else."

Then the music turns more traditional. Lehua does a hula most island girls know—"Mahina Hokuo," "Moon and Stars," a staple of Aunty Lovey's that Stevie had learned when she was not much older than Lehua. After that, a handful of women led by Lila and her mother do gentle, fluid, freestyle hula in the center of the yard. Stevie joins them; so does Margo, who mimics the motions with surprising ease. Several men get up to dance, too. Stevie loves the incongruity of burly guys like Robert and Johnny doing hula moves with plumeria blossoms tucked behind their ears.

Almost as compelling—though in a different way—is the inventive routine that Sharon performs with her boyfriend, something that might best be described as tantric-couples hula, PG-rated for the kiddies' sake. If this were a scene from Hawaiian myth, Sharon would be Pele, dancing to incite lust in Japhy, the man who had spurned her, and then, when he stayed loyal to Stevie, taking her revenge by turning them both into teetotaling, urine-drinking vegans.

"We don't want to wear out our guest of honor," Kiko tells the crowd. "Hank's gotta be in shape for the World Series, you know. So Aunty Lovey and me, we're gonna wind things up with a silly old sing-along song from a long time ago, when folks on the mainland, they just couldn't get enough of everything Hawai'i. It's 'Princess Pupule,' and it goes like-a-this."

After a slow run-through of the verse he repeats like a chorus, Kiko has everyone trained to join in:

"Princess Pupule has plenty papaya,
She loves to give them away.
And all the neighbors say,
Oh me-ya oh my-ya you really should try-ya
A little piece of the Princess Pupule's papaya.
Zazza zazza zazza zazza zay."

When most of the guests have departed, Margo kisses Hank's cheek. "I'll see you tomorrow," she says.

Stevie's close by, stacking chairs that Japhy brings her. "I know you're not going out to sample all the hot Kaua'i night spots, Margo, because there aren't any."

"No, but for somebody with skin like mine, this is the best time to walk the beach. Robert says there's the perfect place in Po'ipū."

"Say hello to Hina for me."

"Who's she?"

"Goddess of the moon. Pele's sister."

"Goddesses everywhere," Margo tosses over her shoulder on the way to Robert's truck, "and I haven't even left my uncle's yard yet. I love that about this place."

Hank unhooks his cane from the back of his chair and speaks to Stevie. "Thanks, honey. That was some last luau."

"Doesn't have to be the last," she says. "We can have another when they win the Series."

"If the Cubs win the Series," Japhy says, "we'll have to roast a billy goat instead of a pig."

Another grin from Hank as he plants his cane, but getting to his feet is such an effort he won't be able to manage stairs on his own. Stevie drops the chair she's holding to rush over, but Lila's already there. "All right," Lila says, draping Hank's arm around her shoulders. "Let's get you to bed."

A helpless ache overwhelms Stevie as she watches her father enter the house—with even more difficulty than on the night of his fall. How long ago was that? She digs around in her head for the date of her Chicago garden opening: September 7. Just three weeks. Impossible! The only way to make sense of so many changes in such a short while is to consider time as something more elastic than she'd ever thought. But what about her? Can she keep stretching without snapping? It doesn't feel like it, not right now. "Maybe the luau wasn't such a good idea after all," she tells Japhy. "All those people. It was too much for him."

"Don't go there. Hank had a great time. You did a lot of good."

"We're getting closer than ever. I don't want him to die."

"I know," he says. "It's the hardest thing. Maybe even harder than dying yourself. What's going to happen is going to happen, though. You can't predict it, not in any way that matters. And you can't change it, either. If you try, you might miss out on something you'll cherish in the end."

"Margo says I should be ready for Dad to go. Is that what you're telling me, too?"

"Nope." He holds out a hand and draws her over to sit on the lanai steps with him.

"You're just saying that," she says, easing down, "because if you didn't, I wouldn't park my ass next to yours."

"Well," he says, "it is a very nice ass. But I'm just being truthful. From what I know, doesn't matter if death's sudden or expected. There's a world of difference, sure. Still. Nothing prepares you for that void."

"Do you mean the person who's dying, or the person who doesn't want that person to die?"

"Both. You have to find your own way through. But other people can help. Especially if they love you. So. On that basis, I figure I qualify."

Stevie pulls back to look him in the eye. "Did *they* just say what I think they did?"

"They didn't want to scare you."

"It is scary, though. Makes you vulnerable."

"Can you handle it?"

"I hope so."

"I'll take that for a yes."

"What about you?"

"Me? I hope so, too." Japhy loops an arm around Stevie's waist and presses his lips against the damp spots on her cheeks. "Tears of heaven," he says. "There ought to be a Hawaiian name for *that.*"

Lila shows Stevie how to operate the oxygen tank should Hank awaken and ask for it again, as he did before falling asleep with Pip in the crook of his arm. "I expect he'll go through the night just fine," Lila says. "But I can stay out on the lanai if you want."

"No, I'll manage, Lila. You've already done so much today."

It's still early, not yet ten o'clock. Japhy helps Stevie put another load in the dishwasher and store leftover food. Together they finish off the last of Lila's *liliko'i* pies. "You're right," he says. "More lemony than Hamura's. Better, too."

It's clear by now that Margo won't be home anytime soon. "I'd be pissed," Stevie admits to Japhy, "if it were anyone but Robert."

"Guess it's a good thing rascally sleeping isn't a crime around here anymore. If that's what they're up to."

Stevie laughs. "Rascally sleeping—is that what we've been doing?"

"You bet. Only sex in the marital bed was legal. According to missionary law, anyway. They enforced it, too—till land and labor issues made the courts too busy for peeping and pursuit."

"You mean till the missionaries went into business for themselves."

"Or their children did. Speaking of sleep, though, I better head out and get some. Have to be up early tomorrow."

"Oh, right," Stevie says, disappointed.

He brushes hair back from her forehead and kisses the space where frowns form. "I know you don't want to leave Hank alone—"

"But I don't want you to go, either. Stay?"

"Was just going to suggest that myself."

Comfortable as Stevie is in Japhy's arms following their own hushed, satisfying spell of rascally sleeping, she can't seem to reach anything but a drifting, superficial kind of slumber, nowhere near deep enough for dreams. It's from worry over Hank needing oxygen again, and on top of that, the fact that she's never shared a bed while here—not even when she came to Kōloa on her own, much less with a terminally ill father down the hall.

And so she finds herself studying breath—the breath she can feel moving through Japhy, the breath she can hear huffing in Rainier on the floor beside the bed, the breath she can see in the rise and fall of Hank's chest when she throws on a robe and gets up to look in on him, as she does twice. Breath. What the *ha* in "Hawai'i" means. Grandpa had taught her the significance of every syllable. *Wai* means water, and *i* stands for *ike*—supreme knowledge or intuition from your line of ancestors, your wise people. Another word that's a poem, as Grandpa would say, like *haole.*

One reason *haole* were thought to be without breath, Grandpa told her, was that they'd arrived here so compressed in collars and corsets it seemed as if they'd have a great deal of trouble taking any but the smallest sips of air. Then too, traditional Hawaiians breathed one another in by way of greeting, and so couldn't imagine *haole* gaining any satisfaction whatsoever in that department, either. While this last thought meanders through Stevie's head she inhales Japhy's breath, and as she does, a familiar tinkling sound fills the bedroom, nearly a whole bar of "Lovely Hula Hands," emanating from the music box that Grandpa gave her so long ago, the music box that's been broken for over a decade. It can't be a dream; light-headed as she suddenly is, she's definitely not asleep. She'd think herself hallucinating if it weren't for Japhy awakening with a start before the music mechanism slows in its last run of notes and the revolving platform with its miniature painted palm tree and hula girl once more freezes. "What's that?" he mumbles.

"I'll tell you in the morning," she whispers. "Go back to sleep."

Stevie takes the music box out to the lanai. There's some give in the winding mechanism now, but only a little—hardly a bar's worth of juice—and even when she's rewound it, not another note plays.

Covered with chicken skin, she feels compelled to check on Hank yet again. He looks so frail in the moon glow, so much weaker than when awake, and somehow, having heard the music box go off makes that easier for her to accept.

Stevie crawls back into bed and molds her body to Japhy's. Growing drowsy, she decides a great deal of common sense lay behind the custom of Hawaiians chanting their genealogy. Not because the ones who are gone or whom you never even knew are more valuable than the mortals you're left to contend with in the flesh, but because, like it or not, you're stuck with the energy of their hopes, their fears, their secrets. That screwing up the ancestor chant meant an automatic death sentence—something she'd always found gruesomely funny: "*Aloha*, tell us who you are," then, "Oops, sorry, gotta kill you"—now seems more like the moral to a story: if you're all screwed up in understanding your lineage, well, it might not kill you, but there's damage done. Is that why she feels fortunate to know so much more now about the people her father came from? Probably.

Stevie lets out a huge breath of her own, and soon enough tumbles into sleep, all the way down this time.

Japhy's still in bed early the next morning when Stevie, freshly showered, begins dressing in the darkened room. She grabs a pair of panties from the jumble of laundered clothes piled onto a bedside chair, then pulls them on as Japhy stirs, yawns, and stretches. Stevie raises the blinds, letting in a shaft of buttery light.

One eye open, Japhy regards her at the chair again, fishing out a clean bra. "Me, too," he says.

She pauses, bra in hand. "You, too, what?"

"I'm agreeing with your underwear."

"Well, good, I guess. Are you often incoherent in the morning?"

He shakes his head and points at her crotch. Stevie looks down to see that the pink bikini briefs she's wearing bear a legend, imprinted in red: *I ♥ My Cunt.*

"Sheesh," Stevie exclaims. "Margo threw some things into the load I washed yesterday. She must have missed these."

"They're not yours?"

"Mine? No way. This is not a wardrobe item I would ever own."

"Hmm," he says.

"Hmm," she repeats. "What's that supposed to mean?"

"It's what I'm saying to be tactful. Instead of 'That is *exactly* the sort of wardrobe item you *ought* to own.' "

"Why?"

"Good question." He props up on one elbow, a thoughtful frown at odds with his dimples. "Suits your secret side, maybe."

Stevie's thumbs are already under the waistband, but instead of stripping, she ends this exchange by giving the elastic a brisk, declarative snap. What could be sillier than arguing with a pair of panties? Wearing them, maybe. But so what?

Before leaving for Hanale'i, Japhy goes outside to load trash for the recycling center. Stevie, brewing coffee in the kitchen, sets out two blue mugs painted with hibiscus blossoms and stops to watch him. It's as though she's inside Japhy, able to feel every muscle he's using, alert to every one of his senses, animated by his thoughts. He didn't come to Kaua'i expecting anything like what's happened, not any more than she did. Death had been what blew them both across the Pacific. Not to claim them, not yet. But to reveal something about being alive.

Then the rumble of an engine in the near distance and here comes Robert's truck. Stevie watches while Robert walks around to open the door for Margo, says something that makes her smile, then takes her by the shoulders as they slowly plant cheek kisses. Clearly, they've made a connection. Rascally? No. Intimate? Yes. Of that, Stevie's certain. It seems she can feel inside them, too.

So many different kinds of love at her father's house this morning.

As Robert drives off, Stevie lifts a hand to wave, not so much to greet

Margo as to remember her own separateness. It doesn't work. When she glances up at the crimson-crested cardinal trilling at the tip of a monkeypod tree, she might as well be that bird, warbling for its mate. The strange part of her brain Japhy had pointed out the other night—her posterior superior parietal lobe, her defective global-positioning device—must be asleep still. And yet she's standing solid, not teetering between her different worlds.

Margo sails into the kitchen asking after Hank.

"I keep looking in on him," Stevie says. "His breathing's been steady since he went to bed."

"Good."

"What do you make of Robert?"

"He's sharper than all my professors put together. And I like his terminology better, too. I mean, 'My family conflates love with anger' sounds so dry and clinical. But the way Robert says it—love and *huhū* stuck together—well, it's so much more *human.* We talked all night on the beach and went out for breakfast at dawn."

Margo takes her coffee into the bathroom, and in a few seconds, Stevie hears the shower running and Margo singing, off-key, "Princess Pupule has plenty papaya. . . ."

Outside, Stevie sets mugs down on the table between the Adirondack chairs. As Japhy approaches, she smiles. "Waimakalani."

"Will that make sense after coffee?"

"I'm just guessing, but that might be how you'd make a name, to say it."

"Waimakalani?"

"Uh-huh."

Japhy raises his mug for a sip. "Still not sure what you mean. Isn't Makalani your Hawaiian name?"

"Yeah. All I did was give my name some water. Some *wai.* And there it is. Waimakalani. Tears of Heaven."

Chapter 21

Stevie's first glimpse of the Līhu'e park site will be from the rear of a helicopter she climbed into with Margo and Hank at the Līhu'e airport. If, that is, she can bring herself to look down. Flying inside a Plexiglas bubble always begins for her with a terrible attack of vertigo—a close neurological relative, no doubt, of her directional handicap. She braces against the flimsy-feeling copter door with one hand and grabs Margo's arm with the other, so that she feels anchored enough to lean over and gaze downward.

Stevie didn't have exact parameters for the pilot, only the kind of directions that locals give, along the lines of "Turn left at the second palm tree, right after the *lauhala* grove, cross the stream, and there you are." In this case, her landmarks were the sparse set that Japhy provided. A narrow bridge at the site's bottom, a modest waterfall at the top. The *mauka* plateau and gently sloping *makai* hill. Stacks of lumber and tin from torn-down plantation facilities. Most helpful, though, is the old cane field flume, easy to spot, since three orange tube boats are now barreling down, carrying tourists.

"That's got to be the place." Stevie's voice carries through the microphone built into the required headset that she wears. As the copter swoops in, its nose dips low, and once again the bottom falls out of her stomach, just as it did on liftoff from the Līhu'e airport.

Her father rides up front with pilot Mike O'Connor, the owner of this tourist helicopter fleet and a buddy of Hank's from Coco Grove days. Hank took a pain pill before they left, and Mike twisted the rules to allow an oxygen tank on board, just in case. The canister sits at Hank's feet, its plastic breathing tube coiled around the dial. While Stevie hopes that neither Mike's training in emergency medicine nor the medical equipment he has stowed will be necessary, such backup reassures her.

This parcel of land below, as best Stevie can make out, is smaller than other parks she's worked on, but so enticing that for a moment she forgets about her vertigo. Surprising, how little interest she has in changing the land's contours. She's already proven to herself that she can control landscape just as precisely as an architect controls a building or an artist controls a sculpture. Now the whole idea bores her. Now the fascinating thing is to be confident enough to work with what she *can't* control. Now she can't wait to get her hands on the sort of ornery, shaggy, rebellious plants that will thrive wherever she decides to put them, but will also insist on pushing back with their own existence.

"Want me to circle again?" Mike asks.

"No, thanks. I've seen enough."

"Well," Hank says, "what do you think, Stevie?"

"I think it's incredible."

"Want the job?"

"Yes," she whispers.

"What?"

"If you could see her face, Uncle Hank," Margo says, "you'd know she wants it."

Hank turns to regard Stevie. "They couldn't pick anyone better."

This must be the kind of remark her father always makes about her to *other* people, the reason why she's so often heard how proud of her he is. But it's the first time he's ever said such a thing in her presence. "You wouldn't think I'd failed, coming back here to work?"

"Failed?" he barks. "It's not like you'd be cleaning out toilets. Besides, the whole point of building a reputation, if you ask me, is getting to where you call your own shots."

"Thanks, Dad." It's impossible to keep her voice from quavering. Which comes not so much from his compliment as from the impulse she suspects is behind it—his need to know her life's not stalling out on his account.

"I'd like to see what you do with the place."

"I'd like for you to see that, too."

"Well, then. You better get cracking."

Stevie feels a keen surge of anticipation even as she wonders if Hank believes he'll live long enough to see the park through completion—provided, of course, she gets the job. He must. After all, as he pointed out over breakfast, he doesn't yet require morphine and he's still got an appetite. "Plus," he'd said, "scrawny as I am, I don't have that cadaverous skin-and-bones look I've seen on other guys right before they croak." She understands. He doesn't want her hovering, timing his death like a boiled egg. But if she reverts to her old knee-jerk response to a shove from Hank, which is to pedal like crazy, she'll miss out on too much with him.

The copter rises again, setting off on the tour that Hank had insisted Margo take before going home, much as he had advised countless hotel guests to experience Kaua'i's splendors from the air. "You can't spend all your time here watching baseball with a sick old man," he'd told Margo.

The Cubs won last night's game in Atlanta, the first in their best-of-five series against the Braves. Not only did Kerry Wood pitch a dazzler, but he drove in the winning run. "The first Cubs pitcher to do that in a postseason game," Hank had pronounced, "since Orval Overall in the 1907 Series." So many Cubs fans were in the Atlanta stadium going crazy that the commentators called it Wrigley South. And now, well, Hank's wearing yet another layer of excitement over his letterman's sweater, like a kid thrilled to be in the copilot seat with all those gauges and controls.

Stevie had forgotten how much he enjoyed swooping over the island this way. He first took her on a ride when she was a child, and she knows from those early trips that queasiness disappears once she accepts that no matter how low the copter nose dips, she will not tumble out. Today the calmness comes as they cruise Waimea Canyon, red soil radiant in the clear late-morning light, and no matter which direction Stevie leans or looks, nothing lurches inside her. The second she lets go of Margo's arm, her cousin, who evidently got the comfortable-at-perilous-heights gene, springs into action, uncapping her camera to click away as they ascend to the wet, cloudy heart of the island, with its cleft, labial waterfalls and rainbow ribbons.

Crossing into the Na Pali coast, they dip down between spires of majestic mountains and hover over forbidding fluted ridges and impenetrable forests. Such otherworldly splendor! No wonder, Stevie thinks, that Kaua'i's supreme landscape architect returns from time to time to admire her work. It's Madame Pele's permission she ought to ask before making designs on any portion of her firstborn island. And so she does, silently supplicating as they descend over the giant elephant toes of cliffs that seem to be wading into the sea, then circle over hammering surf at Polihale Beach, with its sands bleached like royal bones.

"That's Bali Ha'i," Stevie informs Margo, indicating the steep mountain they pass while heading for Na Pali's lush northern tip.

"As in *South Pacific*?" Margo asks.

"Right," Mike says. "They used trick photography to make it look like a separate island. All the beach scenes were filmed on this end, too. The one we're over now is Ke'e. Hikers take off into the jungle from Ke'e, and a stone shrine marks where the most important hula school ever once was. For more than a thousand years, people from all over the islands came to study."

"The Ka Ulu a Paoa Hālau," Stevie adds. "They say Pele herself danced there."

Mike glances at her with a grin. "Hey, that was *my* line. Didn't expect a big-city girl like you to be such a fount of knowledge, Stevie."

"Oh"—she shrugs—"I've been reading up a little."

Yesterday morning, she'd done a strategic raid on the Borders store in Līhu'e, buying so much stuff that the clerk who tallied everything asked if she needed help getting it all out to her car. In her bags were books about Kaua'i's myths, traditions, and history. Memoirs and novels pertaining to the island. Music CDs—everything from Gabby Pahinui slack-key to traditional *mele* to loony *hapa haole* songs like "Princess Pupule." Even DVDs of movies shot here, including *None but the Brave,* the World War II picture Sinatra was making when he almost drowned. Usually, Stevie gathers research materials only after she's won a project, but this project is different. With this project, she's driven to deepen her gut-level, island-girl understanding before she even makes a bid.

There's a reason why only elderly Kauaians and Sinatra fanatics remember *None but the Brave,* she'd discovered while watching it with Margo last night, after Hank went to bed, and they'd laughed themselves silly over the scene where Sinatra, as a boozing medic, wisecracks his way through amputating a soldier's leg. Still, it was intriguing. Not just for its locations, but for being shot the year her father first came to Kaua'i. When digging her way into a new site, experience has taught, every little personal connection matters. Even a hokey movie filmed here is an exercise in island storytelling. In its own wordless way, that park should be one, too.

"There was no written language before the missionaries came," Stevie goes on for Margo's benefit. "So chants and hula preserved everything. Purists today would never dance on a stage, or at a mall, or even at a luau. Dancing is a sacred rite for them, not entertainment. They have to be out in the elements they're expressing or it isn't authentic."

"Hula *kahiko,*" Mike says. "That's what they call those old-style dances. Didn't used to see 'em much till the seventies. Big revival then of everything traditional."

Turning inland, they fly over taro patches near Hanale'i, the river that feeds them, and go *makai* again toward more sugary beaches.

Margo points downward as they pass enormous houses with extensive grounds. "That must be where the celebrities live."

"Uh-huh," Stevie tells her. "That's *Haole*-wood."

Mike laughs. "You'll have to clean up your act, Stevie, if you ever want to be a tour guide."

Margo gives Stevie a quizzical look. "I thought you said the word *'haole'* was poetic."

"Poetic?" Mike hoots again.

"Well, it is," Stevie insists. "Unless accompanied by stink-eye, in which case it's definitely nasty."

"Stink-eye or no, can't talk *haole* to tourists if you're in the business," Mike says. "It is just not the *aloha* spirit."

Margo points again. "And look at that huge fancy hotel! I can't imagine ever coming here and wanting to stay in such a place."

"I almost feel sorry for people who do," Stevie says. "So many never slip out of that hotel cocoon. It's like we have hundreds of flavors, and they're willing to settle for just the few that come with their package."

"It wasn't like that at the Coco Grove." Hank's voice is uncharacteristically thin and reedy through the mic, as though he's already speaking from the beyond. "Not in my day. Oh, I suppose we served up our share of Hawaiian cornball. That lagoon we called a royal fish pond. The wedding chapel. Lighting torches every night. But it was still an intimate place. The lobby had a bunch of framed Matson Line posters from the twenties. Back then, the only way to get to neighbor islands was by boat. Pretty boats, too—nothing like today's giant cruise ships, dumping out pale plump people by the thousands."

"Hank," Mike says, "you're as bad as your daughter. You'd be surprised how many of those pale plump people care about the culture."

"Well"—Margo sniffs—"at least I'm not plump."

"Don't get me wrong," Hank says. "I don't begrudge them. It's just that now those posters seem so exotic. But when I got here, it all still felt that way."

Stevie's been so taken by aerial views that only then does she notice how Hank has the plastic breathing tube hooked over his ears and into his nose, his hand resting on the oxygen tank dial.

She reaches over to touch Mike's arm, and nods toward Hank when she gets his attention. "Not to worry," he says. "Checked the big guy's pulse over Princeville."

As they swoop down toward the airport, Stevie's even woozier than she was on takeoff, almost nauseated. The feeling passes quickly, though, and once they've landed, Hank turns off the oxygen and suggests a quick early lunch at Hamura's, before Margo checks in for her flight home.

"Sure you're up for that, Dad?" Stevie asks.

"I'm hungry. The oxygen must have given me a boost."

Even so, Stevie makes certain Hank only has to walk very short distances, dashing off for the Defender to pick him up by the tarmac and driving straight to Hamura's door, where she lets him and Margo out before parking.

It's early enough that they don't have to wait for vacant seats. Stevie, suddenly ravenous, orders the large special instead of her usual medium, plus a double order of chicken sticks.

"Quite the appetite you've got," Margo observes.

"I'm hungry. Falling in love must have given *me* a boost." With Margo sitting between them, Stevie speaks loudly enough to be sure Hank's heard. Because this, it seems, is something he would want to know, too. Though his only comment is to the waitress: "I think I'll have the teriyaki today."

"Wish you could have stayed longer," Hank tells Margo as they stop to drop her off outside the airport.

"Uncle Hank, as short a time as we've had, I feel like I got an adult dose of exactly what I needed. You, your daughter, the island. Everything."

Hank leans down for his cane, but Margo stops him. "No, don't bother getting out. I'll come to you."

As Margo opens the passenger-side door and reaches in to embrace him, Hank says, "Will I see you again, honey?"

For once, Margo seems speechless, eyes glazed with tears. "I hope so, Uncle Hank."

"Then we don't have to say goodbye. We can just say *aloha,* and *a hui hou.* Till next time."

Stevie walks with Margo to the airport entrance. "I know I talk a good game," Margo says, "but I'm not ready for him to die, either." Margo stops to reach into her bag for a Kleenex. She blots her cheeks, puffs her nose, and then takes Stevie by the shoulders, training those sharp, blue-as-Hank's eyes on hers. "Listen, let's make a deal—to never stop speaking, no matter what."

Returning Margo's gaze, Stevie's positive that in any future they might share, her cousin will, upon occasion, be exasperating, annoying, and confusing to boot. But that seems just another part of the bargain. "Okay, Princess Pupule," she says. "Deal."

Margo stops again, diving into her bag to find another Kleenex, this one for Stevie.

Chapter 22

It's still dark when Melveen arrives for the early morning shift at Hank's house and Stevie sets out for the Līhuʻe site. After parking the Defender on a service road, she shoulders her backpack and climbs to a high, breezy hilltop. There she uncaps her thermos of coffee and sits to watch the sunrise over the ocean. Then she walks the site's perimeter in slow, jagged, ever-smaller circles, stopping to sip water, jot notes, observe birds in flight, consider the sun's seasonal drift. It's midday by the time she's finished.

Hot and sweaty, she cuts through jungly overgrowth to the waterfall's modest pool, where she slips off her pack, sets her clipboard down, strips, offers the appropriate request for permission to enter, and wades in to swim. Only while floating on her back, gazing up toward the water's mountaintop source, does she realize that this park, like the Chicago park, will also have a fountain, and she's already in it. Her job, if she's chosen, is just to glorify the work of Pele and her crew of fire, wind, water, and time.

Later, while she's drying off on the bank, it comes to her what a womanly shape this piece of land has. Hilly breasts for vistas and picnics. A big-bowled belly for music performances and hula. Generous thighs and arms, perfect for embracing garden paths. And here she is, perched at the womb's mouth. That slashing flume, which had struck her as the most difficult element to integrate, now seems more like a scar. Not an ugly thing to be hidden, but another narrative track to honor. *From here poured down water to feed the cane.* Something along those lines—though no local needed a sign to explain such a thing, and visitors who cared enough to seek the place out would already be aware of the flume's original purpose. So what if tube boats crash through from time to time? Tourism is just as much a track in this island's story as sugar. And for everyone like Lila who used to trespass over company property to slide down the flume, there's another track still, a memory track, crackling with excitement, danger, and—who knows?—probably even the thrill of first sex. Stevie hadn't lost her own virginity with an island sweetheart, but she could imagine others who did after such an adventure.

By sunset, she's traced the route of a hide-and-seek stream that runs from the waterfall pool, diving under the earth and breaching up again. She's also got a map in her mind of all the ways light and shade play throughout the day, a template for every remaining element. She departs with her clipboard legal pad full of notes, but the attached global positioning device hadn't been necessary. There's no deficiency to compensate for here. The only orientations that matter are *mauka* and *makai.* Her island-girl sense of direction is all she needs.

Over the next few days, while Stevie works on her proposal, Japhy moves out of his cottage and Lila moves in.

One of the reasons Hank had wanted Stevie to consult his attorney, she's learned, is that while his Kōloa residence will go to her when he dies, as will the condo in Seattle, the cottage is willed to Lila. And with

Japhy moving out to Waimea, Hank saw no reason not to effect the cottage transfer ahead of time. It wasn't fun, discussing Hank's death in property terms, but this arrangement delights Stevie—and not just because it puts Lila even closer by to visit, monitor Hank, and spend the occasional night. She's never seen Lila so bowled over as when she learned of Hank's bequest.

Now Lila can earn extra income by renting out her other house, and someday she'll no doubt use her good fortune to defray the high cost of island living for a grandchild who might otherwise be forced to move to the mainland. In the outer suburbs of Seattle, San Francisco, and Los Angeles, there are sizable enclaves of islanders exiled for economic reasons. Kaua'i real estate has become so pricey, with affordable new housing so scarce, that the more property a local family has, the more likely that family is to stay together. And as unorthodox as Lila might be in her relations with men and motorcycles, she's a traditionalist when it comes to looking out for family.

When Stevie meets with the Līhu'e park's consortium principals in a conference room at the Sheraton Hotel, they're quick to bring up the Chicago controversy, and no wonder. They had only to Google her name and there it was. Her selection is no slam dunk. It helps, though, that Christopher Caldwell wrote a long Sunday thumbsucker after the community forum, reevaluating everything but her benches in a positive light, and it's a bigger plus when the drawings and ideas she lays out for the park are in sync with those of the principals. So is her budget. Her portfolio helps clinch the deal, but not nearly so much as being island-born.

"Who else applied?" That's what Arthur Stewart wants to know when she calls New York to tell him about clinching the deal.

"No one," she admits.

"Why am I not surprised? Is this a grief move, Stevie? Did your father die?"

"No."

"Good. Then he's stabilized."

"It's hard to tell. I hope so."

"Then why don't you come back for a while? I want you out front on the Anacostia River redevelopment in D.C. It's major."

"The Līhu'e project is major," Stevie said.

"How can it be major if no one's ever heard of it?" He doesn't yell, but his tone is that of someone at the end of his tether with a backward child.

"It's major for Kaua'i."

"Look, the whole point of that forum was to put a positive frame around Chicago. It worked, you did it. You don't have to make a lateral move, much less fly under the radar like this."

"Don't worry, I won't use the firm's name."

"That," he says, "is not what worries me." Then he hangs up.

Stevie understands what worries Stewart—that she's lost the drive he hired her for. And though she doesn't feel like calling back to convince him otherwise, she is, after all, still driving. Just in another direction.

Stewart's attitude makes all the sweeter Japhy's insistence on celebrating at his place tonight. This is her first visit to his new home, and she drives from Kōloa bearing gifts: drought-resistant plants suited to the hotter, drier climate of Waimea. In the rear of the Defender are a small red wiliwili tree, Cape honeysuckle, and purple lantana for ground cover. She also thought to bring a bag of soil, some mulch, a spare set of gardening tools, and her binoculars. Crossing the river that Waimea's named for, Stevie makes one of the mental language equations she performs constantly these days: *wai* = water, *mea* = reddish brown.

In the town's tiny commercial district there's a generic Big Save grocery store facing off with the locally owned Ishihara Market. Stevie can still sing Ishihara's corny old radio jingle, and she does, keeping an eye peeled for the turn to Japhy's house.

There it is, just as he'd described it—plantation-style, painted a light, lemony color, close to the beach. Parking alongside Japhy's truck, she catches sight of waves breaking on the soot-colored sand, the sun in its slow-motion dive toward the island of Ni'ihau. It's a privilege, having a view of Ni'ihau, because a view of Ni'ihau is the only access most people are ever allowed.

Only the few hundred pure-blooded Hawaiians who live on or come from Ni'ihau are officially entitled to set foot on its beaches, and their routine trips to and from Waimea are bumpy three-hour rides in the sort of LSTs that stormed Normandy on D-day. Yet the entire island is owned by an old-time sugar family that acquired it in a deal with Kamehameha V. Complicated, like every other element of postcontact history. Now, for prices few visitors can afford, the current owners run in occasional flights for day trips of hunting and touring. By all reports, Ni'ihau resists innovations from not only this century but most of the last, and Stevie's touched by how here in Waimea, where postcontact history began, spectral sunsets bathe the only island to retain such mystery.

Rainier charges out of the house ahead of Japhy to dance around the Defender, and when no little brown terrier appears, she butts her head against Stevie's thigh. "Sorry, girl, but Pip's in demand elsewhere."

"Come on," Japhy says, with a kiss. "I'll give you the tour."

He points out the system he's installed to collect, filter, and pump rainwater. There's solar water heating, too, and a bright new light-colored roof that won't absorb heat, plus long eaves providing plenty of shade—not only where the sun hits hardest, but also the windward side, to keep incoming air cool. The yard's sprinkled with hardy, lantana-friendly local grasses. A trellis by the lanai will be perfect for honeysuckle. When Stevie presents Japhy with all his botanical gifts, he picks up the red wiliwili, asks her to decide on the best spot for planting, and sets down the tree to mark her choice. "I'd like flowers, too," Japhy says. "I know you're not a gardener by trade, but maybe you'll have some ideas."

"It would be fun to garden here, starting off with such a clean slate."

Then they go inside, where there are louvered interior doors, ceiling fans, and floors of bamboo and tile. Such an energy-conscious place! As an LA who works with eco-issues all the time, Stevie ought only to admire this virtue, not have her heart constrict at how Alana-inspired it seems. So babyish of her. Who says it's a contest, winnable only by a dead woman? *Nobody but me.* That's what she'd *like* to believe.

Although Japhy's house is twice the size of Hank's rental cottage, it has the same sense of unfussy ease. Stevie notices a small shelved alcove with an ocean-facing window. There it is: the photo of Alana and Megan that she remembers from before. A few others, too. Tempting for Stevie to breeze right by, since Japhy doesn't point out the alcove and it's a separate-enough space to ignore on a walk-through like this. What a cowardly idea. No, she must go to the alcove and take time for these images, fully absorbing the moments they capture.

"Such a little beauty," she says, taking hold of Japhy's hand. "Her mother's face and her father's dimples. It's good you've made a special place for them."

"I'm glad that's how you see it."

And it *is* how she sees it, deep down. But that doesn't keep doubts from dancing back into her head. Love unclouded by apprehension—she's tasted that with Japhy. What keeps her from making a real meal of it?

Out on the deck there's a grill filled with charcoal and chunks of *kiawe*. A small picnic table is already set, with a bowl of floating plumeria blossoms at its center. Stevie runs back to the Defender for her binoculars, and when she returns, Japhy pours two rum drinks from a pitcher in the refrigerator. Then they walk out to his property's edge, where the beach begins and two lounge chairs are situated for watching the sun's last burst of cloud-kindled fireworks. "You're so quiet," Japhy says after a while. "Did the photographs bother you?"

"No," Stevie says. "It's just that I can see how you might want to be a father again. And I hope you don't think I'm being presumptuous or crazy for mentioning this now, but my feelings for you . . . Well, if I don't, it's going to be like some kind of time bomb inside me. The thing is, I've got problems there."

"What kind of problems?"

"Fertility problems."

Japhy's voice is so low and soft it almost fades into the sound of breaking waves. "That must have been hard for you to tell me. But Stevie, it doesn't matter."

"Not now, maybe. But it might later."

Japhy shakes his head slowly. "I don't think so."

"Why?"

"It's hard to explain. But I'm thinking about this fight Alana and I had. It was right around Christmas, not long before we went to Mexico. When I got home, Megan waved her hand and said, 'Owie, hot!' Then I saw these tiny white blisters on her fingertips, and I just went nuts, demanding to know how this could have happened to her. Well, we had a gas fireplace with a glass front in the living room, and we usually lit it only at night, when the temperature dipped and Megan was already asleep. But on this day it was chilly, and a windstorm knocked out power for a while. So Alana took Megan to the living room to play, turned on the fireplace, and gave the 'hot, don't touch' lecture to Megan when the glass front heated up. Megan was old enough to understand—she was so bright, and already good about that sort of thing. But the flames must have intrigued her, because during a few seconds when Alana's back was turned, she touched the glass anyway. So that's the kind of father I was, being a real asshole to Alana because my daughter needed to learn a tough lesson and I couldn't prevent her pain. And then come to discover that the world's much more dangerous than I'd ever imagined. Not just the crash, either. Other terrible things, too. One right after the other. With nothing I could do about any of them." He sighs. "I'm not putting it well."

"Falling in love again isn't as frightening as having another child to protect."

"Or lose. Mostly lose." He gives her a penetrating look. "How are you with that?"

The territory he's just laid out seems like lava not yet cool enough to step on. Stevie takes a small, meditative sip of her fruity drink and decides to walk around it instead. "This is hard to explain, too. The ideal thing for me is enough balance. So that having a baby—however someone like me might be able to do it—is a free choice. No huge pressure one way or the other. I love kids, and back in New York, I borrowed my friends' at every opportunity. But I'm used to how my life doesn't look like everybody else's. It doesn't bother me. I guess I even like it that way. The one neat part about getting older is knowing that nothing is ever ideal. And this might sound funny, but I'm not sure I need a child of my own to feel complete."

"That could change."

"True. It could change for you, too."

"There's a lot we don't know yet, that's for sure. I guess what's important is, we're happy with how things are."

"I agree. One step at a time."

As the sun slips behind Ni'ihau, Japhy points out to sea. "Quick," he says. "Might be spinners out there."

Stevie uncaps the binoculars, adjusts the focus, and looks in the direction that Japhy indicated. She's just in time to catch one dolphin's spectacular double pirouette through the air, then another's. She hands the binoculars to Japhy. "Definitely spinners."

After a while, he shakes his head. "Must have been a last sunset rally. But I'm glad *you* saw them."

"Do you know why they spin?"

"I've heard theories. That they've got suckerfish attached, and they're jumping to get rid of them. That they're showing off. But I bet only the dolphins know for sure."

Her best answer yet. "Yes," she says. "That's my feeling, too."

Japhy can sleep in with Stevie because his radio show Sunday morning is a prerecorded phone interview with a naturopathic vet he knows in Seattle. It was past midnight when they'd finished their bathtub stargazing to step out all shivery-skinned, wrap themselves in towels, and warm each other in bed. "Damn," Stevie says when they awaken so late that the *Paradise for Pets* program is already over. "I wanted to see what it felt like, listening to you on the air while you're naked here with me. Pretty weird, I bet."

But she seems only mildly disappointed, and he's glad to have her all to his in-the-flesh self, without having to share her with his on-the-air self. Stevie isn't due at her father's house until this afternoon, when they'll join Hank and Lila to watch the Cubs in their final, tie-breaking game against Atlanta. It's the most leisurely morning the two of them have spent. Making love, drinking coffee in bed, showering together. How abnormally normal it all seems. It's as if his spine, after a long spell of contortion, had suddenly slipped back into alignment.

After breakfast, they walk to the Waimea Hawaiian Church, which Stevie's never been to before. Japhy drops a donation in the *lauhala* basket by the door and they slide into a rear pew. The church is so plain that its founding missionaries' Puritan ancestors would have felt right at home. No stained glass, no statuary, no altar cloth, no carved pews, no organ. Just a simple wooden cross on the wall, a vase filled with ferns, and four ceiling fans lazily stirring the air.

"Everyone's from Ni'ihau," Stevie whispers.

"How do you know?"

"The necklaces."

Casually as all the congregants are dressed, many of the women wear shell lei, the sort of intricate, handcrafted pieces that Japhy, hunting for Stevie's Christmas present, had examined in a jewelry store the other day. Each one exquisite, strung with impossibly tiny, perfect shells gathered after winter storms on Ni'ihau, none larger than a pigeon pea. Half of every harvest broke in the piercing process, which explained how expensive the necklaces were. The older woman seated on the other side of Japhy wears a choker much like the one he'd bought, strung with shells of red and white to resemble heliconia flowers. Stevie must be right. These women in church didn't purchase their necklaces. They're wearing treasures culled from home.

Before the service begins, a young couple arrive with their newborn, who's passed all around to be held and cooed over, another communal treasure. For a moment, Japhy feels left out. He wants to marvel over that baby, too—feel that once-familiar warm, sweet-smelling, animated weight in the crook of his arm—and then, without a shred of misgiving, hand him back to his parents. Who are young—very young, probably not yet twenty—and won't be crippling their infant with fear. Or so he imagines. He glances at Stevie, smiling in the baby's direction without any evident longing. He'd like to think this is another way they're well suited—her fertility problems an interlocking piece for his aversion to fathering another child. No conflict there. He remembers blowing out his knee on the ski slopes, how his recovery from surgery was far more painful than expected because of the excessive scar tissue his body had manufactured. Even though in his dreams he skied perfect runs again, and knew he could in reality if he wanted—plenty of people did—he could never bring himself to risk another blowout, another surgery. Starting another family is like that, only worse. Much worse. Just the thought leaves a hollow, queasy feeling.

Japhy picks up a book of Hawaiian-language Bible verses from the holder in front of him. When he opens it, out falls a photograph of a young girl in braids and an older woman who might be her grandmother. As he tucks the photo back in, he sees that the woman beside him, reading verses in her own book, also holds a photograph—of someone who looks to be a sister. Worshipers here bring their dead to church. The first time he visited, this custom was a big part of what had made him feel at ease. Not something that any crusty New England missionary had taught Hawaiians to do, that was for sure. But they had brought something of the old religion to the new, just as they beautified staid Congregationalist hymns with ethereal Hawaiian harmonies.

The service is as simple as the church itself. After the minister reads through a hymn, everyone sings. Japhy's neighbor points out the hymnal page so that he and Stevie can join in—which Japhy is too shy to do, being unfamiliar with all the rules of Hawaiian pronunciation and never much at carrying a tune. But Stevie is more confident. Her soft, low voice easily rides the harmonic waves.

The sermon's in Hawaiian, too—blessedly so, thinks Japhy. He'd been put off formal religion by the dull, droning, endless services he was forced to attend as a child while visiting his grandparents. He wouldn't have described himself as a man of faith before the crash, and especially not after. But he's never seen a minister deliver a sermon while waving a crimson blossom in the air, as this one does, and Japhy rather enjoys wondering what he'd say himself if he were the one up there with that hibiscus in his hand.

Deep in their roots all flowers keep the light.

A line from Roethke, the only nature poet his mother enjoys quoting more than Gary Snyder, the circuitous inspiration for Japhy's name. Then another bit of Roethke comes to mind: *Love is not love until love's vulnerable.* Though it's not looking at the flower that reminds him of this. It's looking at Stevie in her pale green linen dress, her face luminous, and all that thick, wavy hair piled into a recklessly artful heap.

While everyone in the congregation takes turns standing up to read a Hawaiian Bible verse, Stevie shows Japhy prayer book pages written in English, telling of how Henry Opukahaʻia arrived in New England in 1809, became a Christian, and died at the age of twenty-six. If the prayer book has it right, none of them would be here this morning if it weren't for Henry. His death inspired the first boatload of missionaries to set sail from Boston; they arrived on the Big Island of Hawai'i six months later, determined to spread the Gospel first where Henry had been born.

"Such a dry version of the story." Stevie says this after the service has ended, on their return to Japhy's house. Instead of going back through town, the way they'd come, they're taking a more leisurely beach route, carrying their shoes and walking close enough to the incoming tide that the dark sand beneath their feet is hard and damp. "Henry was just a child when he saw his parents massacred in a tribal fight for control of the Big Island. He was kidnapped, ransomed by an uncle, and later, in the middle of training to be a *kahuna,* he ran away to sign on with a Yankee whaling ship. Didn't have a word of English when they set sail, but he wound up living in New Haven—first with the ship's captain, then with the president of Yale. What he died of was typhus. Islanders had no immunity."

"Something tells me we're in Michener territory."

"Yeah, his book starts with the missionaries coming."

"Whenever I think of Michener's *Hawai'i,* all I can see is Julie Andrews on the boat, puking up bananas."

Stevie laughs. "I know, that one's burned into my brain, too. But it doesn't end there. A few years ago, Henry Opukaha'ia's descendants moved his remains from Connecticut back to Kona, into a vault overlooking the sea. Beside the church those missionaries built. The church Henry'd hoped to establish himself."

"So he came full circle."

"His bones did, anyway. In a jet that made the trip in less than ten hours."

"Is this more of your basic Kōloa Grammar School history?"

She shakes her head. "Mostly homework for the park."

"How does Henry tie in with the park?"

"He doesn't—not directly. But holding as many island stories as I can in my mind makes me feel more qualified, somehow."

"Do you feel like you have to have an opinion?"

"About what?"

"An imposed religion that suppressed indigenous culture. I've heard people argue all night about that one."

"Me, too," Stevie says. "All the good missionaries accomplished—

establishing written Hawaiian and an amazing literacy rate—versus everything they quashed. And do we really want to go back to human sacrifices, a *kapu* system that was so harsh on women and everybody who wasn't royal or chiefly?" She sighs and shrugs, though not in a dismissive way. "It can go round and round. What I feel is sad that the missionaries laid so much nasty heathen-pagan shame on Hawaiians, but glad that what's wise and beautiful survived anyway. Just wanting to find the middle path, I guess."

Japhy starts to speak, but the flood of feeling that overtakes him is tactile, not verbal. The flat of his hand finds the small of Stevie's back. She spins into his arms like a dancer, and when he presses her body against his, they stand that way for a long while, swaying as though moved by the rhythm of waves now lapping at their feet.

Back at the house, Stevie changes her clothes to saw leftover shingles into a planter box for holding honeysuckle. Japhy settles onto the living room couch and dials Kate's number in Seattle. "Hi, Mom," he says, eyes on Stevie.

"Japhy! Guess what—I heard your radio show on the Internet this morning."

Athletic as Stevie looks in her purple running shorts and tight white tank top, her breasts and hips seem lush—even lusher than he remembers from that first glimpse of her in a bikini at Māhā'ulepū. "Unbelievable," he tells Kate. "You got up at five a.m. just to listen?"

"That's how much I miss my number one son—I'll take him any way I can get him these days. Even prerecorded. What a nice show you do!"

Stevie pulls a pencil out of her tousled hairdo to mark the last board she'll need, then zips Japhy's small circular saw through with a single motion, clean as the cut of her long, slender limbs. "Well, it's livelier when people call in. One of my callers from last month is here right now. Stevie—doing a little carpentry outside." She picks up a hammer and pounds the first nail into place.

"Yes, I can hear."

"Stevie found an abandoned puppy that I'm neutering next week. A terrific little terrier mix named Pip." As Stevie's back turns to Japhy he remembers how, when he awakened ahead of her this morning, he'd stood at the side of the bed for a few moments to admire her bare bottom's heart-like shape.

"Pip? Pip as in *Great Expectations*?"

"Uh-huh."

"This Stevie," Kate says, "sounds like my kind of guy."

Japhy smiles to himself as "this Stevie" puts down the hammer for a moment to wipe perspiring palms on her shorts. "You're probably right about that."

"Does it feel like home there yet?"

After dropping a nail, Stevie squats to retrieve it—as graceful a squat as Japhy's ever seen, with knees together, spine straight. "More and more. I've been thinking about the holidays. If it's not too late to pull it all together, let's see if we can find a place to rent near me that's big enough for everyone."

"I don't want to guilt you into having a family thing if you're really not up to it, Japhy. Are you sure?"

"Positive."

"I'm so glad. What changed your mind?"

"Lots of things. Mostly a talk I was having with Stevie. I don't want you all feeling like I've run away, but I'm not ready to come back yet, either. This seems like a good middle path."

By the time Kate catches Japhy up on how everybody else in the family is doing, Stevie's finished with the planter. Sweaty and satisfied-looking, she sets it down by the trellis. Such energy she has. Not mindless or exhausting to be around, but always aimed, somehow. Busy, that's what she is, with an almost childlike sense of absorption in whatever's captured her attention.

Kate's in the middle of describing her own latest project—editing a collection of haiku-inspired poetry about the moon—when Stevie kicks off her flip-flops and opens the screen door. Japhy holds out his free hand to grab hers as she pads into the house. "Want to take another shower with me?" Stevie says, leaning over the back of the couch to smack him loudly on the lips. Then, "Oops, sorry—I thought you were off the phone."

Japhy hears helpless laughter, the sort that ends in Kate having to wipe her eyes dry. The sort he hasn't incited for years. "My kind of guy," Kate repeats. "You're such a tease, Japhy."

"I wasn't teasing," he protests. "I just didn't bother to correct your sexist, gender-based assumptions."

Which just gets her laughing harder. "You've got me there, love," she gasps. "You've got me there."

Hank's in his bedroom with the door closed when Stevie arrives with Japhy an hour before the game begins. "Melveen's with your father," Lila says as Pip runs circles around Stevie's feet, yipping until she picks him up.

Stevie frowns. "You and Melveen here at the same time? Why?"

"Because she's giving Hank a sponge bath, a shave, and a shampoo." Lila's voice is light, but firm. "He specifically asked for Melveen, so me? Just trying to keep out of the way."

Still holding Pip, Stevie charges off for the bedroom, and she's about to knock when Lila swoops in to stop her. "Wait, *ku'uipo.* He'll want privacy for this."

Through the door, Stevie hears Hank. "Ah, that feels nice, Melveen." His new thin, reedy voice makes her want to weep.

Lila walks Stevie to the kitchen, where Japhy's at the sink, filling a water bowl for Rainier. "He wanted Melveen 'cause he's not ready yet to be that fragile with me." Lila sighs in mock exasperation. "Always the problem for us, yeah? Our close time came after I got divorced, too. Before he grew back that shell of his and took the job in Seattle. When you were old enough to tell, well, nothing much *to* tell. Except for a little spark every now and then, it was mostly in the past."

"I thought it might have gone like that," Stevie says. And she did, on some barely conscious level—the only level where she could imagine *any* of Hank's liaisons. Easier to understand how, when the romance fell away, he and Lila would still be bound by feelings for Stevie. Or was that looking at things like an egocentric child? Whatever the glue, there was no lingering bitterness, as with Beryl. "You do," Stevie adds, "have the distinction of keeping him as a friend. And never once calling to pump me for Daddy news."

"You ought to let those other ladies know when his time comes. Not to mention your mother. Have you talked to her yet?"

"Not about this." Lila drills her with a what-are-you-waiting-for look that Japhy clearly catches. Stevie's sure that, later, he'll be eager to hear more about Lila and Hank; so far, he seems to enjoy piecing together her background. But now, Stevie wants more information about Hank. "Has Dad been reading today?"

"Sleeping, mostly."

"Eaten anything?"

"A little oatmeal."

"*Māmaki* tea?"

"Just some fizzy water, cut with juice."

Japhy exchanges an easily read glance with Lila. *Uh-oh, here she goes again.* It doesn't help. "Why didn't anyone call me?" Stevie demands. "I could have gotten here hours ago."

"Oh, my girl," Lila says, "you could have been here the whole time, dogging him like Pip, and still no difference. It's not like Hank's dying any minute, I promise. He just doesn't have the energy to do for himself today. This happens."

Pip jumps out of Stevie's arms as Melveen opens the door to Hank's room; she nearly trips over the little dog as he charges for Hank's bed. "We got him all suited up for the game," Melveen reports.

Lila pats her cheek. "Thanks for squeezing us in, Melveen. I'll go give him the once-over. And, Stevie? Why don't you put together a milk shake? Toss in some of that protein powder on the counter—two scoops."

"I can walk the dogs," Japhy offers.

"You don't have to stay," Stevie tells him.

"Are you throwing me out?"

"No, but I'd understand if you'd rather get back home or go to the beach. There's a really good wind today."

Japhy is already at the door, calling Pip. "I'll get another bottle of champagne at Sueoka's," he says. "If Hank's not up to drinking, we can spray him with it after the Cubs win."

When Stevie brings the milk shake to Hank's room, Lila is sitting in a chair pulled up to the bed, holding Hank's right hand in both of hers. "Ah," Hank says. "Another member of my harem arrives." He looks so weak that Stevie doubts he'll ever get out of bed again. She takes a moment to steady herself, inhaling the scents of soap and shave cream, and before she can find her voice, Lila, in a slow, fluid whoosh of motion, sets the milk shake glass aside, transfers Hank's hand into Stevie's, and guides her into the chair. "I'll just go get a straw," Lila says.

When was the last time Stevie held her father's hand—just held it, with no reason but to be near and loving? Never. Or not ever that she remembers. But even though it took Lila to show her how, it seems like the natural thing to do at this moment, creating enough ease for him to convey his condition and for her to absorb it without any resistance. A new place for them both. "Listen," Hank says after a while. "It's just a game."

"If you say so."

"And the good news is, looks like I'm going to live long enough to watch it."

She's certain he wants her to laugh, and she does. Though the funny thing is how genuine it feels.

"Maybe I never told you," he muses, "but I wasn't ready for you coming along."

"Should have been more careful then."

"I *was* careful," Hank insists. "The thing is, I know I wasn't a perfect father."

Stevie squeezes his hand. "Who is?"

"But I never once regretted having you. You were such a determined little thing, from your very first breath."

"You weren't in the delivery room."

"Speaking metaphorically, kiddo. You were born on Bastille Day. Appropriate, don't you think?"

"How so, Dad?"

"You're such a groundbreaker—no pun intended. So independent. So much your own person."

There's no push to his words, only appreciation. Can this be the same father who wanted always to toughen her up, prepare her for the world's hardness, not teach her to find its soft edges?

"Never thought much of those other guys," Hank continues.

Stevie rolls her eyes. "Now he tells me."

"You didn't want to hear it then."

"Might have done me good, though. Knowing you cared enough to meddle."

"Honey, in this life, you have to make your own mistakes. Anyway, what I'm getting to here is Japhy. He's different."

"So you think he's a keeper?"

"A keeper? He's a hold-on-to-for-dear-lifer."

"Oh, Japhy's got his stuff, Dad. Big stuff, too."

"If you say so. Just do me a favor. Try not to give him too hard a time."

"You think *I'm* the difficult one, don't you."

"Well," Hank says, "you're not your old man's daughter for nothing."

A comment that just yesterday would have set off swells of pain, anger, defensiveness. Which probably goes to prove Hank's point. But now, hanging on to his hand, she feels only his concern for her happiness, and all she can do is nod, giving that hand a small, tender shake of agreement.

Stevie's hand slips back into Hank's throughout the game—when Ramirez puts the Cubs up four to nothing with a two-run homer in the sixth, when Kerry Wood leaves the mound after holding the Braves to one run on five hits over eight innings, when Hank's eyes mist as thousands of delirious Cubs fans stand up in the Atlanta stadium to sing "Take Me Out to the Ball Game" over and over again.

"Just four more wins, Hank," Japhy says, "and your Cubs are in the World Series."

Hank raises an equivocal eyebrow. "We'll see. The Marlins are worthy opponents."

The Marlins! Of course, Stevie knew that if the Cubs won today, they'd go on to play Miami for the pennant. It's only hitting her now, though, that she'd dreamed of a marlin her first night here with Hank. But what was it that *happened* in the dream? She can't remember until she flashes on herself fishing from a pier, and then it all comes back. She'd caught a marlin. And then she let it off the line because she didn't want a trophy fish. A *trophy* fish! And then her father tipped over, into the water. She's tempted to tell everyone about her marlin dream right then and there, but she's too superstitious, and too unsure of the dream's meaning. Margo, who had called three times during the game, would no doubt tell her that this dream had nothing to do with baseball; the marlin was a symbol of her drive to achieve, a drive instilled by

Hank, and with Hank dying, she'd need to find new purpose to her life. Or so Stevie imagines.

"Something wrong?" Japhy asks her.

"God no. That was a swell game."

"Swell?" Hank says. "The Cubs win their first postseason series in ninety-five years and all you can say is 'swell'? That game wasn't swell, Stevie. That game was . . ."

"Magical?" she offers.

"No. *Historic.*"

Chapter 23

On Monday morning, before Hank awakens, Stevie puts in a few hours on her park plans. It was sweet of Japhy, rejiggering his schedule to do Pip's neutering surgery today, his usual day off, just because that worked best for her. Though when she thanked him for it, he said, "Makes sense for me, too. If I work today, I can watch a game with you guys later this week."

When Melveen arrives, Stevie does the bulk of weekly grocery shopping. Later, when Hank is up, she installs a handrail in his shower with the help of a handyman recommended by the hospice director. That rail, plus a plastic garden chair, allows him to bathe on his own, though Melveen stands by, just in case.

Hank shakes off all the breakfast suggestions Stevie makes. He announces that what he wants instead is a cheeseburger with

French fries, plus a Coke, "a *real* Coke, the kind that comes in those little curvy glass bottles, poured over crushed ice." Such specific cravings—like a pregnant woman's, Stevie thinks. What's more, he wants to eat out. She's too relieved by this return of energy and appetite to lobby for healthier food, and so at eleven a.m. they become the day's first customers at the Po'ipū Beach Broiler, an open-air restaurant with the atmosphere of an old beach house.

"We've got your crushed ice," the waitress tells them, "but our Coke's from a vat."

So Stevie dashes out to the nearest grocery store for a couple of bottles. On her return, she finds Hank talking baseball with Gary Yates, the Broiler's owner. There's a lot to discuss, since Mr. Yates's son Tyler, once the pride of Kaua'i High School's team, is not only a minor league player, but a fireballer who hits a hundred miles an hour on the radar gun. Which is how he tore ligaments in his throwing arm last year.

"He's come back strong after surgery," Mr. Yates says.

Hank squints seaward for a second before turning back to Mr. Yates. "I predict the Mets will call Tyler up as their fifth starter next year."

"Man, you are right on the money! They're just starting talks. How'd you know? Somebody on the inside tip you off?"

"He's got new pitches," Hank says, "right?"

"A real sweet changeup and the curveball. As of this season."

Hank nods his approval. "Can't be testing his speed on every throw or he'll blow that arm out again. Such a big guy—looks more like a linebacker than a baseball player. Helps with the intimidation factor."

The waitress reappears with two enormous burger platters. "Well, good luck with your Cubs, Hank," Mr. Yates says. "Hope they do it for you this time."

"Me, too. It's their last chance."

At that Stevie winces, but once they're alone again, she turns a baffled stare on Hank. "How *did* you know about Tyler, Dad? I mean, it's not like you follow the minor leagues."

"Search me." Hank uncaps his burger to slather on mustard. "I just had this picture in my head of the Mets' rotation with Tyler on it."

"You're putting me on!"

"Getting psychic in my old age, maybe."

It's a lot of food Hank's ordered, but he puts away more than half of what's on his plate. "God," he says as the table's cleared. "What I'd give right now for a cigarette."

While Hank rests that afternoon, Stevie lies down for a short nap that turns into two hours of deep, difficult-to-awaken-from sleep. There's a dream in her head as she stirs and stretches, an extended version of an earlier dream, the one where Japhy's cruising her Pineapple Street apartment. This time, she doesn't yell at him for picking up the hula girl music box, and the action keeps unfolding. He sets the music box down, opens her closet door, shoves clothes aside, and leads her into empty rooms that she never knew existed. Even now those rooms feel real, and she's still amazed over paying rent on unused space, amazed that her home was so much bigger than she'd realized. Stevie's pretty sure this dream isn't about Brooklyn real estate. But her muzzy mind can't pin it down any further.

It's not like her, sleeping in the middle of the day. Maybe it's the heavy lunch. Or maybe she's just energetically tuned in to Pip, who must be woozy after surgery.

Stevie bought a new hedgehog (Ralph III) for Pip as a post-op treat. But when Japhy brings the puppy back that night minus both balls—the one that was visible, the other hidden—Pip shuns not only the toy, but her and Japhy as well, welcoming only Hank's attentions. "He's pissed off," Stevie says while they finish drinks out on the lanai.

"He's just groggy from the drugs," Japhy tells her. But as he goes to the kitchen for more ice, Stevie shakes her head. "It's not the drugs," she tells Hank. "He's punishing us for what happened to him today."

"And I don't blame him." Hank cradles Pip against his shoulder and coos into a floppy ear. "We have something in common, little guy. We're both the last of our lines." He shoots a look at Stevie. "As far as I know, anyway."

"Dad," Stevie reprimands. All Japhy needs is pressure from her father to sire an heir. But even though Japhy gives no sign of having overheard, her edginess lingers. From the oddness of hearing Hank lobby to become a grandfather—if that's what he was doing. From her own reluctance to confirm his hunch. But most of all, from her ongoing inability to imagine the world with Hank gone.

❋

The next afternoon Stevie watches with Hank as the Cubs lose their first home game to the Marlins, and her father's condition seems to dive with his team's fortunes. He takes oxygen throughout the final innings, then heads straight for bed on two Loritabs, reading his Roosevelt biography for only a short while before dropping off.

"Should I wake him for dinner?" Stevie asks Lila when she stops by after work.

"No, let him rest. But cover him so he won't catch a chill."

Together they decide that, beginning tomorrow, they'll set up a cot in the hall near Hank's bedroom and take turns sleeping near his open door so that someone's close by if he should call out.

"That's a silly plan," Hank says the next night as Lila throws sheets on the cot for her first shift. Stevie wonders if he's right. The Cubs crushed the Marlins today, sixteen to nine, and for this game, her father didn't require oxygen. "Just humor us, Dad," she tells him.

"You're the one doing *us* a favor, Hank," adds Lila. "We'll sleep better not having to worry about you wandering around without your cane."

There's no baseball on Thursday, when the Cubs and Marlins travel to Miami for their next pair of games, and as soon as Hank gets up, Pip insists on being wherever he is, happy to go outside only when Hank is stationed in his Adirondack chair, reading and enjoying his new, improved view with a blanket shrouding his knees. Even then, the puppy's curled into a doughnut on his lap. Stevie has to use chunks of raw sirloin to lure Pip into taking walks, keeping him on a leash since he's not supposed to run until a week after surgery. Though Pip gives no indication of wanting to run anywhere but back to Hank. The same behavior holds through Friday, when Japhy comes over to join them in watching the Cubs bury the Marlins again.

"Interesting," Japhy says when she remarks on Pip's clinginess while they're reading in bed.

"Interesting how?" But for that he evidently has no answer—or none so vital as the impulse to set their books aside and kiss her. It's a good impulse. His mouth on hers is so delectable that it makes her forget all about whatever's driving the little dog.

❄

On Saturday, the Cubs are ahead by one run in the ninth inning, so the game keeps everybody—Hank, Stevie, Japhy, Lila, and Johnny—tense until the final out, when a rush of jubilation propels Stevie off the couch. "What could be sweeter?" she shouts, dancing around the lanai. "The Marlins are dead in the water. The Cubs are cooking, they're on a tear. One win away from the Series with their best pitchers ready to go in Wrigley Monday night? It's in the bag!"

Nobody, not even Hank, refutes her. Though she can tell that, for him, this requires enormous restraint.

Japhy drives home to Waimea after dinner, as Stevie had insisted; she's sleeping on the cot tonight, Japhy has a live radio show early tomorrow morning, and after the excitement of the Cubs' last three consecutive victories, all of them could use a quiet Sunday without baseball, especially Hank.

Stevie's just finished cleaning up in the kitchen when Margo calls. "Guess what?" Margo yelps. "Kenny's got tickets—we're going to the next game!"

"Cool." Stevie walks to Hank's room with the phone, mouthing her cousin's name. Hank holds up a finger, signaling her to wait while he finishes reading a page in his Roosevelt biography. Then he closes the book and sets it aside without marking his place. "Finished?" Stevie asks.

"Yep," Hank says.

"Already? It's such a big book. I didn't want—I mean, I didn't think you'd finish so soon."

"Me neither. But it was really good." Hank removes his reading glasses and scoots Pip out from under his arm to alongside his hip. But instead of taking the phone from Stevie, he leans back against the pillows and closes his eyes. "I'm all done here. Give Margo my love."

"I heard that," Margo says. "Make sure he knows we'll be there cheering for him."

"And we'll be looking for you in the stands."

"I'll bring one of those posters people wave for the camera. Mine'll say, 'Do it for Hank.' "

After hanging up, Stevie fetches a glass of ice water and sets it on Hank's nightstand. "I'll get the oxygen," she says.

"No, I'm good to go." He gives her a glance before closing his eyes again. "I was already dreaming. Of when I was a boy in Paradise."

"Paradise?"

"Paradise Springs, Wisconsin. Evvie and I used to go with my aunt every summer. She rented rooms at a farm that boarded city people. I remember fishing for bass there. And swimming to the dock in the lake. And my first kiss, up in a hayloft."

"How romantic. How old were you then?"

"Twelve."

"Who was the girl?"

"Sally Becker. Her hair was so pretty, so soft. She washed it in rain-water."

"This Paradise of yours sounds like a pretty nice place."

"It was. Wish I could show you."

Stevie leans down and kisses his forehead. "Maybe you can dream yourself back there."

"I'd like that." Hank takes a long, slow inhalation. "One more game, Stevie," he says. "Just one more game."

Whatever dream Stevie's having flies from her head when Pip awakens her with a plaintive bark, paws on the cot's edge. She leaps to her feet, flips the hall light switch, and goes straight to her father's bed.

Despite Pip's noise, Hank's eyes are closed. His arms are rigid, his hands knotted into fists by his sides, and there's a tight, lopsided grimace on his face. Yet the center of his body seems caved in, deflated, somehow.

"Dad?" Stevie says. No sound from Hank but the rasp of labored breathing. She turns on his bedside lamp, dives for the oxygen tank, adjusts the dial, and hooks the plastic tubing around Hank's ears, guides it into his nose. Then, stifling a sob, she sits on the side of his bed to take hold of his hand, gently tracing the path of each vein running from wrist to knuckles. His exhalations ease. His arms soften. His hand relaxes into hers. All signs, she hopes, that he's not in pain, because there's still nothing stronger than Loritab in the house. "That's better now," she says, "isn't it?" Though Hank's eyes remain closed and he can't seem to speak, she's sure he still hears her voice, still feels her touch. It's tempting to call in Lila so she won't make any mistakes—won't make this any harder on her father than it already is. But every cell in Stevie's body insists that this moment belongs just to them, that mistakes aren't possible now, not if her motive is love. And how could there be any messenger more true than her own very substance, grown from Hank's?

A breeze blows lady-of-the-night fragrance into the room. Pip jumps onto Hank's bed, noses open his left hand—the one Stevie's not holding—and lays his head in the palm.

Willing reassurance into her fingertips, Stevie shifts her steady, rhythmic touch to Hank's arm, then his head, then each side of his face. "It's okay, Dad," she says, pressing her lips to his cheek. The feel of his dry, cool skin and its strange, sweet chemical scent tells her everything she needs to know. His lingering grimace is not from pain but from fear, and on top of that, anger. So hard for him to navigate these emotions in life. How's he supposed to manage them now, in death? He can't. That's what he needs her for. Not to heal him, but to help him go where he's headed. Stevie closes her own eyes for a second, wondering what to say. Lila would know. Grandpa, too. *So does Makalani,* she can hear him tell her, and then the words flow effortlessly, in a soft, steady stream.

"I know it's sooner than you thought, Daddy. I know you wanted more. But it's all right for you to leave. Your body's all worn out, but your spirit's still strong. You won't disappear, you won't. It's like going back to Paradise. It's like going home. No rush, just go easy, one step at a time." Her cheeks are bathed in tears that pour from her like these words, without a sob, without a shudder. "Remember how I walked for you that day in the hospital, how you walked for me? It's the same. Only this time, I'm right behind you. You don't have to worry about me anymore. I'm ready whenever you are."

Gradually, Hank's face loses all tension. Stevie glances at the clock radio dial, which reads 3:48 a.m., and turns back to Hank as a lone tear slips down his cheek. Then she moves in closer, listening while he takes a breath different from any preceding breath, a breath she's certain will be his last. Air enters Hank's body in a sharp, surprised, openmouthed gasp, but leaves sounding like an awestruck whisper.

Chapter 24

"How are you doing, Stevie?"

It's a constant question in the days following Hank's death, especially at the Coco Grove dinner she hosts to celebrate his life.

I'm grateful I was with him.

Glad he made such an elegant exit.

Relieved he went out with the Cubs on top, and didn't have to watch them blow it.

Grateful, glad, relieved—all true enough. But since there's no concise answer to how she's doing that begins to scratch the surface of all her sorrow and loss, each soon becomes its own epic.

At first this is soothing, spinning her heart out into stories meaningful enough to make a difference—not just to her but to whoever cared enough to ask in the first place. But coming at her again and again, day after day, the question morphs into one that drops her down on some strange planet where gravity's so dense with grief that every step is like walking through mud in weighted hip boots.

And there are so many steps necessary, she discovers, when a loved one dies—more than she'd ever imagined. Japhy helps her take some major ones. Lila, too. After that, "*What* are you doing?" becomes a far easier question for her to handle.

The answer: "Not much." Which is less embarrassing than admitting to her two major, almost obsessive grieving rituals: listening to Rory Block sing "Ain't No Grave" with the volume cranked up high as it'll go, and sleeping. Her attraction to the song makes a certain kind of sense, but sleeping? Must just be an escape. A way to give her body a chance to build up more fluid for tears.

She can't seem to get enough sleep, or find enough places *to* sleep. She sleeps on beds, sleeps on beaches, sleeps on hammocks and lanai. She even dozes off while floating on her back in the ocean at Salt Pond Park. She sleeps just about everywhere except behind the wheel, and she's had to snap herself out of more than a few dangerous nods while driving, too.

It feels like an endless hunger, this urge for sleep.

Then Hank appears in a dream, standing atop a hill on the Līhu'e site, young and tan and athletic-looking, wearing shorts that bare two good legs. He walks down to the thatched-roof gazebo where she sits in a loose white gown making a lei of red *lehua* blossoms. At her feet is the ceramic urn containing Hank's ashes.

"But you're dead!" she cries out.

Her dream father just shakes his head with a grin. "No I ain't, kiddo. You can't keep a good man down."

It sounds just like him! But awakening in her father's Adirondack chair, Stevie's confused. Did she just dream Hank, or did Hank just dream her? That's the question she puts to Lila.

"Doesn't matter," Lila says. "Either way, you're getting that he's in a better place than he expected."

"But he never expected to be *anywhere.*"

"I know, my girl. That's what I'm telling you."

Whatever her dream means, seeing Hank again this way seems to be the purpose of all that sleeping, because finally, twelve days after his death, she feels energy start to stir. When Lila asks her to Kiko's Thursday-night hula class—one of many such invitations—this time, Stevie says yes.

Straddling her Nighthawk, Lila starts the engine. Stevie straps on Lila's extra helmet, swings her leg over the bike, wraps her arms around Lila's waist, and off they fly into the twilight for Kiko's *hālau* in Kapaʻa, their bodies in sync, echoing turns in the road as if they're dancing together already. Stevie wouldn't be surprised if Lila chose the Nighthawk because it has such a happy-sounding engine, full of throaty chuckles as they breach a hill, singing with laughter on open flats. When they reach the *hālau,* Stevie's so exhilarated by the ride that she wants to keep going.

"I know," Lila says. "It's addictive. But dancing will do you good, too."

While everybody else on the *hālau* lanai puts on a homemade gathered green practice skirt of thick, palm green cotton, Stevie steps into an old white skirt of Lila's, sewn from the same pattern. These skirts are a far cry from the wispy, sexy little numbers made of synthetic grass that luau entertainers wear, but Stevie's surprised by how sensuous her hips feel, hugged by that extra weight, as she raises first one, then the other.

She recognizes some of the women here: Leilani Chong, Lila's daughter-in-law Amy, and Sharon, the gorgeous urine-drinking health nut with her scent of ylang-ylang and geranium. Stevie feels self-conscious as Lila introduces her to the rest—like an interloper among all these barefoot hula sisters who are so plainly attached to one another—and an old knee-jerk response from schoolyard teasing compels her to count who's *haole* here. Just three, apart from her mostly *haole* self. Nobody gives her any stink-eye, but she senses a certain reserve, and her awkwardness increases as Kiko signals that it's time for class to begin and the women launch into a Hawaiian chant. With her sharpening translation skills, Stevie can tell they're asking permission to enter the *hālau*—as if hula were as elemental as an ocean to plunge into, a flower they would like to pluck.

As they file inside, Stevie at the rear, Kiko notices her with a yelp. "How are you doing, Stevie?"

"Don't ask."

"Don't want to say, or not sure?"

"Both."

"No matter. Just be wherever you're at, just do whatever you can. Don't push. It'll be sweet, sistah."

She stations herself at the rear of the room so she can follow the others as they move to the beat Kiko establishes on his *ipu,* warming up with swoops and dips across the floor. The most difficult step for her is a low stoop and rise combined with knees fanning in and out. An elegant quiver as executed by the other women, while Stevie's is more of a lame, funky chicken. But once she's mastered it, she becomes lost in movement. Her skirt, so heavy on steadily rocking hips, seems to anchor everything earthward, creating a rhythm, while freeing everything from the waist up to find a fluid, airborne melody. As the class progresses, Kiko teaches the beginnings of a hula to the moon goddess, Hina, in which the goddess escapes the world's drudgery by ascending to her domain on a lunar rainbow. It's plain that Kiko is a gifted *kumu,* just as encouraging as Aunty Lovey but far more demanding, with a knowledge and openhearted, spiritual reverence to his teaching that's all his own.

Stevie hasn't been this alive to her body since Hank died. By the time class ends, she understands that it's not just grief that has made her so sleepy, and it's not the approach of an overdue period that has made her breasts feel so tender, and it's not stress or her lone, unreliable ovary that has delayed her period, but it's what happened with Japhy by the birthing stone.

It's her hormones. It's life inside her. But where? In the right place? Which would be her womb, of course. Or the wrong? Stuck within her remaining ovary or fallopian tube, where a fertilized egg's rapidly multiplying cells are doomed to die.

And now, a whole new series of tasks for Stevie—not just necessary tasks, urgent ones.

1. Keeping herself from mentioning anything to Japhy, even though she can't imagine getting through the night without the comfort of his body close by in bed.

2. Slipping off to his bathroom first thing in the morning to pee on the stick that turns blue.
3. Inventing an excuse to head back to Kōloa right away, before coffee, even, so Japhy won't notice she's not in her right mind.
4. Finding a doctor willing to see her a.s.a.p. and shoot her straight through whatever tests are necessary to determine just where this tiny embryo is embedded.
5. Calling Lila, who, thank God, has the day off, so she can tell her face-to-face what's going on.

"This is hard to explain," Stevie begins as she pulls out a chair from Lila's round, tiled kitchen table, set up in the same spot where Japhy had his—the one they were sitting at when he told her about Alana and Megan. A memory that only ties this pregnancy all the more tightly to Japhy's losses, making her own dilemma feel small. Although didn't he admonish her to never, ever, make such comparisons? Yes—while they were making love, in the bedroom now decorated with the familiar, cozy clutter of Lila's quilts and shells and baskets. Even so, Japhy couldn't have anticipated a loss like the one that she's more than half expecting. Again. And could the timing be any worse? It's only a few weeks since they've advanced to the stage where "I love you" is spoken directly, not by implication, and even then, the feeling's conveyed like a newborn thing itself. Precious, yes, but a long way from walking around on its own.

"Spit it out," Lila prompts. "Don't mince words."

Stevie gets up to throw cold water on her face, grabs a fern-sprigged kitchen towel to blot, sinks back into her chair, and lets loose with a gusher. "Okay, so I'd been feeling crampy, and I thought my period must be finally coming because it was definitely late, only I knew the lateness didn't have anything to do with sex because there wasn't any—with Brian, I mean. But it couldn't have been cramps, it had to be from how I'd stopped running and put on some weight and so, finally, I was ovulating again—on the night you gave me that killer *pakalolo* to smoke, so of course, that was the one time, the *only* time, I didn't plan ahead."

Now that it's out, Stevie's heart pounds as if she's just raced a marathon. Only Lila doesn't get her point. "What are you telling me?" she asks.

"That after I got back from Chicago, I might as well have left my birth control in the box."

"So you're pregnant!"

It's tempting to match Lila's excitement with her own, just to see what that would be like. So womanly, Stevie imagines. Joyous, too. But she resists, answering in a dull, flat voice. "Yes."

"How far along?"

"Six weeks, maybe five, I'm not sure—I've been in such a haze. But Lila, I don't know what kind of pregnancy this is. It might be just like the last one."

"Might be," Lila says. "Might not, too."

"With my history and age, the odds aren't good. Can you come with me this afternoon to find out?"

"Why not the daddy?"

"Isn't that obvious? It's such early days for us. And he's afraid of being a father again."

"Japhy has another child?"

"I know what you're thinking, but this is nothing like with Brian. Japhy had a little girl, a beautiful little girl. Megan. Just a baby when she died—killed with her mother coming back from a vacation in Mexico. That terrible crash, remember? Four years ago, I think. Alana, she was Japhy's wife."

Lila rocks against her chair, hand to breast. "Oh, oh, oh. Such suffering."

"I feel bad even telling you. It isn't something he wants people here to know, not unless he tells them himself. But now do you see? If he's still in denial over *that,* how's he going to deal with *this*?"

Scooting close to Stevie, Lila wraps an arm around her shoulders. "Still, *ku'uipo.* You can't live in fear. Fear just brings out the worst in us. What would you do about this if you weren't afraid?"

"I don't know! I'm too scared to figure that out!"

"Well, *I* know. You would tell him."

"I'm not saying a word until I know for certain if this one's ectopic."

"So if it isn't, you'll want to have this baby?"

Stevie shrugs out from Lila's embrace. "Don't ask me that, please. I don't want to go there yet, I *can't*—not before I find out if it's even possible for this to *be* a baby."

❋

Dr. Tamar Pearce enters the small air-conditioned room where Stevie, in a hospital gown, perches on the edge of an examining table, gripping its sides so her hands won't tremble. Lila extends her own steadier hand to the doctor. "Lila Wei," she says. "I'm a nurse and this sweetheart's aunty, here for moral support."

Dr. Pearce can't be more than five feet tall. No older than Stevie, she looks like a fragile doll of the Dutch persuasion, with a chin-length fringe of silky blond hair. What she lacks in size, though, she makes up for in authority. "It's good you're here so early on," she tells Stevie, "and without any symptoms. If this pregnancy does in fact turn out ectopic, the egg will still be small enough that we can give you a shot of methotrexate to dissolve it." Stevie's stomach wobbles, although she knows this information is meant to be reassuring. "I've read the history you gave us," Dr. Pearce continues, indicating her clipboard. "You won't have to experience the kind of pain you had before, Stephanie."

"It's Stevie"—words that come out in a croak.

"Was this pregnancy planned, Stevie?"

Not by me, she thinks. *By something totally oblivious to my screwed-up plumbing. The Night Marchers, maybe. Or my father—his spirit looking for a way back before he even died. If that's possible. And if it is, what about Japhy? Souls on his side could be looking to reincarnate, too.* But since this just makes her feel possessed on top of terrified, she only shakes her head.

"Then you've got enough on your mind," Dr. Pearce says. "I just don't want you worrying at this point about a worst-case scenario where you lose your left ovary, too."

"That's what I told her," Lila says. "Last time was such a nightmare."

The doctor glances at Stevie's whitened knuckles. "Why don't you get over here and hold her hand, Lila. Not that my pelvic exams hurt. In fact, that's the big advantage of having hands as small as mine. Or so my patients tell me."

Her patients are right, Stevie decides when the pelvic's over. She hadn't felt much besides the plastic speculum ratcheting open, and Dr.

Pearce had executed that particular maneuver with as much sensitivity as all the rest. Even her stirrups are comfortable, wrapped in lamb's wool.

Now Dr. Pearce says, "So far, so good," and she extends the examining table. "Let's have you scoot up to the pillow and lie down." Then she folds back Stevie's gown and papery blanket to bare her belly. "One more scar on your right side than I was expecting. Appendix?"

Stevie nods. "Ruptured when I was a kid—forgot to write that on the form."

While Dr. Pearce returns to her clipboard to make a note, Lila slaps her forehead. "Why didn't I think of that myself?"

Stevie swivels her head around. "What?"

"Your appendix—" Lila begins.

"There *can* be a correlation between a ruptured appendix and ectopic pregnancy," Dr. Pearce says. "But I think it's best if we don't get too far ahead of ourselves." She rubs her hands together to warm them before pressing on Stevie's abdomen, paying particular attention to the neighborhood of her sole surviving ovary, on the left. "Any pain, Stevie?"

"No."

"Tenderness?"

"No. Is that a good sign?"

"Good, but not definitive. Neither is your blood test, although it does tell us you're absent the low levels of HCG that are usually associated with ectopic pregnancy. That's a hormone produced by the placenta—human chorionic gonadotropin. Okay, we're done. You can sit up now."

"What's next?" Lila asks.

"Ultrasound. Ever had one, Stevie?"

"No. Or not that I remember, anyway. They might have done one before my last surgery. I was pretty out of it by then."

"Entirely painless. Just some cold jelly on your abdomen and an instrument rubbing through it, bouncing sound waves. The computer translates those into an image of interior organs. If that doesn't show anything, the next step is a transvaginal ultrasound."

"Is that the kind," Stevie asks, "where you have to drink a bucket of water and then they squiggle some sort of alien probe around inside while you try not to think about how bad you have to pee?"

"Not exactly how I'd explain it to anyone I didn't want to run screaming out of here. It's a little uncomfortable, maybe, but also painless."

Stevie groans, tightening her grip on Lila's hand. "I've been dreading that test ever since my doctor in New York told me about it. Which probably means I'll need it. But then we'll know for sure?"

Dr. Pearce gives her a regretful smile. "Not necessarily. It might be too soon to get our answer with ultrasound. And if it is, why, we'll just keep monitoring your condition every few days until we *are* sure."

Another groan from Stevie. "Is it possible for me to just check out of my body until this is all over?"

"Afraid not. But I can teach you how to do yogic breath—that might help."

"What a good idea," Lila says.

And so Stevie learns how to inhale through her nose—slowly, to a count of eight heartbeats—and exhale by the same route, to the same count, vibrating air against her throat with an audible rasp. Just doing a short round in the examining room calms her anxiety. On a scale of one to ten, she's down from off-the-chart to six by the time Lila accompanies her into another examining room, this one in Wilcox Memorial Hospital—*the hospital where* I *was born,* Stevie can't help thinking—for her ultrasound.

Lila knows the technician—Joy Apostol, an old friend from high school—and it's a comfort for Stevie, feeling Joy's fondness for Lila extend to her.

Lying on the table, Stevie cranes her neck to see the screen that Joy watches while moving the wandlike probe over her jelly-coated belly. Just a vague, shadowy blur, nothing at all like the clear-cut illustrations of reproductive organs you see in women's health books, with everything such a promising shade of pink, branching like a healthy plant. From the way Joy keeps circling over the same spots again and again, Stevie can tell she hasn't found her egg. A high-tech egg hunt—that's what this is, isn't it? *Maybe he's hiding,* she thinks. *Maybe he doesn't like being bombarded by sound waves.*

He? Where did that come from? Stevie never had such a gender specific sentiment last time. Of course, she hadn't allowed herself to feel much of anything last time except all the physical pain. Which is probably why she's being so ridiculous now. As if a tiny fertilized egg is capable of hiding! *Stop,* she tells herself. *It's attached wherever it's attached, and going all goo-goo isn't going to help.* But a different, less rational part of her keeps sending another, much sweeter message. *Please be in a good place, little one.*

Joy switches off the computer screen. "Not enough detail, Stevie," she says. "How about you drink water for me and we'll take another look from the inside?"

As Joy presents Stevie with cup after cup of water, Lila keeps up a running commentary. "Imagine you just ate a big ol' plate of *poke*—all that salt! And nothing to wash it down till now. . . . This is how much we're supposed to drink *every* day, yeah? Only who ever does? . . . Think what a nice picture we're gonna get when your bladder's full, plumping everything up in there. And then it's only three feet to the bathroom, but forget about that for now."

Once Stevie's done drinking, it's off with her panties and back into stirrups. Joy covers the probe in a sheath of latex. When it's inside her, Stevie's eyes squinch shut; her throat's so tight that it's difficult to sound a rasp on the exhale. Dr. Pearce was right—the procedure isn't painful. But Stevie was right, too. This feels like something that's done only after you've been abducted in a spaceship. Joy is no alien, though, and with Lila holding her hand once more, Stevie takes enough complete yogic breaths that she's able to open her eyes and look at the screen.

"Aha!" Joy says, her long red nails clicking on the computer keyboard. "Got that ovary real good now."

"Is it normal?"

"Except for a cyst on the outside. Common, this type—nothing malignant. But only doctors are supposed to say so for sure."

"Does that rule out ectopic?"

"Not like finding a yolk sac."

"You mean my egg?"

"Uh-huh. But might be too early."

The screen goes blank again as Joy moves the probe. Another picture emerges, clear enough for even Stevie to tell that it's her uterus. This is torture for a visual person like her, having graphic evidence in her face and not being able to read it.

Joy gets three different angles before she stops, removes the probe, swivels the screen away from Stevie, then starts clicking on the keyboard again. Giving up on yogic breaths, which have lost all effect anyway, Stevie swings her legs over the side of the table and hops to her feet—not so she can run to the bathroom, though she's never had to pee worse in her life, but so she can look over Joy's shoulder.

"Well?" Stevie demands. "Did you find him?"

Chapter 25

Stevie manages to put off Japhy for almost an entire week after the ultrasound.

First she pleads the need to grieve Hank alone, at his house, where her father's energy is so strong still. Not completely true, considering how focused she is on life—*new* life—and also how her father doesn't feel nearly so absent now as he did before she peed on that stick. Still, she speaks to Japhy with conviction, and then feels guilty because there's nothing but the warmth she's come to depend on in his response. But only until she convinces herself that, in this case, ends really do justify means.

When Japhy checks in with Stevie by phone on the third day, she thanks him for his concern—rather formally, sounding to herself more than a little like Beryl—before mentioning how behind she is with plans for the Līhu'e park; if she doesn't work almost around the clock for the next few days to finish designs for basic elements like the benches, lighting, and band shell, it will be impossible to get everything fabricated in time for the park to open in September. An even better excuse, since it happens to be *completely* true. Once again, Japhy acquiesces without a murmur of protest.

But on Thursday morning, when Stevie calls Japhy to make a case that seems feeble even to her—she needs *more* time alone to recover from the exhaustion created by her first two excuses—he responds with obvious aggravation. "Fine," he tells her. "I just hope you'll let me know when you figure out what's really going on." Then he hangs up without saying goodbye. It's difficult, resisting the urge to call back. But whatever pain he's feeling, it's small compared to the pain she's saving him from.

After pulling herself together, Stevie sets off to inspect trees and plants at two different botanical gardens, each so vast that she's arranged private tours. Her guides are knowledgeable, full of practical advice on everything from watering systems to candidates for her on-the-ground crew. It's time for dinner when she heads back home. Another solid day's work. But setting aside her dilemma hasn't helped a brilliant solution bubble to the surface, which is usually how it goes for her with *design* problems. If anything, she's more stumped than ever.

What she ought to do is return to New York, where she can pass the execution phase for the Līhu'e park to someone junior at the firm, ponying up for the travel costs out of her salary if Stewart objects. Assuming she can carry this baby to term, it would be better if her body billowed out on Pineapple Street rather than here on Kaua'i, where the only decent way for her to show love for Japhy is by denying it altogether. A line of reasoning that makes her feel, by turns, frozen inside and insane. Adding to this swing's wildness is the tsunami of delight that hits when she lets herself imagine a baby boy at her breast, on her hip, even in a backpack, coming along for the ride when she's out on a job. She sees him as a toddler, too, his fat, dimpled hands picking wildflowers. At that moment, it seems such a gift that she might bear a child. A phenomenon, really, and one that, according to Dr. Pearce, may be unrepeatable; this could be her last chance at conceiving without major medical assistance. As remarkable a talent as Stevie has twice shown for having unprotected sex at the precise moment when a ripened egg might meld with some vigorous spermatozoon, the odds of such a thing occurring again dip almost daily. While she can't quite bring herself to think of what's happened as lucky—not with the timing so premature in relation to her romantic career with Japhy—the Hawaiian word for gift does come to mind. *Makana.* Might be a good middle name for this baby. Which she remains convinced is male, despite the fact that when Joy at last located the yolk sac and fetal pole, it was much too early to determine gender.

No sooner does her pleasure peak, though, than it's as if some unseen hand hits the reset button and the whole damn emotional cycle starts up for her all over again: soaked in despair, lathered by craziness, rinsed with delight. There seems no way to stop it, either. No way at all.

After going home to feed and walk Pip, Stevie takes him with her on the drive to Kiko's *hālau,* leashing him on the lanai in a spot from which he can see her inside during class. In the first few days after Hank's death, Pip turned into a poster puppy for canine depression, lying around with his head between his paws, picking at his food. Japhy said that he'd heard from an animal psychic that if you mentally transmit to a dog the image of the person it's missing bathed in blue light, the animal will be put at ease. He sounded dubious, but Stevie was concerned enough to try anyway, and it did seem to help. At least Pip regained his appetite and stopped sleeping on Hank's bed, atop his pillow. But he still wails, inconsolable, whenever she leaves him.

Dancing tonight only seems to intensify Stevie's internal whirring, not put a stop to it, and afterwards, all she wants is to be alone again. Lila and Kiko, however, won't hear of this. They both insist that she come with them and everybody else to the beach. "You have to, Stevie," Kiko says. "You can't miss out on the *ho'olauna.*"

"We do it every year," Lila tells her. "Didn't you get my message?"

Stevie nods, but she's in no mood for socializing, which is her understanding of what a *ho'olauna* entails. To be friendly—that's the word's meaning. She expects a bonfire, night swimming, the presence of husbands and boyfriends and children, too. "The way I feel, I'd just wreck the party for everybody."

"The *ho'olauna* is not a *party,* Stevie!" Kiko says. "It's where we set our intentions for the whole next year. It's what makes you a sistah, sistah. It's a *ceremony.*"

On the mainland, it's not uncommon for food to punctuate the end of some momentous event. After the wedding, the funeral, the christening, the bris. But in Hawai'i, you always eat *before* doing something important. A well-known rule that further emphasizes the intended significance of tonight's ceremony.

Before it begins, Kiko fires up the camp stove he's set on a picnic table so that everyone can be served with hot cocoa and a bowl of pilot crackers. Island comfort food, going all the way back to the tall ships and seamen who required bakeries to prepare cheap, plentiful, long-lasting rations of hardtack. And since in later years the stuff jibed with plantation workers' meager means, they created their own meal by buttering their pilot crackers, sprinkling sugar on top, then breaking them into bowls of either cocoa or hot coffee—depending on whether they were serving a child or an adult, closer to awakening or to going to sleep—with dollops of Carnation canned milk as the finishing touch. When Stevie was a kid, she considered this dish a rare treat; Lila had to prepare it on the sly because Beryl didn't want her daughter eating something she considered low-class and bereft of nutrition. For Beryl, pilot crackers and cocoa was a slippery slope that led to pidgin, useless superstitions, believing too much in what couldn't be seen, and precocious sex.

"Mmm," Lila says, sipping from her bowl with a blissful expression. "Exactly how my *tūtū* made it." All the other local women murmur in unison: "Mine, too."

Everyone sits by banyan trees at the remaining picnic tables, positioned close to the beach. The moon tonight hangs golden and fat, not quite full. It soon will be, though—on November 2, according to Stevie's calendar. Which would have been Hank's seventy-first birthday and seems as if it ought to be a deadline for *something.* But what?

Kiko clears away the cocoa pot and box of crackers, then sets out three bowls, filling the largest of them with an orange, ginger-brewed liquid. Then he explains, for the benefit of Stevie and the other women who have joined his *hālau* since the last *ho'olauna,* just what the ceremony entails.

"It's soooo simple," he says. "When I hand you this little bowl, you stand up and give your genealogy back to grandparents, then you share something about who you are. After that comes the best part—you get rid of stuff you don't want anymore. The stuff you don't need. For everything you get rid of, you use the little bowl to scoop up *'olena* broth from the first big bowl. Then you toss that away into the second big bowl. When you toss, we all say a little blessing. Not just a blessing, but a promise, too. That everything we hear tonight is a precious treasure, something we hold inside very delicately, with a great sense of value. Just 'cause we have to get rid of stuff, well, that don't make it trash. What's trash is talking trash. What's trash is bad faith and gossip. I know you know what I mean."

Stevie's tempted to grab Pip and slink off into the night. Just the notion of losing anything else—necessary or not—is unbearable yet familiar, as though loss lies at the root of her soul and she's doomed to keep re-creating the conditions it requires. But soon she's so moved by the stories these women rise to tell that all her whirring thoughts wind down.

What's no longer needed, it becomes clear, are ways of being that have ceased to serve. Ways of being that have walled off hearts, choked imaginations, paralyzed energy. Ways of being that come from a child lost to drugs, a marriage grown rancorous, a broken friendship, a brush with cancer, the legacies of suicide, abuse, prostitution. Subtler circumstances, too, trailing their own insidious tendrils. There are no comparisons made, though. No discussions or exchanges of any kind. But with each thrown-away barrier, each toss of broth into the bowl, Kiko leads an affirming whisper that echoes the sound of surf behind them: *"Haaaa, haaaa, haaaa."*

When everyone else has spoken, Stevie stands. Telling who she is turns out to be easy enough. She even shares her Hawaiian name, how it came to her, and speaks of her feelings for Lila, for Kiko, and her gratitude to them for bringing her into the *hālau.* But when it's time to get rid of what's no longer needed, she freezes.

"Breathe plenty *ha,*" Kiko tells her. "Say *aloha* to *mana*. Ask for help. The words'll come."

He's right. They do. "I want to get rid of my grief," Stevie says. "My grief from being torn away from Kaua'i when I was young." Then, she dips and splashes.

"Haaaa, haaaa, haaaa."

"I want to get rid of my fear. I'm afraid I'll lose this pregnancy just like the last, and if I don't, well, I'm afraid of going back to New York and having this baby on my own, which is what I have to do if I don't want to tear a bigger hole in someone's heart than the one that's there already. I want—no, I *need*—to get rid of my fear." Another dip, another splash.

"Haaaa, haaaa, haaaa."

"The last thing I want to get rid of is Stephanie Pollack the well-known minimalist designer, so I can let my work be more free."

Who here has more than a slender notion of what she means by "minimalist designer"? But searching all these attentive faces bathed in moon glow, Stevie sees not just glimmers but beacons of understanding, and as she empties her last bowl of *'olena* broth, the response comes with even more conviction than before.

"Haaaa, haaaa, haaaa."

After Stevie's done, Kiko ends the ceremony. "Don't be surprised if what you threw away tries to sneak back in on you again," he says. "It's one thing to have the insight, the intention. Another to do the work. Be patient, yeah? With yourselves and your hula sistahs, too."

One by one, the locals Stevie had felt shunned by at the *hālau* approach to ask about her time with Lila as a child, to tell of happy conclusions to their own difficult pregnancies. All the while, their fluttering hands light on her head, her arms, her shoulders, drawing her into embraces. It's as if she's become real to them. As real as they've become to her. Now she wants to stay on this beach with everybody forever. But the other women slip away until only she and Kiko remain, perched on top of a picnic table, staring out to sea.

"First of all," Kiko says after a long while, looping his arm through Stevie's, "you *are* having this baby and you're having it here, yeah?"

The *ho'olauna* afterglow dissolves. Kiko was right. Everything's sneaking back in again. "I'm not going to force anybody—"

"And when it's time, I'm gonna be right there, catching that kid. Don't look so spooked. I'm a certified midwife, they let me into hospitals. You won't have to deliver at home."

"But I don't know if—"

"Next thing. How long did you plan on waiting before you tell the guy?"

"I'm not a teenager, Kiko. I can take care of myself."

"Running away—you call that taking care of yourself?"

"It's not running away. I have a career, and I'm almost kind of famous for what I do. Maybe you should wonder if I'm not running away because I haven't gone back to New York. Tons of unfinished business there for me, and I've just been phoning it in."

"Oh, this ain't about ego or jobs. It's about trust. Put on your solid-ground shoes, sugar—trow dose eggshell shoes da dump!"

"Eggshell shoes? Where did *that* come from?"

"Search me. Just some Kiko pidgin, especially for you."

"Thanks. But what does it mean?"

"Means don't be so scared of making mistakes—just drives you *lolo.* Means you got me, babe, and don't you forget. Means I'm not letting you go home tonight without a better plan. You're not being so very nice, Stevie—not to Japhy, and 'specially not to yourself. I might be some crazy *mahū* with burned-off eyebrows, but let me tell you a couple things. For one, we not only have us a full-grown man here, he's a medical guy—knows all 'bout the birds and the bees. For another, I hold to the definition of love that says it's willing the good of the other. So, yeah—that's what you *think* you're doing, not laying this on him outta love. But what you're really doing is laying down all *your* stuff, the deep-down stuff you *don't* want to throw away, just for carrying his. And that's no good for nobody."

He stares at her for a second, eyes fierce, then throws back his head and laughs. "What a blowhard, yeah? Just when you were enjoying yourself, what happens? This fat-ass hula-head turns into a freakin' *missionary*!"

The best plan Stevie can come up with to free herself from Kiko is to promise to call Japhy and set a tell-all date. "Do it now," Kiko says.

"Can't, don't have my cell phone."

"Use mine."

"No. I need the drive home to gear up for this, Kiko. I'll call soon as I get there, I swear."

What Stevie likes best about this plan is that it gives her time to rehearse what she'll tell Japhy, so that instead of seeming needy or asking too much of him, she'll come across as solid, adult, capable of handling everything from natural childbirth to colic and three a.m feedings on her own. Which is not quite what Kiko had advised. But you don't toss thirty-six years of stress strategies out the window just because traditional Hawaiian wisdom doesn't endorse them, and chief among Stevie's is to imagine the worst, then protect herself accordingly.

Pulling the Defender into the drive, she spots Japhy's truck outside the carport, then turns to see him in Hank's Adirondack chair, lit enough by the moon for her to catch the antagonized fold of arms and the backward tilt to his head, face set not just for receiving, but for delivering bad news. Even the dogs are affected, wandering far off before romping in their usual way.

An angry man in Hank's chair. All possibility for mature behavior escapes Stevie like vapor dispersing. She stands by the car waiting for Japhy to say something, and when he doesn't, she walks over to settle into the other Adirondack with the air of someone who expects to be strapped in and executed. "I was going to call you tonight," she says, voice not just defensive but choked with guilt.

"We're not getting anywhere on the phone, Stevie."

"I only wanted to work out when we could get together. I can't go into it now." Although she doesn't quite force a yawn, it's not entirely natural, either. "I'm so—"

"Exhausted. Yeah, I know."

"Well, it's the truth." She reaches for his hand, but his palm flattens in a traffic-stopping gesture.

"Look, if you want this to be over, I need to hear it. I can't do another day like this, wondering what the hell is bothering you. All week long, I've been trying to make up a *good* story about what you're doing, but I can't. Nobody *ever* makes up a good story when they're left in the dark. And what I'm thinking is, well, you needed me to get through Hank dying."

"How can you even say that?"

"I'm not saying it was conscious."

"Which would make me not only selfish, but stupid. Gee, thanks."

"I'll make it easy. You don't want to hurt me, but you need to get back to your real life, not hang around some pissant island out in the middle of the Pacific Ocean with some pissant vet who doesn't play in the same big league you do."

"Don't tell me how I feel!" She lurches forward, ducking her head into her hands, willing herself not to cry. If she cries, she'll only get angrier, then end up saying more than she's ready to tell. More than Japhy's ready to hear, riled as he is. Well, there's no fixing that now. Her eyes sting from fatigue, her legs feel leaden. She hasn't got the energy to deal with her own rage and soothe his, too. Better to come off childish than as the chaotic, knocked-up, man-wrangling woman she's so terrified of Japhy perceiving her as. Better to call it a night than risk humiliating herself further. "I think it's best," she says, "if we both calm down and talk in the morning."

Without waiting for a reply, Stevie heads for the house. As she reaches the steps, Japhy's behind her. "I don't want to calm down," he says. "I don't want to talk in the morning. I don't want to leave things the way they are. All I want is for you to be honest about what's tearing you up. I can take it, darlin'. You don't scare me."

There it is—all the aching openness she'd stop a bullet to protect. Stevie melts down toward the steps with Japhy and onto his lap. "Well," he murmurs into her neck, "at least that's over. First fights are always kind of sloppy."

"Embarrassing, too."

As Stevie turns to press her lips to his, Japhy's fingers weave together across her belly. She feels the warmth of his palms through her thin cotton shirt as they trace a slow, sweet circle. Then his mouth goes slack against hers and when he pulls away to look her in the eye, she can tell that once again, his hands have read her body. "Damn, Stevie," he says. "So that's what this is all about."

"I know it's not what you wanted. I know you're not ready. I don't expect—"

"Hush." His hold on her tightens. "It's a whole new ball game now, isn't it?"

Chapter 26

In the first days after Flight 261 nose-dived into the Pacific, relatives of those on board traveled to the California crash site. Japhy was not among them. He had no hopes of Alana or Megan or anyone else surviving—the plane had plummeted from too great a height. And even then, before reports of airline negligence broke, rage enflamed his grief. For Alana's parents and sister, though, the trip to Port Hueneme was an emotional necessity. And so they joined the community of bereaved compelled to be there as Navy vessels salvaged debris and human remains. They took a chartered boat out to where the jet hit water, and as they arrived, a family of dolphins bounded through the oil and foam still roiling to the surface. They prayed onshore by the light of eighty-eight candles. They watched as eighty-eight doves winged their way toward fog-shrouded islands. And then they left Port Hueneme, filled with despair beyond the reach of dolphins, doves, and candles, but telling Japhy they wished he'd been with them.

Now, on January 31, four years after the crash to the day, to the hour, to the minute, Japhy stands on the beach of Port Hueneme—with Kate, with Alana's parents and sister, with a memorial throng of hundreds. Afternoon light breaks through a thin layer of clouds, illuminating trails of white vapor from planes taking off at LAX. As bagpipers play "Going Home," Coast Guard cutters from the rescue effort float close to shore. Holding Japhy's arm, Alana's stalwart mother walks them both down the beach, joining a procession toward the water. Barefoot, they step into this cool side of the Pacific to lay on the outgoing tide the last of their roses; all the rest smother the base of a monument just dedicated, a tall bronze sculpture of three dolphins leaping around a sundial.

"You need to do this," Kate had told Japhy, convincing him to come. "These won't be people who *say* they know what you've been through. These will be people who have been through it themselves."

But there isn't anyone here in quite his position. Japhy is the only person in attendance who lost both spouse and child. There's another surviving parent he met briefly in Seattle during the blackest days—Thea, a woman whose only two children were killed with her ex-husband, who'd taken them on vacation. But Thea didn't come. Possibly for reasons similar to the ones that had kept Japhy away till now. Or maybe she couldn't bring herself to mourn at the dolphin monument because it was funded in part by a donation from the airline. Something he'd wrestled with, too. Just as he'd wrestled with dipping into the blood money that the airline settled on survivors in order to buy his place in Waimea. He'd already put a lot into environmental causes Alana had embraced. Working up a grant for the writer who would take on her book. Investing in the Līhu'e park consortium. Setting chunks aside for a dozen other efforts that were hard to keep straight without the paperwork in front of him. But the purpose of it all was clear enough. To keep Alana's and Megan's spirits moving through the world somehow, not trapped forever in mourning.

Still, he finds himself wishing Thea could have put her anger aside. More than anybody's, her adjustments to outliving loved ones must resemble his. They might have given each other the sort of explicit comfort that's missing for him in all this ritualized remembrance. But would he have been able to tell *her* about how he's expecting the birth of another child? Probably not. He's too leery of appearing as if it's his mission to replace the irreplaceable. Which is why he hasn't broached the subject with Alana's family, even though Stevie's four months pregnant. Even though now that her exhaustion has passed, along with a painful interlude from pressure on her ovarian cyst, everything's going well.

It hasn't come to him yet, the right way of conveying their situation's complex truth. *I'm still dating the woman I got pregnant because we don't want to rush things.* He can just imagine how, hearing this, his in-laws wouldn't know whether to laugh or to cry. Neither does he, most of the time. It occurs to him, though, that Stevie, who's so keen on there being two-way traffic between them, would want to alter his explanation. *You didn't get me pregnant,* she'd chide. *We did.* She'd probably mention the birthing stone and the Night Marchers and the *pakalolo,* too. Everything that helps her feel their baby is meant to be. But it's good that she doesn't try to win him over to her perspective. Trusting fate is a concept that shatters the moment he considers the crash.

Kate didn't need to hear about Stevie's pregnancy from Japhy. She'd figured it out while in Kaua'i over Christmas. "When is Stevie due?" she asked one morning as the two of them walked the dark, mica-speckled Waimea beach.

"Due for what, Mom?" But he might have known Kate wouldn't dignify a pretense like that with any response other than a slight rolling of her gold-flecked hazel eyes. After all, growing up under Kate's scrutiny was what had taught him the futility of subterfuge with women. He could never fool her. Still hard to tell, though, whether this was because of his being such an easy read, or her being such a sharp reader. "How did you know?" he demanded.

"Oh, it just came to me. Some break in the time-space continuum, I guess."

"No, really."

"I've seen her in a bathing suit."

"She's hardly showing."

"Oh, Japhy. That's not the only way to tell."

He had flashed then on everybody staying at the sprawling white plantation house he'd found for his family to rent—a mansion, really, with fluted columns and a porte cochere, built by a long-ago sugar baron. Big enough to house Kate and Jack, his jovial archaeologist stepfather, plus Japhy's father and stepmother, and Japhy's siblings along with *their* families. Even if Japhy wanted to break his news, there would be no intimate way of doing it. He'd have to stand up, clink his glass, and give a speech. "I hope you haven't mentioned this to anyone else," he told Kate.

"Not a soul."

"Good. Don't. Stevie's not ready."

Kate peered at him from under the bill of her lime green baseball cap, imprinted with the word "onomatopoeia." "Because of Alana and Megan?"

"Because it's not quite three months. She's still nervous about going to term."

"What about you?"

"I think she'll be fine."

"What about the two of you together, Japhy?"

"We're still working on that one."

"Guess I better spell it out. What about your, well, underlying compatibilities?"

"Our *what*?"

"Okay, okay—it's a terrible expression, takes the 'r' right out of 'romance.' But you know what I'm talking about. The long-haul assets so notably absent with your father and me. The love that shows up in kindness, conversation, companionship. Have you had enough time with each other to discover all that?"

"If I'd wanted Dr. Phil to come for the holidays, Mom, I would have asked him."

Kate flashed a smile punctuated by those genetically dominant dimples of hers. "Give me some credit, dear. I have a *much* bigger sense of mystery than Dr. Phil. What about Stevie?"

"I'd be surprised if Dr. Phil was even on her radar."

Another impatient look from Kate. "What's *Stevie's* spiritual side like?"

"Oh, just like the baby, I'd say. Getting bigger every day."

He'd been hopeful then. But now, on the beach at Port Hueneme, surrendering his last rose to the ocean is difficult enough, and what feels impossible is becoming a father again—hurling himself into *that* sea. Which is nothing if not a sea of trust. Here, his feet still in the lapping waters of violent death and remembrance, the prospect jangles every cordal component of his nervous system. For the rest of the afternoon, he has little to say apart from goodbyes at the airport.

Then, mechanically, he clears security, buys a coffee and scone at a concourse Starbucks, and walks to the departure gate for his flight to Lihu'e. The waiting area is predictably crowded for a Hawai'i-bound flight on the last day of January. There's only one seat left vacant, at the end of a row in sight of the jetway door, beside a grandmotherly woman knitting a sky blue baby sweater.

It seems that, despite all good intentions, Japhy's capacity for trust is something like used-car mileage, and there's only enough left in him for what's growing with Stevie, apart from the baby. He's ready to roll with the trust required there. Looking to what she aspires to be as well as what she is, assuming that she'll do the same for him. Keeping best traits and talents in sight while seeing the real person clear. Laughing about all the inevitable imperfections, glitches, pouts, and childish carryovers—the biggest struggle of all with Stevie, given her tendency to crouch into defensive postures at the smallest provocation. Though, to her credit, she informed him just the other day that anytime she's hormonal or pissy or just plain weird, addressing her as "darlin' " or "sweetness" (her favorite endearments from him) is guaranteed to have a soothing effect. He's tried it, and she's been as good as her word. And now she's expecting him to come home cleansed by the ceremony of all lingering trepidation.

Japhy's cell phone rings. It's Stevie. He has to force himself to answer.

"I just felt him kicking!" she announces. "While we were clearing brush for the hula garden."

Japhy wills his mouth to work. "Really? Wow."

"Yeah." A long, disappointed pause on the other end. "I had to call because, well, I thought, today of all days, you know? It seemed like a sign from the universe, a reminder that awful as life can be, good things are coming, too. But maybe I should have waited."

As Japhy swallows hard, there's a loud announcement—the usual initial boarding invitation for first-class passengers, those needing assistance, families with small children.

"Is that your flight?" Stevie asks.

"Yes. It is."

"I'll let you go, then. Just wanted you to know. See you at the airport."

Japhy sits rigid, staring straight ahead as a couple bustles over to the jetway door, the woman holding tickets and bottled water, with a baby asleep in the sling tied around her waist, the man toting their carry-ons, a baby-supply bag, and a folded-up stroller. The same drill he remembers performing with Alana and Megan on their last trip together. The woman looks at him and waves, a small, sad smile on her face. Why would she do that? He has no idea. But her gesture prompts a wash of sweaty anxiety, then all the tears he couldn't cry on the beach, where they would have been not only appropriate but understood by everyone around him.

As the woman disappears into the jetway, Japhy gasps for air, shoulders shaking. He reaches blindly for the Starbucks bag, dumps the scone, and bends over to breathe into the bag long enough to stop gagging. When someone touches his knee, he sits up with a start. It's the woman who waved, come back alone to kneel at his feet. "Take my seat," the knitter beside Japhy tells her. "Our section's next."

After she sits, the woman leans in close to speak. "I recognized you from the memorial. You lost your wife and baby. I'm Megan. I lost my parents."

"Megan," he says, taking the Kleenex she offers to mop his face. "That was my daughter's name. I'm Japhy."

"I know. I hope you don't mind my coming back."

He shakes his head. "Of course not. It's just that seeing you all . . ."

"I could tell. We're going to Po'ipū. My in-laws have a time-share there. And you?"

"I live in Kaua'i now."

She reaches inside her shirt to pull out a chain from which a heavy ring dangles. "My father's," she says, fingering the ring. "They found remains for my mom, but none for my dad, so it's all I have of him."

"The Coast Guard found his ring?"

"Not the Coast Guard. A fisherman, coming in with his catch." Slipping the chain over her head, she hands the ring to Japhy. "It's a Masonic ring. Inscribed with the name of Dad's lodge—Raphael number 162, see? And the guy who found it—*his* name was Rafe, short for Raphael. He could have been arrested for not turning the ring over to the authorities, but nothing would do for him but flying up to Tacoma and delivering it to me in person."

"Brave man," Japhy says, handing the ring back.

"Yes, he is. This ring's more than a keepsake, though. When I was little, Dad and I, we made a deal. When he died, he'd send me some sign if, you know, death wasn't the end of everything. For me, Raphael was part of that sign. Do you know your saints and angels?"

Japhy shakes his head. "I'm not really religious."

"Well, Raphael is the angel who heals. Not just patron saint of doctors and the sick, but overseer of souls in the afterlife. Dad's ring gave me the most comfort of anything till my daughter was born. But none of it keeps me from wishing my baby could grow up knowing her grandparents."

"I'm expecting a baby, too. A boy—just found out for sure from an ultrasound."

"That's great, Japhy. Congratulations."

"Only, I don't think I have the courage to raise him. How am I ever going to get on a plane with him and his mother? Or, even worse, put them on a plane without me? How am I ever going to tell him about his half sister, how she was killed with *her* mother, how he wouldn't exist if they'd lived? Not that I'd ever put it that way. But how do I give him that part of myself so he's not afraid of terrible things? How do *I* stop being afraid *for* him? Do you know what I mean?"

"Yes, of course. I think a lot about the right way to tell that story, too. The strange thing for me is, I probably never would even have *had* a child if my parents were still here. I'm forty-two—the outer edge of the envelope for a first-time mother. It's not as though one life can ever restore another. And my daughter makes me miss Mom and Dad every bit as much as she makes me feel closer to them. But *we're* not dead yet. Doesn't that mean we go on with, well, beginning things?"

"I used to think so. Now I don't know what to think."

"We don't have to decide now." She nods toward the jetway, where a flight attendant picks up a mic to announce the next section's boarding. "Right now, all we have to do is get on that plane." She leans over to pick up the boarding pass that fell from Japhy's pocket when he was hyperventilating and hands it to him. "Are you ready?"

"They haven't called my row yet."

"Okay, then." She pulls him close for a hug so filled with kindness that his eyes brim again. "See you on board."

Japhy watches her walk back down the jetway, wondering if he'll be able to follow.

Chapter 27

In her eighth month of pregnancy, Stevie's still dancing on Thursday nights at Kiko's *hālau,* wearing a practice skirt with a drawstring waist tied over the top of the baby she carries, looking like a bulging beanstalk. All the weight she's gained has gone to her belly—the sure mark of a boy, according to Kiko, Lila, and the expectant mothers she meets in Dr. Pearce's waiting room.

Tonight, with the first flap of her knees in warm-ups, Stevie feels a mild fluttering just beneath her ribs, where the baby's head is. Another spell of in utero hiccups, no doubt, although this almost never happens except when she lies down to sleep. Her baby seems to have inherited his mother's lousy sense of direction, refusing to flip over in preparation for the normal head-first exit into the world. What helps such breech babies go bottoms up, according to Hawaiian lore, is lots of swimming. Another de-breechifying technique, shared by hula sister Sharon, is lying on your back with knees to chest, or as close as they'll come, several times a day. Still another, advocated by one of Stevie's baby books, is crawling on all fours. And so she takes routine breaks from work at the Līhu'e site to swim, crawl, and hug her knees. At home, she tries other methods, gleaned from the Internet, each more nonsensical than the last: lying head down on a slanted ironing board, shining a flashlight on her belly, pinching her little toes. If her son doesn't cooperate soon, Dr. Pearce will take a crack at manually turning him in the womb, and if that doesn't work, she'll perform a cesarean. Stevie's had to allow for both possibilities in the birth plan she just finished writing, with copies for Kiko, Dr. Pearce, and the hospital. But at this point, dwelling on another scar added to her abdominal collection, or on the official, scary-sounding term for baby turning—external cephalic version—can't be wise. Her baby's still got time to turn himself around. And if he doesn't, well, as Kiko's pointed out, Stevie can be grateful for living in modern times instead of ancient ones, when babies who didn't come out easily were assumed to be evil, as were the mothers—usually a death sentence for both. Gruesome information, but she'll take perspective any way she can get it these days. Meanwhile, hula hip-rocking, better than warm baths or lovemaking (something there hasn't been much of for months), seems to ease the aches and pains of her expanding pelvis.

Stevie concentrates on the beat of Kiko's *ipu*, wondering if her hiccupping baby's ears are connected well enough for him to hear it, too. With the next knee flap, she feels a sharp kick against her bladder, a cramp at the base of her spine, and then, like a crescendo to the kick and the cramp, water gushes out from between her legs. Stevie freezes, causing Lila to jump out of line to keep from bumping into her. "Lila, my water just broke."

Lila calls out to Kiko in the same calm, efficient, confidence-inspiring manner that Stevie heard her use so often with Hank. "Stevie's water broke. Let's get her to the hospital."

All the other dancers swoop into action. One calls Dr. Pearce while another calls Japhy. Sharon fetches a stack of Laundromat-fresh towels from the hamper in her jeep, passes some out so that the floor can be wiped, uses some others to dry Stevie, and places the rest between her legs. Then the dancers divide themselves among three cars to follow Kiko's Toyota, with Lila and Stevie in the back seat, to Wilcox Memorial.

"You're only a few weeks early," Kiko says on the way as Stevie starts to moan. "You'll both be *fine.*"

"But he hasn't dropped yet! Can he still be turned? I—" She cries out from the pain of what must be her first contraction. Lila and Kiko don't need to be told what's going on.

"That boy of yours, Stevie," Kiko says. "He's wantin' to pop out and say howdy *wikiwiki.*"

"No way Dr. Pearce will try version with contractions starting up, *ku'uipo,*" Lila adds. "A quick C-section, then he's in your arms. But you can't have a whole bunch of people with you for a section, Stevie. Just the daddy or your midwife or a friend. A camera's okay for after the baby comes out, but they don't allow movies with surgery."

Stevie throws her head against the seat, biting back tears. All that pelvic expansion and ache for nothing. No brave sips of *māmaki* tea to ease her labor. No playing the compilation music CD she's burned to carry herself through the hours. No sitting up, as per Kiko's midwifery guidelines, for the easiest possible delivery, with camcorder switched on for the moment her son's head crowns. Instead, the exact opposite of her ideal birth, with everyone but Stevie calling the shots. She reaches for her bag, pulls out her cell phone, punches in Japhy's number, and hands it to Lila. "Tell Japhy what you just told me. If he's not going to be there, I want you."

Stevie doesn't have to hear his end of this brief conversation to know its effect: another worry added to those already clouding his heart. "Well?" she says when Lila clicks off.

"He's on his way, of course. What did you expect?"

"Don't make me laugh." Stevie swipes at her eyes with the back of her hand.

"What do you mean, honey girl?"

"What I *expect* is a joke," she spits out. "It hasn't got anything to do with what *happens.*" Now is not the time for delving into Japhy's apparent inability to speak of what's eating at him, leaving her with no option but to apply an ancillary to the Golden Rule—the Platinum Rule, maybe, for troubled couples: Do unto others only what they wish to be done. Japhy's wish, she could tell, was for her to refrain from poking at his deeper feelings. At least those feelings haven't kept him from being thoughtful. Back rubs and foot rubs have been hers for the asking. He's learned her favorite dishes and prepares them often, including his own tangy version of *liliko'i* pie. Since the Kōloa house is so much closer to the hospital than his, he's been pushing to move in with her for the final month. She would have agreed by now if he hadn't seemed to be making the move offer more out of loyalty than in joyous anticipation of their son's birth. Margo knows the whole story by now. "I've booked a ticket a week before your due date," she said on the phone this morning, "so don't worry. Whichever way this goes, you'll have all the help you need."

Even in her third trimester, it struck Stevie as smarter—more loving as well—to limit her time with Japhy to what a "normal" couple would be spending together after less than a year of knowing each other. Which translated roughly into three or four nights a week maximum, never more than two of them consecutive. If not for the baby, there is no doubt in her mind that they'd already be living together. Maybe his earlier-than-expected arrival will flush everything out into the open.

Stevie's next contraction ignites a wild, unreasonable bolt of fury. Where did it go, the vast psychic real estate that had opened up with her first real rush of love for Japhy? What a no-brainer. To the baby, of course. She just hadn't been prepared for all the territory she'd happily surrender as he colonized her body. And damned if she's going to surrender even more to a man who will only father him out of some tortured sense of duty. Who will only abandon her. As Kiko pulls up in front of the hospital, Stevie feels a crazed need to ask questions that might at least restore some semblance of control. How much time does recovery from a cesarean section require? How old does an infant have to be before he can safely fly to New York? Even though she sent her letter of resignation to Stewart five months ago, after she got everything in Chicago under control, Stewart had made it clear he'd take her on again if she moved back to the city.

But everything happens so fast—check-in, Dr. Pearce's operating room examination, a shot to stop contractions, connecting her to the fetal monitor that blessedly shows no sign of distress—there isn't time to ask. In fact, Stevie forgets all about her questions until she's in a morphine haze, sitting up with her arms around Dr. Pearce's shoulders while the anesthesiologist inserts a needle into her spine. The strangest uncomfortable sensation she's ever experienced. As numbness spreads, Stevie interrupts Dr. Pearce, who's assuring her that with the right attitude, a cesarean birth is every bit as empowering for a mother as a vaginal one. "How long will it take me to recover?"

It's Japhy's voice that answers. "Let's not worry about that one now, darlin'."

She remembers telling Japhy how using this endearment was guaranteed to make her melt. But as he enters her line of vision—already gowned, carrying her music and mini sound system, handing his camera to one of the attending nurses—she's a long way from melting. In fact, when he leans down to brush back her hair and plant kisses, first on her forehead, then on her lips, it's as if all the feeling leaving her body below her breasts rockets up for blast-off in her chest. Oh, she can still see trepidation behind Japhy's eyes. What takes her by surprise is the glimpse of soul shining through that dark morass, intensifying what's exploding inside her until it seems a wonder that the baby doesn't come shooting out through her sternum right then and there.

Since Stevie's separated from all the action by a blue drape over her belly, she can't see the surgery, but Dr. Pearce asks one of the nurses to narrate. "It's a magical operation, really," the nurse says in a soft, reverent voice. "The doctor finishes making the incision. . . . She plunges her hands into your abdomen, then your uterus, and . . . voila! Out comes your baby boy."

"Your *beautiful* baby boy," Dr. Pearce adds. "Congratulations."

A perfect moment accompanied by the perfect, gentle slack-key music—"Pupu Hinuhinu," the shiny-shell lullaby. But the moment ends when Stevie feels Japhy tighten his grip on her hand and she glances up at his face, realizing at once what's troubling him. There's something wrong with their son. Instead of a lusty wail with his first gulps of air, nothing but weak whimpers. She can feel the baby's strain as though he's still inside her. He's trying too hard to cry, to breathe. Stevie, unable to speak, digs her nails into Japhy's palm, waiting for Dr. Pearce to explain.

"Your boy is no preemie peanut, I'll tell you that," Dr. Pearce says. "Longest legs I've seen on a newborn in ages. We've got a future basketball player here, I think." Even in her drugged, maternal fog, Stevie knows a "good news, bad news" windup when she hears one. "Wish we could give him to his momma and daddy right away, but this little one's lungs need extra help. So we're going to clean him up and get him set to go on oxygen while we put you back together, Stevie." Oxygen. Oh, God. He's coming in the same way Hank went out, desperate for air.

"I'm sorry you have to wait to get your hands on him," Dr. Pearce continues, "but this isn't unusual, especially with a C-section. Nothing our special-care nursery here can't handle."

Stevie doesn't trust what she's hearing. Doctors minimize terrible situations all the time, don't they? It's part of their training. "No, honestly," Stevie cries. "What's the matter? Is he a blue baby?"

"Absolutely not. His heart is perfectly fine. He's just got some fluid left in his lungs, stuff that would've been squeezed out of him if he'd had more time and come through the birth canal. If this were severe, we'd be flying him to the neonatal intensive care unit in Honolulu. Let go of that daddy there, Stevie, so he can come see your son weighed and measured—give you the blow-by-blow."

"Go," Stevie croaks.

She wishes Japhy would run, not walk as though wearing antigravity boots, weighted by this shared, newly minted panic added to his older horror. But in a few seconds, he calls out to her in a voice cracked by emotion. "Six pounds, Stevie. Nineteen inches long! A little put out with us all for making him breathe on his own, maybe, but he really is . . . beautiful. Amazingly beautiful."

Dr. Pearce's eyes flash at Stevie over her mask. "I call that an accurate report," she says.

"A name," Stevie says. "He can't go to that nursery without a name. They have to know who they're taking care of. You're looking at him, Japhy. Is he Michael Makana, or Gabriel Makana?"

"Michael or Gabriel," Japhy muses. "Gabe or Mikey."

"They're both angels," offers the narrating nurse, who picks up

Japhy's digital camera to snap the close-up that will be Stevie's first good look at her baby.

"But I don't think either one's quite right for this little guy," Japhy says. "He feels more like a Rafe to me. What do you think, Stevie? For Raphael?"

The name ratchets around in Stevie's head like a pinball bouncing over all the highest-scoring spots. "Rafe," she murmurs. "Raphael Makana."

"A gift," Japhy says, "from the angel of healing."

Exactly what they all need.

During her initial recovery, while Japhy camped out by the special care nursery, Stevie can only think or speak of Rafe. But there's just one topic that the nurses who pop in and out of her room want to discuss: gas, as in "Have you passed any yet?" After saying no for the tenth time, Stevie looks up from Rafe's photo on the digital camera and rolls her eyes at Kiko, who's massaging plumeria-scented lotion into her still-rubbery legs.

"I know you're just doing your job," Kiko tells the nurse. "But her baby's in *Matrix* mode right now, hooked up to tubes so he can breathe and eat, and all you care about is *farting*?"

Which at least makes everybody in the room laugh, and relieves Stevie from having to hear yet another explanation of why the nurses' question matters. Kiko's massage is meant to be a distraction from the nurses as well as from how hungry she is—not surprising, since her last meal was lunch the day before, a half sandwich. She won't be allowed to eat again until she answers in the affirmative, and she won't have the strength to visit Rafe until she eats again. Which makes them both prisoners—Rafe in his Isolette, her in this room. All she can do to ease the dilemma's awfulness is bring herself up to speed on every parameter of Rafe's progress: oxygen levels, ventilator pressure, blood gas numbers, lung expansion ratios. Provided his weight is sufficient, Rafe will be released as soon as his lungs are strong enough for him to take full, complete breaths on his own. Meanwhile, what Stevie hangs on to is the mantra she hears from everyone around her, from specialists to loved ones: "All he needs is time."

But it's hard for her to keep hold of this mantra as a certainty when, at last, she's cleared for a visit to the hospital's special care nursery. It's a tiny place, with room enough for a few Isolettes, and Rafe is the only baby there. It rips her heart, seeing him propped up on his side with the ventilator tube taped across his entire mouth, the umbilical IV lines delivering fluids, the pulse oxymeter on his finger. His sea blue saucer eyes are open, miserable looking, and the closest she can get is to lean in and kiss the top of his head, covered with a blue knit cap. Stevie's arms ache to hold him, her breasts ache to feed him.

"He's a fighter," Japhy says. "You'll see."

As Stevie gains enough strength to be discharged, Rafe weakens. He loses weight. He's plagued by persistent spells of too-rapid breathing. On the evening of his third night on earth, fluid continues building in his lungs.

Stevie and Japhy are evicted from the nursery so he can be treated with a diuretic. The diuretic was Japhy's idea, diplomatically advanced so the hospital doc would comply.

Stevie keeps her cell phone on the counter at Hamura's while she and Japhy have dinner, in case a nurse should call. Not wanting to be more than five minutes away from the hospital, they leave Hamura's to check into a Līhuʻe motel, where they are alone together for the first time since before Rafe's birth. But not really. The baby's there with them every second, the invisible object of all the breath, all the spirit, they might will into his long, skinny, pale little body.

Lying awake after Japhy falls asleep, Stevie sheds quiet tears that slip down her cheeks onto the stiff, scratchy motel pillowcase. There was nothing Japhy could do to keep from losing his baby daughter, and now, it's as though he's studying to be a neonatal pulmonologist to keep from losing his baby son. *Falling in love again isn't as frightening as having another child to lose.* That's pretty much what Japhy told her in that other life they lived, when the subject seemed so far away and theoretical. Has all his apprehension been intensified by the jeopardy that Rafe is in? Maybe she could tell if her own fears weren't so enormous.

When they arrive at the nursery the next morning, the ventilator is no longer by Rafe's Isolette. The sound of that machine working is by now in Stevie's mind the sound of her baby breathing. He must have worsened in the night and been taken away—that's the thought freezing her in place. Japhy doesn't look worried, though. Why not? Then, as he pulls her along, she understands. On the other side of the Isolette is a pleated plastic hose attached to Rafe's nose. He's so improved that he doesn't need the ventilator anymore.

Stevie gets her first good look at Rafe's sweet little rosebud mouth and sees, when he makes a small digestive grimace, that he has not only Hank's cleft chin, but Japhy's dimples, too. His color is pinker, his body temperature stable enough that his thick shock of coal black hair is uncovered. The IV lines in his belly button are gone, replaced with a single feeding line into his foot. He can sleep on his stomach now, which the nurse allows since he seems more content in this position, and since the top priorities for Rafe are sleep and weight gain.

It's a long day full of firsts. For the first time since he was born, Stevie and Japhy hear their son cry—a hearty-lunged squall. Rafe has his first taste of mother's milk on a nubby stick resembling a Q-tip. Stevie changes her first diaper, and at nine o'clock that night, she's allowed to hold Rafe skin-to-skin against her chest for the most peaceful thirty minutes in both of their entire lives.

On the fifth day, Rafe's removed from every tether but the feeding line, and the medical professionals caring for him all agree he's ready to try nursing. The trouble there is that every time Stevie gets him in her arms, he goes to sleep. "That's cute, Rafe," Japhy says, holding him while Stevie buttons herself back together. "Everybody loves a sleeping baby who can breathe all by himself. But the sooner you eat on your own, buster, the sooner you get to blow this pop stand. Let's get with the program, what do you say?"

On the sixth day, Rafe finally latches on and is officially pronounced "a good feeder." On the seventh, he's vaccinated and circumcised. On the eighth, he has only to pork up by a tiny fraction of an ounce in order to be released. Stevie gets in two good nursing sessions before he's taken from her to be weighed, all naked and squirmy before his judges. She stares at the digital scale as Rafe hits just the mark required, not one hair higher.

"He can go home now," the nurse in charge says. No sooner are the words out of her mouth than Rafe lets loose with a geyser that, if it had come a moment sooner, would have kept him in the nursery for yet another day. He finally put it all together, the breath of *ha* and the water of *wai,* maybe with a dollop of help from *i,* for *iki,* ancestors who stamped his passport to this world, this island that's his earthly home. He is the next loved thing in his lineage. Everyone's laughter at her son's feat rings in Stevie's ears like an impassioned amen.

While Rafe is whisked off to have his vitals recorded for release, Stevie turns to Japhy. She has a question that needs answering, right away. Does "home" mean just Rafe and her, or all of them? Before she can ask, though, Japhy smothers her in the most wholehearted embrace they've shared since Rafe's first prenatal kicks. "That's our boy," he says, and for now, it's answer enough.

Chapter 28

When Rafe is three months old and thriving, Stevie makes dinner reservations for two at a fancy Po'ipū restaurant perched on the shore, touted for both its chef and sunset views. It's their first night out alone since Rafe was born. Lila is babysitting, and they drove here from her house, where they left a supply of Stevie's breast-pumped milk in the fridge. A little romance, that's what Japhy figures Stevie has in mind. A break from the cocoon of baby-centered days at his Waimea house. *Their* Waimea house now. Hank's place is designated for guest lodging and Stevie's office, extended to include another bedroom and worktables on one side of the lanai.

Japhy can't help thinking that sunset displays in Waimea are more stunning than this restaurant view, with its lazy pastel palette. But if it's romance Stevie wants, he can handle that. He can handle popping out of their cocoon, too, though time with his son is such a joy that he's partnered up with another vet so there'll be more of it. But if Japhy's right about Stevie's intentions for this dinner, why does she look so troubled as she scans the menu? He reaches across the table to lace his fingers through hers. "Pricier than you expected?" he inquires.

"No, no. That's not the problem."

"Is it Rafe? He couldn't be better fixed for tonight."

She sighs and puts the menu aside. "It's not Rafe I'm worried about. It's you."

Japhy takes a mental scan of the last few days. There's been no tension he's noticed, no sign of moodiness or irritation. They made love just last night, and that wouldn't have been anywhere near so impassioned if she'd been worried about him then. "What's up?"

"There's a reason why I wanted us to come out on our own like this," she begins.

"You're tired of home cooking."

"Nope."

"You'd like to enroll Rafe in military school."

"Yeah, right."

"You want to propose to me."

Unlike most only children he's known, Stevie takes his teasing as the act of affection he intends. It most often puts her at ease. But all he can get out of her now is a fleeting smile. She withdraws her hand from his to fidget with her earring, a large gray pearl that almost matches her eyes. "Actually," she says, "I'm just traditional enough to believe that kind of proposal is *your* job. I have another kind of proposal for you tonight."

Their waiter appears with Japhy's mai tai and the first glass of wine Stevie's allowed herself since discovering she was pregnant. After they order dinner, she takes a sip and sets the glass aside.

"Shoot," Japhy tells her.

Stevie takes a long breath. "There's an LA firm in Seattle that's interested in collaborating. I don't have to move to do it, either. They want me to head up design for the plaza at a new courthouse there."

"Do you want the job?"

"I do. The space has great potential. But here's the thing: I'd have to travel. Not like I did before. I mean, I'm not going to spend half my life in airplanes the way I used to. Once a project gets under way, I can pull off the development phase with a good crew on the ground, e-mailing photos and FedExing plans. But Japhy, I *do* have to go to Seattle to meet with all the principals on this job, and I have to go soon. Rafe's so young, I want him with me. Which will be hard for you, I know. Even terrible, maybe."

She's right. It feels terrible already, almost as bad as when he started hyperventilating in the L.A. airport. His mouth goes dry; invisible bands contract around his throat, his chest, his belly. Willing steadiness into his hands, he takes a swallow of water. "You go, Stevie," he says. "I'll be fine. You'll be fine. So will Rafe. I better get used to this."

Stevie's face falls as her eyes dart away from his. He knows that expression. She's on the verge of tears, and not happy ones, either. What's wrong? Can't she tell how determined he is to get over this fear? Didn't he just give the thing she was asking for, his okay for her and Rafe to fly away without worries about him falling apart?

Then it comes to him, the difference between what she's asked for and what she needs. What she needs is something she doesn't know *how* to ask for, not when it involves such loaded words as "airplane," "baby," "Seattle." What she needs is a man who's there for her so she doesn't have to handle everything on her own, the way she always has. What she needs is their son's father—to tote Rafe's gear, to help her through first-flight jitters, to hold him during that long trip when she has to eat or sleep or go to the bathroom.

The moment Japhy realizes this is when his body starts to relax. His way through the fear is so much simpler than he'd imagined. It's loving Rafe. It's loving Stevie.

As ribboned clouds of pink and gold blaze at last into crimson and orange, Japhy takes her hand again. "Maybe what you'd really like," he says, "is for me to go with you."

"Yes!" she cries.

The next thing he knows she's in his lap, kissing him full on the mouth. There's a burst of applause from diners at nearby tables. "For the sunset?" Japhy says, his lips still on Stevie's.

Then there's a chorus of congratulations aimed at their table. Stevie laughs. "They think you just asked me to marry you."

Chapter 29

Stevie walks into the water at Salt Pond Park with six-month-old Rafe naked on her shoulder. When the water reaches her waist, Rafe kicks his feet in anticipation, then crows like a muffled island rooster as she dips him in a few times, wetting his face. She's been here with Lila and Rafe every day for a week, and now, on this warm late-November morning, Japhy wants to see the results. "Okay," Stevie tells him as she eases Rafe into the water, fingers laced beneath his belly, "stand about a yard away from me."

"That far?" Japhy says.

"Uh-huh. That far."

"Are you sure? He can go that long a way?"

"No worries, I know what I'm doing here. So does Rafe. Don't you, Rafe?" Another crow as Rafe's palms smack the water. "Okay, little one, off you go."

The second Stevie releases Rafe, he starts paddling. But he's only traveled a few inches when Japhy reaches out for him. "Oh, sweetie pie," Stevie says. "You don't have to do that. Let him come to you."

It's torture for Japhy to wait, she can tell. But as Rafe arrives with steam to spare, two sets of dimples are on display. Japhy spins Rafe overhead before setting him back in the water for a return trip to Stevie, who steps even farther away.

"Look at him go," Japhy yelps. "He's really swimming, isn't he? A regular water baby."

"An *exceptional* water baby, I'd say."

After one more round, Stevie leaves Rafe with Japhy so she can have a solo swim. Close to the reef she dives down, eyes open, for a look at all the wrasses and butterfly fish clustered around the coral. Glancing up, she spots a sea turtle ride in on a breaking wave. The first *honu* she's ever encountered at Salt Pond. An unsought omen for her wedding day.

It surprised no one more than Stevie when the Līhu'e park got written up in a prestigious architecture journal by Christopher Caldwell, who just happened to be honeymooning in Kaua'i as the place neared completion. Funny, really, how in the least career-oriented year of her life since college, she received her best, most meaningful review:

> As so often happens with promising artists whose reputation outweighs the totality of actual achievement, Stephanie Pollack made her big breakthrough at precisely the moment when she thought nobody was looking. Although Pollack is justly known for designing spaces with brilliant features, her latest project, on the Hawaiian island of Kaua'i, is her first thoroughly brilliant space.
>
> This public park, on acreage purchased with private funds, incorporates not just an emotional connection to Pollack's birthplace, but a reverence for its native plants, myths, and sincere, openhearted culture. There is a heretofore untapped abandon in her undulating gardens, one of which consists solely of native species, many threatened, and another composed of trees and fo-

liage revered by practitioners of ancient hula. There is understated sophistication in her incorporation of existing water elements that is echoed in the shapes of band shell, outbuildings, informational displays, and seating structures. Most unexpectedly, there is playfulness, too—in a snail-shaped rock garden made from what Pollack calls bad-luck lava rocks, a bounty she incorporated upon discovering that the state's park service had in its possession an unwanted, burgeoning collection. Each rock was mailed back to the islands by a tourist who claimed he or she had been punished by Pele, the volcano goddess, for taking it away. Benches by the rock garden incorporate text from letters written by the afflicted. Adding a splash of zest to the composition is a bed of tropical flowers in Pele's colors, red and black. If not for the park's spectacular orienting vistas of mountains and sea, one could easily become lost amid the swirl of Pollack's paths, the passion of her engagement with this land and its bounty. Which is, one suspects, exactly what Pollack intended.

By the time the article appeared, Stevie had already established a solid working relationship with the firm in Seattle. Now she has her pick of interesting projects. If she stays selective enough, everything will be manageable. Not perfect, not without ambivalence and angst. But manageable. And, often enough, delightful. *Everything*—still a novel concept for her. Work, motherhood, life in Waimea with Japhy, and also marriage. Especially marriage.

Before the afternoon ceremony begins, Stevie sits in the Līhu'e park gazebo she designed—very much like the one where Hank appeared in her dream—and safety-pins a red *palaka*-cloth bow tie that Lila made to the collar of Rafe's T-shirt. She wishes her father and grandfather had lived to attend this wedding, but plenty of relatives and friends are here to see her and Japhy marry. Margo and Kenny are staying at the Kōloa house, as are Japhy's mother and her husband. Margo's kids are camped out in the living room. Lorna and her family flew in from New York and are bunking at Lila's.

Beryl made it, too—her first trip back to Kaua'i since the divorce.

Stevie didn't expect she would want to stay at the house of her first marriage, but Beryl accepted the offer to sleep on the lanai with the same warmth and excitement she emanated taking Rafe into her arms. Hard to square such behavior with elegant, remote Beryl. Although she had only bottle-fed Stevie, Beryl would bare a breast and nurse this grandson of hers, if that were possible. "It's likely genetic, love," she'd told Stevie. "Your grandfather never had a lap for me to crawl onto, and look how he doted on *you.*"

"Well, dote away. He's lucky, having two *tūtūs* gaga over him. But I have to tell you, this baby boy and *his* mother, we're staying tight. No way am I ever going distant on him." Which is, in no small part, thanks to Lila.

Lila, mother of her soul, stands behind Stevie in the gazebo now, threading plumeria into Stevie's upswept hair. Softly, she sings along with the slow, sexy slack-key rendition of "Ku'u Sweetie" they can hear Kiko playing as the last arriving guests take their seats. Around Stevie's neck is the Ni'ihau shell lei Japhy gave her. On one wrist she wears her Hawaiian name bracelet, and on the other, a band of *kukui* nuts she picked and polished herself in honor of Rafe's conception. Having forgotten to bring a mirror, she looks to Lila for her final bridal checkout, wanting to make sure nothing's smudged on her face, and that her tea-length ivory-colored dress of lace-bordered batiste isn't askew or smeared with milky mashed-banana baby drool.

"You look," Lila says, "exactly how you should. Lovely. Happy in your heart."

When Kiko shifts into an old Sons of the Pioneers instrumental number, Lila leads Stevie from the gazebo to the wedding march starting point, taking leave of her with slow, inhaling kisses on each cheek.

All eyes turn to Stevie, standing at the end of a grassy aisle. Only Rafe will take this walk with her, riding her hip, not to give Stevie away so much as seal the deal that brought him into the world. She remembers Grandpa telling her how Hawaiians speak of their dead in the present tense. That's how she thinks of Grandpa now: *He is with me.* Hank's here, too, and in more than just spirit, in her blood and Rafe's. He's also here in multicolored anthuriums that grow from a bed of soil enriched by his ashes, encircling the area where Japhy now stands, waiting for her. Japhy's own dead, she has a feeling, are in attendance, too, sustained at last in peace.

At Japhy's feet sit Pip and Rainier, *palaka*-cloth kerchiefs tied around their necks, and beside him is Robert Kapahana, chosen to perform the ceremony on account of being who he is, a *papa kanaka kahuna,* but also legally qualified to officiate on account of being a licensed local official. Lorna, Stevie's matron of honor, stands next to Robert; she's holding an orchid bouquet and Japhy's wedding band.

As Stevie starts walking, she smiles at everyone watching her arrival. Hula sisters, cousins, Lila's kin, Japhy's slew of relations, soon to be hers. Hardly the standard-issue family she'd grown up hankering for, but more wonderful than that, for blossoming from her life in such an unpredictable way.

"Psst, Stevie," Margo hisses from the front row of seats.

Stevie turns to see her cousin wave a baby-size Cubs cap that she plants on Rafe's head. "He can wear the 'something blue' for you, okay?"

Stevie laughs. "I know better than to argue with you over Cubs attire."

Kiko puts down his guitar as Stevie hands Rafe to Lorna and takes her bouquet, leaning close to whisper.

"First words, Lorna, first words. Japhy's were, 'How can I help you?' "

Lorna beams. "Perfect," she says. "Not just lover, but helpmate, too. Exactly what you need."

Stevie nods and turns to Japhy, feeling herself inside a sunlit jewel box.

Just before dusk, Stevie parks the Defender beside a stand of drowsy palms dipped over the beach. Blissful as this day has been, she's not accustomed to being the center of such unwavering attention. Now she needs some time for herself, just to take it all in and prepare herself for tonight's feast. A beach walk, that's her plan. Maybe some shell gathering, too, since the tide is out. And she's brought binoculars in case anything's jumping and spinning out there in the sea.

Stevie opens the rear of the Defender and hefts two Coleman coolers—one filled with iced drinks and the other packed with marinated meats for grilling. Then she drags the coolers one by one across the sand, leaves them in the open-air shelter where everybody will dine, and heads down the beach.

As though one creature, a flock of seabirds lifts off the water to fly screaming overhead. Sharks must be feeding. Which means red wiliwili must be in bloom. Stevie raises her binoculars and turns away from the ocean to check, soon spotting a stand of spiky blossoms. She also sees a large, barefoot woman wearing a red muumuu, her back turned to Stevie, stacking logs in a bonfire pit. Her hair is long and loose and wild and gray.

Pele the Crone?

The thought raises chicken skin, filling Stevie with the same sense of wonder she felt in the presence of that strange beauty all those years ago, transporting her straight into timeless time. *The only question that matters,* she can hear Grandpa saying, *is why Pele chose you.* Pele the Beautiful didn't stick around long enough for Stevie to ask, and after Pele the Invisible swept Grandpa off into the beyond, Stevie could never figure out a convincing answer. But Pele the Crone? *She* might be patient enough to explain.

Or so Stevie thinks, until she gets closer to the fire pit and can see the face of the woman she's been staring at. It's Lila. "Finally," Lila says as she looks up from laying one last stick of wood. "I was waiting for you to light the fire."

Stevie nods, understanding that she's with Lila, but unable to shake the sense that she's speaking to Pele.

"If you do it now," Lila tells her, "we'll have plenty good coals for grilling when everybody gets here."

"All right. But I don't have anything to light it with."

Lila stoops down for her bag and hands over a box of Diamond strike-anywheres. "I do."

After staring at the box for moment, Stevie reaches in, pulls out a match, and sets the wood aflame.

Acknowledgments

It is a great pleasure to arrive at the point where I get to thank all the generous souls I've leaned on, learned from, was inspired by, and whined with while writing this book.

Like Stevie's father, mine was a fierce Cubs fan, and since he'd "left the building" (as the obit writers say) when novel number three began, I counted heavily on my big brother, Mark Coburn, who's been to Wrigley Field far more times than I, for reliably true, philosophically sound, and comically keen baseball input.

As a tribute to the remarkable work of landscape architects Kathryn Gustafson and Shannon Nichol, who were kind enough to share their expertise, I've fictionalized elements from their signature designs for Stevie's South Side project. The discerning would do well to seek out the real things. My buddy Jack Mackie, a nationally known public artist, was a big help in laying out how design teams function.

A writer needs rituals, and so I thank L.C.'s Kitchen for providing the delectable cheeseburgers, fries, and salads that Jack Remick and I split on Wednesdays before putting our pages on the table; Hedgebrook Cottages and the Oregon Writers Colony's retreat for allowing me return visits; the Seattle Seven for fellow-author kibitzing at Victrola Coffee House; and readers/listeners who lighted the way, especially Libby Burke, Nick Fennel, Beverly McDevitt, Silvia Peto, Valerie Brooks, Barbara Branscomb, Ki McGraw, Carol Craig, Chip Hughes, and Bette Lee Coburn.

I am grateful for the unwavering excellence of my editor at Ballantine, Linda Marrow; all the expert aid I received from editorial assistants Daniel Mallory and Junessa Viloria; and Janet Fletcher's superb copyediting. Thanks also to agents Suzanne Gluck and Erin Malone for their indispensable support and savvy, and to Kent Carroll for bountiful provisions from his vast store of literary as well as publishing wisdom. Finally, heartfelt appreciation to Borders Bookstore in Līhuʻe and Kohala Books in Kapaʻau for their fine Hawaiiana sections.

About the Author

Randy Sue Coburn is a former newspaper reporter whose articles and essays have been published in numerous national magazines. She is the author of *Owl Island* and *Remembering Jody,* and her screenplays include *Mrs. Parker and the Vicious Circle,* the critically acclaimed Cannes Film Festival selection that received five Independent Spirit Award nominations, including Best Screenplay. She lives in Seattle.